BATTLE OF THE FANG

MAGNUS HAD COME. The daemon-primarch was at the foot of the stairway, attracting tracer fire in glowing, angry lines. The ordnance seemed to explode before it hit him, blooming in starbursts of angry red and orange around his massive frame. The Long Fangs and heavy weapons squads had unloaded all they had at him, pouring streams of flame at the monster's head and chest.

It had no discernible effect. Magnus was a giant, a five-metre-tall behemoth striding through the clouds of promethium like a man pushing through fields of corn. He was radiant, as splendid as bronze, dazzling amid the shadows of the mountain. Nothing hurt him. Nothing came close to hurting him. He had been created for another age, an age when gods walked among men. In the colder, weaker universe of the thirty-second millennium he was unmatched, a walking splinter of the Allfather's will set amid a fragile world of mortal flesh and blood.

A WARHAMMER 40,000 NOVEL

BATTLE OF THE FANG

CHRIS WRAIGHT

BLACK LIBRARY

*For Dan Abnett and Graham McNeill, the Magnus and Russ of
Black Library (but which one's which?)*

A Black Library Publication

First published in Great Britain in 2011 by
The Black Library,
Games Workshop Ltd.,
The Black Library,
Nottingham, NG7 2WS, UK.

10 9 8 7 6 5

Cover illustration by Jon Sullivan.
Internal illustration by John Blanche.
Maps by Chris Wraight and Adrian Wood.

A CIP record for this book is available from the British Library.

UK ISBN 13: 978 1 84970 046 7
US ISBN 13: 978 1 84970 047 4

See the Black Library on the internet at
www.blacklibrary.com

Find out more about Games Workshop
and the world of Warhammer 40,000 at
www.games-workshop.com

Printed and bound by CPI Group (UK) Ltd, Croydon, CR0 4YY

IT IS THE 41st millennium. For more than a hundred
centuries the Emperor has sat immobile on the Golden Throne
of Earth. He is the master of mankind by the
will of the gods, and master of a million worlds by the
might of his inexhaustible armies. He is a rotting carcass
writhing invisibly with power from the Dark Age of
Technology. He is the Carrion Lord of the Imperium for
whom a thousand souls are sacrificed every day, so that
he may never truly die.

YET EVEN IN his deathless state, the Emperor continues
his eternal vigilance. Mighty battlefleets cross the
daemon-infested miasma of the warp, the only route
between distant stars, their way lit by the Astronomican,
the psychic manifestation of the Emperor's will. Vast
armies give battle in His name on uncounted worlds.
Greatest amongst his soldiers are the Adeptus Astartes,
the Space Marines, bio-engineered super-warriors. Their
comrades in arms are legion: the Imperial Guard and
countless Planetary Defence Forces, the ever-vigilant
Inquisition and the tech-priests of the Adeptus
Mechanicus to name only a few. But for all their
multitudes, they are barely enough to hold off the ever-
present threat from aliens, heretics, mutants - and worse.

TO BE A man in such times is to be one amongst untold
billions. It is to live in the cruellest and most bloody
regime imaginable. These are the tales of those times.
Forget the power of technology and science, for so much
has been forgotten, never to be re-learned. Forget the
promise of progress and understanding, for in the grim
dark future there is only war. There is no peace amongst
the stars, only an eternity of carnage and slaughter, and
the laughter of thirsting gods.

PROLOGUE

STRIKE CRUISER GOTTHAMMAR powered smoothly through the void, its vast engines operating at less than half capacity, its wing of escorts keeping pace comfortably across the ten thousand kilometre-wide patrol formation. The cruiser was gunmetal-grey against the deep well of the void, its heavily armoured flanks emblazoned with the head of a snarling wolf. It had translated from the warp only hours earlier, and the last residue of Geller field shutdown still clung, glistening, to the exposed adamantium of the hull.

The *Gotthammar's* command bridge was located near the rear of the gigantic vessel, surrounded by towers, bulwarks and angled gun batteries. Void shields rippled like gauze over metres-thick plexiglass realspace viewers, under which the bridge crew laboured to keep the ship on course and with all its systems working at their full pitch of perfection.

Inside, the bridge was a huge space, over two hundred metres long, a cavern carved out from the core of the vessel. Its roof was largely transparent, formed out of the lens-like realspace portals arranged across a latticework of iron. Below that were gantries ringing the edges of the open chamber, each of them patrolled by kaerls hefting *skjoldtar* projectile weapons. Further down was the first deck, across which milled more mortal crew. Most were clad in the pearl-grey robes of Fenrisian ship-thralls, though kaerls moved among them too, stomping across the metal decking in blast-armour and translucent face-masks.

The floor of the first deck was broken open in several places, exposing deeper levels below. Bustling tactical stations clustered down there, and rows of chattering cogitators, and poorly-lit trenches filled with half-human servitors. Many of these were hardwired into their terminals, their spines or faces consumed in a mass of pipework and cabling, with exposed patches of grey skin the only reminder of the humanity they'd once enjoyed. Their service was different now, a demi-life of lobotomised servitude, shackled for eternity to machines that kept them alive only as long as they performed their numbing, mechanical tasks over and over again.

Above all those levels, set back at the very rear of the bridge cavern, was the command throne. A hexagonal platform jutted out from the vaulted walls, ten metres in diameter and ringed with a thick iron rail. In the centre of that platform was a low dais. In the centre of the dais stood the throne, a heavy, block-shaped chair carved from solid granite. It was far larger than a mortal man could have sat in comfortably, but that didn't matter much because no mortal man ever ventured on to that platform. It had been empty for many hours, though as the *Gotthammar* closed in on its target, that was about to change. Giant doors behind the throne hissed as brace-pistons were withdrawn. Then they slid open.

Through them walked a leviathan. Jarl Arvek Hren Kjarlskar, Wolf Lord of the Fourth Great Company of the Rout, massive in his Terminator armour, strode on to the dais. His battle-plate hummed with a low, throbbing menace as he moved. The ceramite surface was covered in deep-scored runes, and bone trophies hung from his huge shoulders. A bear-pelt, black with age and riddled with old bolter-holes, hung from his back. His face was leathery, glare-tanned, and studded with metal rings. A distended jawline was encased in two night-black sideburns, lustrous and predator-sleek.

With him came other giants. Anjarm, the Iron Priest, clad in forge-dark artificer plate, his face hidden behind the blank mask of an ancient helm. Frei, the Rune Priest, in sigil-encrusted armour, his stone-grey hair hanging in plaits across the neck-guard. The doors slid closed behind them, isolating the trio on the command platform. Below them, the decks hummed with unbroken activity.

Kjarlskar grimaced as he surveyed the scene, exposing fangs the length of children's fingers.

'So what do we have?' he asked. His voice rose rattling from the vast cage of his chest like a Rhino engine turning over. He never raised it, so they said, even in the heat of battle. He never had to.

'Probes have been launched,' said Anjarm. 'We'll see soon.'

Kjarlskar grunted, and took his place on the throne. For such a giant, nearly three metres tall and two across, he moved with an easy, contained fluidity. His yellow eyes, locked deep within a low-browed skull, glistened liquid and alert.

'*Skitja*, I'm bored of this,' he said. 'Hel, even the mortals are bored of this.'

He was right. The whole Fourth Great Company fleet was buzzing with frustrated energy. Thousands of kaerls, hundreds of Space Marines, all chasing shadows for months on end. Ironhelm, the Chapter's Great Wolf, had kept them all busy pursuing the target of his obsession across the fringes of the Eye of Terror. Every system in the long search had been the same: abandoned, pacified, or home to conflicts too tedious and petty to bother with.

Running after ghosts was crushing work. The hunters needed to hunt.

'We're getting something,' said Anjarm, his head inclined slightly as he checked his helm's lens-feed. As he spoke, a semi-circle of pict screens hung around the command platform flickered into life. The incoming data from the probes emerged on them. A brown-red planet swam into view, growing larger with every second. The probes were still closing, and at such vast range the image was broken and distorted.

'So what's this one?' asked Kjarlskar, not showing much interest.

'Gangava system,' answered Anjarm, watching the picts carefully. 'Single world, inhabited, nine satellites. Final node in the sector.'

Images continued to come in. As he watched them, the Jarl's mood slowly began to change. The thick hairs on the exposed flesh of his neck stiffened slightly. Those yellow eyes, the windows onto the beast, sharpened their focus.

'Orbital defences?'

'Nothing yet.'

Kjarlskar rose from the throne, his gaze fixed on the picts. The visual stream clarified. The planet's surface was swaying into view, dark-brown and streaked with a dirty orange. It looked like a ball of rust in space.

'Last contact?'

'Before the Scouring,' said Anjarm. 'Warp storm activity recorded until seventy standard years ago. Explorator reports list as desolate. We had this one low on the list, lord.'

Kjarlskar didn't look like he was listening. He was tensing up.

'Frei,' said Kjarlskar. 'Are you getting anything?'

The planet continued to grow as the probes took up geostationary positions. Angry swirls of cloud shifted across the surface. As the Rune Priest looked at the probe-relays, veins began to pulse at his shaven temples. His mouth tightened, as if some pungent aroma had risen, stinking, from the screens.

'Blood of Russ,' he swore.

'What do you sense?' asked Kjarlskar.

'*Spoor*. His spoor.'

The clouds were breaking open. Beneath them were

lights, laid out in geometric shapes, revealing a city, vast beyond imagining. The shapes were deliberate. They hurt the eyes.

Kjarlskar let slip a low growl of pleasure, mixed with anger. His gauntlets clenched into fists.

'You're sure?' he demanded.

The Rune Priest's armour had started glowing, lit up by the angular shapes carved into the plate. For the first time in months, the wyrd-summoner looked excited. Probe-auspexes continued to zoom in, revealing pyramids in the heart of the city.

Massive pyramids.

'There can be no doubt, lord.'

Kjarlskar let slip a savage, barking laugh.

'Then summon the star-speakers,' he snarled. 'We've done it.'

He looked from Anjarm to Frei, and his bestial eyes shone.

'We've found the bastard. Magnus the Red is on Gangava.'

PART I:
OLD SCORES

CHAPTER ONE

VAER GREYLOC HUNCHED down, keeping upwind, letting his naked fingers graze against the packed snow. Ahead of him, the plain stretched away north, bleached white, ringed by the peaks beyond.

He sniffed, pulling the frigid air in deep. The prey had sensed something, and there was fear carrying on the wind. He tensed, feeling his muscles tighten with readiness. His pin-sharp pupils dilated slightly, lost in their near-white irises.

Not yet.

Down below him, a few hundred yards away, the herd huddled against the wind, stepping nervously despite their size. *Konungur*, a rare breed. Everything on Fenris was bred to grip on to survival, and these creatures were no different. Four lungs to scrape the thin air of Asaheim of every last molecule of oxygen, huge ribcages of semi-fused bone, hind-legs the width of a man's waist, twin twisted horns and a spiked spine-ridge. A kick from a *konungur* could take the head off a man.

Greyloc stayed tense, watching them move across the plain. He judged the distance, still down against the snow. He had no weapon in his hands.

I am the weapon.

He wore no armour either, and the metal-lined carapace nodes chafed against the leather of his jerkin. His mouth stayed shut, and only a thin trail of vapour escaped from his nostrils. Asaheim was punishingly cold, even for one with his enhanced physiology, and there were a thousand mutually supportive ways to die.

The *konungur* paused. The bull at the herd-head stopped rigid, its majestic horned profile raised against the screen of white beyond.

Now.

Greyloc burst from cover. His legs pumped, throwing snow up behind in powdered blooms. His nostrils flared, pulling air into his taut, lean frame.

The *konungur* bolted instantly, rearing away from the sprinting predator. Greyloc closed fast, his thighs already burning. His secondary heart kicked in, flooding his system with adrenaline-thick blood. There was no *mjod* in it – he'd been fasting for days, purging the battle-stimulant from his frame.

My pure state.

The *konungur* galloped powerfully, leaping high through the wind-smoothed drifts, but Greyloc was faster. His white hair streamed out over his rippling shoulders. He outpaced the slowest, tearing alongside the herd, fuelling its panic. The group broke formation, scattering from the bringer of terror in their midst.

Greyloc fixed his eyes on the bull. The beast was two metres high at the shoulder, over four tons of pure muscle moving at speed. He plunged after it, feeling his legs sear with the sharp pain of exertion. The fear of the beast clogged in his nostrils, fuelling the blood-frenzy pumping through his system.

It veered suddenly, trying to shake him off. Greyloc leapt, catching the creature's neck with his outstretched hand and swinging round to grapple it. The bull bucked, trying to break the hold, kicking out with spiked hooves and bellowing a series of echoing, coughing distress calls.

Greyloc pulled back his free fist and sent a punch flying at the *konungur's* skull. He heard bone crack, and the creature staggered sideways. Greyloc dug his claws into the ice-hard flesh, pulling at the cords within and dragging the beast to the ground.

The *konungur* screamed, collapsing in a flurry of limbs. Greyloc bared his fangs and buried his face in the animal's throat. He bit down, once, twice, ripping and shaking like a dog. He sucked in the hot blood, feeling it wash over his teeth, and the kill-pleasure poured into him. The body beneath him spasmed, kicked a final time, then shuddered still.

Greyloc flung the limp head of the bull aside and let his own fall back.

'Hjolda!'

Still pumped from the chase, Vaer Greyloc roared his triumph into the empty air, spitting out flecks of blood and hair. The rest of the herd were far away by then, bolting across the ice for higher ground.

'Fenrys hjolda!'

His cry echoing around the plain, Greyloc looked down and grinned. Endorphins raged through his bloodstream and his hearts hammered in a heavy, thrilling unison.

My pure state.

THE CARCASS BEGAN to steam as blood welled up from its flank. Greyloc ripped the shoulder open with his bare hands, feeling the hot, wet slabs slap apart. He ignored the bull's glassy eye, now vacant and cooling fast. He tore strips of flesh free and gorged on them, replenishing the energy expended during the chase. *Konungur* meat was rich, rich enough even to satisfy the demands of his predator's frame.

It was only as Greyloc ate that he saw the snow ahead of him disturbed. He looked up from his feast, blood running down his chin. Something was coming.

He snarled with displeasure and stood. The beast within him was still roused and alert, still running with the kill-pleasure. In the distance, dark against the pale sky, a flyer was approaching. It came quickly, wheeling across the plain and descending sharply.

Greyloc wiped his jaw, which did nothing but spread gore across his white hair. Every sinew was still tight, every follicle erect. He growled with frustration.

This had better be good.

The blunt, snub-nosed flyer came closer, skirting the

drifts. It was a four-man *skarr* gunship, open-sided and armed with twin-linked bolters under the wings. A single figure stood in the exposed crew bay, hands free and long red hair streaming out from the turbulence of the descent.

'Jarl!' the newcomer bellowed over the roar as the flyer came to rest, bobbing a metre from the ground. The tilted engines thundered deep wells into the snow, melting and evaporating it and turning the drifts into slush.

'Tromm,' snarled Greyloc, not bothering to hide his anger. He was still pumped.

The Wolf Guard Tromm Rossek was in full battle-plate. He looked as bulky and ebullient as ever, and there was something joyous in his eyes.

'News from Kjarlskar! Ironhelm summons you!'

Greyloc spat a mix of blood and saliva on to the snow.

'Now?'

Rossek shrugged, still braced against the swaying movement of the gunship.

'That's what he said.'

Greyloc shook his head and shot a rueful glance at the mauled corpse of the *konungur*. Kill-pleasure was replaced with a numbness, the dull pain of frustration. With difficulty, he reeled in his hunt-state. He felt the hairs on his forearms relax even as he took a running leap and hauled himself on to the crew bay of the hovering gunship.

'Good kill?' enquired Rossek, a broad smile across his expansive, tattoo-laced face.

'Get me back to the Aett,' muttered Greyloc, slumping

to the metal floor as the kaerls in the cockpit fed power to the burners.

It had been.

THE GUNSHIP WENT north-east, banking between the ever-rising peaks. All of the Asaheim plateau was high, thousands of metres up, and even down on the prey-plains the air was perilously thin for mortals without rebreathers. Ahead of the flyer, fresh mountains were piled on top of one another, massive shoulders of ice-locked rock jumbled in a climbing pattern, ever higher, ever steeper. The engines of the gunship whined as they powered it upwards.

Greyloc hung on to the edge of the exposed platform casually. He could feel the blood on his face begin to crystallise. He was near-naked and the chill would immobilise even his body soon, but still he stayed on the edge, letting the frigid air tear at his death-white mane.

'So what's got him roused?' he asked at last, adjusting easily as the gunship banked sharply.

Rossek shrugged.

'Jarls are in the chamber. Something big.'

Greyloc grunted, and shook his head. The subsidence of the kill-pleasure was like a drug withdrawal. He felt surly and blunted.

The two figures on the gunship platform were physical opposites. Rossek was huge, red-haired, bearded, thick of limb and with a heavy-set face. His nose was flat and broken, his neck broad and banded with muscle. A dragon tattoo snaked across his left cheek, terminating at his temple where six metal studs protruded from the bone. In another Chapter that might have indicated six centuries of service. Rossek wasn't that old – he just liked studs in his skull.

His lord was hewn from different stone. Greyloc was lean, rangy, and his flesh clung tight to the bone. The Wolf Lord's face was drawn, as if preserved and stiffened by the ice-dry winds. Out of his armour, the tautness in his frame was evident. He was a prey-stalker, a plains-killer, fast, pale, and deadly. The brutish camaraderie of the *Vlka Fenryka*, the superhuman warriors of Fenris, sat uneasily with him. All the Aett knew his prowess in the hunt, but they didn't trust his brooding, and they didn't trust the shade of his hide. He was white, and his eyes were the colour of steel.

Like a ghost, they said. Snow on snow.

'Are all the others there?' Greyloc asked, still standing in the face of the wind. He could feel ice creep across his exposed forearms and ignored it.

'Three Great Companies are off-world still, but Kjarl-skar's one of them.'

Greyloc nodded. Ironhelm had been mustering his forces on Fenris for a long time, and the endless expeditions to hunt down his old adversary had seemed – at last – to be in abeyance. The Great Wolf's passion for finding Magnus had become an obsession, one Greyloc had argued against before. There were a thousand other enemies to hunt, and many of them would stand up and fight rather than shrink away into the aether when the noose closed.

'We'll see, then,' Greyloc said, watching as the mountains loomed.

The massive precipices were coming to a head. Vast beyond imagining, a single peak was rearing up on the horizon. As if the core of Fenris had been shoved through its mantle into a terrifying, unmatched pinnacle, a conical mountain-mass soared up into the darkening sky. Its flanks were sheer, snow-clad on jagged shelves of rock, glossy with ancient, undisturbed ice. In every direction, lesser summits crowded the view, clustering close to the broken skyline in the shadow of the Great One, the Shoulder of the Allfather: the *volda hamarrki*, the World Spine.

Against the gathering dark of the dwindling atmosphere, tiny lights shone at the distant summit. They marked the habitation of the Sky Warriors, the abode of the demigods, itself a tiny fraction of the bulk of that vast peak. The inhabitants of that place, whether kaerl or Space Marine, called it the Aett.

To the rest of the galaxy, awe-struck by half-snatched legends of Russ's fortress and never likely to see it, it was just the Fang.

Greyloc looked at the approaching lights impassively. There were other flyers coming in, at least three of them. Ironhelm was pulling all his forces back to the hearth.

'Perhaps he's given up at last,' said Greyloc, watching the flickering lights of the docking platform draw closer. 'Can that be too much to hope?'

'WYRMBLADE! ENOUGH SPLICING.'

Odain Sturmhjart strode into the laboratorium, pushing aside fleshmaker-thralls impatiently. The huge Rune Priest, clad in sigil-encrusted armour, slammed his staff on the ground and ripples of excess power discharged against the stone.

Thar Ariak Hraldir, bearer of the Wyrmblade that gave him his name, looked up from his work. The low light made his eyes look like pools of resin-rich amber. The Wolf Priest was irritated, and his ragged, ugly face twisted into a scowl. A pair of curved fangs snagged his lips as he exhaled loudly. Slowly, aching from the hunched pose he'd held for so long, Wyrmblade straightened.

'Bone-rattler,' came the caustic reply. 'This, especially, is not a good time.'

Ahead of him, vials containing clear fluid were arranged in long rows on a metal table. Each was labelled with a single rune. Some stood alone, some were connected to one another by microfilament, others were linked together with strands of conductive plasfibre.

Wyrmblade gestured with a finger, and the lights in the laboratorium rose. Strip lumens exposed white-tiled rooms, surgically clean, each leading off from the other like chambers in a den. Blast doors to the inner rooms closed, obscuring the view of what lay beyond. Before they snapped shut, there was a fleeting view of banks of equipment humming around glistening centrifuges, of picts updating steadily with rows of runes, and of man-sized tanks of translucent fluid against the walls. There were dark shadows suspended within those tanks, motionless and silent.

'You tell iron-arse that,' said Sturmhjart, and his ruddy cheeks glowed with mirth. 'He'll flay your skin off to cover what he's missing. I've come to save you from that.'

The Rune Priest was built like all the Adeptus Astartes

– solid, heavily muscled, broad and stocky. He had a circuit of augmetics around his left eye and a thick grey beard, stiff and matted from age. Bone talismans hung in chains from his breastplate, carefully arranged to channel his power over the elements. The pattern of runes on his armour might have looked random, but it was nothing of the sort, and every carving and incision had been made after days of scrying and casting. His cheerfulness was misleading too – Sturmhjart was the Chapter's High Rune Priest, and wielded power of a terrifying magnitude.

'He could try,' muttered Wyrmblade, casting a final look over the vials before leaving them. As he walked from the long table, a drawer full of steel instruments closed with a smooth click. 'Then he'd remember who pulled him off the ice, and who gave him his first scars.'

The Wolf Priest moved silently and slowly, carrying his bulk with an accomplished ease. He was old, and the centuries hung heavily on his ravaged features. Black, straggling hair framed his long face, and the tattoos on the flesh had turned scab-brown with age. His skin looked as tough as plascrete, weathered and beaten down by over five hundred years of ceaseless combat. Though ancient, his eyes were still keen and his grip still strong. His armour was as black as his hide, hung with ancient bones and covered in a second skin of gouges, plasma burns and blade-scores. Every one of his movements radiated a deep, old power, tested and tempered in the fires of war.

Two Priests. So opposite, so alike.

Sturmhjart cast a sceptical eye over the ranks of vials.

'Making progress?'

'You've never understood the importance of this. If I failed to convince you a decade ago, I won't do so now – you're both older and more foolish.'

Sturmhjart snorted a laugh, and it echoed from his chest like an erupting *krakken*. 'Older, yes, though there's more than one way to be foolish.'

'You seem to know them all.'

The two Priests strode out of the laboratorium. As they turned down the long corridor leading to the transit-shafts, lit only by flame torches against the polished rock, black-robed fleshmaker-thralls shrank back respectfully and inclined their heads.

'I don't know how long Ironhelm's going to tolerate this research,' said Sturmhjart. 'You haven't been off-world for a year.'

'He'll tolerate it until it's done.' Wyrmblade turned his dour, sunken-eyed face to the Rune Priest. 'You'll tolerate it too. The work's essential.'

Sturmhjart shrugged.

'Don't interfere with the wyrd, brother,' he said. 'I've warned you before. If the fates permitted it, it would have been done already.'

Wyrmblade snarled, and the hairs on the back of his arms rose. Deep within him, he could feel his animal spirit glide to the surface. If Sturmhjart noticed that, he showed no sign.

'Do not presume to give me an order, brother,' Wyrmblade responded, coming to a halt. 'You're not the only one who can see the future.'

Heartbeats passed, and neither figure moved. Then Sturmhjart backed down.

'Stubborn old bastard,' he muttered, turning back down the corridor, shaking his ragged head as he stalked between the torches.

'Never forget it,' said Wyrmblade dryly, following closely. 'It's why we get on so well.'

THE CHAMBER OF the Annulus was high up in the pinnacle of the Fang, in the Valgard near the very summit of the huge fortress, surrounded by a seam of pure granite. It had been one of the first halls to be delved from the living rock by the Terran geomancers brought to Fenris to establish the VI Legion in the time of legends. In that age, tech-adepts had been able to level the very mountains and raise them up again, to shape the continents and quell the tumults of the death world's seasonal upheavals. They could have made Fenris a paradise if they'd chosen, and it was only on the primarch's orders that the planet was never altered from its fearsome character. Russ wished for his home world to remain the great proving ground of warriors, a crucible in which its humanity would be tested and honed forever.

So, as it had happened, only one mountain out of the hundreds on Asaheim had been changed from its primeval form, its chambers hollowed out and wrought by ancient devices of forgotten, terrible power. Now the knowledge brought by those long-dead artificers was fading fast, and no citadel of comparable strength and majesty would ever be built again. The Fang was unique in the Imperium, the product of a genius that was slowly bleeding out of the galaxy as humanity stumbled and unlearned the lessons of the past.

Within the Chamber, twelve figures stood around the Annulus, the huge circle on the floor with the sigils of the Great Companies inscribed on panels of stone. Eight of them were Jarls – Wolf Lords – including the pale figure of Greyloc, now in his war-plate and cleansed of the blood of the hunt. Three other Wolf Lords were off-planet, though Ironhelm had sent astropathic messages to their fleets advising them of Kjarlskar's discovery. Standing beside the Jarls were the three High Priests: Wyrmblade, Sturmhjart and Iron Priest Berensson Gassijk Rendmar, resplendent in his foundry-enhanced armour.

That left one place remaining. It was filled by Harek Eireik Eireiksson, Heir of Russ and the Great Wolf. Wearing his customary Terminator battle-plate, he cut a vast, ominous figure at the head of the council. His black hair and beard were long and full, the forks braided and sealed with bone totems. Aside from Wyrmblade he was the oldest warrior present, having led the Chapter for three centuries and served for at least another hundred years before that. The blood of his victims had stained his battle-garb for so long that the grey had long since shrunk to darkness. Only the curved sheet of metal implanted across the right hemisphere of his skull glinted from the firelight of the torches, the legacy of the bloody duel that had earned him his iron implants and given him his nickname. In the semi-light of the Chamber, Harek Ironhelm looked as joyless and brooding as a spectre of Morkai.

'Brothers,' he said, fixing his gaze on each of the Wolf Lords in turn. His voice carried a permanent undertow of rumbling, grinding aggression. 'The hunt is called.

Jarl Arvek Hren Kjarlskar has uncovered the lair of the Traitor, and now, at last, we will have completion.'

As he spoke, a shimmering green hololith emerged over the centre of the Annulus. It was a planet, rotating gently. Points on the hololith were marked with warship battle-signs, all of them Fenrisian. Kjarlskar had blockaded the world.

'Gangava Prime,' said Ironhelm, relishing the words as they left his cracked lips. 'What orbital defences there were have been destroyed, but void shields shelter the major settlements. Kjarlskar estimates tens of millions in the principal city alone.'

As Ironhelm talked, his voice became more animated. Greyloc saw the Great Wolf's right hand, enclosed in its heavy gauntlet, flex into a fist as he spoke. A subtle kill-urge pheromone marked the air.

He's combat-roused. Already.

'We'll take the Rout,' Ironhelm announced, baring his thick, chipped fangs in a chill smile, as if daring any to disagree. 'All of it. We strike, hard. This prize calls for the full wrath of the running pack.'

The hololith flickered as tactical overlays showed landing sites and ingress routes. The primary target was a massive urban sprawl on a high northern latitude, hundreds of miles across. The swirls of citylight were uncomfortably arranged, and as Greyloc looked at them a hot sensation broke out behind his eyes. He heard low growls around the chamber as the others recognised the mark of corruption in the architecture.

'How far?' demanded Morskarl, Jarl of the Third, his question muffled by an archaic Heresy-era face mask.

'Three weeks in the warp. The fleet is being made ready.'

'And you're sure he's there?' asked Iron Priest Rendmar in his strange, metallic voice.

'Kjarlskar's Rune Priest confirms it. The Traitor waits for us, confident in his strength.'

'He invites the attack,' said Jarl Egial Vraksson of the Fifth, narrowing his eyes across a heavily scarred brow and scrutinising the tactical display. 'Why?'

'There are over two million troops in the target zone. It's fortified, and there are armament works within. He's building a new Legion, brothers. We've caught him before he's ready.'

'A Legion with no fleet,' said Greyloc softly.

He suddenly felt hostile eyes sweep across him. Ironhelm's enthusiasm was infectious, and they didn't want to hear contrary counsel.

'And what of that, whelp?' demanded Ironhelm. The term 'whelp' had been used in the past as a joke, a way for the older Jarls to poke fun at Greyloc's relative youth, but there was a sharper edge in Ironhelm's speech this time.

Greyloc looked back at the Great Wolf coolly. The entire chamber was alive with a rush for completion. The hunters needed to finish the job, and they were straining like hounds on the leash.

'You think the Traitor didn't foresee this, lord?' he said, keeping his voice low and posture respectful. 'How many false signs has he left for us already?'

Rekki Oirreisson, Jarl of the Seventh, a hirsute monster with a heavy jawline and bunched shoulders, grunted his displeasure.

'The Rune Priest has ruled,' he said. 'Magnus is there.'

'And if he is?' replied Greyloc. 'For all his degeneracy, he is a primarch. If Russ, honour to his name, couldn't kill him, what hope have we?'

At that, red-eyed Borek Salvrgrim of the Second took a step forwards, hand reaching for his weapon-belt. There was a chorus of low, angry growls from other Wolf Lords.

'Jarl, you forget yourself,' warned Ironhelm, his powerful voice echoing around the Chamber.

For a moment, the danger lingered. The suggestion – even the intimation – that there were limits to the vengeful capability of the Rout was perilous.

Then Salvrgrim withdrew the challenge, grudgingly, casting a dark look at Greyloc as he did so.

'We are committed to this,' said Ironhelm, speaking to Greyloc as if demonstrating an axe-grip to a child. 'It is blood-debt. It is completion.'

That word again. Like all the others, Greyloc knew the importance of it. They were hunters, the Wolves, and nothing was more important than bringing the chase to a kill. Plenty in the Imperium thought of Russ's warriors as savages, but that betrayed their ignorance of galactic history – the Wolves did what was necessary to complete the task, whatever it was. That was the trait they'd been bred for. To leave a slaying unfinished was a cause for deep shame, something that burned in the soul forever, chewing away until the ache was cleansed.

'There are other considerations,' interjected Wyrmblade, too old to be daunted by disapproval. His lined, cynical face looked up at Ironhelm's. 'My work, for one.'

'Do not mention that here,' muttered Vraksson, glaring at Wyrmblade. 'This is a council of war, not a discourse on your blasphemy.'

Wyrmblade gave the Jarl a cold smile.

'Perhaps your pattern could have done with some tweaking, Egial.'

'Enough,' hissed Ironhelm.

Greyloc watched the Great Wolf carefully, noting the dilated nostrils and glistening irises. The kill-urge was powerful now.

This council will only endorse one outcome.

'Disgust is strong in me,' said Ironhelm. 'We have him – the Crimson King, the architect of our dishonour – in our grasp and hesitate before taking the chance. For shame, brothers! Will we cower forever here, huddled around the fires while the deeds of our fathers keep us warm?'

There was a fresh murmur of agreement around the Chamber. The pack-scent had turned from one of surly belligerence to one of impatience. Greyloc saw how skilfully Ironhelm spoke to their pride, and remained silent. There would be no contesting the coming verdict.

'We have our full strength gathered,' continued Ironhelm. 'No force remaining in the galaxy can stand against us when mustered together. Kjarlskar has him pinned, and, as we join him, Gangava will bleed under our claws.'

Guttural noises of approval came from Salvrgrim, whose vehemence for the chase was ever paramount.

'This is it, brothers,' snarled the Great Wolf, raising his

clenched fist before him. 'Do you not sense it? Do you not feel it in your blood? This is when we destroy the last dregs of Prospero!'

There was a sudden, massed roar from the assembled Jarls at that, a thunderous sound that rebounded from the cold stone around them.

Greyloc exchanged a quick glance with Wyrmblade, his only ally in the Chamber. The Priest's expression, as ever, was sour.

'And who will man the citadel, lord?' the old Wolf Priest asked, timing his question to puncture the euphoria around him.

Ironhelm looked at Wyrmblade, and a mix of scorn and exasperation marked his features.

'You, then,' he spat. 'You and the whelp, since your stomach for fighting is so weak. But no more than that. Only one Great Company will remain – the rest I will commit to this.'

He spun back then, facing the circle of huge armoured figures around the Annulus, and there was a murderous smile on his ravaged face.

'For those who join me, honour beyond measure. We shall do it, my brothers! We shall do what even our dread father did not.'

His smile grew to a wide, expectant grin, exposing his fangs of tooth and metal.

'We shall take the Crimson King,' he growled, his voice grating deep within the curve of his breastplate, 'and tear him from the face of the universe.'

CHAPTER TWO

THE CHAMBER'S LIGHTS were dim, barely above the level a mortal would need to see by. Apart from the glow of floor-level lumen strips there were only four *prakasa* floating below the ceiling. They swam through the air lazily like jewels, tiny points of slow-spreading illumination in the warm darkness. From below the floor, the low hum of the ship's warp engines made them shiver like leaves in the breeze.

Ahmuz Temekh would have been able to read the text before him even in near-complete darkness, but the soft blush of colour was satisfying. He reached for the corner of a fragile page and turned it gingerly. His oversized fingers worked carefully, avoiding the rips that had already disfigured the ancient manuscript.

His violet eyes gazed down on the script. He knew

what was written there. He knew what was written in all the books still possessed by the Legion. Only Ahriman, perhaps, had delved deeper, and he was gone.

'You should not have strayed, brother.'

Temekh spoke aloud, feeling the shape of the words slip around his cultured lips. He spoke in Telapiye, the xenos language of the book's long-dead authors. Even with his superhuman control of musculature, he couldn't recreate the full range of sounds necessary – for that, he'd have needed two tongues, each with more prehensile range than his own. Still, that even his rough approximation was heard in the universe was something. Since the last of the telap had been exterminated, it was entirely possible that Ahmuz Temekh was the only speaker of the million-year-old language left.

A faint chime rang out from the corridor outside Temekh's private chamber. He felt a flicker of irritation, quickly quelled. Aphael was only doing his job.

'Come.'

As he spoke, a panel in the darkened chamber withdrew silently and slid open. The *prakasa* swelled into more light and their beams swept around the room, showing up the eclectic contents. A *hauxx* writing desk from Karellion, an aquarium of feldspar crystal populated with sparkling cichlids, a wraithbone sword-holder from the extinguished Saim-Arvuel craftworld.

So many trinkets. On ancient Terra, they'd have called him a jackdaw.

'Still reading, brother?'

Herume Aphael ducked as he entered the room. He was arrayed in full battle-armour, which made him a half-metre taller than Temekh. His plate was deep blue, decorated with bronze swirls at the joints; only his bald, smooth head was exposed. The Pyrae sorcerer-lord spent much of his time in armour these days, and Temekh couldn't recall when he'd last seen him without it.

'There's plenty of time,' Temekh replied, putting the book down on the desk in front of him.

Aphael grunted, and stood opposite him. He was emanating impatience. There was no surprise in that – they were always impatient, his kind. That was the gift of their order, and what Magnus continued to value them for.

'Why are you here, brother?' asked Temekh, not wanting to waste the precious days before system-fall made anything but thoughts of combat impossible.

'What are you reading?' countered Aphael, looking at the book with distrust.

'Nothing of value to the current campaign. The author's light has been taken from the universe. By Angron, I believe – one of his many exercises of tolerance.'

Aphael shrugged. 'He's as barbaric as the Dogs, but keep your mind focused on the matter at hand.'

'It is, I assure you.'

'You would do well to assure me. You've become distant.'

'If I have, it is in your imagination.'

Aphael smiled without humour. 'And you'd know all about that.'

The Pyrae shook his head. As the flesh moved against the interface nodes in his armour's neck-guard,

Temekh could see the puckering, the slight reflectiveness. Was that an early sign, a giveaway symptom?

Oh, no. Not you too.

'In any case, the assault plans are now advanced,' Aphael said. 'You should join the command group, or your absence will cause more comment among the conclave.'

At that, Temekh let his mind detach briefly from the physical, abstracting himself into a local vector within the immaterium. From his privileged vantage he saw the fleet around them as it powered through the warp. Strike cruisers, bristling with weapons, readied for the orbital war to come. Behind them, vast troop ships, crammed with thousands upon thousands of mortals bearing the single eye on their breastplates.

And in the holds of the great battleships were the Rubricae, Ahriman's creations. They waited, silently, animated by nothing but the wills of those who led them. They would feel no hate against the Dogs as they killed them, the ones who had reduced them to their state of eternal, silent horror. For them, the years since the Betrayal were nothing. Even for Temekh and the others who had retained their souls, mere decades had passed since Prospero had been sacked, whatever else might have happened in the universe of mortals. For Magnus's children, the wounds were still raw, still weeping.

He relaxed, and his soul snapped back to its physical bounds.

'The fleet is in good order,' he said. 'You are to be congratulated.'

'I don't need your approval. I need you on the bridge.'

Temekh bowed his head.

'I will come, then. And we will refine the instruments of our revenge together.'

Aphael frowned at Temekh's weary tone.

'Do you not wish to see them burn, brother? Do you not relish the pain we will cause them?'

Temekh almost replied with the words he had been reading a few moments ago.

There is a symmetry of pain in revenge. When a man will not withdraw his emotion from those whom he wishes to destroy, then even in victory he destroys nothing but a part of himself.

'Causing them pain will not bring back Tizca,' he said, gazing absently at the cichlids as they darted through the weeds of the aquarium. 'But if we have been so diminished that our only remaining satisfaction is in their destruction, then it will have to do.'

His violet eyes flickered back up to look at his comrade.

'So they will burn, brother,' he said bleakly. 'They will burn in ways they do not even begin to comprehend.'

Only to himself, silently and within the privacy of his psychically shielded mind, did he complete the sentence.

And so will we.

FREIJA MOREKBORN HAD the Blood Claw by the throat, and she wasn't letting go.

'Damn you,' she spat, before landing her knuckles on his slabbed, stupid face, breaking teeth and splitting skin. The Sky Warrior looked up at her blearily, arms limp. *'Show. Some. Respect.'*

'Daughter!'

Freija heard the voice from far away, interrupting her dreaming. Somewhere deep in her subconscious, irritation stirred. She was enjoying this one.

'Daughter!'

This time, her shoulder was grasped. Unwilling, grudgingly, she was shaken awake. Her last dream-image was of the broken Space Marine sinking to the floor, beaten in combat, humbled and humiliated in a way that could never happen in the waking world.

She opened her eyes, seeing her father leaning over her. Her bedchamber was still dark, lit only by a wavering tallow candle set high into the rock walls.

'What is it?' she mumbled, shrugging off his rough hands. She could make out the familiar line of his shoulders, feel the calloused flesh on hers.

'Get up,' he said, turning from her and looking for more light.

Freija pushed herself up from the disarranged furs of her bunk. Her sand-blonde hair fell in unruly clumps around her face. The tiny chamber was ice cold, but she ignored it. Everywhere on Fenris was ice cold.

'What's going on?'

Morek Karekborn managed to find a working glow-sphere and sent it spinning up into the air. A thin grey light flooded across the untidy space. His blunt, honest face was thrown into stark relief, and the worry lines around his eyes looked deeper than ever.

'Change of plan,' the old warrior said, running a tired hand over his cropped head. 'The Eleventh has been called off-world. We're back on duty.'

'*Skítja*,' Freija swore, rubbing her eyes and trying to

banish the heavy weight of sleep. 'Again?'

'Don't question it. Just get into uniform.'

Freija looked at her father with concern. Morek was a rivenmaster, leader of five hundred kaerls of the Aettguard. His duties drove him hard, and he drove himself harder. He had the shadows of long-term fatigue in his face.

They're killing him, she thought. *And they don't even know it.*

'We've just come off rotation,' she protested, swinging her legs from the hard bunk and staggering over to the grey tunic thrown across the floor. 'There are other detachments that could do this.'

Morek leaned against the wall.

'Not any more. The Twelfth is the only one staying. Get used to it – we've got weeks of this to come.'

Freija still felt thick-headed from sleep as she pulled her tunic over her head and tried to drag the worst of the tangles from her hair. Weeks of being driven into punishing defensive exercises by the Sky Warriors, of being ordered around by whooping Blood Claws who'd forgotten what it was like to have a mortal body and mortal weaknesses.

'Great,' she said coldly. 'Bloody great.'

'Freija, my daughter,' said Morek. He came up to her and put his hands firmly on her shoulders. 'Be careful this time. Think about how you act, think about what you say. They've been patient with you because of me, but it won't last forever.'

She almost shook him off. She hated his lectures, just as she hated his blind faith in his masters. He worshipped them, even though he knew that they'd all been mortal once. The Sky Warriors barely knew mortals such as he and she existed, even though without the loyal service of the Aettguard they'd be unable to keep even half of the Fang's huge maze of chambers in operation.

'Don't worry about me,' she said, dropping her fledgling defiance. 'I can fight. That's all they care about.'

Morek gave her a hard look. She knew how he felt. Like so many fathers, he wanted to protect her all the time. She was the only thing left for him. Part of her wanted to give him some kind of reassurance, some kind of certainty that she'd follow in his path, diligently doing her duty to Russ and the immortals. There were times when indeed that was all she wanted, but they made it so damned *hard*.

'You show your feelings too much,' he complained, shaking his head.

'And what do you want me to do?' she blurted, shaking free of him and reaching down for her boots. 'If they wanted meek, shrinking servants, they've got the wrong planet. *Fekke*, I'm a daughter of Fenris, and my blood runs hot. Mortal blood, at that. They can drown in it.'

She looked up then, suddenly worried she'd overstepped the mark, only to see her father gazing at her with an odd expression.

'Aye, you're a daughter of Fenris, all right,' he said, and his brown eyes shone. 'You make me proud, Freija. And sick with fear.'

He pushed himself from the wall and made to leave.

'Get into armour quickly, and get your squad together. We have an hour to take over from the

Eleventh. I don't want to look bad in front of that bastard Lokkborn.'

'So what's going on?'

Morek shrugged.

'No idea. No idea at all.'

HIGH UP AT the summit of the Valgard, ships blasted off from launch platforms like crows leaving a roost. Thunderhawk gunships mingled with the Chapter's few remaining Stormbirds, forming an endless stream of jagged shadows against the nightshade-blue sky. Among them were the much larger *hlaupa*-class escorts, heavily armed variants of the Imperial Navy's Cobra destroyers. Vessels of such size would not normally have been able to dock within a planetary atmosphere, but the sheer altitude of the Valgard landing stages made it possible for them to make planetfall on Fenris. Twelve of them had left already, and the fabled hangars were swiftly emptying. Only seven days had passed since Kjarlskar's discovery on Gangava and already the fleet muster was drawing near to completion.

Far above the procession of surface-capable vessels hung the spacegoing fleet. Each warship buzzed with activity on all decks as the thralls prepared the plasma drives to power them to the jump-points. Some ships were new arrivals at the muster, having been recalled by Ironhelm only days before from long-range duty. Others had been held above Fenris in readiness for many months, waiting for the Great Wolf's call to arms. The serrated outlines of the strike cruisers glided amongst the swarms of lesser ships, each of them marked with the symbol of a Great Company and the black wolfshead of the Chapter.

At the centre of the muster, picked out by steady columns of gunships waiting to enter the cavernous launch-bays, was the pride of the Chapter, the colossal *Russvangum*. Built to a design now lost in the cataclysm of the Heresy, the massive vessel hung motionless in the void. Strike cruisers, themselves capital ships, passed under its shadow and were utterly obscured. It dominated local space just as the alpha-beasts of the plains dominated their packs. Like all such Space Marine vessels, it was designed to do one thing only – unleash overwhelming, morale-destroying, nerve-burning fury onto the surface of a recalcitrant world from high orbit. It had done such work many times, and its drop-pod and torpedo arrays were charred black from heavy use. All the *Vlka Fenryka* were predators, but the *Russvangum* was perhaps the most potent expression of their awesome reach and power. Only the legendary *Hrafnkel* had carried a heavier punch, and that was now just a memory in the sagas.

From his tower high on the flanks of the Jarlheim, Ironhelm watched the final preparations for the muster take shape. He could see the launch trails of the Thunderhawks, thin and graceful, as they broke atmosphere and headed to the muster-points. Around him, tactical displays showed the positions of the ships as they moved slowly into convoy formation. It would not be long before he too took his place on the flagship.

So many of them. So much power. All in one place, all directed at a single point.

A familiar thrill animated his gene-forged limbs. It would be days – weeks, even – before he'd be able to channel his eagerness properly into the battle-rage, and by then his whole being would be at a fever-pitch of readiness. Thinking of the carnage that he would unleash, a cold expression broke across his ragged face.

They have forgotten just what we are capable of. Reminding them will give me much pleasure.

All enemies of the Allfather engendered hatred in a son of Fenris, but Magnus was placed in a different category of loathing. It had always been that way with the Thousand Sons. The sagas still recounted in the caverns of the Aett told of the sorcerers' betrayal, their condescension, and – worst of all – their escape. The Legion hadn't been destroyed at Prospero, only crippled. That shame had hung over the Wolves for over a thousand years, staining whatever deeds they'd accomplished since and marking their failure like spoor-trails in the snow.

Perhaps, if the traitor Magnus had disappeared into the Eye of Terror and never re-emerged, that shame might have been bearable. But he hadn't. He'd returned over the following centuries, leaving devastation in his elusive wake. Precision strikes on Imperial worlds had continued, each aimed at retrieving some valuable piece of knowledge or esoterica. Despite the grievous damage Russ had inflicted on them, the Thousand Sons still had the potential to launch raids into protected space, and the knowledge of that burned at Ironhelm. It had burned at him for decades, until nothing else seemed important.

Despite all the resources he devoted to hunting Magnus, the chase had always come up short. There were always signs left behind for them to find, mocking hints, challenges to catch the originator of the ruin and bring him in. On Pravia, on Daggaegghan, on Vreole, on Hromor. The Traitor had left his calling cards behind, taunting the Wolves who ever snapped at his heels.

We have been patient. We have waited. And now the trap closes.

Out of the corner of his eye a rune flashed over the doorway.

'Come,' he said, turning away from the view of the fleet.

Sturmhjart stalked into the chamber. The Rune Priest's eyes blazed with fury.

'Why?' he demanded.

Ironhelm spread his hands expansively.

'Odain,' he started. 'This is–'

'Tell me why.'

The Great Wolf sighed, and set the door to close with a flick of a finger.

'You know Wyrmblade's work. He needs watching.'

Sturmhjart snarled, pulling back his lips.

'Like a child? That's more important to you?'

'Only you can restrain him. He plays with forces that could destroy us all.'

'You let him.'

'Because he may succeed.'

'Tell him to wait. Tell him to stop until the Rout is called back from Gangava. I will not be denied this honour!'

Ironhelm shook his head.

'This is a critical time. The whelp is his protégé, and I need a wise head to keep the Aett in line. You will not be coming with us.'

Sturmhjart growled, and a flicker of yellow energy snaked across his chest. Ironhelm could sense the furnace of frustration hammering inside the Rune Priest's body.

'Do not do this,' he insisted, his fist gripping his staff tightly.

Ironhelm's eyebrow rose. Sturmhjart had never defied an order.

'You threaten me, Odain?' he said, letting a challenge-note enter his speech.

For a moment, Sturmhjart stood still, glaring at him, face contorted with anger. Eventually, reluctantly, he dropped his gaze, spitting on the floor with disgust.

'You don't understand,' he muttered. 'The witches. They take the elements and corrupt them. These are *my* enemies.'

Ironhelm looked at the Rune Priest carefully. Sturmhjart was a warrior after his own heart, a bloody-minded, fearless cutter of threads, but he had to know who dominated the pack.

'They are not. They are prey for all of us. Frei will be there, and the other Rune Priests, but I need you here.'

Sturmhjart balled his fists, and fresh slivers of elemental power rippled over the gauntlets. He was reeling his anger in, but it pained him.

'As Wyrmblade's nursemaid,' he spat bitterly.

'No, brother,' said Ironhelm. 'Wyrmblade has

delved deep, and he holds fate in both hands. If he falters, you must be there. You must watch over this.'

Sturmhjart's expression shifted awkwardly from frustration to surprise.

'You heard me,' said Ironhelm. 'Whatever Greyloc thinks, you're to be my sword arm here. We must remember the Wolf Brothers, their failure and the reasons for it. I will not see that path trodden again.'

Sturmhjart's eyes flickered in doubt.

'You think he's–'

'Wyrmblade's as loyal as Freki,' said Ironhelm, relaxing as he saw the Rune Priest's anger retreat. 'But we have to watch for the future.'

He came up to Sturmhjart and placed a heavy hand on his shoulder.

'I do this because I can trust you, brother,' he whispered, drawing his head close. 'Most out of all my Wolves, I can trust you. Seek the truth in the wyrd if you want, and you will understand – the Tempering is our destiny.'

Sturmhjart looked back into Ironhelm's eyes. He was still not reconciled, but he would take the order.

'So I have full sanction, lord?' he asked.

Ironhelm smiled grimly.

'We always have full sanction,' he said.

THE FANG WAS vast beyond comprehension – a huge network of tunnels, shafts and chambers that riddled the highest levels of the peak. Even so, the fortress proper was dwarfed by the full bulk of the mountain, and only the very upper reaches had ever been delved into habitation. For the most part, the Wolves dwelt underground, their lairs hidden under kilometres of solid rock. Only at the very pinnacle, the terminus of the Valgard level, did artificial structures break the surface in any quantity. It was there that the mighty landing stages and docking berths had been constructed, clustered around massive towers that thrust from sheer cliffs hundreds of metres tall. Ancient drive mechanisms powered service shafts a kilometre deep, hauling materiel and wargear from depots in the heart of the mountain and delivering them to the transports waiting in the hangars. They were always busy, those places, testament to the restless spirit of the Wolves and their ceaseless voyaging into the sea of stars.

Haakon Gylfasson stood on the edges of one such hangar, watching the scores of thralls and servitors crawl over the steaming hulls of ships like vermin on a corpse. Dozens of vessels had left already, and most of those that remained were earmarked for the warfleet. The ships left to the Twelfth were few, and for the most part the slowest and least well-armed. Only a single strike cruiser, the *Skraemar*, would remain in orbit to defend the planet, and it would have fewer than a dozen smaller craft in its escort.

That struck Gylfasson as entirely reasonable. What didn't strike him as reasonable was the commandeering of the *Nauro*. That was personal, an affront, and in a way that most of his battle-brothers would struggle to understand.

'I'm sorry, lord,' said the kaerl for the third time, staring hard at the data-slate in front of her and trying to avoid eye contact with Gylfasson. 'This is part of the requisition. The Great Wolf–'

'Let me tell you something,' said Gylfasson in his dark, feline drawl. He didn't speak like a typical Space Marine, and had none of the overt, bristling threat about him that they did. His colouring was dark, and his facial hair thick and matted. He was slighter than most pack members, even when kitted out in his full array of Scout's carapace armour. Only his eyes truly gave him away, the circles of amber pinned with black. No one but a son of Russ had those eyes. 'I'm not a nice person. I don't have the generosity of my brothers. I don't hang around them much, and they don't hang around me.'

The kaerl looked like she'd rather be anywhere else herself, but listened respectfully.

'So don't think I won't take this personally. Don't think I won't find out who your rivenmaster is and get you placed on external patrol in Asaheim for a month. I need this ship. It's my ship. It stays here.'

The kaerl looked back at her data-slate earnestly, as if some new information on it could possibly help her. Fifty metres behind her loomed the *Nauro* itself, sitting on the hangar apron and steaming gently. It didn't look like any of the other vessels waiting on the plascrete. It was jet-black, untouched by the gunmetal grey that coloured the rest of the fleet. Its classification was uncertain – too small to be a frigate, far too big to count as a transatmospheric craft, and just under five hundred crew. It sat low against the ground, narrow and unusually slender. Nearly a third of its length was taken up by plasma drives, a ratio that made it colossally fast. Which was exactly why Gylfasson liked it.

'You won't find what you're looking for there,' said

Gylfasson patiently, watching the kaerl play for time.

She looked up with a desolate expression on her face. The woman was built like most Fenrisians, heavy-boned and broad-shouldered. She'd seen combat, from the skulls woven into her uniform, so most things in the galaxy wouldn't shake her. Bartering with a Sky Warrior obviously did.

'Leave her be, Blackwing,' came a metallic voice from behind the kaerl.

His armour humming at a low, grinding pitch, the Twelfth's Iron Priest Garjek Arfang came pacing across the apron. He had his ancient Mk IV helm on, but Gylfasson could sense the amusement emanating from him. Somewhere, under all those layers of plate and augmetics, he was smiling.

'Stay out of this, Priest,' warned Gylfasson. 'This is my ship.'

'You're a Scout,' said Arfang bluntly. The kaerl took advantage of the interruption to withdraw. 'None of these ships are yours.'

'No one flies her like I do.'

'That is true. So be pleased that Jarl Oirreisson doesn't want it. He's taken a *hlaupa* instead. It will fall apart the first volley he fires, but when it comes to technology, he is a man of poor taste.'

Gylfasson looked at Arfang suspiciously.

'So it's not been requisitioned?'

'Not any more.'

'Then what's happening to it?'

There was a grating sound from behind Arfang's helm as the Iron Priest issued what passed for a laugh with him.

'Jarl Greyloc wants you on system patrol. You and the rest of the Scouts. He doesn't, I ascertain, like the Aett being under-manned.'

Gylfasson smiled broadly.

'Back on void-duty,' he said, looking over at the *Nauro* with satisfaction and thinking of the long, empty hours away from the reek of the Fang. 'You have no idea how pleased that makes me.'

GREYLOC STOOD IN the Chamber of the Watch, bathed in a column of cold light descending from the roof. The summit of the space was lost in darkness. In the shadows, thralls hurried to and fro, handing over data-slates and speaking in low voices. Picts placed around the edge of the chamber flickered with rapid updates, marking the movement of the fleet to the jump-points. One by one, green indicators turned red.

'Open a channel to the flagship,' Greyloc ordered.

Thralls scurried to comply. An icon-blink told him communication had been established.

'Lord,' he said, maintaining the deferential tone he'd adopted in the council. 'We have muster-complete signals. You're clear to break orbit.'

'All confirmed,' came Ironhelm's crackling voice from the bridge of the *Russvangum*. 'We'll be gone soon, and the Aett'll be nice and quiet. Just how you like it.'

Greyloc smiled.

'Indeed. I have hunting to catch up on.'

There was a rough burst of static from the other end. It might have been a snort.

'You're missing the best of it.'

'Maybe so. The hand of Russ ward you, lord.'

'And all of us.'

The comm-link snapped closed. Greyloc stood immobile for a few moments, his lean face pensive.

Then the picts began to update with fresh data. Position trackers showed massed movement. The fleet was underway.

A thrall approached the static Wolf Lord and bowed.

'Orbital grid overview prepared, lord,' he said, keeping his eyes on the floor. 'You may inspect when ready.'

Greyloc nodded, hardly seeming to notice the figure before him. His white eyes were fixed on the rock walls beyond. The stone was still as bare and unadorned as it had been when first carved.

The centuries had done little to adorn the Aett. It was the same size as it had been in Russ's time, still cold, half-empty and sighing with the incoming ice-wind of Fenris. Sections of the lower levels had fallen into disuse, and even Wyrmblade didn't know what had been left untouched in the deepest places.

We have not evolved. We remain the same.

The thrall hovered for a moment longer before scuttling back out of the light. He was replaced by a larger figure, and the heavy tread of Rossek echoed across the chamber.

'Tromm,' said Greyloc, snapping out of his thoughts.

'Jarl,' replied the Wolf Guard.

'You've kept the Claws busy?'

'They're knocking Hel out of each other in the cages.'

'Good. Keep them at it.'

'And after that?'

Greyloc scrutinised his subordinate carefully. Rossek was normally so ebullient, so full of energy.

'You don't agree with my decision,' he said.

The Wolf Guard kept his expression level. 'Someone has to guard the Aett.'

'You don't think it should have been us.'

'Since you make me speak, no.'

Greyloc nodded.

'Say more.'

Rossek looked him directly in the eye, as always. There was reproach there.

'We do not have the trophies of the other companies, lord,' he said. 'There are whispers that we lack spirit. They say your blood's cold.'

'Who says so?'

'Just whispers.'

Greyloc nodded again. The whispers had always been there. Since ascending to Blood Claw he'd had to fight for his honour against the slurs that he wasn't a real wolf, that the Helix hadn't taken properly, that he was more ice-wight than true flesh-warrior of the Rout. The days when such news would have concerned him were long gone.

'They've said as much before. Why are you listening now?'

Rossek held his gaze.

'We need to be careful,' he said. 'The other Jarls–'

'Forget about them.' Greyloc placed a gauntlet on his Wolf Guard's arm, and the ceramite clunked dully. 'We have no reason to hang our heads, and there are more ways to fight than those recorded in the sagas. The galaxy is changing. We must change with it.'

Greyloc felt the uneasiness stirring within Rossek. The Guard didn't like such talk. None of the Wolves, with their reverence for tradition, did. Only the two warriors' long brotherhood kept Rossek from speaking out more, from protesting against the manner of war Greyloc had imposed on the Twelfth Company.

'Do you trust me, Tromm?' asked Greyloc softly, maintaining the grip.

A hesitation.

'With my life, lord.'

His amber eyes were unblinking. Greyloc took some satisfaction in that. There were doubts there, like ravens clustering around carrion, but his core was loyal. So it had ever been, even after Greyloc had narrowly beaten him to replace old Oja Arkenjaw as Jarl. If the vote were held again, he had no doubt Rossek would have the numbers. The old warrior had always claimed not to want the honour, but every mind could change.

'Good,' said Greyloc, releasing his hold. 'I need you, Tromm. I need all of you. When Ironhelm returns from this mad *skraegr* hunt, things will have to change. We can't let these shadows blind us forever, keeping us chasing after ghosts of the past. You will see the truth of it, if you look.'

Rossek didn't reply. Such talk made him uneasy, and Greyloc knew he couldn't push too hard.

Across the picts placed around the chamber walls, the last of the fleet signals dimmed as the rearguard departed for the jump-points. Greyloc felt a surge of satisfaction then, and some of his preoccupation receded.

Ironhelm's latest campaign had embarked. The Aett was his.

CHAPTER THREE

KYR AESVAI, THE one they called Helfist, laughed hard, sending flecks of spittle from his semi-distended jaws.

'Russ, you're slow,' he mocked, then leapt back into the attack. He whirled his axe round and hurled it down at his enemy's shoulder.

Ogrim Raegr Vrafsson, the one they called Redpelt, sprang away from the incoming weapon.

'Quick enough for you,' he panted, falling away and bringing his own axehead into play. He kept it out wide, making room to swing, watching for the momentum of his opponent.

Crunches and impact sparks rang out further down the long row of iron training cages. The pair were not the only Blood Claws sparring in the pens – the entire infantry contingent of the Twelfth had been ordered into intensive drills in the days since Ironhelm's fleet had left. Greyloc was a cold one, but no fool – he knew how frustrated his company would be at missing the action at Gangava, and made sure he kept them busy.

Helfist pressed the attack, stepping warily. His jawline was still basically humanoid, though his facial muscles betrayed the gigantism common to all Space Marines. His cropped hair was a dirty blond, and stubble ran across his tattooed cheeks. He retained the brutal energy of a *hmanni* tribesman, and he carried himself with a strutting, confident menace.

'Nope,' he grinned, circling. 'You're too damn slow.'

Redpelt could have been his twin were it not for the messy shock of auburn hair and straggling sideburns. His fangs were similarly short, not yet extended by the long working of the Helix. He had an iron ring in his lower lip which glinted from the glow-globes above them. When he let slip his savage smile, which happened a lot, it dragged against his teeth like scree clattering down ice.

'Stop talking,' he said, beckoning Helfist on. 'And start fighting.'

Helfist darted left, then checked back and dragged the axe-blade up, aiming for Redpelt's torso. The two weapons impacted in a shower of sparks, locking the shafts. Helfist pushed two-handed, throwing all his massive strength into the shove.

Redpelt held it for a moment, then stumbled back, knocked off balance.

'Ya!' yelled Helfist, and pounced.

The axeheads clashed, then clashed again, each blow sending ripples of terrific force slamming into the defensive parries. Helfist was indeed the faster, and his uncovered arms moved in a blur.

'Coming for you now...' grunted Helfist through gritted teeth, his face a mask of concentration. Beads of
sweat had formed on his temples, even though the
fight-cages were winter-cold and glittering from the ice
on the metal.

Redpelt didn't reply, kept busy fending off the furious
assault from his pack-mate. Both Blood Claws were out
of armour, wearing leather tunics and greaves lined with
exquisite knotwork. The axe-blades were blunt for training, but were still capable of breaking bones and tearing
flesh. That was the way the overseers arranged it, to instil
the proper respect for the blade and to discourage reli-
ance on battle-plate.

Redpelt slammed against the cage wall, feeling the
unyielding iron press into his back. He rolled away as
Helfist's axe arced through the space where his chest had
just been.

From outside the cage, a torrent of raucous laughter
rang out.

'Skítja,' swore Redpelt, picking out the dark shapes
of other Blood Claws standing out of the range of the
glowglobes. He'd got an audience. A low jeering broke
out as Redpelt evaded another swipe and scrambled to
get out of range.

'Slow, slow, slow,' taunted Helfist, swaggering after
him, breathing heavily, his face running with moisture.
Redpelt took some satisfaction from the fact he wasn't
making this easy.

'You'd fight better if you didn't talk so much,' Redpelt
muttered, trying to regain balance and take the initiative
back.

'Think that if it makes you feel better,' crowed Helfist, stalking after him, hefting the axe-shaft lightly. He had the superior smile of victory, and closed back into swing range.

'Yeah,' growled Redpelt, coiling for the spring. 'It does.'

He thrust suddenly upwards, hurling himself at Helfist's advancing torso and barrelling him back. Helfist had come in too close, too confident, and couldn't get his axe down in time. Redpelt wrapped him in a bear-hug and propelled him further, running him into the far wall of the cage. They hit it with a resounding clang.

Helfist's axe dropped from his clutches and he balled his fist, poised to deliver the crushing blow that had given him his name. Redpelt was quicker, and head-butted him full in the face. There was a crack of bone against bone, and the metallic tang of fresh blood.

Helfist's head rocked back, and his glittering eyes went glassy. Redpelt let his own weapon fall and clubbed the reeling Blood Claw with a flurry of punches, hammering him down to his knees.

A roar of approval rang out across the iron cage, punctuated by whoops and howls. Weapons were dragged along the bars, echoing up into the roof space and making the entire chamber reverberate.

The cacophony was so loud it almost obscured the gong that signalled the end of the fight. Feigning ignorance, Redpelt got in one more bone-crunching uppercut before the cage doors were slammed open and Brakk lumbered in to break them up.

'That's enough,' he snarled, pulling Redpelt off the

reeling Helfist and hurling him back across the cage. Even out of power armour the Wolf Guard was far stronger than either of them. 'This is blade-practice, not a brawl.'

There was a chorus of disappointed boos as Redpelt clambered back to his feet and Brakk hoisted Helfist up against the cage wall.

Redpelt's whole body ached. A hot trail of blood ran down his face from where the skin over his forehead had broken.

He felt drained, bruised, battered, fantastic.

Helfist was beginning to come round, his head lolling and eyes still out of focus.

'That was stupid,' growled Brakk. 'Am I going to have to beat the stupidity out of you, Blood Claw?'

'You could try,' drawled Helfist, punch-drunk against the iron.

Redpelt grinned, limping over to his adversary. Brakk spat on the floor.

'Get yourself cleaned up,' he said. 'The Jarl wants reports on your combat readiness, and you're going to have to work a whole lot harder.'

Brakk stalked off out of the cage, pushing his way through the crowd of spectators clustered outside. Redpelt caught Helfist before he could collapse to the floor again and pulled him back up roughly.

'Like I said. Too quick for you,' he said.

Helfist's vision was clearing. The blood in his wounds had turned dark with clotting. It took a lot to knock him over, but even more to keep him down.

'This time, brother,' he replied, and grinned across blood-soaked teeth. 'Only this time.'

Redpelt laughed, a throaty roar of feral enjoyment. The two fighters slammed their right fists together, and the bruised fingers clenched fast.

WYRMBLADE SLUMPED BACK in his throne, feeling bone-weary. The work was exhausting, even for one with his gene-forged physiology. Days at a time of testing, refining, testing again, splicing, looking for the hidden flaws, rooting out the false positives and bearing down on the secrets wound within the vials and vessels. All around him, the low hubbub of the laboratorium continued – thralls diligently poring over sample trays, cogitators chattering, vials of fluid gently bubbling at precisely controlled temperatures.

Nine days. Nine days since Ironhelm had left, emptying the Aett of the Great Companies and leaving the corridors sparse and home to whispers. In that time, almost nothing had been achieved, and much had been undone. Every step forwards was accompanied by many more backwards, sideways and down. It would be easy to despair, easy to lose hope.

Except, of course, that despair was as alien to a son of Russ as peace and stillness.

The secret eludes me only because I draw closer. Like prey on the ice, it can sense the hunter.

The analogy helped him. There had been times when intractable problems had been solved through the imagery of the hunt. The kill-urge could be sublimated, turned into a source of pure mental determination. That gave him hope, too. There was so much that he didn't understand, but so much that he was beginning to see clearly. That the kill-urge had such origins was a positive sign.

Do I dare too much? Is this forbidden? Perhaps. But then we have never been ones for following the rules. Leave those to Guilliman's sons.

He reviewed the evidence again. The pattern he'd been pursuing over the past few weeks was breaking down. Not irretrievably, but with severe consequences for the model he'd placed so much faith in. It would need another week of work to put right, to untangle the snarls. Not for the first time, he found himself in awe of the original architects, the ones who'd put the elements together, who'd forced the river of humanity into its new and lasting course.

Is this forbidden? he asked himself again, knowing the answer already.

Of course it was.

A rune blinked on his armour-collar, alerting him to Sturmhjart's presence nearby. The Rune Priest, for all his power on the battlefield, was an unsubtle spy. Wyrmblade sighed, stowing the data-slate in the arm-recess of the throne. He gestured to a nearby thrall, and the leather-masked mortal nodded his understanding. The blast-doors deep in the laboratorium complex slid closed, masking the contents of the rooms beyond. Pict screens of sensitive results cleared, replaced by standard looking rows of runes.

Wyrmblade rose from the throne, wearily preparing to meet the scorn and suspicion of his brother.

He fears much, and guesses much, thought Wyrmblade, pacing through the interconnected tiled chambers in his awkward, age-corroded way. *Let him. If he guessed more, he'd fear more. Only Greyloc sees the potential, but his soul is strange.*

Wyrmblade neared the entrance chamber to the laboratorium and saw the hulking figure of the Rune Priest waiting for him, his rich, sigil-encrusted armour an odd counterpoint to the sterile realm of the flesh-makers.

I just need more time.

Wyrmblade forced the familiar hooked smile on to his wrinkled features and went to greet his brother with the expected irascible banter.

A little more time.

THE THOUSAND SONS flotilla flagship *Herumon* began to slow, making ready to break the seal between the warp and the materium. All around it, the rest of the fleet matched pace, fifty-four blue and gold warships and troop carriers grinding down to translation speed.

On the bridge of the *Herumon*, Temekh and Aphael stood side by side, Pyrae and Corvidae. The other members of the senior command retinue – Ormana, Hett and Czamine – stood around them. All wore full battle-plate over their robes and their helms had been donned. Most of them had spent the long, boredom-filled hours on the Planet of the Sorcerers honing and altering their suits. The helms now bore crests and flutes of gold and bronze, and their greaves were engraved with florid scripts invoking long forgotten epigrams.

Temekh regarded them tolerantly. Of his companions, only he seemed to see how far they'd fallen.

We have lost our taste. We are becoming parodies of ourselves.

His own armour was relatively unmodified Mark III, re-coloured sapphire to reflect Magnus's orders, but otherwise much as it had been before the Betrayal. He still wore the neatly clipped beard he'd adopted on Prospero, still kept his white hair trimmed close. He found himself wondering whether Amon, Sobek and Hathor Maat had done likewise. Those who had joined Ahriman's breakaway cabal had always been the most headstrong and those with the most power. The rump that had remained faithful to the primarch were the second-rate, the ones who had not dared to join the casting of the Rubric.

Not that it had mattered. The counter-sorcery had affected them all anyway, preserving less than a hundred of the Legion's sorcerers and condemning the rest, the Rubricae, to dust. Now the remnants of what had once been the Emperor's most finely crafted weapons were scattered into petty bands of raiders, vengeance-seekers and knowledge-thieves. This grand fleet, this gathering of disparate forces, was the final gesture, the last echo of a disaster that had taken place over a thousand years ago.

'Lord, we are preparing to make translation.'

The speaker was a shaven-headed crewman with heavy kohl around his eyes. He wore the robes of a senior watch officer, and must have served in the fleet for many years. Most of the mortal crew were much more recently drafted, the products of a long programme of cult-planting on a hundred Imperial worlds.

Aphael turned to Temekh.

'And what do you see, prophet?' he asked, his voice

distorted by an elaborate vox-grille.

Temekh suppressed his irritation at being asked again, and cast his mind's eye out on to the Great Ocean. The occult relations between warp space and realspace unfolded before him like the branches of an equation, moving subtly against one another, falling in and out of balance.

He tracked the location of the fleet and traced it to its destination. The margins were slight. If they maintained their current orientation, they'd be coming in very close to Fenris.

'You're taking us in hard,' said Temekh, snapping back into the present. 'Too hard.'

Aphael laughed.

'You want to give them time to prepare?' The Pyrae shook his armoured head. 'Remember how our orbital stations were taken down? In *seconds*. That's the way to burn a world. The Ocean has been calmed for us, smoothed apart to let us drop right in on top of their heads.'

Temekh could sense Aphael's smiles under his helm, could feel his eagerness for the clash ahead.

'There's nothing to worry us in the warp, brother,' Aphael continued. 'If you looked yourself, you'd see the Dog-fleet is already days away and beyond recall. With *speed* we will do this thing.'

'Fine. Just don't hurl us into the heart of the planet.'

Aphael didn't laugh at that.

'Time to translation?' he asked, turning to the officer.

'Imminent, lord.'

'Then activate the screen.'

Ahead of the command group, a curved mirror rose

gracefully from the bronze-plate floor. The glazed surface swam with colour, shifting and breaking like oil on water. Temekh looked at it with distaste. It was a crude representation of the aether, the result of looking at it through machine-spirit eyes.

'Begin,' ordered Aphael.

Across the fleet, warp drives powered down. The fifty-four ships acted in unison, their plasma drives growling into life and their void shields rippling into place.

The shifting vision on the mirror sheered away, replaced by the void. Ahead of them, terrifyingly close, was a single ball of pearl-white. It rushed toward the approaching ships, growing larger with every second. The Thousand Sons fleet, guided by its peerless scryers, had emerged from the warp closer and faster than any mortal-guided ship could have managed.

Temekh felt a low foreboding creep across his stomach. So this was it, the target of Magnus's long and bitter planning. It looked smaller than he'd hoped for, a dirty ball of howling gales and cracked ice.

Aphael radiated savage energy. Ahead of the *Herumon*, other ships of the flotilla were becoming visible through the realspace viewers. Streaks of superheated plasma scored across the heavens as the strike vessels raced to compass the target. In their wake, the heavy troop carriers lumbered into position. There were no mistakes, no botched rematerialisations.

'Fenris,' Aphael breathed, held rapt by the unfolding spectacle in front of him. Terrible forces spread out across the cosmos in tight formation, the kind of forces not seen together since before the Betrayal.

Temekh, seeing the same vista unfold, felt nothing but a weary dread. He'd wept over the destruction of Tizca, but that did nothing to fuel his sense of revenge. By contrast, Aphael's eagerness felt vulgar and empty.

We have lost our taste.

The Pyrae was heedless. He walked toward the mirror, watching as the isolated globe filled the screen ahead.

'This will hurt you,' he murmured. 'Oh, this will hurt you *so much*.'

ADAMAN EARFEIL'S LAST day alive did not start well. Few of the astropaths manning the communications spire in the Valgard were Fenris-born, which made him one of only a dozen or so off-worlders on the entire planet. His native subordinates were rude, malodorous and given to making foul-mouthed jokes about his witchery. They didn't like the use of psyker powers, even though their own bone-rattlers leaked enough aether-born power to level a manufactorum. Even after forty years' service, he still hadn't thrown off the ways of his home world, the hive-planet Anrada. He hated Fenris. He hated the stink, he hated the boredom, and he hated the cold.

After little more than two hours' sleep, the chime summoning him to the astropathic gantry was infuriating. The entire choir had been busy enough over the past few days transmitting material for the muster. He emerged from his cell blearily, wiping the sleep from his sightless eyes. In the corridor beyond he felt the press of bodies hurrying back and forth.

There was a low, concerned chatter over vox-beads. Something had got the spire roused.

Once in the Sanctum Telepathica, Earfeil strode confidently through the mass of kaerls and thralls around him, judging where they were from smell and sound alone. The passages from his cell to the transmitter thrones were as well known to him as the outline of his own body. Ever since waking, though, he'd felt a dull pressure mount behind his eyes, dragging at his thoughts and making his work difficult.

He took his station, feeling terrible. Thick-headed, lethargic and irascible.

A servitor creaked up to assist him into his transmit-throne, and he winced as he felt the cold steel of the interface implant itself into his wrist input nodes. There was no damn reason for that to be so painful – if the savages on this forsaken world had cared about anything like comfort, they'd have installed new equipment years ago.

'Water,' he croaked, knowing that it would take the servitor an age to retrieve a cup and bring it back, frigid and with an aftertaste of grit.

Clumsily, his headache getting worse, he began to decipher the programme of work ahead. All around him, he could hear more chatter as other astropaths began their litanies.

'Blessed Emperor, Protector of Humanity, Lord of the Heavens, guide my thoughts in Your service and clear the landscape of my mind...'

Earfeil began to recite while adjusting the series of dials and levers on the console in front of him. The machinery felt warmer than usual – normally, his desiccated old flesh would stick to the ice-cold metal.

As he spoke, the itinerary began to appear in his mind. He couldn't see the text exactly, but the sending was clear enough as a mental image.

'May my body endure and my soul remain pure, my Inner Eye remain clear and my Outer Eye remain dark as the eternal mark of Your favour...'

He kept speaking the familiar words as the iron hood, bristling with needle-slender probes, descended over him. He kept speaking as the probes threaded through the steel-ringed holes in his bald skull and came to rest in their allotted places. He kept speaking as the voices of the rest of the choir drifted out of focus.

My head is killing me.

There was no sign of the water. Earfeil pulled up the first transmission. Standard inter-world communique, something about convoy escorts on one of the Wolves' protected systems.

'Maintain the ward of Your protection... dammit, Fror, why is this list so long?'

There was a crackle of broken static over the channel to the superintendent, a Fenris-born over two hundred years old.

'Fror?'

Earfeil gave up. Senile old goat. The pain behind his eyes got worse. It felt as if the burned-out nerves had somehow reconnected.

What in Hel is doing that?

He considered calling for an apothecary, pulling out of the contact, then changed his mind. They all thought he was weak anyway, a soft-fleshed off-worlder with a smattering of unholy magick.

He opened up his mind.

The aether rushed in. A single eye stared back at him from the void, ringed with a circuit of crimson.

'Holy Empe–' he started, and then the pain really began.

Something massive entered his consciousness, something vast and ancient, something of such magnitude that Earfeil immediately knew he was a dead man.

'Fror!' he screamed, maybe out loud, maybe mentally. Dimly, he could hear other noises coming out of the darkness around him. There were heavy footfalls as someone ran across the chamber. Then there were screams. Then all was lost in the pain – the crushing, mind-bending pain.

He briefly thought about struggling against it. For a moment, a horrifying moment, he was taken back to the soul-binding on Terra. Back then he'd been exposed to sentience of such magnitude that it had burned out his eyes and seared his soul shut.

This is the same force.

No, it wasn't. Not quite the same, though kin to it. Even as he writhed in his bonds, pinned down in his seat by the electrodes running through him, he could make out familiar shapes in the warp signature.

Close the link!

It was too late for that. Earfeil could feel his organs popping inside him, slapping open with hot, agonising explosions. Blood was running down his face, dribbling into his open mouth, frozen in a soundless rictus scream. The eye blazed at him, rippling with casual menace. This thing wasn't even trying hard.

+What are you?+ he sent, and his message was like

shooting a microlumen into a star.

The eye didn't waver, but piled on more agony. It was then that Earfeil knew it was doing the same to all the astropaths. That should have been impossible – there were wards against infiltration across the spire, and the psykers were all soul-bound. This thing was tearing them apart as if the protection didn't exist.

He juddered in his throne, feeling awareness leave him. His nerves were burned away, giving some release from the pain.

This will isolate us, he thought as he fell towards death. *It wants us mute.*

That was the penultimate thought Adaman Earfeil ever had. The last one came hard on its heels.

And whatever it is, he realised, his burned body spasming in excruciation, *it's just like the Emperor.*

CHAPTER FOUR

WOLF SCOUT HAAKON Gylfasson, the one they called Blackwing, sat in the command throne of the *Nauro* and surveyed the scene before him smugly. The landing stages were already far behind and the dark of the sky from the realspace viewers had sunk into star-flecked black. The neon-white curve of Fenris fell away as the starship climbed higher, its engines straining against the powerful pull of the receding planet. It had taken many days of preparation to fit the *Nauro* out for an extended system patrol tour, but now the irritating wait was over and he was back where he belonged.

In the servitor pit below him, a dozen hardwired automata laboured at their stations. On the gantries above, six kaerls were strapped into restraint harnesses until the atmosphere was cleared and gravity generators could compensate properly.

'Master, report when ready,' ordered Blackwing casually, enjoying the feel of the ship as it thundered into low orbit range. The metal floor shivered slightly under him. The vessel was like a hunting-hound – lean, trembling, taut in the slips.

'You're pushing her hard,' came the reply over the comm-link from the engine chambers. The ship's Master was a veteran of working with Blackwing, and there was no confidence in the mortal's voice that his warning would be heeded.

Blackwing enjoyed making him uncomfortable. He enjoyed making everyone uncomfortable. That was the joy of piloting an interceptor with a crew entirely composed of mortals – the absolute power, the knowledge he could drive this thing as hard as he wanted. It was a beautiful ship, a thoroughbred, and there was no fun in keeping the ascent within safety parameters.

'Treat her mean, Master,' he replied. 'That's the way she likes it.'

There was a muttered expletive from the other end before the link cut out. Blackwing grinned and summoned a hololith from the arm of the throne. The tactical display flickered into life in front of him, a swivelling sphere representing local space.

'We'll buzz the grid on our way out,' he shared with the Tacticus, mentally plotting a trajectory that would take them to within a few kilometres of the first orbital gun platform. 'It'll take their minds off their tedious lives.'

'I can't raise them,' replied the grey-suited Tacticus,

seated at a console just below Blackwing's position.

'What do you mean?'

'I mean I can't raise them.'

Blackwing frowned and cut into the channel. There was a hiss of static.

'Are our comms shot?' he demanded.

'We're fine,' replied the Tacticus, his fingers playing across a control panel that looked more like an organ. 'It's them.'

Blackwing flicked his eyes at the hololith display. The first of the gun platforms was swimming into augur range, a single rune floating within the emerald sphere.

'What's their problem?' he asked.

The Tacticus turned away from his array and shrugged.

'System failure,' he suggested. 'That, or they're being jammed.'

Blackwing laughed harshly.

'Yes, like that's–'

The wolf-spirit within him suddenly stirred, as if uncurling from sleep. He felt the hairs on the back of his arms rise under his armour.

'Keep trying,' he ordered, and expanded the range of the tactical display. The figures within the sphere rushed into tiny points as the scope widened. More orbital platforms swept within the augur ambit.

'Can we get the *Skraemar*?' he asked, not liking what he was seeing.

'Not responding.'

The sphere kept expanding as the sensor arrays took in more and more of local space. Then, at the edge of the range, more runes appeared. Lots of them. None with Fenrisian sigils.

'How're our shields?' asked Blackwing, clutching the arms of the throne a little tighter.

'Fine.'

'Keep them fine. Now bring auxiliary plasma banks online.'

The Tacticus turned to look up at him, staring as if he'd gone mad.

'We're still within the gravity–'

Blackwing fixed him with a withering look.

'I want attack speed. Now. Then signal the Valgard and tell them to throw everything they've got up here. Then get your prayers in.'

Blackwing turned to the tactical display and dug his fingers into the control arms of the throne. He poured on more power, and felt the febrile machine-spirit whine in protest.

'Get used to it,' he growled, gouging at the metal under his gauntlets. 'It's going to get a whole lot worse soon.'

SOMETHING HAD STIRRED within Greyloc's mind even before the warning runes started to come in. He was deep in the Fang, working on the edge of his axe-blade Frengir, the one he'd taken from his life and kept by his side. The Wolf Priests didn't like remnants of mortal days being retained, but a blade was a sacred thing, and now he was Jarl they had less power to turn that displeasure into sanction.

He'd been honing the killing blade with a whet-stone, working carefully to maintain the murder-edge. The head of it was iron, far softer than any axe he'd used as a Space Marine and useless for proper combat.

Still, he'd kept it in pristine condition over the years, never letting the metal blunt or degrade. Scrapes of swarf littered the bare floor by the whetstone, scattered at his feet as he worked.

Then the runes glowed into life, set high up on the walls of the forge. At the same time, red sigils burst out across the collar of his armour, smaller versions of the data-feeds his helm would have given him had he been wearing it.

Greyloc put the axe down.

'Jarl,' came a voice into his earpiece. 'We're under attack. Multiple targets closing in, defensive grids coming under fire. Transmission spires compromised, casualties taken.'

The change was instantaneous. Greyloc grabbed his helm from its mounting and strode from his cell into the corridor beyond.

'All pack leaders to the Chamber of the Watch,' he snapped back over the comm. 'Including Wyrmblade. Enemy numbers?'

'Over forty major targets closing,' came the response. It was Skrieya, the Wolf Guard he'd stationed in the Chamber. 'Possibly more.'

'*Forty?* From where?'

There was a hesitation.

'Unknown, Jarl.'

'Make sure Sturmhjart's there,' snarled Greyloc as he broke into a run, his whole body tensing. 'Hammer of Russ, there'd better be a reason why he didn't see this.'

RIVENMASTER GREGR KJOLBORN of the Reike Og orbital platform ran down the plasteel corridor to the command module, half-deafened by klaxons blaring from every angle. There was a massive, shuddering boom, and his world tilted several degrees.

He slammed against the near wall and spat a curse.

'Where in *Hel* did they come from?' he muttered as he regained his feet. The doors to the command module had jammed open, and he could see the mess within before he'd burst past them.

'Status!' he panted as he took up position on the dais in the centre.

The command module of the gun platform was seven metres wide and circular. Realspace viewers dominated the ceiling. Normally they would have opened out on to blank space. Now the plexiglass looked out on to an inferno. The whole structure, several thousand tons of plasteel and adamantium, was listing dangerously. Across the floor of the module, kaerls and servitors worked at a cluster of linked consoles, all of them alive with flashing danger runes. Far below, the curve of Fenris's northern hemisphere glowed ice-white in the void.

'Primary shield failure imminent,' read out his huskaerl, Emme Vreborn. Her voice was flinty and unwavering, something that did her credit as the burning console in front of her spat sparks. 'Power ten per cent above minimum. We've got a few minutes.'

Kjolborn nodded, feeling his blood continue to pump around his system. 'Weapons?'

'Critical,' reported another kaerl.

'Great.'

Kjolborn tried to take in the situation. Seven minutes ago there had been signals picked up on the long-range scanners. Two minutes after that the signals had turned into battleships. Either there was a serious problem with the augur array, or a fleet had come out of the warp staggeringly close to Fenris's gravity well. There'd been no warning, no warp wakes detected, and no time to do anything other than power up the weapon batteries and prepare to return fire. As it had turned out, that response had been pitifully insufficient.

A wall of ships had swarmed at them at full speed, sending arcs of energy tearing into the linked network of orbital platforms. Several guns had gone down almost immediately, taken out by the massed volume of fire, their void shields overloaded and cracked apart in a blaze of released energy.

The defenders' counter-attack had been sporadic, with no time to coordinate proper firing solutions. In the wake of the initial assault, enemy fighters had spun out of the shadow of the larger ships, screaming into range and strafing the surviving elements of the defensive grid. It had all been too fast, too overwhelming. Now the outer network was in flames, burning and falling into the upper atmosphere, and what was left was going to do little more than slow the bulk of the fleet closing in on it.

'Has the Aett been warned?' asked Kjolborn, looking at the carnage around him, his mind racing.

'Oh, they know all about it,' replied Vreborn.

'Lucky them.'

For a moment, Kjolborn thought wistfully of the saviour pods slung under the planetside face of the platform. If he'd been bred anywhere but Fenris, he might even have contemplated trying to reach them.

'Divert all power from the shields and feed to the forward battery,' he ordered, running his gaze over the swirling pattern of light on the tactical displays.

'Sir?'

There was a second crash as something massive hit the platform from underneath. The lights failed, leaving nothing but blood-red backups. The crew of the command module looked like shadows of the Underverse in the gloom.

'You heard me. I want one shot before we go.'

The kaerls complied without further query. With an involuntary shudder, Kjolborn watched as the platform's void shields shrank back across the realspace viewers. The withdrawal left a shimmering trail in its wake, and then the blade-sharp unmediated view of the void.

'Lock on incoming *Fyf-Tra*, bearing 2.-2.-3. Once you've fixed, hit it.'

Kaerls hurried to comply. Out of the corner of his eye Kjolborn saw another platform explode in a huge ball of hot white plasma and its signal wink out from the tactical display. He ignored it, concentrating on his target. Amid the sea of oncoming ships, an enemy frigate, already reeling from some other impact, was turning to bring a prow lance to bear. It caught the reflective light from the half-disc of Fenris on its armoured prow, and the sapphire plating flashed briefly.

'Gotcha,' said Kjolborn grimly, careless of the las-fire coming in from a squadron of fighters hard to port-nadir.

'Solution ready,' reported the second kaerl, working to compensate as the incoming fire sent the platform lurching again.

'Knock it out of the void.'

Eye-watering fluorescent beams leapt across the gap, slamming into the frigate a hundred kilometres distant and breaking open the shell of void shielding. Massive, silent explosions rippled along port-ventral galleries of the vessel as the lethal energy cut though the hull-plates and ripped them aside. The ship stopped turning and began to spin down into an aimless death-spiral. More explosions broke out as something within the structure ignited and set off a chain.

Kjolborn watched the target die with a cold satisfaction. More enemy fighters homed in on the dark disc of the platform, tearing up the physical shielding with heavy las-fire.

'What have we got left?' he asked, wincing with each blow his platform took.

Vreborn smiled wryly in the dark, her face under-lit red.

'Nothing,' she reported. 'That finished us.'

Kjolborn laughed savagely, watching as vengeful enemy contacts surged towards their position. Other gun platforms were firing more frequently now, but they were being destroyed as quickly as they were taking down their targets. The void was aflame across every viewer, punctuated with the dark shapes of broken hulls and the incandescent burn of debris falling planetward.

'Worth a shot just to piss them off,' he said to

himself, watching fresh signals close in on his position and bracing for further hits. A squadron of gunships was wheeling toward them now, weaving between a slow-moving phalanx of larger ships to get a clean shot.

Vreborn wheeled around to face Kjolborn, suddenly animated.

'The saviour pods,' she said.

'You're not going to get to them in time, huskaerl.'

If the lights had been up, Kjolborn would have seen her look of injured scorn.

'They're projectiles.'

Kjolborn realised what she had in mind then, and shrugged. 'If you can spin it, do it.'

The gunships, wedge-nosed sapphire Thunderhawks, raced into position, battle-cannons primed to fire. Kjolborn watched them come, wishing he'd had the time to get drunk before taking his seat. Just because he didn't fear death didn't mean he liked the idea.

And I don't even know who's doing this.

Vreborn worked furiously, tilting the platform upwards. The platform's low-power manoeuvring drives had been shot to nothing, and the cumbersome disc swung round only slowly. As it turned, Kjolborn heard heavy clamps shoot back on the level below, releasing the saviour pod docking claws.

He stood up from the throne, watching death come for him from the stars.

'This isn't the way I wanted to go,' he announced to the others in the module. 'But you've been a better than mediocre crew. I mean that. There are only two others I'd rather have died with, and one of them–'

They were the last words spoken on gun platform Reike Og before the incoming Thunderhawks of the Thousand Sons unleashed their main cannons on the listing target. Without shielding, the end was almost immediate, and the fragments of metal, plasteel and bone that weren't immediately vaporised in a cloud of atoms spun into the upper atmosphere, lit up, and burned into nothing.

So it was that huskaerl Vreborn would never know that, of the seven empty saviour pods jettisoned milliseconds before the explosion, four made it down to Fenris, two more were immolated by the backwash from another platform destruction, while one of them, against all probability, found its target. A Thunderhawk, roaring under the destroyed gun platform at full attack velocity, could do nothing to avoid the punching fist of adamantium-braced metal that had been ejected at the last possible moment. It was hit hard in the cockpit, flew wildly out of control and tore into the upper atmosphere at lethal, unrecoverable speed.

Just like the debris of the platform it had killed, it lit up like a meteorite before dying in a blaze of promethium-fuelled destruction.

GREYLOC STORMED INTO the Chamber of the Watch, seconds behind Rossek and Wyrmblade. The Rune Priest Sturmhjart was already there, as were six of Greyloc's Wolf Guard. One of them, Leofr, was still being enclosed in his armour by a dozen thralls, and the sound of drilling echoed around the dark space.

'Tell me,' the Jarl growled, taking up position within the column of light. From that vantage he could see every pict screen that lined the Chamber.

Greyloc could feel his mind working quickly, poised to tease out possibilities, assessing every scrap of information. There was no fear, just a rapid, mechanical process of appraisal. All around him, his Guard stood ready, expectant.

'Fleet is engaged, Jarl,' reported Hamnr Skrieya, turning from the screens to face him. The blond, hulking Wolf Guard had a warrior's shame etched on his face, and it made his speech savage and clipped. '*Skraemar* has taken heavy damage but holds position. Grid is down to twenty per cent.'

'Who dares this?'

Skrieya let a flicker of hatred mar his intense expression for a second.

'Archenemy, Jarl. The Sons.'

Greyloc froze for a second.

The Thousand Sons! Ironhelm, what have you done? You were the prey for this trap.

He shook his head to clear it and looked at the tactical hololiths. For a moment, even he, a veteran of a hundred void engagements, was taken aback. The invasion fleet was huge. Around the fifty-four points of light indicating capital vessels, hundreds of smaller signals swarmed and harried. The red lights indicating defensive assets were beleaguered. Even as he watched, three of them guttered out.

'How did they get in so close?' he demanded, feeling frustrated anger suddenly rise up within him. 'Where was the warning?'

There was a distant rumble across the walls of the Chamber as the Fang's defensive batteries opened up, sending salvos of ship-killer missiles hurtling into the void above.

'We've been blinded,' said Sturmhjart. Like Skrieya, his face was written with shame. 'I saw nothing, the augurs saw nothing.'

'Damn Ironhelm!' spat Greyloc. He felt the urge to lash out, to slam something heavy into the screens that reported the carnage above. 'Can we contact him?'

'No,' said Skrieya, bluntly. 'We can't contact anyone. All astropaths are dead, all system exits blockaded.'

'We need to join the void war,' urged Rossek, looking away from the tactical display and preparing to leave. 'There are Thunderhawks still in the hangars.'

'No.'

Greyloc took a deep, ragged breath. The tactical displays were unequivocal. Though it had been raging for less than an hour, the war above was already lost.

'Prepare the Rout to defend the Aett. We cannot stop them landing.'

'Jarl–' began Rossek.

'Open a channel to the *Skraemar*,' he ordered.

A crackling link was established. Over the background of it came huge, shuddering crashes. The strike cruiser was taking heartbreaking levels of punishment.

'Jarl!' came a Space Marine's voice over the comm. It was thick with fluid, as if blood had welled up in the speaker's throat.

'Njan,' replied Greyloc. He kept his voice soft. 'How long can you hold them?'

There was a crude laugh. 'We should already be dead.'

'Then cheat it a little longer. We need time.'

A reverberating crash distorted the comm-link, followed by what sounded like a rush of flames.

'That's what we had in mind. Enjoy the fight when it comes for you.'

Greyloc smiled coldly.

'I will. Until next winter, Njan.'

The link broke then, suddenly cutting off the reports of distant carnage. All that remained to indicate the struggle above them were the points of light on the tactical displays.

Greyloc turned to face his commanders, his white eyes burning.

'We can debate how this happened later,' he said. 'For now, get ready to fight. Ready the Claws, ready the Hunters. When they get down here, we'll rip their throats out.'

There was another rumble as the Fang's colossal defence batteries sent death roaring into orbital space. Greyloc allowed the wolf within him to rise to the surface, and fixed the assembled Wolf Guard with an expression of pure animal loathing.

'This is our place, brothers,' he snarled. 'We'll teach them to fear it.'

THE NAURO CORKSCREWED through the crimson blooms of detonating charges at full tilt, weaving a path through the shells of dying vessels and spinning away from the flickering tracery of incoming las-fire. In the cold silence of the void, the manoeuvring had a sharp-edged beauty to it, an exhibition of peerless ship-mastery.

Within the ship, activity was frenetic. Crew members raced to combat the fires raging on the lower decks while kaerls struggled to keep the void shields from buckling completely. The plasma drives were dangerously hot from being overburned, and the ventral augur arrays had been almost completely shot away. Any more big hits, and they'd be fast moving junk.

'Get those lances back online!' roared Blackwing, sending his ship plummeting steeply to avoid a barrage of plasma bolts.

The two underslung energy lances, the only significant offensive weapons the ship had left, had been knocked out of action after a collision with a huge, spinning chunk of somebody else's prow-shield. The *Nauro* was already painfully exposed, and the inability to fire back wasn't helping.

'We can't save them both!' shouted a crewman from the pits below him. Blackwing couldn't see who he was – he could barely see anything other than the dancing lights on his hololith display. Piloting a single vessel in three dimensions through a maelstrom of plasma and las-fire was a nightmare, even for a pilot with his superlative reactions and training.

'Get me one, then!' bellowed Blackwing, pulling the prow round just in time to thunder past the shattered, blazing hull of a Space Wolves frigate as it rolled gently into destruction. 'Just one. Morkai's hairy balls, that's not asking for much.'

He wrenched the *Nauro* into a rare corridor of open space and tried to make sense of the tactical situation. His launch path from the Valgard had sent him straight into the orbital battle as it was breaking out.

The Wolves, unprepared and massively outgunned, were being taken apart. The first rank of gun platforms was now cold and dead, a circuit of dark, drifting metal. The second and final layer was holding for the moment, but it had taken a horrendous mauling. Every successful hit from the defenders had provoked a hurricane of return fire. The Thousand Sons' rapid strike vessels were quickly gaining the space to move with impunity, clearing the way for the larger battleships to take their places and pile on the pain.

The arrival of the *Skraemar* and her escorts had briefly halted the carnage, but the defending fleet was still outnumbered many times over. Only a handful of the Space Wolves, frigates were still operational, and once their protective chain was broken the *Skraemar* would take the full force of the onslaught.

'Starboard lance semi-operational, lord!' came a triumphant cry from below the command throne.

'Semi?' snarled Blackwing, wheeling away from a wing of enemy fighters and exposing his less-damaged starboard flank to them. The telltale juddering in the ship's frame told him that there were still flank gun batteries in operation, which was something. '*Semi?* What does that mean?'

'We've got one, maybe two shots. Then we're all burned out.'

'Another kill – that's all I'm asking.'

He knew then that they were going to die. It would happen in the next second, or the next minute, but not long after. The planetary defence had turned into a bloody-minded attempt to take out as many of the enemy as possible before they were all turned into orbiting streams of dust. Despite all of that, not one of the Twelfth's ships had turned and run. Not one.

Stubborn bastards, thought Blackwing, glancing at the forest of warning runes on his console with mild interest. *Stubborn, magnificent bastards*.

'Lord, I've got a link from Fenris,' reported a kaerl manning the comms platform. 'You should hear this.'

Blackwing nodded, his attention still fixed on piloting his ship through Hel, and blink-clicked to received the feed.

'*Nauro, Sleikre, Ogmar*,' came the broken, dry voice, filtered through the ship's internal systems. It was a recording – how long had they been trying to get through? '*Astropathic communications are down. Repeat: Astropathic communications are down. Break blockade and translate for Gangava System. Rendezvous with Great Wolf and demand urgent recall. Repeat: Demand urgent recall.*'

Blackwing cursed under his breath.

'They'll think we're running out on them,' he muttered, already looking for possible exit vectors. The *Nauro* was in the middle of the swirling mass of ships, and there weren't obvious escape tactics open to them. Beyond the immediate layer of attack craft there were larger vessels closing in. The net had a fine weave.

Ahead of him, close to the edge of the sprawling engagement sphere, he saw an enemy destroyer recoil from a direct lance hit. That was good – at least some of the platforms were still dealing it out.

'Lock on to that one,' growled Blackwing, already planning his attack pattern. 'Prepare the ship for warp transit, but we're not leaving till I get that kill.'

* * *

KLAXONS BLARED DEEP inside the massive walls of the Fang, echoing down the snaking corridors of stone and making the bone trophies on the walls shudder as if still alive. Shouts rose up from the deep places, the shouts of mortal men mingled with the roars of their superhuman masters. The Aettguard, the body of kaerls committed to the defence of Russ's fortress, had been mobilised. Hundreds of heavy boots drummed the floor as entire rivens mustered in their garrisons throughout the Hould level, reporting to armouries to collect additional ammunition belts and blast helms.

The Hould was the beating heart of the Aett. The thousands of mortal warriors, craftsmen, technicians and labourers who maintained the massive citadel lived out their entire lives there. They rarely left the Fang unless taken out of it by troop transports; the air was thin even for natives at that altitude. Their skin was as pale as the ice that covered the upper slopes, and they were all Fenris-born, of the stock that still roamed across the ice-fields below Asaheim and provided the recruits for the Sky Warriors. Their breed had been taken into the vast halls of the Aett when the first chambers had been hollowed out, and all could trace their lineages back over thirty generations or more. Only some – the kaerls – were kept at arms at all times, but all knew how to wield a blade and fire a *skjoldtar*, the heavy, armour piercing projectile weapon favoured by the Aettguard. They were children of a death world, and from the youngest infant to the oldest crone they knew the art of killing.

Higher up, past the huge, shadowy bulwark of the Fangthane, was the Jarlheim, the abode of the Sky

Warriors. No mortal remained on those levels except on the orders of his Sky Warrior masters, for it was here that the twelve Great Companies were housed. The halls of the Wolves were often empty and silent, since they were ever called away on campaign to some far-flung corner of their galactic protectorate. At least one Great Company always kept the hearths burning, however, tending the sacred flames and paying obeisance to the wards that kept maleficarum from entering the Fang. In the Jarlheim were the war-shrines to the fallen, the totems collected by the Rune Priests from distant worlds, the armouries full of sacred weaponry. In the holy places, tattered banners from past campaigns were laid to rest amid the dusty rows of skulls, armour and other prizes.

As the klaxons flared across the Twelfth Company's demesne, the narrow ways were lit with a savage fire. The masters of the mountain had been summoned, and it was as if the earth itself had been shaken into sentience. The stone reverberated with a deep tremor as the massed wolf-spirits were goaded into life. Armour was strapped on and drilled into place, beast pelts reverently draped over the ceramite, runes daubed on shoulder guards in thick animal blood, charms hung piously over necks and wound around armoured wrists.

Deep within the centre of the maze of shafts, galleries and tunnels, there came the beating of the great drum. It underpinned all other sounds, thumping out a heartbeat rhythm of dissonant savagery. Other drums joined it, working against the single note in a cacophonous, barbed disharmony. The vibrations

coloured everything, making the entire labyrinth reso-
nate with a growing crescendo of hatred and energy.

There were few sights more intimidating in the
entire galaxy than a Space Wolf Great Company kindling the murder-make. One by one, their armour
bolted into place and sanctified by Sturmhjart's subordinate Rune Priests, the Grey Hunters emerged,
hulking and strapped tight with lethal energy. They
went softly like the hardened infantry they were,
their red helm lenses glowing in the oily dark. Behind
them came the ranged-weapon Long Fang squads,
shadowy and bulkier, their faces heavily distended
into the maws of beasts, hefting their massive weaponry as if it weighed no more than an axe-shaft.

Then, last of the infantry to emerge from the armour-
ers' care, were the Blood Claws, the raw recruits.
Bellowing curses at the enemy they lusted to engage
with, the red-and-yellow streaked armoured giants
jostled with one another to get to their mission-points.
They were the most human of all the angels of death,
still only half-changed by the moulding power of the
Helix-enabled gene-seed, but their eyes burned hottest
with the ferocious delight of impending violence. They
lived for nothing but the joy of the hunt, the winning
of prestige at arms, the delight in the stink of blood
and fear in those they'd been unleashed on.

Amid them, joined to Sigrd Brakk's pack, came Helfist
and Redpelt. The superficial injuries of their duel had
long since faded, as had the others they'd incurred
during the days of constant training. The pack, twelve
strong including the Wolf Guard packleader, jogged
down a wide, semi-circular tunnel as the drumbeats

thundered in their ears, shoving aside kaerls and thralls too slow to get out of the way.

'Morkai,' spat Brakk, his voice filtered through the battered grille of his helm. 'To get you bags of dung...' He shook his head, and bone totems rattled across the armour like dreadlocks. 'Just die quickly, or don't hold me up.'

Helfist grinned.

'We'll be hauling your pelt out,' he laughed savagely, flexing his power claw. Like all of the pack he wore his helm – the near-void altitude of the Fang was too punishing for the bare-headed bravado he preferred.

'If we think we can get something for it,' added Redpelt, raising his bolt pistol and checking the ammo counter as he ran. His pauldrons had been drenched in blood-red and the jaws of his helm had a row of teeth running along the lower edge.

'Where's this old man taking us, anyway?' asked Helfist. A shock of straw-pale horsehair hung from his helm and the two Runes of Ending, Ymir and Gann, had been etched on his breastplate.

'Sunrising Gate,' snarled the packleader. 'The only thing on the planet harder than your skulls.'

'Was that a joke, brother?' enquired Helfist.

'An insult, I think,' replied Redpelt.

Brakk came to a halt as the tunnel roof suddenly soared above them into emptiness. Ahead, the floor petered out into a pier overhanging a huge, dark shaft. The pit below was massive, wreathed in shadow and lit only by scattered red glowglobes. The beat of the drums rose out of it, deep and threatening.

'Don't we have Aettguard for gate-duty?' demanded another Blood Claw, Fyer Brokentooth. His voice was thick with the wolf-spirit, guttural, throaty and aggressive.

'You think we're waiting for the bastards to get to the gates?' asked Brakk, turning to face the pack and backing toward the shaft. 'Russ's arse, lad, grow a pair – and then a brain.'

Then he was gone, sweeping down through the thermals, descending hundreds of metres a second, swooping from the Jarlheim levels to those of the Hould.

Helfist looked at Brokentooth.

'I thought it was a fair question.'

Brokentooth ignored him and followed the pack-leader over the edge. Helfist's helm signals showed the two of them plummeting toward the gate level.

'Try to keep up, brother,' he said to Redpelt, joining the remainder of the pack and stepping lightly over the edge.

'Try to stop me,' said Redpelt, taking up the last position and spreading his arms to control the descent.

Hurtling like scree in an avalanche, the Blood Claw pack sped toward their zone of engagement. Above and below them, the beat of the drums hammered out the fresh, urgent call. On every level, in every passageway, figures took up their allotted positions. Bolter batteries swivelled into fire-locks, Land Raider engines gunned throatily into life, and throughout the Aett packs of grey-armoured warriors raced to their stations.

The Wolves had been challenged in their lair, and like ghosts loping across the ice they swept to answer the call.

CHAPTER FIVE

BLACKWING HAD LOST track of the damage done to his ship. After so many runes across the console had gone red, it started getting hard to differentiate between them all. The picture was bad, though. The *Nauro* had never taken pain like it. Even if every remaining shell, las-beam and torpedo somehow managed to miss them, the battered vessel was probably doomed from the damage it had already taken.

Still, the message from the Valgard had shaken things up a bit. Unlike his more hot-blooded brethren, Blackwing had never been too keen on the heroic last stand. He was a dark wolf, a hugger of the shadows, and that bred a powerful sense of self-preservation. It was why the Claws and Hunters disliked him, and why he disliked them. The seed of Russ was bountiful, though, and provided for the whole range of killers – his knife-hook from the gloom was as lethal as a bolter-round in the daylight, after all.

The destroyer he'd targeted lurched into view on the ventral screens. It was in a bad way too, having been hit directly by a gun platform. Those things spat out terrifying amounts of energy, and when one got you, you knew it. Apart from its heavy structural damage, the enemy ship seemed to have lost engine control and had begun to spin away planetwards. A long trail of rust-red plasma ran out to its starboard-zenith. Blackwing could see the pricks of light along its flanks as it tried to power up its broadside batteries, but it wasn't getting them online any time soon.

'Do we have that shot?' demanded Blackwing, rolling the ship to bring his starboard guns in line with an incoming wing of gunships.

'Affirmative,' barked a kaerl at the gunnery pulpit, sounding more confident than he had done a moment ago.

'Then get a lock, and do it,' snapped Blackwing, watching with irritation as he lost power to his port shield generator. Something was badly broken down there, and there was nothing he could do about it.

'Twenty seconds.'

Then Blackwing saw death coming for him. A wing of Thousand Sons frigates had broken from the dogged assault on the *Skraemar* and its escorts and was sweeping back to clear up the remainder of the scattered Wolves fleet. The ships were moving fast. Too fast. At least three of them would be in range before he'd be able to pull away from the fleet action and break for open space. Gunships were one thing; frigates another.

'Lord, we have–'

'Yes, thank you, I have eyes. Lock trajectory to target and give me assault speed.'

That time all the kaerls looked up to stare at him, even those busy wrestling with fires on their consoles.

Blackwing gave them a cool stare back.

'Or will I rip your throats out, one by one?' he asked, pulling his bolt pistol from its holster.

The crew hurried back to their tasks. The *Nauro* yawed badly as the engines were goaded even further and the attack vector was replaced by an interception course. The targeted destroyer loomed larger. It was getting much closer, much faster.

'Ten seconds.'

'Need it sooner,' said Blackwing, gripping the sides of his chair and watching tensely as the target raced into proximity. He could see the plumes of flame along its sides, riddling the ornate gold trim of the decks. The ship's captain was trying to get it out of the way, but with its crippled engines it was as becalmed as an ice-skiff in the doldrums. The gap between the vessels shrank further.

'Five.'

The frigates were now within range, and sensors across Blackwing's console registered their forward lances powering up.

'*Skítja.* More speed!'

He briefly imagined the frantic comms between the destroyer and the incoming frigates. For all the world, it looked like he was on a suicidal ramming course, which was just the thing a barbarous savage would do.

By then, Blackwing could see the decoration on the destroyer's baroque prow. It was called the *Illusion of Certainty*.

How apt.

'Firing!'

The *Nauro* buckled as its remaining forward lance blazed into life, sending a searing beam of sun-white, ship-carving energy screaming toward the destroyer. It hit direct amidships, tearing through the weakened shields and burying deep into the structure. A ball of metal-laced flame burst outward, cracking the destroyer in two.

'We're going to hit!' screamed a kaerl.

The *Nauro* plunged straight into the inferno. Far too close to pull out at such speed, it spun right through the heart of the disintegrating structure.

'Incoming!' cried another kaerl frantically, diverting scarce power to the front shields.

'Hold your nerve!' roared Blackwing, piloting the ship through the expanding globe of shattered adamantium at full tilt. A flaming section of the destroyer's decking, itself almost as long as the *Nauro*, swung across to meet them. Blackwing flung the ship into a downward plummet, only to bring the head back round as a rotating spine of struts and bracing swept past on the port side. Debris was everywhere, rolling into their path and clattering against the weakened void shields like daemon-fingers on the Geller field. Something massive and heavy hit them hard under the hull, making the ship buck like a steer before it careered into another storm of shattered plating.

'And we're through!' he whooped, pulling the *Nauro*

into a sharp starboard-zenith climb and feeding the engines everything he had left. Tongues of plasma snaked after him as he broke through the orb of devastation, curling away in his wake like whips.

Emerging from the far side of the destroyer's death throes had given him precious seconds of time. The frigates would assume he'd destroyed himself in the ramming action. When they realised their error, the plasma trail would distort their targeting cogitators for a few seconds more.

A few seconds was all he needed in a ship this fast. He was on the edge of the orbital battle, and open space beckoned ahead.

'Faster!' he bellowed, trying to see what damage had been done on the passage through the destroyer's ruin. It looked like he'd lost most of his shields, and there was a major breach across his dorsal enginarium. 'Dammit, push her harder or I'll still rip your throats open!'

The *Nauro's* machine-spirit screamed its anger, protesting at the insane demands put on it, threatening to shut down and flush the life-support. Blackwing ignored it, screwing every last terajoule of power, wrenching every last plasma-burn of speed.

'Status on *Sleikre* and *Ogmar*,' he snapped, watching for the lance-salvo from the frigates that would make all his audacity worthless.

'Destroyed, lord.' The kaerl's voice, though grudgingly appreciative, implied *And so should we be*. 'We're on our own.'

Blackwing grinned. Something about cheating death at the expense of others appealed to his darker nature.

'Maintain course and speed,' he ordered. There was no sign of pursuit from the frigates, which in any case were too slow to catch him now. He looked over the tactical hololith, watching as the swarm of ships fell further behind. Against all expectation, they'd punched their way free. 'Get us to the jump-point, and calculate translation vector for Gangava.'

He turned to the row of console runes that he'd been ignoring for the past ten minutes. All still red. Technically, that meant the ship was almost certainly doomed. If it didn't shake apart in normal space, then the warp would probably finish it. No shields, no weapons, shedding atmosphere and with nine decks on fire. Not a happy state to be in.

'I'll take it,' said Blackwing aloud, unable to shake off his gruesome smile. 'Blood of Russ, I'll take it.'

THE SKRAEMAR WAS an ancient, powerful warship, tempered in the long decades of the Great Scouring and bearing the scars of a hundred conflicts since. Some of her encounters had gained sector-wide fame: she'd defied a whole squadron of the Archenemy for two weeks in the Aemnon Belt until heavy support could arrive to turn the engagement, had taken out the much larger eldar Corsair flagship the *Or-Iladril*, and had led the breaking of the blockade of Pielos V at the tip of a desperately underpowered Imperial Navy spearhead. Her machine-spirit was old and star-cunning, and every inch of her machinations was known by her Iron Priest Beorth Rig. She was fast, packed a deadly punch, and didn't die easily.

So when she did die at last, isolated in high orbit

above Fenris and surrounded by foes, the death was not quick. There was no sudden warp core breach, no decisive detonation of promethium tanks. She was cut in a thousand places, broken open by a million separate stabs of white-hot las-fire, raked by a score of torpedo impacts and turned black by clouds of burning plasma. They kept coming at her, wave after wave of gunships, dancing around the crushing columns of spitting energy thrown through the void by the looming battleships.

The *Skraemar* never stopped firing, even at the end. With her hull cracked, leaking fire and blood, she wallowed in a tide of incoming ordnance, swivelling on broken engines to maintain a firing lock on the Thousand Sons warships around her. With her frigate escorts all turned to atoms and the last dregs of the orbital grid collapsing in smoke and sparks, she was alone, a single gunmetal-grey island in a swarm of sapphire and gold.

The *Skraemar's* forward batteries thundered a final time, sending a torrent of whip-fast, spitting hatred toward a wounded Sons destroyer, the *Staff of Khomek*. All of her remaining power had been put into the volley. It ripped the enemy vessel apart from prow to stern, shattering the void shields with pure, overwhelming power.

The *Staff of Khomek* was a minor kill, joining the *Achaeonical*, the *Numeratory* and the *Fulcrumesque* in oblivion. The *Skraemar* had exacted a heavy toll with its defiance, but the end was coming quickly. Gliding through the tide of gently spinning scrap like a predator of the deep ocean, the massive profile of the

Herumon emerged from the shadows and into firing rage.

The *Skraemar* turned. Unbelievably, leaking oxygen into the void in great, jetting plumes, the crippled strike cruiser saw the danger and somehow managed to obtain a firing solution. On every deck, its remaining kaerls shouldered the burden of survival, performing acts of heroism merely to keep the plasma drives from exploding and the hull plating from crumpling inwards.

Njan Anjeborn, the one they called Greyflank, the only survivor amid the wreckage of his command bridge, still piloted the crippled strike cruiser, preparing for another salvo, knowing there would be no kill this time, but striving to draw his final tithe of blood.

Pitilessly, smoothly, the *Herumon* maintained its course. Taking no chances, lining up the ranked batteries with cool precision, the Thousand Sons flagship rounded down the options to a single, remorseless singularity.

It took position, opened fire, and the void became light.

As the brilliance cleared, the broken-backed *Skraemar* spun with a glacial agony away from the impact. The last of its shields buckled and fizzed out of life. A line of explosions ran along the port flanks, writhing against space like clusters of snakes. Other ships closed in, aware now that the Wolves flagship no longer had the teeth to so much as scrape the paint from their plating.

On the command bridge, Anjeborn struggled from the cat's cradle of ironwork around him, dragging his blood-drenched body back to the control pulpit. The pict-screens were all down. Vital systems shuddered and gave out, condemning the surviving crew below to suffocation or freezing. He looked around, searching for one last gesture before the incoming spears of energy cut the last of the life from his command.

There was nothing. The machine-spirit was cold and unresponsive. Anjeborn looked up, out through the plexiglass of the realspace viewers and into space. His last sight was the golden hull of the *Herumon* sliding across his field of vision, blotting out the destruction beyond. He saw at close quarters the rows upon rows of drop-pod launchers, the pristine launching bays stuffed with landers, the banks of void-to-surface immolators and the bronze lips of the torpedo tubes, all still unused.

The weapons that would bring Hel to Fenris.

As the explosions from below crashed their way up to his position, shattering what was left of his ship and sending debris far out into nothingness, Anjeborn watched his death coming for him. Clambering from his knees, he faced it standing, shoulders back, fangs bared, brazenly contemptuous of an enemy that hid behind such odds.

'By your deeds are you known,' he snarled as the final hammer blows struck and the vacuum rushed in at last. 'Faithless. Traitors. Cowards.'

THE WOLF GUARD had departed for combat. Rossek, Skrieya and the other elite of the Twelfth had left for their stations, each in charge of their own packs. Only three Wolves remained in the Chamber of the Watch, and they would not linger there long.

'The orbital defences are gone,' said Greyloc grimly, turning away from the evidence of their destruction. 'Counsel?'

Wyrmblade scratched at the back of his leathery neck, his hook-nosed face crumpled into a grimace as he ran through the options. Augur statistics shone from the pict-screens, showing movements in space above them.

'They'll bring the troop carriers down out of range of the guns and come at us overland.'

Sturmhjart looked at him questioningly.

'They have control of space – why not bombard from there?'

Wyrmblade cracked a crooked smile.

'Stick to your charms, priest. The shields over the Aett were built to last a siege from fleets four times as big. The witches don't have that firepower, not since we crippled them on Prospero.'

'In any case,' said Greyloc quietly, 'they have not come to hurl death from afar. They want to take this place, to desecrate it.'

'I sense nothing,' muttered Sturmhjart. He looked from Wyrmblade to Greyloc with doubt etched on his face. 'I sense nothing at all.'

The Wolf Priest shrugged. 'They are masters of the wyrd.'

'They know nothing of the wyrd!' blurted the Rune Priest.

'And yet they can blind you, and all your acolytes. Something powerful is protecting them.'

None of them said the name out loud.

'But there are defences,' said Sturmhjart, looking sullen. 'The Aett has wards in the stone, hundreds of them. Signs of aversion have been carved into the rock and infused with the world-spirit. No sorcerer can enter here, not even the mightiest of them.'

Greyloc nodded.

'Your brothers have tended them with exceptional care. Now we must preserve them further. How many Rune Priests remain?'

'Six, but four are acolytes and their powers are untried. Only myself and Lauf Cloudbreaker have the power to match a Thousand Sons sorcerer, should one gain the portals.'

Greyloc found himself cursing Ironhelm again, though he hid his emotions.

You were warned, Great Wolf. The signs were there. Magnus has played you for a fool, and I should have been stronger.

'Then they'll have to learn quickly. Ensure the wards are sanctified, and that the Aettguard rivenmasters know their significance. These will be where the defence must be strongest.'

Sturmhjart bowed.

'It will be done,' he said, turning to leave. As he went, he walked with less of a swagger than normal.

'He feels his failure,' said Greyloc once the Rune Priest had left.

'He shouldn't,' said Wyrmblade bluntly. 'You know who's directing this, and the one who left us open to it is not on Fenris.'

'We will endure. Did any of the ships break the blockade?'

'The last, Blackwing's ship, was destroyed ramming the enemy. We are alone.'

Greyloc drew in a long breath. He lifted his gauntlet up and gazed at it for a moment. The armoured fist was scored with many wounds, all inflicted as he'd crunched it into the bodies of his enemies over countless engagements. He looked at it for some time, as if trying to conjure up some power locked within it.

'Packs will disrupt the landings,' he said at last. 'They will not set foot on Fenris unopposed. In time, we will have to meet them here, and I will need you then, priest. I will need you to keep the mortals strong.'

Wyrmblade nodded.

'They will not falter. But the Tempering–'

'I know. Do not let it cloud your judgement. The whole Aett will require your fire.'

Wyrmblade looked like he was going to say something else, then backed down. The pooling shadows under his eyes were dark as he bowed.

'It will be so, Jarl. And when they get here, they will learn what that fire can burn.'

Greyloc nodded.

'That they will, priest,' he said. 'I will count on it.'

THE SPACE ABOVE Fenris was conquered. Aphael felt warm satisfaction flood through his body. He hadn't felt this good since... well, there had been many strange sensations over the decades, some of them more recent than others.

He sat on the command throne of the *Herumon's* bridge, his crested helm removed and lying in his lap, and watched the last of the Wolves' debris drift planetward before being consumed by the re-entry. He'd lost more ships than he'd planned, but none of the troop carriers had been touched. He briefly contemplated the contents of those massive vessels, reflected on what they could do and how many of them there were, and felt a further glow of satisfaction.

'Lord, blockade has been achieved,' came a voice from below.

A Spireguard captain stood to attention on the golden steps leading up to the control pulpit. Aphael looked down at him with amusement. He hadn't felt this good for weeks.

'Do you know why you're called *Spireguard*, captain?'

'Lord?'

'Answer me.'

The man looked confused.

'That is my designation.'

Aphael laughed.

'And you have no further curiosity? My friend Temekh would be disappointed. To blindly accept what you are given is not our way – it is the way of those we punish.'

The man looked fearful for a second, swallowing against the strap of his tall golden helm.

'There was a place once,' Aphael explained, letting his mind's eye wander. 'There were real spires, watched over by thousands of men such as you. Many thousands.'

He looked back at the captain. The man was nothing like a Prosperine warrior. He was short, wiry, with hard, pale skin. All of his comrades were the same. They'd been taken from high-altitude worlds and conditioned for the extreme cold, and when they went into action they'd be wearing heavy plate armour, masks and rebreathers, not breastplates of burnished gold and crimson. Fenris was not a place that rewarded elegance in war.

'Forgive me. These things were not long ago, at least as I see it.'

The captain waited patiently. They all did, these new mortals. A thousand cults, on a hundred worlds of the proud Imperium, now drawn together to create the Last Host, the bringers of revenge. They'd been taught that the Thousand Sons sorcerers were gods, heralds of a new dawn of learning and enlightenment amid the darkening shadows of ignorance and blind faith.

We were, once. We really were.

'You may prepare for the landings,' Aphael said then, turning to more prosaic matters. 'Position the carriers over the Ph'i sector and take your orders from Hett. Are the bombardment flotillas in place?'

'They are, lord.'

'Good. They may commence when ready. And what of the interceptor? The one that broke the blockade?'

The captain signalled his regret with hesitation.

'It made the jump-point before we were able to run it down, lord. But it will be destroyed before it reaches Gangava, as the fates will it.'

Aphael raised a quizzical eyebrow.

'The *Illusion of Certainty* had a squad of Rubricae onboard, led by Lord Fuerza.'

'This matters how?'

'The Dog vessel's shields were down as it passed through the wreckage. For a microsecond, I am informed, there was transporter activity.'

'You're certain of this?'

'No, lord. The augur records are incomplete. But Lord Fuerza is a skilled master of the technology.'

'That he is. Go back and find more detail – much may rest on it.'

The captain bowed and retreated back down the steps. Across the cathedral-like space of the bridge, other crew members went about their business quietly and efficiently. There were faint echoing taps across the marble floor as white-clad orderlies handed dataslates to the Spireguard on duty. Sweeping lines of bronze edged the tall realspace windows, all fashioned from transparent *yyemina* crystals. The hum of the *Herumon's* engines was low and sonorous, blending into the myriad other soft sounds of competence.

Aphael swept his gaze across the scene, running through the itinerary to be completed before he would join his forces on Fenris. The curve of the planet itself hung low in the port-nadir viewers, looking untroubled despite the carnage unleashed across its upper atmosphere.

Then he felt it again, the urgent itching. The skin across his neck rippled and he snapped his head back. Sweat broke out across his body, clad as it was in robes of silk and sapphire armour.

He looked around watchfully, checking to see if anyone had noticed. The crew carried on unperturbed.

Gingerly, fingers moving slowly, he ran his hand up to the nape of his neck, feeling around the tender flesh where the collar of his armour rubbed against skin.

It was getting worse. There were spines there, and the beginnings of some curls of soft matter.

Feathers. Sweet Magnus, feathers.

He withdrew his hand and set his jaw. He could combat this. The Rubric made them immune, and he was one of the warriors, the Pyrae, strongest in body and least exposed to the warping of the Great Ocean.

Temekh must not see it, though. Above all, Temekh must not see it. It was time to don his helm again in any case. Combat would not be far away, and it reinforced the distance between him and the mortals.

'I *loathe* you,' he hissed suddenly, curling his bronzed lip at the realspace viewers where Fenris hung, cold and inviolate. 'This is what you have forced us to become. This is what you have made us.'

He rose from his throne, taking his helm in his fist, ignoring the crew around him, his blue eyes going flat. His moods seemed to change so quickly.

'You will seek to purge your own corruption, and you will fail,' he breathed. 'We will prevent you. We will leave you crippled, as we are. We will leave you broken, as we are. And when the Time of Ending comes, as it must do, you will be weak and alone in the face of the Annihilator.'

He bowed his head then, wondering, just for a moment, where his fury was really directed.

'As we are,' he breathed, weakly.

THE HALL OF the Fangthane was the link chamber between the Hould and the Jarlheim. It had been delved centrally, right in the inner core of the mountain and directly below the landing stages of the Valgard. One of a number of bulwark points within the Aett, it was the only route from the one region to the next. Any enemy, should they somehow make it inside the Fang at the gate level, would have to pass up through the Fangthane to enter the higher galleries.

In a fortress of wonders, the Fangthane had an awe-inspiring quality all of its own. Its walls soared high up into the dark, hundreds of metres, curving gently toward a roof lost in penumbral gloom. The entire populace of the Hould, hundreds of thousands of souls, could assemble in its cavernous space, filling the frozen chamber floor with the warm breath of humanity. They entered from the west, ascending the huge Stair of Ogvai, lined with its images of ancient heroes carved from the mountain stone and lit by flickering torches.

In the chamber itself, images of Fenris had been delved into the walls, each more than fifty metres high and adorned with the intricate knotwork that was the glory of the stone-shapers. There were symbols of the Great Companies of old – wolfsheads, broken moons, claws, axe-shafts and bleached skulls. Monumental images of Fenris's elemental powers – the storm-spirit, the ice-bringer, the thunder-heart – were picked out in the flickering light, seeming to move in tandem with the flames and leaping shadows. Above them all were the runes, the sacred sigils that channelled the soul of the death world into the sphere of the living and warded against maleficarum.

The thralls came silently to the summons, all knowing the hallowed wyrd of the place. There was none of the coarse banter that normally rang through the corridors of the Hould, the routine obscenity and throaty, growling laughter. The Wolf of the Watch, the Twelfth Great Company Jarl, had called all those who had not been drawn to arms already. Such a thing had not happened in living memory, nor in the sagas known by the thralls, nor in any rumour passed from one hearth to another, and the deathly quiet was tinged with unease.

So the ranks of grey-clad men and women marched between the two massive granite statues of Freki and Geri that guarded the west gate, each ten metres tall at the shoulder and crouched ready to pounce. Ahead of them they saw the chamber yawn away into the distance, vaster than any cathedral, lit only by racks of blood-red fire in man-sized braziers of iron. At the far end, most brightly lit of all, there was the mightiest of all the many statues, the colossal image of Leman Russ. The size of a Warhound titan, the granite primarch gazed across the space with a snarl on his craggy features. He had his sword Mjalnar clutched in one hand; the other was clenched into a balled fist. Other primarchs might have been rendered in a more contemplative pose, but not Russ. He'd been carved by the stone-shapers as he had been in life: an engine of war, a living god, a rolling, consuming furnace of violent, focused kill-urge.

Morek Karekborn waited in the front rank of the crowd, less than a hundred paces from the statue, feeling the reassuring weight of his *skjoldtar* in his hands. His riven, just under five hundred kaerls, lined the galleries all round the walls of the Hall, placed to keep order.

His heart was still beating from the hurried progress of the muster. He'd seen the Wolves leave, had watched them stream from the Fang like grey shadows. He'd seen others fire up the Thunderhawk transporters or begin deploying the heavy armour throughout the Aett. They'd worked with quick, blunt efficiency.

As ever, he felt the inadequacy of his mortal response. His spirit had sunk when he'd been instructed to guard the Fangthane while the muster reached completion, though he'd voiced no protest.

There will be no battle here, no murder-make. I cannot serve the Masters within the Aett.

He suppressed the complaint. It was unworthy. The wyrd would be interpreted by the Sky Warriors, and they had ways of reading it that were hidden from him.

I will learn to accept it. There are other ways to serve.

And yet, if battle was coming, he deserved the chance to stand at the forefront of it. He'd earned that, over the decades. Surely, at the least, he'd earned that.

A huge gong sounded from ahead of him, resounding through the gigantic space and throwing echoes back and forth across it. Another sounded from the far end of the chamber, and the stone beneath his feet vibrated.

What little chatter there had been faded into nothing. Vaer Greyloc, Jarl of the Twelfth, resplendent in the massive shell of his battle-plate, strode on to the platform at the feet of Russ. A mortal would have been dwarfed by the figure of the primarch towering above him, but the Wolf Lord had a presence that refused to be dominated. In the scant hours since the first council of war, Greyloc had donned Terminator armour and wore wolfclaws on each hand, each rippling from the power fields enclosing the talons. He wore no helm, and his ice-white eyes shone in the shifting firelight.

Like a shade of Morkai. Snow on snow.

'Warriors of Fenris!' cried Greyloc, and his voice rose above the dying echoes of the gong. Whether it was augmented by some auditory effect or simply projected beyond the ambit of mortal vocal cords, it reached to all corners of the hushed chamber.

'I call you warriors, as all those born on Fenris are warriors. Whether man or woman, whelp or elder, you all carry the spirit of Russ in your blood. You are killers, bred on a world that only respects killing. The time has come for you to take up that mantle.'

His pale eyes swept across the motionless ranks. Morek shifted his weight, letting his attention flicker up to check his men were at their stations. They were all paying full attention. It was rare for any of the Sky Warriors to address mortals in such a fashion, and they were soaking up his words.

'The Archenemy is here. They will land on this world soon, in numbers that have not been seen for a thousand years. They come, so they believe, to take this place, to burn it, to defile the home of your fathers. Not since the days when the Allfather walked the ice has an enemy come to Fenris with the power to shake these halls. I will not hide the truth of it from you. That day has come again.'

The thralls made no response, but remained flinty-eyed and impassive, listening intently. Morek had been on distant worlds during campaigns and seen the way other mortals were. There were places where such speech would have induced panic, or provoked fist-pumping denunciations, or weeping, or collapse.

Not on Fenris. They accepted the wyrd, and endured.

'You are sons of the eternal ice, so I will not say "do not fear", because I know that you will not. You will defend your hearth with all the strength that is in your bones and fists. And you will not stand alone. Even as I speak to you, Sky Warriors have left the Aett, hunting for the first Traitors to make planetfall to burn their landings and bring death among them. Where the need is greatest, when it comes to the walls of the Aett, they will come among you too. The storm will fall here, that we may be certain of, but when it comes we will be in the eye of it with you.'

Morek felt his heart quicken. These were the words he yearned to hear.

They will come among us. The Sky Warriors, fighting with us. This is the honour I crave.

'You will all be armed,' continued Greyloc. 'Even now, weapons are being brought from the armouries. Kaerls will instruct you in their use. Wield them as you once wielded axes. Every one of you will be called to fight. This is our time of testing.'

I welcome it. I glory in it. We will be tested together.

'Little time remains before the storm hits. Use it well. Remember your hate. Remember your inner fire. The Traitors come to challenge you in our own lair. They are numerous, but they know nothing of the wrath of Fenris. We will show it to them.'

Greyloc's words gradually rose in volume. As he

spoke, his fists crackled more brightly with the vast energies held within them.

'Do not disappoint me,' he snarled, and the threat of his wrath ran like a chill wind around the chamber. 'Do not spurn this faith shown in your spirit and determination. These interlopers will be hurled back into the void, whatever pains we endure to accomplish it. You will be a part of it. You will do this!'

The claws rose in unison.

'You will do this for the Allfather!'

The crowd began to press forwards. Their blood was stirred.

'You will do this for Russ!'

Growled murmurs of acclamation broke out.

'You will do this for Fenris!'

The muttering defiance rose in volume.

'You will do this, because you are the soul and sinew of a death world!' Greyloc roared aloud, and his talons blazed into swirling life. It was as if his ice-cold demeanour had been cast aside like a cloak, and what remained was white-hot, burning with a fierce intensity.

As one, the crowd slammed their fists on their chests. The heavy, thudding sound rolled across the Hall like a peal of thunder on the distant peaks.

'*Fenrys!*' cried Greyloc, tapping into the waves of rage.

'*Fenrys hjolda!*' they thundered, and the wall of noise was deafening.

Drums broke out from hidden places in the Hall, and the driving rhythm rippled across the seething masses.

'*Hjolda!*' shouted Morek with the others, feeling his blood begin to pump harder. The murder-make was being roused, the animal spirit of the people of Fenris. It was a fearsome, wonderful thing. No other human world could match it, and the thrill of the impending hunt began to run through his veins.

Morek gazed at the lone Sky Warrior ahead of him even as he screamed out his words of defiance. The Terminator-clad leviathan was the representative of all he venerated, all he worshipped.

A god among men.

'*Fenrys!*' rang out across the Hall. The fires exploded into red, angry life, licking the stone and iron around them like writhing beasts.

'*Fenrys hjolda!*' repeated Morek, hefting his weapon and crying the words with feeling.

They will fight among us.

As the Hall descended into roars and bellows of untamed aggression and the pinions of war descended over the Fang, Morek Karekborn looked on the image of the Wolf King and felt his faith blaze like a comet in the empty skies.

This is what they cannot understand, he realised, thinking of the faithless who came to despoil the Aett in their folly and madness. *We will die for the Sky Warriors, for they show us what we can become. Against this certainty, they can have nothing. Nothing.*

He smiled through his shouting, feeling the hoarseness in his throat, welcoming it as the badge of his devotion.

For the Allfather. For Russ. For Fenris.

PART II: WAKING THE DEAD

CHAPTER SIX

TWELVE HOURS AFTER the destruction of the orbital defences, fire came to Asaheim.

The Thousand Sons warships *Alexandretta* and *Phosis T'Kar* assumed geostationary orbit one hundred kilometres above the Fang and prepared their payloads for dispersal. The two ships had minimal crew – fewer than two thousand each – and virtually no void-war armaments. They'd been shielded from the battle by a dozen frigates and kept away from harm by ships more suited to close combat. In form, they resembled huge cylinders on a vertical axis wedged through the clinging superstructure of a conventional warship. Everything on board the two ships was designed to feed those cylinders, to keep them supplied with huge amounts of promethium and heavy plasma-derivatives they needed to operate. The curved muzzles were aimed planetwards, ready to unload the energies already cradling within their polished walls.

Aphael called them *planet-scourers*. They were capable of levelling cities and razing continents, and there was nothing left in Fenrisian space to hinder their operation.

Orders went out over the fleet mission channel and the devices began to power up. Within the narrow corridors around the cylinder housing, unearthly whining gave way to a low rumble. Chain lightning leapt across the empty gulf between the cylinder walls, cracking against adamantium bulwarks and breaking out into the void. Generators geared up, pumping energy into enormous converters and channelling it through to the devastation engines.

The escorts withdrew, opening up a gap of several hundred kilometres. The entire fleet kept its distance, like a crowd of frightened prey huddling out of range of the hunter.

From his observation cell onboard the *Herumon*, Temekh watched the accumulation of titanic energies gain pace. The gathering of power was heady, and he could sense the bulging, raging torment locked within the weapons as the limits of containment were reached.

'Lord, your chambers have been made ready.'

The Spireguard equerry standing at his elbow broke Temekh's concentration, and he had to suppress an urge to lash out at the mortal. He closed his eyes for a second, maintaining his position within the Enumerations. Some old habits died hard.

'Thank you,' he replied. 'I will observe this before leaving.'

Even as he finished speaking, the planet-scourers reached their firing level.

Massive, snaking columns of gold-silver energy thundered down to the target below, twisting and blazing as they sliced through the atmosphere and slammed into the continental shelf. The torrent kept up steadily, a seamless rain of millions upon millions of plasma projectiles, melded into two pillars of withering, draining power and focused on the apex of the mountain ranges below.

'By the Crimson King,' breathed the equerry, forgetting himself as he watched the lethal quantities of energy unleashed.

Temekh smiled.

'You think that lightshow will hurt the Dogs? Don't fool yourself – this is just to keep them busy while Lord Aphael oversees the landing.'

He turned away from the portal and darkened the viewers with a mental command.

'There are other ways to tear the pelt from them,' he said, walking from his cell toward the chambers that had been prepared for him with so much labour. The equerry trotted after him. 'It is now time to set them in motion.'

FREIJA MOREKBORN HEARD the impact before she saw any evidence of it.

'Hold your positions!' she barked at her six-strong squad of kaerls, keeping the surprise out of her hard-edged voice.

They were operating in the upper levels of the Valgard, assigned to the hangars to assist the armoury staff in preparing the remaining Land Raiders and Rhinos for deployment. The work mostly involved standing guard while interminable Mechanicus rites were performed to prime the machine-spirits, and the waiting around while other squads had been sent to forward combat stations was maddening.

Then the fire came. The hangar was one used by the Thunderhawk transporters and opened directly out to the atmosphere of Fenris. There were powerful shields across the gaping launch bay, both to protect from bombardment and to retain a breathable environment so high up. One moment, the sky outside was the dark blue of the short Fenrisian dusk; the next, it blazed with a seething kaleidoscope of colours, the result of a torrent of hyper-energised plasma hitting the surface of void shields and going crazy.

The hangar, which had been filled with the clang and grind of mechanical equipment and lifting gear, was suddenly dominated by the high pitched hiss and fizz of the shields taking the strain. Warning klaxons from far above their position blared out again, breaking the concentration of the tech-priests huddled over their incense and sacred oils.

'What is it?' asked a young kaerl, a blond-haired recruit called Lyr, hoisting his rifle to his waist instinctively. He was fearless in a human scale firefight, but the vast energies colliding only a few hundred metres away clearly unnerved him.

'Standard bombardment pattern,' said Freija, who had no idea what manner of forbidden technology had been unleashed. 'Stand down, trooper. Until we get the order to fall back, we don't move.'

'Quite right, huskaerl,' came an amused, metallic voice.

Freija whirled around to find herself facing the towering outline of Garjek Arfang, the Twelfth's Iron Priest. She swallowed reflexively, and instantly berated herself for her weakness.

How do they do it? How do they project this aura of intimidation?

'Lord,' she acknowledged, and bowed.

'That's not capable of hurting us,' continued the priest, speaking through his slatted vox-grille. Like all his kind, he had a hulking servo-arm sprouting from the back of his strange, gothic armour. Instead of the usual totems and trophies strewn across the ceramite, he wore the skull and cog of the Adeptus Mechanicus on his breast, interleaved with iron renditions of the cardinal Fenrisian runes. His dark battle-plate was heavy with the patina of wear and combat, and looked like it hadn't been removed for some time. Freija had certainly never seen any of the Iron Priests out of their shells, and it was easy to believe the rumours that what was left of their mortal bodies had irretrievably melded with the arcane technology within. He carried a heavy staff as the badge of his priesthood, crested with the adamantium head of a hammer forged into the likeness of a snarling muzzle.

'They do it to prevent us firing back.'

He walked past her and stood facing the open launch bays, watching the rain of blazing plasma slam into the void shield barrier beyond.

'Our shields are fed by thermal reactors buried kilometres down,' he said, half talking to himself. 'This will do no more than stress the voids, but we won't be able to send any ship-killers up through it.'

He turned back to Freija.

'Inconvenient, no?'

There was a low grating sound from somewhere below his armour.

Growling? Clearing his throat? Laughing?

'Enlightening, lord,' she said. 'Then we are safe to remain on duty here.'

'Perfectly, huskaerl. For the time being.'

The Iron Priest looked from one kaerl to another, assessing Freija's squad for some kind of suitability. He had a strange, clipped manner, and his movements were oddly stilted for a Sky Warrior.

Metal-heads. Even more void-touched than the rest of them.

'I have chosen you,' Arfang announced. 'I will have need of an escort for my thralls, and my tech-priests are fully engaged.'

'At your command, lord,' said Freija, uncertainly. Anything would be preferable to killing more time in the hangars, but he hadn't said what he wanted yet.

The Iron Priest nodded to himself, evidently satisfied. He placed his hammer-headed staff on the ground in front of him, and several hunched figures scuttled out of the shadow of a nearby Thunderhawk. They were servitor-thralls, the half-man, half-machine semi-automata that provided the menial labour for the armoury. Some still had their human faces in place, drooped in a lobotomised, vacant expression of emptiness. Others had rigid iron plates instead of features and their hands replaced with drills, vices, locks, ratchets and claw hammers. Some had bundles of vat-grown plastek muscles bunched across their wasted natural frames, bolted in place with rivets and governed by a tangle of wires and control needles. They were a motley collection of horrors, the result of the dark union of Machine-God and the Fenrisian aesthetic of savagery.

'There are preparations to make. It will take days. When I call you, come without delay.'

'Forgive me, lord. Where?'

The Iron Priest turned his armour-plated head to look at her. His helm-lenses glowed a deep red, as if opening onto smouldering coals within.

'Where else, huskaerl? Have you not heard the war-seers' counsel? The battle-outcomes do not cogitate well. There is mortal danger here.'

That, for him at least, seemed to answer the question. He strode past her, clanking his hammer-staff on the floor as he went. Then he paused, as if considering the possibility that he may not have been entirely clear.

He turned, and Freija thought she detected something like excitement in that flat, unearthly voice.

'Jarl Greyloc has ordered it, huskaerl. We go to wake the dead.'

THE FANG WAS merely the greatest of the many huge peaks that clustered together in the centre of Asaheim. Other summits reared their heads into the icy air around the World Spine, scraping the atmosphere as it thinned toward the void of space. They were piled atop the shoulders of each other, all encroaching on the space of the rest, fighting like the dark *ekka* pines of the valleys to climb toward the light. Everything on Fenris was in conflict, even the tortured, broken land itself.

The peaks closest to the Fang had entered the legends of the *Vlka Fenryka*, etched on their communal consciousness since the Allfather had led them there in the half-remembered twilight of the founding. To the south was Asfryk, white-sided and blunt, the Cloudtearer. To the east were soaring Friemiaki and Tror, the brothers of thunder. To the west was bleak Krakgard, the dark peak where heroes were burned, and to the north were Broddja and Ammagrimgul, the guardians of the Hunter's Gate through which aspirants passed to take the trials of passage.

The ways between the peaks were treacherous and known only to those who'd trodden the paths as aspirants. All were scarred with precipitous drops and deep crevasses. Some hunt-ways were built on solid stone, whereas others were on bridges of ice that would crumble to nothing with the first application of weight. Some led true, taking the hunter from the clefts in the shadow of the summits down to the plains where the prey dwelt; others led nowhere but into darkness, to the caves that riddled the bowels of the ancient landscape, full of nothing but ice-gnawed bones and despair.

For all its majesty and terror, there were islands of stability in that savage land, places where gigantic outcrops of rock created broad plateaux amid the plunging cliffs. These were the sites where the Wolves came to commune with the savage soul of the mountain country. In the Summers of Fire, when the ice was broken across the planet and war came to the mortal tribesmen, great fires were lit in such places and sagas declaimed by the skjalds. Then would the warriors of Russ put aside the demands of battle for a short time and remember those who had fallen in the Long War, and the Rune Priests would delve far into the mysteries of the wyrd, attempting to discern the Chapter's path into the unknown landscape of the future.

It was at such a gathering that a younger Ironhelm had announced the first of the many hunts for Magnus. Further back into the past, the same location had played host to the decision to form the Wolf Brothers, the Space Wolves' ill-fated successor Chapter, now disbanded and a source of hidden shame.

For the Thousand Sons, who knew and cared nothing of this, the plateaux were merely landing sites, places to disgorge the troops and vehicles from their cavernous landers ready for the land assault to come. So, forty-eight hours after the destruction of the orbital platforms, they came in spiralling columns, darkening the skies with their numbers. Heavy, lumbering drop-ships disembarked from the holds of the troop carriers above and thundered down to the embarkation points, guarded by wings of gunships and shadowed by the void-to-surface batteries of the warships in orbit. One after another, the bronze and sapphire vessels broke into the atmosphere, streaking trails of fire as they plummeted.

By nightfall, dozens of them had come, just a tithe of

the many that would follow. Wolf Guard Sigrd Brakk watched the twinkling lights of the latest drop-ship fall toward his position, hard under the shadow of the Krakgard, and his lips pulled back from his fangs. Like the rest of his pack, he was shoulder deep in snow, crouching in the lee of an overhanging drift-curve, waiting for the moment when the plateau he was overlooking was picked by the enemy commanders.

'That one, lads,' he hissed, satisfied, motioning toward the descending ship. 'First kill of the night.'

ASSAULT-CAPTAIN SKYT Hemloq kept a sweaty grip on his lasrifle. Despite his armour and environment bodyglove, the air was terrifyingly cold. That didn't stop him sweating.

His feet crunched through the snow, illuminated by his helmet-lumen, sweeping across the blue-white surface. His squad, thirty strong and all equipped for the soul crushing climate, fanned out beside him.

So this is Fenris, he thought, gazing up in awe at the dark shapes of the peaks above. The nearest of them soared into the night, far larger than anything he'd seen on his home world of Qavelon, and that was reckoned a planet with many mountains.

There was something about the air. It wasn't just the cold – there was something sharp, savage, about it. Even modified through his rebreathers and boosted with oxygen-mix from his backpack, it was thin and caustic. Perhaps it was the alt-clim drugs still swimming through his bloodstream.

It was quiet. The only consistent sound came from the whining engines of the drop-ship. The hulking lander, twenty metres tall and much broader, squatted on the meltsnow-streaked rock, gradually unloading its cargo of ordnance and manpower. Already over a hundred Spireguard had emerged from the cavernous interior, marching with false bravado on to a world that obviously wanted to kill them and looked perfectly capable of doing it soon. They were the first, the ones in the line of fire, the ones charged with establishing the bridgehead.

And yet, there had been no resistance. No movement. Nothing detected on the surveyors.

The silence.

'Stay tight,' Hemloq voxed, fixing his gaze back on the scene before him.

The plateau was over eight hundred metres across on the flat. It plunged down into a chasm on three sides; on the fourth, the rock rose steeply in broken, tumbling terraces. Negotiable, but difficult.

He swallowed, trying not to let his vision get clouded by the myriad points of light across the flat landing site. Fixed lumen-arrays had been erected after planetfall and all the troops disembarking had helmlights on full-beam. The effect was confusing rather than helpful, as the night was broken by hundreds of star-like points and banks of eye-watering brilliance.

The drop-ship sat in the centre of the open space, smoke and steam gushing from its exhausts, a dark outline ringed with whirling tracer lights. Hemloq knew the pilots were eager to take off again. Despite the gunships patrolling the dropsites, they were vulnerable while on the ground, like a prey-bird crouched on its nest.

CHRIS WRAIGHT

Even as he watched, another company of troops disembarked, some of them with heavier weapons in tow. A cumbersome lascannon was unloaded, flanked by a dozen gunnery crew, ready for deployment at the site edges. In time, portable void shield generators and proper anti-aircraft defences would be deployed. When that happened, the place would be something like secure. Until then, they were vulnerable, and all of them knew it.

'Sweep complete,' came a vox from the far side of the dropsite.

'Anything?' demanded Hemloq, speaking more urgently than he'd meant to.

Damn it. Keep it cool in front of the men.

'Nothing, sir.'

'Then hold position. Until we get fixed surveyors online, your eyes are all we've got.'

The vox-link crackled out. Hemloq tried it again, and there was no response. That was just damn rude.

'Keep tight,' he said again. He was beginning to sound ridiculous with his military platitudes. The whistle of the wind in the high peaks, the lack of any response from the defenders, the bone-aching cold. It would have unnerved a man of far greater combat readiness than Skyt Hemloq.

'Trust in the Masters,' he murmured.

On the far side of the plateau, a lumen-bank winked out.

Hemloq stiffened.

'Stand fast, men,' he said, checking on his helm-display to see who was responsible for that section of perimeter.

Another one disappeared.

Shit.

'They're coming!' he cried, uncaring of how shrill his voice had become. 'Pick your targets!'

He hoisted his lasgun to his shoulder, sweeping it round as he peered out into the gloom. Dimly, he was aware of his men doing likewise. His proximity meter was blank. There was no chatter, no feedback.

They're as terrified as I am.

Then, from over to his left, lines of retina-burning las-fire blazed out, followed by the whip-crack noise of their discharge. It was madly angled, fired in haste. Briefly, from the corner of his eye, Hemloq saw something huge and shadowy flit across the snow.

He whirled to face it, firing his lasgun indiscriminately at nothing. There were shouts of outrage as other beams lanced through the night, some of them striking the flanks of the drop-ship.

Hemloq dropped to a frightened crouch, feeling his heart hammer in his chest.

This is a farce. They've got us jumping at shadows.

Then, and from somewhere, from a place he'd never have guessed existed, Hemloq found resources of stubbornness. A defence had to be organised, some structure imposed. The Wolves had a reputation, but they were only men, just as the Masters had promised.

'To me!' he roared, leaping back to his feet, a new note of determination entering his voice. 'Form ranks, and get those–'

A face flashed across his field of vision, something out of a nightmare. He saw two glowing shards of red, a gunmetal-grey helm studded with teeth, hulking pauldrons daubed in blood.

'Shush,' came a wet growl, impossibly deep, sounding more like a leopard's than a human's.

In the instant before Ogrim Redpelt's gauntlet smashed in on Hemloq's vocal cords and ripped them out, the novice assault-captain had time for a realisation that might have been helpful if it had come earlier.

These are no men.

HELFIST TORE ACROSS the landing site, swaying between the flickering las-beams more skilfully than his armour-clad bulk would have suggested possible.

There was little in the arsenal of such mortals that could have hurt him, but he maintained the absolute stealth of the approach and kept his bolter silent. It was a matter of pride – a clean kill, a minimum of fuss. His helm's night-vision showed up the scene in clear lines. It was evident from the confused response of the enemy that they were using no such technology.

A lumen beam swept across him, briefly showing him up against the dark. His helm runes showed six beads locking on to his position, and he checked his barrelling run and turned to face them.

Six mortals, twenty metres off, all dressed in pale grey camouflaged armour, masked and helmeted, with lowered lasguns.

'Fodder,' spat Helfist under his breath, already running fluidly toward them, already relishing the splash of their blood against his armour, already bringing his power fist into the optimal swing-pattern.

One panicked beam got away before he crashed among them. It glanced from his sigil-carved vambraces harmlessly. His fist crunched into the face of one of the warriors, throwing him far into the night. The carry-through crushed the chest of the one behind him.

Helfist spun tautly on his left boot, using the grip of his bolt pistol to smash the visor of a retreating mortal. The air howled in and the man fell to his knees, gagging on a shattered jawline.

The others broke, scrabbling to get away.

'Filth,' Helfist growled, grabbing the closest and snapping his spine with a whiplash shake of his power fist.

His helm showed the position of his battle-brothers carving their way toward the drop-ship. There was las-fire everywhere, cracking and snapping in an ill-focused storm of fear. More of the mortal soldiers had taken up positions across the plateau, trying to organise the defence into something that had a hope of stopping the Wolves. It would do them little good. Helfist could see the incoming signals of gunships, and could sense the charging up of lascannons, but neither would change the odds much now.

Pitiful. It enraged him.

'You come here,' he snarled, decapitating a mortal with a contemptuous uppercut. 'You defile this place.' Disembowelled another with his power fist. The energy field wasn't even activated. 'You dare this.' Ripped up breathing gear, tore open breastplates, broke limbs. 'You insult me with your weakness.' Crushed skulls, blinded faces, ripped out spines, bathed in the blood of the invader. 'This is making me *very angry*.'

A swooping shape rushed past him on his left flank. Redpelt had made a break for the drop-ship. Helfist shook the life out of the man he held in his grasp, cast him aside and joined his battle-brother in the chase. The wolf-spirit within, the avatar of the kill-urge, uncoiled and stretched its claws.

'Fired your bolter yet?' voxed Redpelt over the comm-link, gunning his chainsword and drawing a splatter-filled arc across the panicked mortals in his way.

'No need,' replied Helfist with disgust, shouldering up to a barrage of las-fire at full sprint and ploughing into the terrified snipers. 'They just don't deserve it.'

Redpelt laughed, punching the butt of his pistol heavily into his next target's midriff. The man flew back in agony, stomach burst, blood spilling across the churned snow.

'No argument, brother.'

By the time they reached the open maw of the drop-ship the slush beneath their boots was rose-red. Brokentooth was still some way behind, detained with tearing apart a row of semi-prepared lascannon batteries. Somewhere further back, Brakk was dealing out silent death in impressively brutal quantities. He'd maintained comm-silence since unleashing his pack on the landing site, content to let the Claws take out the principal target while he maximised devastation amongst the infantry.

Caught in mid-deployment, the pilots were trying to take off. Enemy troops were scrambling to get back into the false safety of the interior, driven to a state of blind terror by the armoured shades sweeping through them.

'They sicken me,' continued Helfist, leaping up into the huge loading bay and plunging into the terrified huddle of men within.

Redpelt jumped up after him, pausing only to let the blood slew from his chainsword before flicking it back into life.

'The Wolves are among you!' he roared in Gothic, laughing riotously with the pleasure of the murdermake.

Constricted and cramped, the enemy fell like wheat under the scythe, getting in each others' way, frozen in herd-like horror. Some tried vainly to escape the slaughter and leap past the rampaging Blood Claws and onto the ice, but none made it through Redpelt's gyrating blades. The rest retreated further back into the depths of the hold, postponing death by only few moments, letting loose their ineffective las-fire in panicked volleys.

Then there was a booming detonation, and a thudding, grinding vibration across the steel floor of the loading bay. The drop-ship had managed to take off.

'Cockpit,' snarled Helfist.

Redpelt was ahead of him, charging through the loading bay and racing up the first stairwell he came to. The bulky shoulder-guards of his armour scraped past the narrow walls, drawing huge gouges in the pressed metal.

Helfist blink-clicked a rune on his helm display and his power fist's energy-field sparked into life, throwing an electric-blue discharge across the ship's interior. He slammed the burning gauntlet into the swaying floor and ripped up a sheet of it. With a savage yank, he hauled it back, throwing the first rank of cowering soldiers from their feet and exposing the innards of the ship's structure beneath. He crouched down and pulled out a length of wiring, snapping the connections and shaking the cords loose like entrails pulled from a wounded beast.

With a shudder, the lights died across the bay, plunging the space into utter darkness. High-pitched screams of terror echoed out from the press of troops ahead, suddenly flung back into a maelstrom of shadows and whirling helm-lumens.

'Run while you can, little men,' growled the Blood Claw, stowing his pistol and advancing into the dark, his power fist crackling lashes of disruptive force. 'Now Hel is on your heels.'

REDPELT THUNDERED UP on the next level, his boots denting the meshed metal stairs with every heavy tread. There were armed guards waiting on the plat-form above, and a snap of las-fire cracked against his right shoulder as he emerged.

'Brave,' he snarled, righting himself and sweeping his gore-soaked chainsword into the retreating body of the nearest. 'But unwise.'

He spun into the guards, flailing with his blade. The movements looked wild, but they were noth-ing of the sort – peerless conditioning had given his murder-strokes a deceptive efficiency.

The guards held their ground against the onslaught, and so they died. As he butchered the last of them, Redpelt's helm showed Helfist slicing his way through the hold-level below. From its reeling pitch, it was clear the drop-ship was in the air and climbing.

At the end of the platform was a sealed door. Red-pelt sprinted at it, loosing three rounds as he went, all hitting the intersection. The reactive bolts deto-nated as he crashed into the metal, cracking the doors open and sending the two panels tumbling inwards.

There were four men inside, all seated at consoles, two by two. Cockpit windows lined the far end, showing flashes of the firefight below as the drop-ship struggled to make headway with its loading bay doors open.

Redpelt laughed raucously in triumph, and the horrific sound echoed in the cramped space of the cockpit. Three of the flight-crew sprang up and tried clumsily to get out of the way of his rampage. There was nowhere for them to go. Redpelt's chainsword whirred heavily. Two heavy swipes and all three mor-tals were hacked apart, scattering viscera across the metal-backed seats. Redpelt grabbed the remaining pilot from his flight position, ripping him out of his restraint harness by the nape of his neck. The man's spine broke from the force of it and the corpse went limp in Redpelt's gauntlet.

Snarling with disdain, the Blood Claw hurled the body aside. The control column swayed drunkenly in the absence of a guiding hand, and the drop-ship began to list violently.

'Hel,' he voxed. 'Time to go.'

He plucked a krak grenade from his belt, but then saw incoming danger runes flicker across his lens. Redpelt's head snapped up, just in time to see a wing of four Thousand Sons gunships home in on the plateau, a few hundred metres off and closing fast.

Interesting.

He flicked the grenade back to safety and grabbed the column. It was like a giant's fist closing over a child's toy, but the drop-ship instantly steadied under his touch. Instead of letting it crash to earth, Redpelt dragged it out of its dive and gunned the engines further. With a wail of protest, the tortured atmospheric drives blazed back into full throttle.

The gunships, their pilots looking for targets on the ground, saw the danger too late. The drop-ship rose up to meet them head-on, huge and sluggish.

Redpelt grinned and smashed the nearside window with his chainsword handle. He let go of the controls, crouched, then crashed headlong through the gap, tearing through the metal frame, spinning out into the night even as the swooping gunships veered to avoid the massive chunk of steel and promethium sent lurching into their path.

It was only then that he saw how high up he'd taken it. The plateau was over two hundred metres down, still lit up by sporadic las-fire.

'*Skítja*,' he spat. 'This is going to–'

He plummeted like a stone, barely registering the explosion above him as two of the gunships collided with the stricken drop-ship and the sky was lit with a vast, thundering ball of igniting fuel and ammunition.

'–hurt.'

He hit the rock before rolling away from the impact and skidding across the ice. Both knees blazed with pain, even protected by his power armour, and he felt a sharp, hot whip-crack run up his compressed spine.

He lay immobile for a second, dazed from the heavy impact. Then his vision cleared. Grimacing, Redpelt hauled himself to his feet, ignoring the warning runes indicating muscle damage and a fractured tibia.

Dimly, he was aware he should be paying attention to something else.

'Run, you stupid bastard!' voxed Helfist from somewhere close by.

Then he realised what it was. He broke into an agonised sprint, tearing across the rock as the ball of fire in the sky swung down to his position. The broken drop-ship, directionless and ripped open by the gunship collisions, was slewing back to earth again, streaming flames like an earth-bound comet as its engines gave up the fight to stay airborne.

He ran. He ran like a raging *skeiskre*, pumping his damaged limbs, feeling endorphins pulse through his battered frame.

Russ, you're slow.

There was a crunching, earth-shaking boom as the metal shell thudded into the rock behind him, crushing any residual survivors within and spraying slivers of red-hot metal across the whole battlefield. The ruined ship kept rolling, toppling like a downed beast on the plains, roaring in its death-throes and igniting fresh explosions within its bulbous carcass before it finally, grindingly, painfully, came to rest.

Only then did Redpelt stop and turn, looking over the devastation he'd triggered, aware that his second heart had kicked in and was hammering hard.

Pain-deadeners had started work as his stressed bones began to knit, but the strongest drive within him was the inner wolf, raging and tearing. He felt the rush of the kill-urge sweep over him, a heady mix of adrenaline and gene-rage.

'*Fenrys!*' he roared, whirling his chainsword in a huge loop around his head, glorying in his triumph. '*Hjolda!*'

Then there was another presence at his side. Helfist slapped him hard on the back, laughing harshly over the comm.

'Morkai's arse, you're as thick as an *ungur*,' he said, giving away the wolf-rage within him too. Even through his armour, Redpelt could pick up the kill-pheromones spiking the air. 'Tough as one, too.'

Then Brakk was there too, and the rest of the pack, looming against the burning shell. The las-fire had ceased. No Spireguard had lived to see the drop-ship come down, and the surviving gunships were still coming back round for another attack run.

'Next time just use grenades,' the Wolf Guard growled irritably. 'Next target's north, and they've established a bridgehead. Move out.'

The pack broke into a run instantly, loping across the shattered rock as one, sweeping over it like a grey fluid sliding into the shadows. Power fists were shut down and chainblades were stilled, and once more the Claws drifted into the ghost-like stealth that was the terrifying mirror of their battle-rage.

By the time the gunships came back, flying low over the dropsite, all that remained on it were the guttering flames, the twisted metal, and the already frozen corpses of those unwary enough to bring war to the world of the Wolves.

CHAPTER SEVEN

Auries Fuerza of the Pavoni cult-discipline leaned back against the bulkhead, flexing his pain-drenched limbs. He'd seen death staring at him, the final embrace of the flesh-change, and it had been horrifying. Even now, having finally thrown off the horrors of warp-delirium, he could feel his hearts labour, thumping against his ravaged ribcage like animals trying to claw their way out. How long had he been out cold? Minutes? Hours? Days? In the warp, it was always hard to tell.

Transportation through the malignant currents of the aether was physically demanding at the best of times, but to make a leap at such notice and under such conditions was both painful and dangerous. When he'd seen the Dog vessel hurtle toward his stricken ship, he'd only had seconds to make the decision. Thankfully, the preparations for evacuation had already been made due to the heavy fire the *Illusion of Certainty* had taken. Even so, scrying new warp vectors in the middle of a ferocious void-battle had been far from trivial.

Fuerza could take a certain level of pride that he'd not sent himself directly into the structure of the recipient ship. The fact he was breathing air and not metal struck him as more proof that the pattern of the universe had a design, and one that included him in it.

Only barely, though. His palms had been stripped of skin and now shone like glossy sides of meat in the dark. His breath came in sharp, rattling gasps, and under his mask he could feel the damage done to his face.

There had been four Rubricae with him in the warp bubble, but only one had made it intact. Two must have been lost in the jump, ripped apart by the capricious currents of the Ocean. A third had materialised within a heavy adamantium strut, and black metal rods impaled the soulless creature fast. Flickers of warp residue ran across its broken breastplate, still trying to knit the form of the Thousand Sons warrior back together.

It was hopeless. A Rubricae was one of the toughest mobile structures in the galaxy, immune to pain and despair, able to keep operating even after massive structural damage, but being fused with the hull of a loyalist interceptor had destroyed the integrity of the Traitor Marine's armour-shell. As Fuerza watched, too weak to intervene, the pale light in the broken

Rubricae's helm guttered and died. The spirit of the warrior, such as it was, had failed.

Fuerza felt a profound sadness, an echo of psychic pain within his physical agony.

So few. Now one fewer.

He turned, slowly and with spasms of torment shooting up his compressed spine, to face the survivor. It stood impassively, unmoving. It didn't betray the slightest interest in the fate of its comrades. Not for the first time, Fuerza wondered what kind of attenuated existence the Rubricae had. Did they see the runes running across their helm-displays like he did? Did speech register with them as it did with mortal men?

Impossible to tell. Ahriman, curse his black name, had made them as cold and unfeeling as the graven images of Neiumas Tertius.

For all that, it was an impressive statue. Huge and dominating in its sapphire and bronze battle plate, the Rubricae still held the ornate bolter it had carried into battle on Prospero as a living, breathing Space Marine. Its breastplate displayed the delicate images of serpents and dragons, of constellations and astrological symbols, of obscure sigils and ancient glyphs of power, each a piece of stunning artistry.

The images changed. Fuerza didn't know how, or even notice when, but they were rarely constant for long. The only thing that remained was the Eye, the one symbol that they wore at all times.

'So, brother,' Fuerza croaked, looking around him warily, feeling the blood run down his chin and over his damaged chest. 'What shall we make of this?'

The two of them had rematerialised in a dark corridor

that stretched into shadow in either direction, Fuerza slumped against the wall, the Rubricae standing. The walls were formed of exposed machinery and pipework, unadorned and brutal. The floor was a metal mesh, the ceiling a morass of power cables, coolant tubes and boxy life support modules. It was dark and almost freezing.

Fuerza guessed they were down in the lower levels, since the rumble of the engines felt close. The noise of the warp drives sounded healthy enough, but even in his critical state Fuerza was enough of an empath to detect the hurt the vessel's machine-spirit had suffered. From far above them, there were faint cries, and heavy, resounding crashes. The crew was doing its best to keep the ship from coming apart.

'We're in the warp,' mused Fuerza, licking his dry, cracked lips. 'For all we know, this is the only ship that escaped Aphael's blockade.'

He looked up at the helm of the Rubricae, watching the way the polished ceramite of its crest caught the faint interior light and turned it into a thing of beauty.

'A Wolves vessel,' he continued, trying to construct a mental picture of how the ship would be laid out. 'There may be many of them on board.'

He smiled, suppressing the coughing-up of more blood, and laid a trusting hand on the Rubricae's vambrace.

'No matter, my brother,' he said. 'I can recover from these wounds. You will be my protector in the days to come. By the time this ship leaves the embrace of the Ocean, we will be the only living souls within it.'

* * *

FOR THREE DAYS, the landings in the mountains of Asa-heim continued. For three days, the hunting packs disrupted and burned them, launching attack after attack across the ice. For three days, they racked up victories, preventing permanent footholds, scouring the rock clean of the taint of the invader. Many drop ships were destroyed before landing by clusters of Long Fangs; more were knocked out soon afterwards by the roaming packs.

Despite all of this, the invaders succeeded in estab-lishing bridgeheads. Time wore on, and the Wolves were faced with ever more of the enemy. They could not be everywhere at once, and the battles became fiercer and more protracted. The Thousand Sons established enduring positions at nine points in the mountain ranges around the Fang, landing ever more men and materiel, gradually constructing the strangle-hold from which the main assault would be launched.

As dawn broke over the Fang on the fourth day, the fortress was ringed with fire. Oily black columns, generated by promethium spills that would burn even on the ice, formed a vast, kilometres-wide circle across the mountain chain. The leaguer was closing, forged by the sacrifice of thousands of invading soldiers, each one of their deaths buying space for another drop-ship to land, another lascannon to be unloaded, another tank to rumble down the embarkation ramps.

Greyloc's Thunderhawk, the *Vragnek*, touched down in the Valgard, swooping hard under the umbrella of exploding plasma where the void shields still resisted the constant orbital bombardment. As it came to rest on the rock floor of the hangar, the crew bay doors slammed down and the Wolf Lord himself strode back into the Aett, followed by his Terminator-clad retinue. Wyrmblade was there to meet him.

Greyloc's armour was scorched black across one side and streaked with dried blood. A chunk had been knocked out of his right shoulder-guard, scarring the face of the rune Trysk. His wolfclaws were still fizzing with residual energy, and the crust of gore on his wrists showed that they'd been in heavy use.

'Good hunting?' asked Wyrmblade, looking at the signs of battle with approval.

Greyloc removed his helm with a sucking hiss and locked it under his arm. His white eyes burned coldly.

'Too many of them,' he muttered, striding past Wyrmblade, forcing the Wolf Priest to turn to keep up with him. 'We turn the ice red, but they keep landing.'

Wyrmblade nodded.

'The first rank of drop-ships were to keep us busy. They've landed heavy carriers further out. Traitor Marine squads now march with the mortals.'

Greyloc spat a gobbet of blood-flecked saliva and shook his head.

'Bones of Russ, Thar,' he hissed. 'I wanted nothing more than to keep fighting. I could have stayed out on the ice until my claws were rending their cold, dead bones.'

He looked into the Wolf Priest's eyes, and there was ferocity in his lean face.

'I wanted nothing more. Do you understand?'

Wyrmblade looked back carefully, his old eyes scanning for the tell-tale signs. He scrutinised long, paying particular attention to the white irises.

'Righteous rage, brother,' he said at last, clapping him firmly on the shoulder. 'As it should be.'

Greyloc grunted, hiding his relief badly, and shook himself from the Wolf Priest's grip.

'Then tell me.'

'We're surrounded,' said Wyrmblade. He spoke bluntly, factually. 'The net's closed. If you leave the packs out there, they'll be picked off. There are sorcerers in the ranks of the enemy now, and we don't have the Rune Priests to counter them.'

'They won't be called back easily.'

'Then they'll die. I can show you the auspex scans.'

Greyloc remained silent, grimly weighing up the options.

'We're hunters, Thar,' he said eventually. The harsh edge had left his voice as the kill-urge receded. 'We pursue. They've got us cornered. This fighting won't suit the Claws.'

Wyrmblade smiled, and his mouth hooked like a knife wound in his old, wrinkled face. 'Then we'll learn a new way. Isn't that what you're always saying?'

'I had a vision for it. The Tempering is–'

'They'll learn. You have to lead them.'

Greyloc looked at Wyrmblade coldly. His thoughts were evident across his lupine face, and he didn't bother to hide them.

They do not trust me. I am the White Wolf, the ghost, the bloodless one. They sense what I wish to do, how I wish to transform us all.

'Call the packs back,' he growled, rolling his head wearily from side to side, stretching the muscles that had been combat-tense for days on end. 'We'll meet the attack here. If nothing else, the passage of the Gates will make them bleed.'

THE OPEN SKY was streaked with the dirty trails of incoming shell fire. The enemy had managed to establish firing positions a few kilometres east of Rossek's hold-out, and now spearheads had begun to advance out of them.

'Rojk!' he bellowed into the comm. 'Where's that damned heavy support?'

There was a fizz of static in his earpiece. Either short-range comms were being jammed, or Torgrim Rojk's Long Fang squad had been forced out of combat. In either case, things were getting difficult.

Rossek's squad had assaulted six dropsites during the night, destroying all of them utterly before moving on. In four days his ten Grey Hunters had yet to take a casualty despite slaughtering huge numbers of enemy troops. Only gradually had the truth become apparent. The first wave of landings had been fodder – poorly trained and badly equipped conscripts sent to absorb the fury of the Wolves while the real soldiers were landed further out. The mountains were now crawling with enemy squads. Hundreds of them.

Like the one they were closing in on now.

'Frar, Scarjaw,' he hissed over the mission channel. 'Go wide.'

The two Grey Hunters responded instantly, breaking left from the squad and sweeping up the slope of valley. Rossek's pack had pushed far down a long, narrow cleft in the mountains, using the impenetrable rock cliffs on either side to mask their approach. The broken boulders, some the size of Rhinos, gave excellent cover. At the far end of the valley, only a few hundred metres distant, the enemy was making its advance.

Two tanks were grinding their way toward Rossek's position, guarding a phalanx of marching troops in their wake. The incoming fire was heavy and accurate, shattering the boulders in front of them and sending shards spinning into the air. The vehicles had an unusual pattern. Leman Russ chassis, by the look of them, with autocannons and heavy bolters. They looked like the Chapter's own Exterminators. Infantry killers.

'Eriksson, Vre,' Rossek hissed.

Two more Grey Hunters peeled right, stooping low as they weaved between the shoulders of rock, leaving seven of the pack still in cover on the valley floor.

A huge boulder cracked open several metres to Rossek's right, blasted apart by a long range mortar. Heavy bolter-fire from the tanks ran along the valley floor in rows, creeping ever closer to the Wolves' position.

Rossek checked his helm locator, watching as his troops took up optimal positions.

'Now,' he snarled.

The Grey Hunters on the flanks broke cover and raced toward the enemy lines, sweeping across the broken terrain like bolting *konungur*. They moved incredibly quickly, bounding with assurance across the treacherous landscape. Their boltguns opened up, slamming into the flanks of the swaying tanks and exploding across the front ranks of the infantry beyond.

Rossek watched as the tank-mounted heavy bolters swivelled to meet the flank threats, holding for the few seconds needed to draw fire from the front aspect, then clenched his fist tight.

'*Hjolda!*' he roared, leaping from cover.

His Hunters burst out with him, roaring defiance and letting their pelts stream out from their armour. The time for stealth had passed, and now speed took its place.

Incoming bolter rounds flew past Rossek's shoulder as he weaved toward his destination, his animal senses keeping him one step ahead of the mortals' reactions. He fired back from the waist – short, sharp bursts of twin-streamed fire from the storm bolter held in his right hand. As he closed on the first tank, he thumbed his chainfist into whirring, snarling life.

The vehicles were powerful but slow, hindered by the uneven terrain. The Wolves leapt and ducked as they raced toward the enemy. Despite their huge suits of power armour, they went fluidly, fast and low.

Rossek reached the first tank, leaping high on to its roof, boosted by his armour-servos. The turret whirled to face him, but he jammed his chainfist into the metal, carving it open and sending sparks spinning.

Two Hunters pounced on to the other one, with the rest of the squad sweeping past and laying into the supporting infantry. The heavy bark of bolter-fire quickly drowned out the cracks of returning las-beams.

In a single movement, Rossek mag-locked his bolter, grabbed a krak grenade and hurled it into the gap he'd opened in the turret armour, before leaping from the roof through a hail of return fire. The tank's heavy bolters tracked after him, only to be ripped apart by the muffled boom of the exploding grenade. The tank rocked on its tracks, its armoured panels bulging from within as the explosions blossomed.

Then the other tank blew up, knocked from its tracks when its fuel tanks were breached. Black smoke boiled up from the twin cracked hulls, rolling out of the shattered innards.

The mortals broke then, hurrying back the way they'd come so confidently only moments before, some dropping their weapons in their haste to retreat. Rossek roared his scorn, grabbing his storm bolter again and prepared to reap vengeance.

It was only then that his proximity scanner picked up the new signals, masked by the infantry advance. Further down the valley floor, moving slowly but inexorably, a line of sapphire and bronze figures was marching up the valley. Rossek crouched down behind cover, checking the numbers. Eighteen. Two times nine.

'Comm signal from the Aett, Jarl,' reported Frar breathlessly, clattering heavily against the rock as he sank beside him, his voice heavy with kill-urge. 'Orders to fall back.'

Rossek kept low, magnifying his helm-view and watching the line of Traitor Marines advance through the retreating remnants of their mortal allies. They didn't hide their presence, made no effort to remain in cover. They came silently, arrogantly, as if they'd already conquered the world they walked on.

'Traitors,' he spat, feeling his murder-urge sharpen. The mortals were just meat for his boltgun; these were the real enemy.

'Jarl?' asked Frar. 'Will you respond?'

Rossek found the question irritating. He'd only now seen warriors who were worthy of his blades, ones who wouldn't run like cattle when their cover was broken. Involuntarily, he found himself giving in to a low, wet growl, his finger moving toward the trigger of his bolter.

'No, brother,' he snarled, noting the position of his pack as it clustered around him again, gauging the distance to the advancing Traitor Marines, estimating terrain cover and exposure to ordnance on the way in. 'I will not respond. I would not respond if the voice of the Allfather himself gave the order.'

He turned to the Grey Hunter, sensing the warrior's own readiness for the murder-make. The whole pack had been fighting for hours, and the kill-scent was heavy in his nostrils.

'Kill the comm,' he spat. 'We'll take them. On my mark, bring the wrath of Russ to those that dare trespass on his domain.'

The Hunters tensed, ready for the order, bolters and chainswords clutched fast.

'The wrath of Russ, Jarl,' acknowledged Frar, and as he spoke there was a brutal, guttural joy in the words.

RAMSEZ HETT STRODE through the slush, his pale robes already sodden at the fringes. His golden armour shielded him from the worst of the chill, but the severe cold had a way of penetrating even his atmosphere-sealed battle-plate.

The Heq'el Mahdi dropsite had grown from a few hundred square metres to over a kilometre, a miniature city draped across the ice-bound highlands. It had anti-aircraft batteries, void shield generators, prefabricated assault walls and hastily-dug trenches around the perimeter. Over two thousand Spireguard had been landed and more were disembarking every hour. Among them strode squads of Rubricae, each accompanied by a sorcerer and shadowed by a hundred more mortal troops. Prosperine tanks and mobile artillery ground their way through the grey patches of lingering snow, their engines labouring and letting loose gouts of black smoke in the extreme conditions. Heq'el Mahdi housed a formidable army in its own right, but it was only one of nine secured dropsites. The scale of Aphael's ambition had never been more apparent.

We will never be able to do this again. On this strike, everything depends.

The Raptora sorcerer lord reached his destination. A Spireguard commander, wearing the heavy armour, full facemask and tactical battle-helm that had been denied to the first landers, approached and saluted.

'He's on time, commander?' asked Hett, his voice as rasping as ever. He'd not emerged entirely unscathed from the Rubric, and his vocal cords had stretched beyond mortal tolerances. If the Spireguard noticed the effect, he made no sign.

'Perfectly, lord,' he replied, looking up to the skies.

The two of them stood on the edge of a wide landing platform, cleared by meltas and with the irregular rock smoothed with plascrete. Rubricae stood on guard around the perimeter, as unmoving as the stone about them.

Hett followed the commander's eyeline, seeing

Aphael's ship descending toward their position. It was a Stormbird, one out of many the Legion had once operated, gilded and decorated with images of fabulous mythical beasts. The cockpit was lost in a riot of baroque bronze symbols, geometric and mystical. Above them all was the Eye, picked out in a mosaic of garnet, ruby and beryllium.

Looking at the lander as it touched down on the platform, Hett found himself wondering if Temekh was right about the Legion's loss of taste. The vessel was gaudy. Outsized. Vulgar.

When we lose our judgement, our ability to discern, we lose everything.

The passenger ramp descended, touching gently on the slushy filth beneath it. Lord Aphael strode down it casually, flanked by six towering Terminator Rubricae. His bronze helm, carved with an elongated vox-grille, looked self-satisfied. Every movement the commander made was smug, content, in control.

'Congratulations, brother,' Aphael said as he came up to Hett. 'You have given us the platform we need.'

Hett bowed.

'We lost many men, lord. More than I made allowances for. The Wolves responded quickly.'

Aphael shrugged.

'It is their world. We should have been as eager to defend ours.'

'Nonetheless,' said Hett, turning to walk with Aphael. 'Mortals cannot take on Space Marines. There have been sites of slaughter.'

Hett detected a flicker of irritation from Aphael. For all the commander's surface equanimity, there was something underneath, something fragile. If Hett had been of the Athanaeans, he might have been able to tell what it was.

Not fear, but possibly something like it.

'That is why the Rubricae go to war,' Aphael replied. 'Thanks to our Lord's deception, there can be no more than a hundred Dogs left in their lair. We bring six hundred of our silent brothers. We have two million mortal troops against a few thousand. What numbers would make you more content, brother?'

Hett felt the urgency in the commander's words.

Does he fear failure? Is that it? No. The unease is more subtle. It's something else, something within him.

'I did not presume–'

'Yes, you did,' said Aphael wearily. 'As is your right. You're a commander as much as I am.'

He stopped walking and looked over the expanse of the dropsite, teeming with massed ranks of infantry and the rumble of tank-groups. A wing of gunships flew low across them, some bearing the scars of recent combat. It was an impressive vista, a show of force few adversaries in the galaxy would have been able to stand against.

'If this were not Fenris, I would say that we already have what we need,' Aphael said. 'Complacency in this place, though, will get us all killed.'

He looked back at the Stormbird, where the dorsal loading bay doors had been lowered. Something was emerging down the ramp. Something huge.

'So you'll see, Ramsez, that all precautions that could have been taken, have been taken. We will go into this battle with every weapon the Legion still has in its possession.'

A massive structure lumbered out of the shadow of the loading bay. It stood twice as tall as the Rubricae around it, a mobile mountain of curved metal. Its head was placed directly in the centre of its vast barrel chest, surrounded by tracery of bronze. Outsized arms hefted a cannon on one side and a gigantic mining drill on the other. It moved with crushing, deliberate strides, compensating perfectly for the flex of the loading ramp. The gilded monster exuded a pungent aroma of heavy oils and coolant as it came, but nothing else. It had no soul. Even the Rubricae had more presence in the warp.

Hett gazed at it in shocked surprise.

'Cataphracts,' he breathed, seeing another follow the first down from the open hold. 'I thought they'd all been–'

'Destroyed? Not all. These are the last.'

Hett watched the enormous battle-robots, the product of ancient cybernetic tech-sorcery, reach the perimeter of the landing site and come to a mute standstill. They looked formidable, utterly unshakeable. More followed, a whole squad of death-dealing engines.

'Of course, modifications have been made,' explained Aphael, motioning toward the drill-arms. 'If we have to dig the Dogs out, we will.'

'You think it will come to that?'

'I care not,' said Aphael, and the vehemence of hatred in his voice was unfeigned. For a moment, the timbre was more like Hett's own. 'If they meet us on the ice, we will come for them. If they cower in their tunnels, we will come for them. If they bury themselves in stone, we will come for them. We will hunt them out, drag them into combat, and wound them until their blood stains this place so deep it will never be recovered.'

CHAPTER EIGHT

'FOR RUSS!'

Rossek flecked the visor of his helm with spittle, jab-bing his chainfist, dragging the edge of its blade across the Traitor Marine's breastplate as his body turned. At the edge of his vision he could see his brothers crash into combat, their bolters falling silent as they brought their close combat weapons to bear. The remnants of the mortal army were irrelevant now. All that mattered were the Traitors: eighteen Rubric Marines against an eleven-strong pack of Space Wolves with fire kindling in their clenched fists.

Fair odds.

The Rubric Marine facing Rossek moved as swiftly as he did. Though the sapphire behemoths walked into battle in stately, patient ranks, as soon as combat was joined their bodies sparked into action. Their reactions were those of the Legiones Astartes, swift and sure, poised by gene-forged mastery and that dreadful, arduous conditioning.

Ceramite crunched against ceramite, gunmetal-grey against sapphire and bronze. The whooping, bellowing pack of Wolves whirled their way into battle, bone-totems swinging wildly, their pelt-draped arms landing punches and hammer blows with crunching, precision guided force.

The Traitors responded silently, eerily matching every thrust with a counter-thrust. They spun on their heels as swiftly, traded upper-cuts and deadeners with equal skill, parried the incoming blade and returned the blow with shimmering crystal-bladed power swords.

Rossek towered over all the others, resplendent in his las-scorched Terminator battle-plate. He crashed his way through the guard of the Traitor before him, smashing it back through sheer momentum, swinging huge arcs of devastation with his whirring chainfist.

The Rubric Marine rocked on its heels, stoically fighting against the oncoming storm, driven back, pace by pace, as chunks of its ornate armour were hacked from its frame by the biting blades, never emitting so much as a whisper.

'Death to the Traitor!' bellowed Rossek, feeling fresh spikes of adrenaline pumping through his battle-primed body. The wolf within was foam-mouthed with battle frenzy, howling and slavering. The very silence of his enemy fuelled Rossek's fury, driving the assault to new heights of savagery.

The Rubric Marine stumbled then, staggering over

the rough ground. Rossek pounced, using the brief opening between them to unleash a hail of bolter rounds. As he closed for the kill, the shells impacted, shattering the beautiful armour and smashing the ornamental crests from the Traitor's helm and pauldrons.

'The wrath of Fenris!' Rossek thundered, joining the massed howls and battle cries of his brothers.

This was *life*. This was *perfection* – to bring the battle to the enemy, to fight on the open ice as the Allfather had created him to do. Amid all the anger, the blind fury, the familiar rush of the kill-urge, there was this, too.

Pleasure.

Rossek laughed under the heavy Terminator helm, barely noticing the rune-sigils on the lens display showing pack positions, kill signs and life signs. The beleaguered Rubric Marine reeled under the Wolf Guard's onslaught, unable to answer the raw fury of the charge. What meagre existence it possessed was coming to an end.

Then, everything stopped.

Rossek saw Scarjaw bound across the rocks to his right, hurling himself against two Rubric Marines, his black pelts streaming behind him. The Grey Hunter slowed and froze, locked in an impossible, half-completed lunge.

The rest of the pack succumbed, first dragging as if wading through crude oil, then grinding to a halt.

Rossek whirled round, aghast, before feeling the heaviness pull on his own limbs.

'Fight it, brothers!' he bellowed, sensing the taint of

maleficarum, tasting the unholy stench of sorcery as it sank into his limbs. The runes on his armour blazed red, flaring in defiance against the incoming waves of corruption. His vision wavered, going cloudy at the edges as if mists had rolled across the valley floor with unnatural suddenness. 'Fight it!'

The Rubric Marines suffered no ill-effects. They pressed on with remorseless efficiency, plunging their blades into the static Wolves emotionlessly, ripping open neck-guards to expose the pale flesh beneath, indifferent to the muffled cries of pain as the Hunters died.

Rossek could still move, though slowly. Every gesture was challenging, crushed by a dead weight of heaviness.

Too slow to save them.

'Hnnn-urgh!' he growled, forcing his body to keep fighting through strength of will alone. Perspiration burst out across his tattooed brow, running down his clenched cheeks. Just keeping his fists aloft was a mammoth effort; using them even more so.

Three Rubric Marines closed on him. The one he'd been fighting was among them, looking neither vengeful nor shaken despite its savaged armour. Bringing its sword into a stabbing position, it advanced coolly for the kill.

Agonisingly, Rossek saw the pack-runes on his helm-display wink out, one after another. The warriors he'd led into battle were being butchered, not in the heat of honourable combat, but like cattle.

He clenched his chainfist, gritted his fangs, and raged against it. He felt as if his hearts would burst, his muscles prise from his bones, but he somehow forced his weapons into position.

Then, for the first time, he saw the master of the sorcery. Only metres away, his outline blurred and shimmering, a Thousand Sons magus emerged from cover. Rossek could smell him, feel the pungent sweetness of corruption in his nostrils. There was a flesh-and-blood warrior under those robes, a heart that beat and a mind that could feel malice.

The sorcerer held a golden staff, and pearlescent lightning quickened to its sigil-crowned head.

+As you die, Dog-warrior, know this,+ came a thin, hatred-distorted voice within his mind. The sorcerer lowered the point of the staff at him. +We will do this to every one of you.+

Then Rossek's world filled with pain and light. A vast force threw him from his feet, ripping him from the rocks and hurling him far into the air. He felt his body recoil from the explosion, shocked hard even under the protection of his armour. The impact when he hit the earth again was heavy, dull and crippling. He smelled the sharp tang of his own blood in his mouth, as well as the pungent aroma of burning krak-discharge.

He lifted his head painfully, his vision blurred and shaky, struggling to remain conscious.

Krak-discharge?

'Jarl, do not move.'

It was the voice of Rojk over the comm. Rossek's vision began to clear, just in time to see fresh heavy weapons fire slam into the Thousand Sons squad. The standing Traitor Marines were thrown aside just as the others had been. Huge, rolling balls of fire flared up from the shattering boulders as krak missiles and heavy bolter rounds rained down on the Rubric Marines. He saw Traitors torn apart in the inferno, their armour spinning into shards as the hail of fire detonated across the ceramite. The survivors withdrew, falling back in disciplined silence to escape the torrent of incoming fire.

A few moments later there were sets of hands on Rossek's armour, dragging him from the scene, hauling him across the broken ground.

'My... pack...' grunted Rossek, his vision blurred and groggy.

The motion ceased. A familiar helmet loomed in front of him. Bone-white and carved into the gruesome image of a bear-skull, it was more like a Wolf Priest's than a Long Fang's.

'Only one other life-sign,' reported Torgrim Rojk. There was accusation in the old warrior's voice. 'We've got you both, and we're leaving.'

From somewhere close by, Rossek made out the thudding growl of a Land Raider engine. There was more bolter fire, and the rush of the Long Fangs' volleys streaking through the air.

Rossek shook the hands off him and staggered to his feet. He felt sick. Corrupted.

'The gene-seed,' he slurred, thinking of his fallen brothers. The world still swayed around him, rocking in a hail of contrails and echoing explosions.

Rojk ordered his men to fall back to the open maw of the waiting Land Raider. The veterans withdrew without panic, firing as they went. They carried Aunir

Frar's body with them, unmoving and dripping with dark blood.

'We stay here, we die,' Rojk said coolly. 'Use your eyes.'

Rossek whirled round, nearly falling as he did so. A few hundred metres away, past the kill-zone where his slaughtered pack lay amid the stone, he saw the surviving Rubric Marines begin to regroup. Behind them, further down the narrow valley, more troops were hurrying to join them, mortal and Traitor. Beyond that, hazy in the distance, were tank groups, far larger vehicles than the ones he'd destroyed, grinding up the boulders under massive treads.

The spearhead had been caught up by the main battalions; the Thousand Sons advance was now underway. He'd lingered too long. Above it all the stink of maleficarum was still strong in his nostrils, pungent and cloying. They couldn't fight that witchery.

Numbly, he let himself be half-led, half-dragged to the waiting transport. Thick smoke was pouring from the exhausts as it powered up for withdrawal. The Land Raider's bolters were already firing constantly, covering the retreat.

Rossek barely felt himself clang to the floor of the troop bay, barely felt the grinding thrust of the drives as they powered the transport back along the rubble-strewn valley floor. The lingering pall of corruption ran through his mind, merging his thoughts, jumbling his instincts.

The Land Raider pulled clear, riding out the storm of fire as it picked up speed. Rossek dragged himself to his knees, his ravaged body working hard against the damaged servos of his armour. Only then did clarity begin to return, some sense of what had just happened.

I killed them.

Then the amber-eyed wolf within him howled, not with battle-lust or glory, but with the horror of grief.

CREWMAN RERI URFANGBORN liked the void. Even when the ship was in the strange hiatus of warp travel with all its sickness and nausea, being a crew member on an Adeptus Astartes vessel was a step up from the average life of a mortal within the Imperium. He knew this because he'd seen other worlds and witnessed the horrors and wonders of the galaxy first hand. He'd seen hive cities of metal and plascrete that reared their heads through acid atmospheres, enormous agri-combines plagued with dust and ceaseless labour, forgeworlds covered in continent-sized manufactorums, choked with oily smoke and riddled with pollution and disease.

So, for all its trials, being stationed for a lifetime in the enginarium of the *Nauro* wasn't a bad result. It was dark and cold, but then Fenris was too. It smelled bad most of the time, but after a few years you stopped noticing it. The kaerls were rough-spoken and didn't think twice about landing a punch with a rifle-butt for sloppy work, but were humane enough beyond that – the current ship's Master had even ordered distribution of *demi-mjod*, the heavily alcoholic imitation of the Sky Warriors' sacred battle stimulant, after the escape from the orbital blockade. That had been good. It had made everybody happier, despite the accidents afterwards.

In the time since then, the workrate had been punishing. It was hard to tell how much time had passed – the internal chronos were unreliable in the warp, and only the Navigator had any real sense of how long it had been since they'd reached the jump-point and powered up the warp drives. Certainly days, at least as Reri's body measured it. The time had been filled more than was usual with work – he'd slept no more than a couple of hours in every cycle before being roused back for the next task. Something was making the commander drive the ship hard, squeezing out more speed even in the face of the damage they'd taken over Fenris.

As a lower deck worker, Reri had no real overview of the whole repair process, but he knew something about engines, and they were still in a bad way. There were leaks all over the place, and three of the four major fuel conduits leading from the tanks to the drives had been ruptured beyond repair. Seven decks were entirely sealed off, making travel between the various levels difficult and time consuming. That said, the faces of the senior crew had reverted from extreme anxiety to merely grim. Morkai was still hard on their heels, but perhaps not quite as close behind as he had been.

Which was good news for Reri Urfangborn. He liked life, even more so since Anjia in the quartermaster's section had finally shrugged off the worst of her diffidence and seemed genuinely willing to spend some time behind the bulkheads with him. He didn't fool himself that there was much affection there – his hunched frame and grey skin, a product of his life's work, didn't exactly make him stand out as paragon of virility – but it was amazing what a near-death experience could do to soften a woman's resistance.

He slunk down the service tunnels expertly, conditioned by years of rattling around in the bowels of the *Nauro*. The light was weaker than normal. Whole sections were liable to be plunged into darkness when the powergrid took a sudden demand from the labouring engines, so he'd strapped two torches on either side of his rusty helmet. As he scuttled, he could hear his own breath, heavy and expectant. It had been a long time, and his palms were greasy with desire and engine lubricant.

He rounded a corner, bent double in the cramped interior, careful to avoid the protruding clumps of exposed wiring. The metal around him vibrated constantly, driven by the heartbeat of the titanic engines above.

Just as he reached his destination, a store-chamber buried deep within the labyrinth of service tunnels, the faint strip-lights fizzed out.

Reri grinned as he flicked his torches on. The twin beams were watery and flickering, but they exposed the way ahead well enough. He dropped down from the service tunnel into the chamber he'd picked, knocking aside a crate of worn-out bearings as he landed. He looked around, his torch-beams running over the chaotic pile of boxes on the metal grid floor.

Anjia was there already, slouched in front of a pile of old machine parts, waiting for him in the dark, her head lowered. Reri saw her red hair flash in the torch-light and felt a pang of excitement ripple through him.

'So you came,' he said greedily, scampering over to her.

She made no reply, and Reri hung back for a moment. Was she ill? Having second thoughts? He crouched down in front of her, gingerly extending his scrawny hand to her fringe. He hesitated, fingers trembling. She was sitting awkwardly.

'Anjia?'

He pulled the hair back, exposing her pale face. Where her eyes had been, there were black holes, running with lines of blood like tear-tracks.

Reri screamed, leaping up and away, blundering wildly into the wall at his back.

Except it wasn't a wall. It was a metal giant, a monster with gilded power armour and a high, crested helm. The behemoth reached down and grabbed him by the shoulder, squeezing the flesh until the blood welled up.

Reri kept screaming until the other one emerged. The second monster had long flowing robes draped over similarly ornate armour curves, though he limped and stooped as if badly injured. His helm had been carved into the likeness of a cobra head, surmounted by a hood of gold. The one with the robes gestured casually and Reri found he could no longer scream. His open mouth made no sound at all, even through the screaming continued inside his head. He struggled, more out of instinct than anything else. He'd begun to recognise the figures for what they were – some kind of debased Space Marine. That told him all he needed to know about his survival prospects.

The one with the robe loomed up over him. Reri's torchbeams flickered across the gold cobra-hood, sparkling from the jewels studded in the metal. Like some half-remembered nightmare, no sound would come out of his mouth. His facial muscles gradually relaxed, until his features took on an expression of mild boredom.

The one with the robes said something to the silent one, but it wasn't in a language Reri could understand. Then the golden helm turned to Reri.

'I am glad you came,' said Cobra-mask, this time speaking in strangely accented Fenrisian. The voice was surprisingly soft. Kind, even. 'Your friend did not survive this process. I assume that you are made of stronger stuff.'

His two gauntlets rose. In one he carried a curved scalpel. In the other were two orbs, glistening with an unholy, pale-green light. Aside from the sheen of witchery, they looked a lot like eyes.

Reri kept screaming. He kept screaming as the torchlights were doused, and he kept screaming as Master Fuerza went to work, and he kept screaming until the Thousand Sons sorcerer-lord had finished. Indeed, though his features remained slack and emotionless, locked into surface equanimity by magicks more powerful than he'd ever be able to comprehend, there was a part of Reri Urfangborn that would never stop screaming again.

HELFIST LEAPED HIGH into the air, the dying light glinting from his armour, snow showering from his body in heavy slabs.

'The Wolves are among you!' he roared, breaking the long, patient silence.

Five metres below him, the column of marching mortals spun round, staring up in comical terror. It had been foolish of them to come so close to the ledge, so enticingly swathed in deep drifts and well situated for an ambush.

Two metres to Helfist's left, Redpelt burst from the snow, roaring with his own note of feral enthusiasm. The rest of the pack broke out with him, led by the bellowing shape of Sigrd Brakk, a looming nightmare of blade and armour in the gathering dusk. The Wolves dropped together like a landslide, crashing into the unprepared forces below.

Las-fire cracked up at them as the mortals raced to withdraw, out from the shadow of the ledge and over the broken, treacherous ground beyond. Many stumbled, breaking ankles and wrists as they fell among the knife-sharp rocks. There must have been over a hundred of them, all well armed, all well armoured. For mortals.

Helfist landed heavily, crushing the spine of a retreating trooper with his power fist, now crackling with its blistering disruption field. He swung round, taking another two clean off their feet, tearing open their masks and leaving them to choke on the thin air. With his free hand, he unleashed a stream of murderous bolter fire from his pistol, carving a corridor of blood through the close-packed soldiers, then bounded after it.

'The wrath of Russ!' Helfist whooped in kill-pleasure, picking his targets among the morass of turning, running figures.

By then Redpelt and the rest of the pack were in the midst of them too, hacking and chopping, releasing short, precise bursts of bolt-rounds. Muzzle-flares and energy fields lit up the gloom of the dusk, outshining the wayward las-beams as the enemy did its best to do more than expire under the onslaught.

'Come to my blades, traitor scum!' bellowed Redpelt, barrelling over the rocks as sure-footedly as a true wolf. 'Feel my–'

A lucky las-beam hit him full in the chest, upending him and sending him sprawling on his back.

The Blood Claws roared with laughter as they swept past him, butchering the mortals beyond with a casual, chilling abandon.

'Feel your *what*, brother?' taunted Helfist, eviscerating a trooper with his bolt pistol before seizing another in his power fist to crush.

Brokentooth chortled even as he whirled his chainsword through a whole cluster of terrified, crawling soldiers, the monomolecular edges slicing apart the plate armour as if it were fabric.

Redpelt clambered back up heavily, emanating embarrassment and fury. Smoke rolled from the black burn on his breastplate.

'Who in *fekke* was that?' he roared, striding back into range, his booming voice rising above the screams and gasping sobs of the fleeing mortals. He sprayed bolt-pistol fire in vicious swathes, cutting down the soldiers by the dozen. 'Try that again. *Try that again.*'

Helfist grinned as he punched a soldier's faceplate in and spun round to pick off more with his pistol.

'I wish someone would,' he said over the mission

channel. 'We're running out of things to kill.'

It was true. Brakk had cut a swathe through the enemy, killing with a precision and skill that surpassed even that of his Blood Claws. As ever, the Wolf Guard had remained grimly silent during the butchery, letting the young bloods get the savagery out of their system while he ensured no escapees. By the time he'd swept round to close on Helfist's position, the terrain was strewn with quickly freezing bodies. The last of the standing enemy were cut down with disdain.

'Enough,' barked Brakk once the tide of murdermake had subsided. He slammed a fresh clip into his boltgun. 'That's completion. We're heading back to the Aett.'

Redpelt was still bristling.

'Why?' he spat, letting his chainsword continue to whirr. 'We could fight all night.'

Brakk snorted. Unlike the other packleaders he'd remained in standard format power armour rather than the bulkier Terminator plate, but somehow he still dominated the warriors around him.

'We're not staying out here for you to fall on your arse again,' he snarled. 'I've got recall orders from the Aett – we're going back.'

Helfist drew alongside Redpelt. His body was still flooded with endorphins. The blood-tally had been high, though the quality of kills had been low. There was still work to do, and being dragged back to the lair was insulting.

'We should stay,' he said, almost without meaning to.

The pack fell silent. Brakk slowly turned to face him.

'Really? And what piece of tactical genius makes you say that?'

Helfist was stung by the sarcasm. He felt retorts running through his mind, sentiments he'd been bursting to express for months.

Our Wolf Lord is too cautious. His blood does not run hot. He keeps us from glory, and makes us the whelps of the Chapter. It should have been Rossek. He would have thrown us at the enemy, unfurled our claws, given us the murder-make we need.

But no words came. Brakk was an old Wolf Guard, adamantium-hard and broken over the anvil of countless campaigns. He was the apex predator, the undisputed master of the pack. The Blood Claws were free to mock that power when their youthful passions drove them, but they would never defy it.

So Helfist bowed in submission, feeling his cheeks burn as he did so.

'There are witches among the Traitors now,' explained Brakk, addressing the whole pack. 'So far from Sturmhjart's wards, we're vulnerable. So we fall back to where we can fight them better. The Jarl knows what he's doing.'

The pack stowed their weapons then, preparing for the loping run back to the Aett. One by one, keeping close together, they broke off, streaming across the terrain as the last of the dusk light faded.

As Helfist made to follow, Brakk came up to him. He laid a gauntlet on the Blood Claw's arm. Not gently.

'I know how you feel,' he said over a closed channel.

'Your fire commends you, Kyr Aesval. There will be more killing yet, and the glory you crave.'

The grip tightened.

'But question an order again,' he growled, 'and I'll tear your cocky throat out.'

AHMUZ TEMEKH LOOKED over the chamber. He was deep in the heart of the *Herumon*, shielded from the void by kilometres of the ship's structure. The room was nine metres in diameter and perfectly circular, its walls polished to a mirror-sheen. Even Temekh's eyes, attuned to imperfection in all its forms, could see no flaw on the surface, the result of decades of labour by his neophytes before they'd even been told about the mission to Fenris. The floor was similarly smooth and reflective. The ceiling, some twenty metres distant, was decorated extensively. Zodiacal figures and the five Platonic Solids were picked out in lines of gold and amethyst, all arranged around the central device of the Eye.

The Eye. When did that become our emblem? Did any of us think about what it says, what it means?

Temekh looked upwards with his psi-sight, scrutinising the design. The images, though rendered beautifully, were not mere decoration – they were placed precisely at certain points in relation to the centre of the chamber, points determined by the harmonics they induced within the aether and the resonances that created.

It was sometimes assumed by practicae and other neophytes that the immaterium and the materium had no precise relationship, and that what happened in one was only imperfectly mirrored in the other. That wasn't true, despite how hazy those relations could appear to the uninitiated. The causal links were more constant and more concrete than any existing purely in the physical realm, though it took a lifetime of study to see how the infinite elements of the sundered universes harmonised with one another. Even master sorcerers needed symbols in order to make sense of those deep meanings; images were a part of that, as were names. So it was that the chamber also had words of power inscribed across the walls, scripted in atom-perfect lines by machinery long forgotten and forbidden in the mortal Imperium.

In themselves, the names had little significance. Placed in the proper order, and treated with the proper reverence, the significance could be terrifying. It was all about relationships, connections, cause and effect.

At the centre of the chamber was an altar, cast in bronze and gilded with more esoteric devices. Temekh stood before it then as he had done for the past twelve hours, motionless, hands clasped, head bowed, in an attitude of silent contemplation. He was high in the Enumerations, as close to disembodiment as he dared to go, mindful of the dangers even as he relished the opportunities.

Above the altar, something was taking shape. Though his violet eyes were closed, Temekh could see the form of it growing. At present there was virtually nothing to take note of. A shimmer here, a flicker there. From time to time, the air would tremble, writhing as if in a heat-haze.

The task was difficult, despite the long preparation,

the painstaking researches, the sacrifices made. Once certain states had been achieved, once a certain degree of physicality had been relinquished, reassuming it was an arduous process. The universe had learned over the aeons to resist the imposition of pure psychic essence. The materium had a soul of its own – this, too, was not widely known – a generalised ability to defer incursions from the other side of the veil. If it had not, then the power of the daemonic would long since have run riot across the mortal galaxy.

In order to do what his master wished, that power had to be neutralised, to be gently, carefully prised apart. Ahriman had once called it *singing the universe to sleep*. It was an apt description.

At the memory of his old friend, Temekh felt his heart slowing, his pulse dropping to a faint beat every hour. The recollection helped him. The procedure was working.

Above the altar, for a brief moment, a pupil flickered into being, deep as the pits of the void, ringed with red. Then it was gone, just an echo amid the other half-recognised shapes swimming above the bronze and gold.

They seek you on Gangava, my lord, thought Temekh, letting a part of his mind play over the irony of it. *As if you were any longer restricted to physical geometry. They do not know how powerful – and how weak – you have made yourself.*

There was a ripple in the warm air then, a backwash of something like irritation, the trivial inflection of some vast, magisterial being, still capable of being offended, still able to have its wounded pride pricked.

Temekh reined his thoughts in. Concentration was required. It would be required for many days yet. Every material atom in the chamber would resist him, every law of physics would flex and struggle as it was violated. The materium could sense the enormous outrage he wished to perpetrate, and so it raged in still-potent fury.

Be still, commanded Temekh, exerting his subtle power across the chamber silently. *My voice is law in this place. My will is ascendant. I am here to do the bidding of my master. I am here to put you to sleep.*

CHAPTER NINE

DAWN BROKE OVER Asaheim, throwing weak golden beams through the mountains, gilding the long kilometres of unbroken snow with a faint sheen. The light ran down the flanks of the Fang as the shafts broke clear of the shoulder of Friemiaki.

It showed up a scene of desolation. The Thousand Sons leaguer was complete, a ring of steel around the isolated peak. The rain of plasma from the fleet in orbit continued without pause, smashing into the fortress's void shields and cascading through the empty air. All passes to and from the Fang were now sealed, blocked by the swollen host of infantry and mechanised units. Heavy artillery had been dug into the cliffs facing the Fang, and every barrel pointed at the lone profile of the Wolves' bastion. Ranks of men were still moving, taking up forward positions, covered by flanking columns of tanks and low-flying squadrons of gunships. Heavy ordnance had already been broken out, and a steady torrent of shells whined across the frozen sky to crash against the distant stone and ice of Russ's citadel.

From a viewing platform high above the Sunrising Gate, Greyloc, Sturmhjart and Wyrmblade watched the unfolding deployment of the enemy. From below came the sound of drilling and hammering, punctuated by the flares of arc-welders and las-burners. The huge batteries above and alongside the gate were being augmented by extra troop-killing arrays dragged up from the armouries. The Gate itself, wide enough for a hundred men to walk through abreast, had been sanctified by the Rune Priests and painted with fresh signs of aversion. The colossal structure of adamantium, granite and ceramite bristled with linked boltgun turrets, rocket launchers and static plasma cannons. The firepower collected there was vast, the kind of arsenal more suited to a battle cruiser group than a land-bound citadel. Within the locked doors of the gates stood the defenders, housed in power armour or sealed within the holds of Land Raiders, waiting for the moment to be loosed from cover. Across the entire structure stretched the shields, glistening faintly as the oblique sunlight slanted through clouds of burning engine oil.

Greyloc augmented his scan of the enemy host, assessing the numbers, the distances, the power they could bring to bear.

We must make them pay for the passage of the gates.

He felt calm, alert, poised. The raids on the landing

sites had given his warriors their haul of bodies and delayed the onslaught of the main mass of troops. There had been losses, but nothing like those suffered by the enemy.

'How have they amassed such an army?' asked Sturmhjart, looking impressed. 'The sagas say we crippled them.'

'More of them to kill,' observed Wyrmblade dryly. 'Be glad of it.'

'They have been planning this for centuries, Wolf Priest,' said Greyloc. 'Ironhelm should have seen this coming. We all should have seen this coming.'

Sturmhjart's nostrils flared under his helm. He had worked with incredible energy over the past three days to bolster the Fang's wards against sorcery, and was still smarting from his failure to read the runes.

Recognising this, Greyloc turned to him. 'I make no criticism of you, brother. Their power to corrupt the wyrd is their infamy.'

'They do not corrupt the wyrd,' Sturmhjart insisted.

Wyrmblade laughed harshly.

'You know what, brother? I really don't give a damn where their witchery comes from. They can burn in the fires of Hel like mortal men well enough, and that's all that matters.'

Sturmhjart gave the Wolf Priest a long look, as if he wasn't sure whether he was being mocked or praised.

'They'll burn,' he muttered, turning his rune-engraved helm to face the distant enemy. 'Oh, they'll burn.'

Then there was a thud of fist against breastplate from behind them, and Hamnr Skrieya joined them on the viewing platform. Like all the Wolf Guard he bore the signs of recent conflict on his armour – his power fist was charred from energy field burn and the pelts on his Terminator suit were no more than scraps of tangled fur.

'Skrieya,' acknowledged Greyloc. 'Is the recall complete?'

'It is, Jarl.'

'The tally of blood?'

'We hurt them, Jarl. Casualties were minimal, but... not insignificant. One pack was lost.'

Greyloc raised an eyebrow. The recall order had been given before the advent of the sorcerers had made the field deadly for his kill-squads.

'A pack? Whose?'

Skrieya hesitated for a heartbeat.

'Tromm Rossek's, Jarl.'

Greyloc felt as if Skrieya had kicked him in the stomach.

Rossek. Of all my elite, Rossek...

'He was recovered, but his pack is gone.'

Greyloc suppressed the rush of conflicting emotion at the news. Even in armour, his pheromone state was still open to the others.

The true Son of Russ, the headstrong warrior, the unstoppable one. My brother, this is why you could never be Jarl.

'He must be disciplined,' said Wyrmblade, coldly. 'His pack would have fought alongside us.'

'Not now,' snarled Greyloc. 'We will need his blades.'

For a moment Wyrmblade looked like he would protest, but then bowed his head.

'As you will it, Jarl.'

There was a frosty silence. In the distance, the

marshalling of the enemy forces continued. With every passing moment, the valleys leading to the gate causeways were filling with the Traitor vanguard. They would be unleashed before the sun reached its zenith.

Greyloc looked back out across the battlefield to come. Under his helm, his pale face was fixed in a grim mask of bitterness.

'I will nothing but for this fight to begin,' he growled, and the hairs on his body rose in readiness. 'Blood of Russ, let them come to me now, and I will show them the meaning of agony.'

ARFANG HAD TAKEN longer than expected to make the summons. For a while, Freija had begun to hope that he'd found someone else to guard his precious servitors, and had concentrated on her other huskaerl duties single-mindedly. There had been plenty of those, including weapons drills with her squad, many of whom weren't nearly at the standard she'd have hoped for.

But the Iron Priest had not forgotten, and even as the Thousand Sons army began to close the stranglehold on the Aett, painfully establishing their forward positions in the surrounding peaks, he came back for her.

'The time has come,' he'd said, and that had been all. So she'd left the Valgard with her squad, asking no more questions, ready for wherever Arfang would take her. Soon enough it became clear. They were headed down. A long way down.

Mortals like Freija, for all their Fenris-born prowess, weren't able to plummet unaided down the vertical shafts that linked the levels of the Fang. Even if she

could have done it, the servitors certainly couldn't –
those plunging drops were only possible for the Sky
Warriors. So the journey down the many hundred
levels from the Valgard at the summit of the Fang to
the lower reaches of the Hould took a long time. The
motley company rode on more than a dozen clattering turbo-elevators, tramped down several long
spiral staircases hewn from the stone and marched
across countless rough-cut chambers glowing with
the embers of old fires. With every level they passed,
the decorations in the rock became less ornate, the
glowglobes a little less close together, the voices a little
more hushed.

They'd swept quickly through the Fangthane, now
teeming with thralls. Freija knew her father had been
charged with its defence, but there was no sign of him
amongst the milling crowds when she and Arfang got
there. Squads of mortals were busy installing gun turrets
at the far end, and there were heavy lengths of waist-
thick cables strung along the floors. That alone made her
blood run a little more chill. The Fangthane was a sacred
chamber, and if the Jarl expected to make war here
then the carnage of the coming assault would surely be
greater than anything unleashed on Fenris before.

Freija found herself wondering if the Sky Warriors
felt even the smallest fragments of trepidation at that.
They'd have to be inhuman not to.

But of course, they were inhuman. Not so much a different class as a different species.

Species. Sounds like I'm classifying beasts.

After the Fangthane, they'd kept going down, descending ever further into the deeper levels of the Aett. The

Hould, the vast and teeming hive of tunnels where Freija had been born and spent her early life, was not the raucous, buzzing place she knew. The thralls went about their business with looks of tight expectation, all of them hefting arms, most led by an experienced kaerl at their head. Barricades were being erected at strategic points in the tunnel network and mobile gun platforms installed at cross-ways. The warding runes, the Eyes of Aversion which guarded every major intersection, were being re-sanctified by the Rune Priests and their leather-masked wyrd-thralls. Munitions were piled high, kept under the watchful eyes of huskaerls as more cases arrived hourly from the huge armouries.

Every so often a Sky Warrior would stalk past them on some urgent errand, streaked with fresh blood on his charred armour. They never acknowledged her, but all nodded respectfully to Arfang before striding off into the shadows. Freija could sense the heightened level of tension in their gestures – they'd already been fighting for days, and were heavily primed for coming battle, their golden eyes blazing, and that made them even more terse and inscrutable than ever.

At the base of the Hould, buried kilometres down into the rock, was Borek's Seal, the largest of the Fang's innumerable chambers. Even more massive than the Fangthane, the enormous cavern was a gloomy and shadow-draped place. Just as the Fangthane guarded the approaches from the Hould to the Jarlheim, Borek's Seal warded passage to the levels below, the Hammerhold and the half-explored Underfang. It was colossal, the size of a battleship's hull, though almost empty of decoration and devoid of the pelts, bones and carvings that adorned most chambers of the Aett. The bare rock walls were unfinished and jagged, a reminder of the primal nature of the Wolves' ancient origins. A few fires burned low in vast circular pits, but their light was weak and the perma-chill was little disturbed by them.

Even as she marched across the yawning cavern in convoy with the chittering, limping servitors, Freija found herself gazing up at the huge columns supporting the far-off roof. Each was the width of a Rhino chassis, a shaft of naked rock that glinted with points of red from the low flames.

She'd never come down this far before. No one she knew had. This was below the Gate level, the limit of the kaerls' patrol circuits, and beyond it none but the Iron Priests went.

'Frightened, huskaerl?' asked Arfang, his staff thudding against the stone as he strode.

Frightened wasn't a state that had much meaning on Fenris beyond a generic, abstract insult. 'Watchful, lord,' replied Freija, as curtly as she dared.

Arfang let slip a grating chuckle.

'Just so. I would not want whelps down here with me. That would not do.'

Freija looked at the Iron Priest carefully. In the dark, his armour was as black as scorched metal, lined with red from the fire-pits.

'Forgive me, lord,' she ventured. 'This is unusual. Kaerls do not travel to the Hammerhold.'

'They do not,' agreed Arfang.

They continued walking. The Iron Priest didn't seem to feel the need to offer any further explanation.

'So, if I may ask–'

'You wish to know why I summoned you, what possible use a mortal could be to me down here.'

'I cannot imagine you needing my help.'

Arfang stopped walking and turned to her. Behind the two of them, the trail of servitors clattered to a halt.

'You think there's no danger in the forges?'

'We are in the Aett, lord.'

'We are on Fenris, huskaerl. We do not eliminate the danger on this world, even though we could. We keep it close to us, learn to live with it, use it to keep us strong. The Underfang has many perils. Some are not known even to the Great Wolf.'

'But we aren't going to the–'

'This is a time of danger, and there are ways from the dark places into the Hammerhold. If I could have chosen, I would have come here with a pack of Hunters. But they are all needed to cut threads, so mortals will have to do.'

He leaned forwards, and his eyes glowed like old stars.

'Waking the dead is difficult,' he growled, his voice low and rumbling. 'It will devour my attention for many hours. While I am engaged, the thralls will need guarding. Can you do that, huskaerl? Or are you afraid of the deeper dark?'

Freija glared back at him, stung by the implied weakness. She felt the flare of rebellion in her breast, the always present urge to lash out at the arrogance of the armoured demigods who dictated every aspect of her life. They only lacked fear because it had been bred out of them by the Helix, yet how quickly they learned to despise mortal emotion, the very core of the humanity they were charged with protecting.

'I fear nothing, lord,' she said, keeping the worst of the irritation from her voice.

The Iron Priest's helm-face was blank, but the subtle movement of his head told Freija that, somewhere under all that battered plate, he was smiling at her.

'We'll see, huskaerl,' he said, resuming his thudding stride. 'We'll see.'

MOREK WALKED ACROSS the floor of the Fangthane, weaving his way between the incoming columns of wounded and returned. Most had been landed by the Thunderhawks higher up in the Valgard, but some had come in through the land gates. The massive hall was filled with sound and movement as kaerls hurried to install more gun platforms even as files of warriors brushed past them, hurrying to other deployment points.

Amid them all came the Sky Warriors. Some walked tall, bearing the mark of victory in their gold eyes, strutting and prowling among the mortals like demi-gods. Other packs had taken casualties, and prickled with shame and an evident desire to get back into the fray. They were all wound tight, the ones who'd suffered, burning with a sullen, dark resolve to make amends. Morek knew well enough to avoid close contact with them. When the beast was active within them, they sometimes had trouble remembering who the enemy was.

'Rivenmaster!' came a throaty, rattling voice.

Morek whirled round to face it, and his heart sank.

A Wolf Guard was limping toward him. The huge figure loomed out of the fire-lit dark in Terminator plate. The armour was cracked and battle-scarred, and the warrior within looked similarly damaged. He'd taken his helm off, revealing a heavily tattooed face ringed by a russet mane. Studs glinted from his temples, and his eyes betrayed a wild, destructive grief.

Beside him on a suspensor platform floated the body of a Grey Hunter, strapped to the mobile stretcher, lying totally motionless. His armour had been carved apart, and long trails of blood ran over the plate. Lights flickered along the suspensor chassis, etching out the shapes of sigils. Morek was no Apothecary, but he could understand the Rune of Ending as well as any other Fenrisian.

'I serve, lord,' he said, bowing.

'Get this warrior to the Lord Wyrmblade,' the Wolf Guard growled. 'Do it now.'

Morek hesitated, just for a moment. He'd been ordered to oversee the preparations for the Fangthane defence. There were countless thralls who could escort a wounded Sky Warrior to the Wolf Priests.

He could have protested. It would have been pointless. The Wolf Guard before him was wounded and was clearly struggling to contain a furnace of sullen, frustrated fury.

'I will, lord,' he said, trying not to think about the many things that would remain undone in his absence.

The Wolf Guard grunted, and shoved the suspensor toward him. It bobbed lightly as it was touched.

Morek could see the extensive trauma on the ruined body, the deep sword wounds and congealed blood. It looked like the Hunter was in what his kind called the Red Dream, the deep regenerative process triggered by the too-close embrace of Morkai.

'Go swiftly, mortal,' growled the Wolf Guard, turning to go back the way he'd come, then hesitating. 'What are you called?'

Morek looked him in the eye. Long experience had taught him that you always had to look them in the eye.

'Morek Karekborn, lord.'

'Guard him well, Morek Karekborn. When this is over, I will seek you out. His name is Aunir Frar, Grey Hunter of my pack. His wyrd and yours are now one. Remember it.'

Morek maintained eye contact, though it was difficult. The Wolf Guard's amber irises seemed strangely out of focus, as if some massive assault had damaged something within him. What could not be doubted was the urgency in the words.

'I understand,' Morek replied, already planning the route of his ascent to the home of the fleshmakers, a place that, before that hour, would have been death for him to even approach. 'His wyrd is mine. My life for his.'

ON THE EIGHTH day since the Thousand Sons had arrived in orbit around Fenris, the assault on the gates of the Fang began.

Though each of the two land portals, Bloodfire and Sunrising, were high up the sheer sides of the mountain, they stood at the termination of massive ridges between the peaks, allowing movement up towards them from the surrounding highlands. The ridges ran up to the citadel gates like huge causeways of stone, each kilometres wide and worn smooth by the endless gnawing of the winds. In the half-forgotten millennia past, the Allfather and Leman Russ had walked on that same stone, planning the construction of the Aett together, seeing how the tortured landscape of Asaheim could be made to house the greatest fortress outside Terra. Russ had made it so that the two Gates overlooked entirely bare approaches, such that any massed advance on them would provoke a slaughter.

As Greyloc watched the massive forces under the command of the Thousand Sons begin to roll forwards, he gave silent thanks for that foresight. The host assembled by the invaders, revealed in the sharp glare of the late noon sun, was beyond anything he'd seen marching under a Traitor's banner. The Great Scouring had devastated the Legions of the Betrayers, and Magnus's own troops had been thinned out during the inferno on Prospero. In the intervening centuries, they had clearly been busy.

The encircling army had coalesced into two hosts, one for each Gate. In the vanguard came the heavy artillery, ranks of them rolling on heavy treads and churning up the snow. There were big mortar launchers among them, and vehicles bearing demolisher cannons, and still more with gigantic plasma weapons mounted high on their lumbering chassis. Further back came even heavier vehicles, swaying like drunkards as they ground into firing range. There were mobile launchers with whole frames of sleek missiles hoisted into firing angles, and vast superheavy assault tanks with siege cannons protruding from bloated turrets.

Between them came the troop carriers, the Chimeras of the mortal troopers and the Rhinos and Land Raiders of the Traitor Marines. There were hundreds of the former, only a handful of the latter. Even so, the first wave of the enemy boasted more manpower than Greyloc had left in the entire fortress, and he knew there were many thousands more held in reserve.

Above the advancing ranks swooped the wings of gunships, flying low and in tight formation. There were bigger atmospheric ships hovering further out on whining engines, each packed with weaponry, poised and ready to sweep over the battlefield.

Somewhere amid that sprawling tide of men and vehicles were the sorcerers, the fallen Space Marines who commanded the whole edifice. They were the key, the handful of witches who held the corrupting power of the warp in their armoured hands.

It was an intimidating force, the last residue of one of the Emperor's own Legions of Death, an army capable of bringing a world to its knees.

But Fenris was no ordinary world, and its denizens were incapable of being intimidated.

'Unleash,' ordered Greyloc.

At the Wolf Lord's command, the flanks of the Fang erupted.

Bolts of plasma and heavy las-fire scythed out across the ice, crackling with enormous, terrible energies as they lanced to their destinations. Heavy bolters thundered out from a hundred positions on the slopes, hurling mass-reactive rounds over huge distances. Autocannons spooled up, spitting lines of armour-piercing shells deep into the enemy columns. Missiles screamed out of their silos, hurtling high into the frost-clear sky before plummeting down into the ranks of the invader.

The oncoming tanks responded as soon as they came into range, and a hail of fire returned, crashing into the walls of the mountain, showering it in an inferno of exploding promethium and detonating shells. The inferno kindled even as the rain of plasma from orbit, the steady column that had shaken the mountain for days, was intensified, and the entire summit of the Fang was bathed in a shifting curtain of flame.

Greyloc remained on the exposed platform, unmoving, watching calmly as the shields before his position absorbed the incoming punishment. An enemy missile spiralled up out of the sea of destruction, exploding only metres from him, sending rippling shockwaves across the void barrier. He stayed motionless, focused on the unfolding barrage below, looking for any sign of weakness or unbalance.

The Thousand Sons advance was neither rash nor unprotected. Even as the Wolves emptied their fury at the oncoming army, the fire was met with the glistening discharge of shields. Something, some sorcery, was warding the tanks from harm. The barrier wasn't perfect – columns of armour were already smouldering and broken – but it was enough to prevent the annihilation of the vanguard. In their wake, the troop carriers were getting closer.

In a hail of flickering plasma-spikes and explosions,

the gap between the Gates and the Thousand Sons closed. Every round of fire from the Fang destroyed a rank of heavy weaponry on the ground, but for every broken chassis another tank took its place, rolling over the burning, twisted metal. The causeways were gradually covered with a carpet of crawling ironwork, throwing fire back at the batteries mounted above them, gaining metres with each painful, wreck-strewn advance.

Then the aerial attack commenced. Wings of bombers and heavy gunships swooped in across the high faces of the Fang, strafing the gun emplacements, weaving between the lines of flak and anti-aircraft fire. With every pass, aircraft were downed by the defending guns, streaking back down to earth in trails of smoke, spinning into their own troops and carving ruin in their destruction. But with every pass, another defensive battery was reduced to ruins, or another void shield was put under critical strain, or another stream of shells was diverted from the onslaught on the land.

The air began to choke from the plumes of rolling, ink-black smoke. The view from the gates was gradually lost. The vista turned from one of cold, clear perfection into a vision of burning, charred desolation. The growing walls of smoke dimmed the light of the sun, locking the mountain in a pall of closing shadow.

Greyloc calmly checked his helm display, noting the positions of his Wolf Guard, the locations of the Rune Priests, the deployment of his key assets, the state of the defence he had designed and put in place.

And now comes the test. The Hand of Russ ward us.

Then the Wolf Lord turned from the platform, his claws bursting into whip-curling life, shimmering with twin disruptor fields, and made his descent to the Gate level, ready to meet the tide of fury as it broke.

THE SOUND OF hammers was everywhere. It ran through the chambers, resounding in the stone, vibrating in the deep shafts, echoing in the hidden vaults. Even over the aural compensators built into her helmet, Freija found the incessant, banging tumult disorientating.

'I see why it was named this way,' she said grimly.

The Iron Priest nodded.

'It is glorious,' he replied, and there was no trace of sarcasm in his vox-filtered voice.

They were standing on the edge of a precipice, far down into the Hammerhold. Ahead of them ran a single bridge of stone, flying out across the abyss, six metres wide and without a rail. It disappeared into the gloom and haze of the distance. Hundreds of metres down, in the huge cavern spanned by the bridge, a vision of Hel had unravelled. Gigantic, hulking furnaces, each the height of Warlord Titan and twice as wide, threw off clouds of blood-red light. Channels of heat-blackened stone carried rivers of fire from one inferno to the next, passing through wheels of iron and plunging pistons. The silhouettes of servitor-thralls, their wire-studded spines curled over from hunching, crept between the colossal machinery, checking flickering pict-readouts and tending brass-lined cogitator banks. The vast space hummed with a low, rumbling activity. Along clattering conveyor belts amid the forges, Freija could just make out the embryonic shells of vehicle plating, artillery barrels, even body-armour parts.

Then there were the hammers. They were borne by rows of muscle-enhanced, metal-ribbed, faceless servitors, chained to their adamantium anvils by segmented nerve-conduits, endlessly working, endlessly beating. There were ranks upon ranks of them, more machine than human, moulded into mindless golems by the uncaring arts of the fleshmakers. They were the perfect workers: tireless, uncomplaining, hugely strong, content to hammer away in the pits of fire until death from exhaustion gave them a final release.

Not much of a life.

'We are wasting time,' said Arfang, prompting his personal servitor retinue to limp across the bridge. The Iron Priest strode out after them, leaving Freija and the kaerls scurrying to match the pace.

'Who supervises them?' asked Freija, unable to take half an eye away from the toiling legions down in the haze of fire and heat below.

'They need no supervision,' replied Arfang coldly. 'They only know one way to serve. Do not disdain that, huskaerl – without them our warriors go to war empty handed.'

'I do not disdain them, lord. I just had no idea there were... so many.'

'And that troubles you?'

It did. It troubled her more than she would ever admit to him. It troubled her that legions of half-dead, semi-mechanised slaves had been toiling under her feet for as long as she'd been alive. It troubled her that she didn't know where they came from, nor why she'd ended up as a huskaerl and they'd ended up as forge-meat. It troubled her that she knew so little of such things, and that the ways of the Aett were so arbitrary and clouded in a fog of tradition that only the Sky Warriors had any access to.

'I am merely curious,' she said.

'A dangerous instinct. Be careful where it takes you.'

It took nearly ten minutes of solid walking to traverse the yawning forge-halls. Arfang set a punishing pace, one that the servitors struggled to match. Even Freija found her battle trained muscles aching by the time the far side neared.

The bridge terminated as it reached a cliff of rough-hewn rock. An iron-lined door had been carved into it, crested with the sign of the two-headed wolf Morkai, the guardian of the dead. The image looked old, far older than anything in the Hould, and the edges were smooth from the hot, wearing winds. The doorway was open and there were no guards. A single, isolated green light winked at the base of the heavy frame.

Disruptor field.

Arfang gave a flick of his finger and the light switched to red. He strode on. The tunnel beyond was pitch-dark, unlit by torches, glowglobes or fire-pits.

Freija adjusted her night-vision visor, and the walls were picked out in a grainy pale green. Though well-used to the cold and dark, she gave an involuntary shudder as she passed the threshold. The chill seemed deeper somehow, more permanent and invasive. As they walked, the sound of hammers receded, replaced by a dead, frigid silence.

They went down. A long way down. Freija saw holes loom up in the walls of the tunnel; tributary corridors, from which the air sighed in frozen gusts. Soon the way forward became a choice from many options, and the path began to twist back on itself, writhing through the deep roots of the mountain. At all times the tunnel remained wide and tall, and a Rhino could have been driven along its length with ease.

She began to lose track of time, and certainly of how far they'd come. The utter dark, and the cold that sank into her bones, gave a strange sense of dislocation to that forsaken place. It was temptingly easy to imagine the rest of the galaxy simply ceasing to exist beside that eternal, primordial darkness.

When the first noise came, it had her scrabbling for her *skjoldtar* and her heart hammering. It was unearthly, a low, purring growl that ran down her spine like mercury on glass. She saw her kaerls tense up, sweeping the muzzles of their weapons across the walls.

'What was that?' she hissed.

The Iron Priest kept walking, untroubled.

'I told you, huskaerl,' he said. His booming voice rang from the walls. 'There are dangers in the dark. Keep your weapons primed, and let no harm come to my thralls.'

Freija swallowed down her expletive. The Iron Priest was annoying her more than ever.

'Worry not, lord,' she said, her jaw tight. 'We are here to serve.'

'I am glad that is how you feel.'

Freija took a quick look over her shoulder. In the far distance, far up the snaking tunnel, she saw two points of light. She blinked, and they were gone. The chill in her bones intensified.

What has been done down here?

And then they were walking again, down and down, further into the deep dark, an island of heart-warmth in an infinite ocean of utter, endless emptiness.

MOREK WORKED HIS way up through the Jarlheim levels, keeping his head down as he went. Most of those he passed were heading in the other direction, hurrying to where the fighting was fiercest. The few going his way were mostly gunnery crews heading for their rotations on the anti-aircraft batteries.

The vibration of the outgoing fire patterns made the elevator shaft shake as he ascended.

How is that even possible? We are hundreds of metres within the mountain. What forces are being unleashed out there?

The suspensor floated behind him in the steel cage, carrying the prone body of the Grey Hunter. Though it seemed disrespectful, Morek had failed to resist the urge to look at the fallen Sky Warrior.

Aunir Frar's face had been exposed when the Long Fangs had removed his helm in the Land Raider. It was proud, severe, sharp-edged. Mature fangs glinted from his open mouth, and the jawline was extended into the lupine profile of a veteran warrior. Perhaps he'd been angling for elevation to the Wolf Guard. The Red Dream still had him in its grasp, and his breathing was shallow, almost non-existent. Parts of his plate had been ripped away, revealing over a dozen deep stab-wounds, including a horrifying, artery-severing gash across the neck. If Frar had been a mortal, there would have been no life left in him to save.

The elevator rattled to a halt. Morek hauled open the doors and exited, pulling the suspensor along behind. Ahead of him were the chambers of the fleshmakers. There were signs of aversion etched into the stone lintels. A caustic, antiseptic smell stung his nostrils. Ahead, the dull red firelight of the Aett was replaced with harsh white lumen-strips. There were tiles on the wall and metal tables covered in instruments of surgery. Unlike the rest of the Wolves' lair, which was littered with totems and bleached animal skulls, the Wolf Priest's dwellings were pristine, cold and unadorned.

Morek entered, squinting against the bright lights, keeping the suspensor close. There was noise from further in, but no immediate sign of anyone about. He kept walking, passing more rows of metal tables, walking through more rooms full of equipment he could barely guess the purpose of. Alongside the machinery of surgery and physical augmentation, there were long banks of ancient looking cogitators, lined with bronze cases, humming gently.

The noises grew. He was getting closer to activity. As he turned a corner, he entered a larger chamber, dome-roofed and even brighter than the others. There were huge, heavy tables there too, and some were occupied. Two Sky Warriors lay on them, both conscious, both being operated on by teams of leather-masked thralls.

The mortals worked quickly and deftly, slicing open flesh, pinning back muscle, working at the wounds with needle probes and pain-suppressants. They all wore iron visors with bottle-green lenses, each of them flickering with points of light.

'Mortal,' came a deep voice, and Morek turned to face it. A Wolf Priest, one of Wyrmblade's acolytes by his look, strode up to him in night-black armour, his exposed hands covered in blood. 'State your business.'

Morek bowed. 'I was charged to bring this warrior, Aunir Frar, into the care of the Lord Wyrmblade.'

The Wolf Priest snorted.

'You think he'd be here? When the Aett is under assault?' He shook his head. 'We'll take him. Go back to your station, rivenmaster.'

Even as the Priest spoke, thralls flocked around the suspensor, dragging it alongside one of the metal tables. Steel threads were inserted into the prone body and scanning devices angled over the wounds. The Wolf Priest turned to his new charge and began to direct the operation.

Morek bowed. He turned and withdrew, walking back through the empty chambers of the fleshmaker's domain as quickly as he could. Something about the place unnerved him. The aromas were foreign, utterly unlike the smells of hide and embers he'd been born into.

Too much light.

He went through another room, then turned left, passing between open doors. He went several more paces before realising he'd come the wrong way. The chamber he'd entered was smaller than the others, though still lined with clinical white tiles. There were three huge tanks in the centre of it, each filled with a translucent fluid. The vessels were cylindrical, no more than a metre wide but running the whole height of the room. Machinery clustered at the base of them, ticking and rattling rhythmically.

He knew he should look away, but the contents of the tanks held him. There were bodies floating in them, dark outlines of men suspended in the liquid. Huge ribcages, bunched-muscle arms, thick necks. The profile was that of a Space Marine, heavy and powerful. They didn't move, just hung, swaying slightly. Dimly, Morek could make out snaking coils of respirator tubes hanging down and covering their lower faces.

He turned away, knowing he'd come too far, suppressing his curiosity.

The curious mind opens the door to damnation.

It was as he did so that he saw the metal table, over to the left, away from the main beams of the strip-lumens. His eyes locked on what was on it, and stayed there.

Slowly, almost unconsciously, Morek felt his feet propelling him towards the table. He passed the tanks by, their contents forgotten. He couldn't look away then, couldn't turn back.

On the metal slab was a body, or perhaps a corpse. There was no breath in its gigantic lungs – at least, not one he could discern. It was like the others, naked, stretched out on its back, arms straight by its sides.

Morek felt the sense of wrongness immediately. For a moment, he couldn't work out what, precisely, was so troubling about the corpse – he'd seen many before

– but then he paid more attention.

The forearms were smooth, almost hair-free. The fingernails were no longer than his own. The jawline was square-cut and blunt, but with no signs of lupine distension. There was no room in that mouth for fangs, just mortal dentition.

Morek moved closer, feeling his breathing quicken slightly. The corpse had its eyes open, blank and unseeing.

They were grey like his, with a pupil like a mortal's. There was no extraneous facial hair across the thick-set face, no heavy bone-ridge across the brow. The musculature was still there, rigid and heavy-set across an outsize skeletal frame, but it was blank and featureless.

Whatever this thing was, it was no Space Wolf. It was a sham, a simulacrum, a mockery.

Morek felt sickness well in the back of his throat. The Sky Warriors were sacred to him, as sacred as the world-soul, as the spirits of the ice, as the life of his daughter. This was an abomination, some dreadful meddling in the changeless order of things.

He took a step back. From behind him, back in the operating theatre, he heard the movement of thralls as they struggled to save the life of Aunir Frar.

This is forbidden. I should not be here.

His sickness was replaced by fear. He'd seen the look in the eyes of the leather-masked thralls, and knew the reputation of the fleshmakers. They did not forgive trespasses.

Morek turned and hurried back the way he'd come, averting his eyes from the floating figures in the tanks, ignoring the banks of strange equipment that lined the walls beyond them, hardly seeing the rows of tiny vials arranged in careful order under the controlled lights.

There were heavy footsteps somewhere behind him, and his heart jumped. He kept going, kept his head down, hoping whoever owned them was headed somewhere else. The linked chambers were confusing, hard to find one's way around, and the sound could have come from anywhere.

The footsteps faded. Morek was back in the reception chambers, the ones with the empty metal tables. Ahead of him was the exit, and the corridor to the elevator shaft.

His heart was beating hard.

The curious mind opens the door to damnation.

He looked down at his hands. They were rough, calloused, hardened by a lifetime of service to the Sky Warriors. They were trembling. For a moment he paused, uncaring if the thralls saw him now.

What was that thing?

He stood still for a few more heartbeats, rendered indecisive by what he had witnessed. The Wolf Priests were the guardians of the Aett, the keepers of the traditions of the *Vlka Fenryka*. If they had sanctioned it, then it must be permitted.

It was an abomination.

He looked back over his shoulder. The tile-lined chambers stretched away from him, each one leading to the next, each stinking of antiseptic and blood. He felt the nausea rise up again, catching in his gullet.

In the Hall of the Fangthane, he had shouted himself hoarse with devotion to the Sky Warriors, the embodiment of the divine savagery of Fenris. As hard as he tried, he couldn't summon that spirit back up.

Shakily, with none of the purpose that had brought him to that place, he walked back to the elevator shaft. Across his open, loyal face the certainty had gone.

In its place, and for the first time in Morek's life, there was doubt.

CHAPTER TEN

BLACKWING SAT SLUMPED at the metal conference table, ignoring the dozen figures seated around him, running his hands through his matted hair. He ignored the flickering strip-lights, the dozen or so kaerls standing to attention by the walls in their dirty uniforms and the sclerotic grind of the damaged engines from below.

He felt cramped, dirty, cooped up. Each day since the escape from Fenris had been a wearying round of emergencies and repairs, all in the cause of keeping the *Nauro* from breaking open and spinning into the void.

It was demeaning work, fit perhaps for mortals, but not for him. He was bred for higher things, for expert slaying in the shadows, for glorying in the contests of void-war. Having to listen to the counsel of greasy

enginarium workers and the doom-laden pronouncements of the ship's tactical crew bored him supremely.

Not that the situation wasn't dire. He knew enough
of starship mechanics to recognise when things were
about to fall apart. Frankly, they ought to have done
so already – the ship was still at least twelve days out
from Gangava, and that schedule was only possible
because he'd continued to thrash the warp drives over
the protests of the ship's Master. A few days ago, he'd
made the mistake of asking the *Nauro's* Enginarius,
a mortal who'd had extensive training from Adeptus
Mechanicus tech-adepts, what the machine-spirit was
doing during all of this.

'Screaming, sir,' he'd replied in his gruff, practical
voice. 'Screaming like an *ungor* with its throat cut.'

Blackwing had given thanks then that he was insensitive to such things.

Then again, he was insensitive to most things.
He'd never gelled with his battle-brothers, had never
forged the friendships that tied squads together. He'd
despised his superior officers, chafing against the
discipline they'd imposed. Even in the Space Wolves
Chapter, famous across the Imperium for its loose
attitude toward the Codex Astartes, that discipline was
severe.

Blackwing had always been different, subject to
dark moods and bouts of a manic, dangerous over-
confidence. The Scout corps had been perfect for him,
allowing him to perfect the arts of lone killing far from
the raucous brotherhood of the Aett. It was in such
isolation that he'd found a kind of contentment.

Now, however, he began to wonder whether that

choice had always been such a good one. None of the mortals on the *Nauro* were capable of making the command choices he had to, of taking the difficult decisions on which their lives all depended. It might have been preferable, perhaps, to have had a brother warrior to consult, someone to share the burden with for a short while.

Not that any of his battle-brothers would have willingly come with him on a mission. Blackwing had created a near-perfect bubble of solitude around him, alienating even those who had no prior dislike of the Scouts.

So be it. That was the path he'd chosen, and it had suited him well enough before now. Not all of Russ's sons could be hollering berserkers.

'Lord?'

The voice was that of the ship's Master, a grey-haired man called Georyth. Blackwing looked up to face him. Even out of armour, the Space Marine dominated the chamber. As his yellow eyes, sunk into their dark-ringed sockets, clamped on to the mortal, Georyth swallowed.

'You asked for a report on the fires.'

'So I did, Master. Tell me the latest good news.'

'I have none to give. Three levels are still out of bounds, even to thrall-servitors. The burning has spread to the drive chambers. As supplies run low, our ability to contain it will diminish.'

'And I know what you recommend.'

Georyth took a deep breath.

'It hasn't changed, lord.'

'You wish us to drop out of the warp, open the levels

to the void, flush out the area and make repairs.'

'I do.'

'And how long would such a manoeuvre take, assuming optimal performance?'

'A week, lord. Perhaps less.'

Blackwing shot him a cold, superior smile. There was no humour in it, just a kind of knowing disdain.

'Too long.'

'Lord, if the promethium lines are–'

Blackwing sighed and pushed himself back in his chair.

'If they're breached? Then we die, Master. Even I, an ignorant warmongering savage with zero enginarium training, know that.'

He fixed his pin-pupil gaze on the man.

'But reflect on this,' he said. 'Without the Great Wolf's forces to relieve it, the Aett will fall. Lord Ironhelm's ships must still be in the warp. If we keep travelling at our current pace, with no pauses or slowdowns, we will arrive at Gangava many days after them. And then, even if I can pass on Lord Greyloc's message swiftly and persuade Ironhelm to return to Fenris, it will be another twenty days before he can possibly do so. Which means that Lord Greyloc, whom I know is held in such unflinching esteem by all this Chapter, will have to hold the citadel, with a single depleted Great Company, for at least forty days. You saw the forces in orbit, Master. You saw what they did to our defences there. Now tell me, speaking honestly, if you really think that army can be defied on land for forty days.'

The Master's face went grey.

'If Russ wills it...' he began dutifully, but his voice lost its certainty, and he trailed off.

'Precisely. So perhaps you will now understand my insistence that we reach Gangava as soon as we can. We have cheated Morkai already on this voyage, and we will have to cheat him for a little longer. Count yourself lucky you're commanded by a Scout, Master. That's what we do. Cheat.'

The Master didn't reply, but slumped in his chair, his expression hollow. Blackwing could see his mind working, already trying to figure out some way of keeping the raging fires from reaching anything explosive. He didn't look confident.

Blackwing turned to look at the rest of the command crew.

'Anything else we need to discuss?' he asked dryly.

The Tacticus said nothing. The man had been driven hard, and his eyes were red-rimmed from fatigue. The Enginarius had already given his assessment of repair work needed in the hold, and the Armourer was dead, killed by an exploding bulkhead hours after translation from Fenris.

Neiman, the Navigator, was the only one still looking calm. He was also the only non-Fenrisian on the crew, a Belisarian from Terra, and was as slim and cold as his crewmates were stocky and vigorous. It was rare for him to leave his work of guiding the ship through the perils of the immaterium. In the presence of non-mutants, his pineal eye was covered in a wrap of silk over a steel patch.

He didn't speak. He was staring intently away from the table, toward the kaerls standing to attention around the walls of the council chamber. His natural eyes were unwavering.

Blackwing found this annoying. He'd not summoned the man to this meeting to have him daydream.

'Is there something you wished to contribute, Navigator?' he asked.

Neiman didn't flinch.

'Who is that man?' he demanded, his gaze locked on a particularly scruffy kaerl. Blackwing shot a glance at the man. He was shorter than the others, a little more hunched, with greasy hair and bruised skin around the eyes. He was a good deal filthier than the rest of them too, but the endless demands of survival had taken their toll on everyone. Strange, though – he didn't look like a soldier.

At all.

'Is this particularly important?' asked Georyth irritably. 'We have other things to resolve.'

The man in question didn't respond. He kept staring blankly, his expression totally vacant. On either side of him, the kaerls suddenly seemed to notice his presence. One of them looked at his sergeant in alarm, as if the man had been functionally invisible until that moment.

Blackwing felt the hairs on his back rise. His mood shifted instantly from boredom to high alertness. Why hadn't he noticed this man before? What had the Navigator sensed?

'Seize him,' he ordered, rising from his chair.

The kaerls grabbed the man by the shoulders. As if a switch had been flipped, the vacant-faced man went crazy. He backhanded the kaerl to his left, slamming him into the wall, then grabbed the neck of the other and launched into a vicious headbutt. Still without uttering a sound, the man spun round, making for the exit doors, knocking aside another kaerl who rushed to intercept him.

He moved with astonishing speed. But, for all that, it was mortal speed. Blackwing was quicker, leaping across the table in a lithe pounce and careering into the man as he raced for the door. Together they skidded along the pressed-metal floor. Blackwing seized the man's hair and crunched his face into the wall, stunning him. He regained his feet quickly, dragging the man up with him.

'Take care, lord!' warned Neiman. 'I sense–'

The injured man turned his bloody face toward Blackwing's. His eyes suddenly blazed a pale, sickly green.

Blackwing felt the build-up of maleficarum. In a single movement he hurled the man away, sending him cartwheeling through space toward the empty far end of the council chamber. Before the kaerl had landed, Blackwing pulled his bolt pistol from its holster and squeezed off a single round. The slug punched through the flailing man's head and detonated, spraying bone and glistening grey matter across the wall.

The ruined, headless body hit the metal with a wet thud. It twitched for a moment, then fell still.

'Teeth of Russ!' swore Georyth, superfluously training his own sidearm on the corpse. 'What in Hel–'

'It knew how to remain hidden,' said Neiman, looking at Blackwing in alarm. 'This is witchery – he was in plain view of all of us.'

Blackwing stooped to pick up something on the

floor. A sphere the size of an eyeball had rolled across the metal. It glowed green, and flickered with a ghostly witchlight.

He rose, gazing at the bloodstained ball in his palm. It felt hot to the touch, almost painfully so. As he looked at it, a dull ache broke out behind his eyes.

Blackwing crushed it with a clench of his clawed fingers.

'It seems we have a new problem,' he said grimly, turning slowly to face the startled ship's council. 'Something else is on the ship. Something that no doubt wishes us harm. And whatever it is, it now knows how weak we are.'

THE IRON PRIEST had gone. In his absence, the dark seemed even colder, even more remote. The concept of daylight was already proving hard to reconstruct, as was the passage of time. Freija had lost track of both. Perhaps the assault had started, or perhaps the Sky Warriors still held the enemy in the mountains. If the battle came to the Aett, would any sign of it penetrate so far down?

She swept her gaze across the chamber. It was big, though hard to say how big – even her night-vision visor didn't pick much out in the far recesses. One wall, the wall her squad had clustered around, had been extensively worked. There were huge doors in the centre of it, once more crested with the twin faces of Morkai. The space around the doors was studded with arcane machinery – coils of coolant piping, statuesque clusters of power transformers, lattices of ironwork covering unidentifiable workings within. Incredibly, given the oppressive cold and distance from maintenance crews, the low hum from the machines sounded healthy.

The thrall-servitors had certainly known what to do with it. After their master had passed through the doors, they'd got to work, attaching themselves to input valves and initiating obscure sets of protocols. Whatever they were doing, it was noisy and repetitive. Lights flickered across the wall of machines from time to time, glinting painfully in the otherwise perfect dark. The servitors not directly attached to the devices had started performing a series of rites in front of the major machine-nodes – anointing the moving parts with pungent oils, reading long lists of benedictions in flat, metal-dry voices, bowing before the inert iron and steel as if it were an altar of long-dormant gods.

They worked methodically, tirelessly, soullessly. There was no communication between them and the Iron Priest within. Arfang was alone, presumably in a place where only the Sky Warriors were permitted. There was no indication of how long his work would take, whether it was going well, or even what he was planning.

Freija fought against a growing weight of boredom. The oppressive dark combined with the dreary intonations of the servitors made it hard to stay sharp.

'Keep your focus,' she warned over the vox-link, speaking to herself as much as her troops.

Four of the six-kaerl squad stood alongside her, facing outward from the machine-wall, the muzzles of their rifles pointing into the dark. Two more were resting, slumped uneasily between their comrades and the unnerving rites of the half-human servitors.

Then she heard the noise again. Instantly all thoughts of boredom were banished, and she felt the prick of sweat under her gloves.

The other kaerls heard it too, and she saw them stiffening. The two on rest-rotation climbed their feet, grasping their sidearms clumsily in the gloom.

It was a low, rumbling growl, glottal and damp, vibrating in the stone of the floor.

'Hold your ground,' she hissed over the comm, trying to see something definite in the grainy feed her visor was giving her.

Behind her, the servitors carried on their work. The guns of the kaerls swept the far end of the chamber, moving slowly and uncertainly. She could sense their tension in the tight, nervous movements.

Suddenly, the distinctive rasping bark of a *skjoldtar* burst out of nowhere, its muzzle flare dazzling in intensity. Despite herself, Freija nearly pulled her own trigger in reflexive shock.

'Cease fire!' she shouted, peering into the shadows. Her proximity meter was empty, save for the group of friendly signals around her.

The echoes of the gunfire took a long time to die. The culprit, probably Lyr – she couldn't tell – shook his head. By now Freija's heart was properly beating. There was something out there, something she couldn't see, something that sounded – *felt* – utterly terrifying.

'Hold your ground,' she said again, feeling her stomach twisting.

Get a grip, woman. You are a daughter of Russ, a child of the storm.

'We're not getting a good feed from the visors,' she said. 'I'm walking out.'

None of her troops responded. They stayed where they were, locked in a semi-circle around the oblivious servitors.

Freija took a deep breath, and began to advance. She went slowly, feeling her heavy breathing quicken. Ahead of her, she could see nothing but static.

Then it came again, nearer this time, thrumming and resonant. It wasn't emanating from one of the tunnels beyond. It was in the chamber, there with them, watching. Somewhere.

Freija had gone ten metres by the time she stopped. She looked over her shoulder briefly, checking for the presence of her squad. They were still there, still surrounding the wall of machines, still guarding the doors.

She turned back.

Less than a metre away, a pair of golden eyes, pinned with black, liquid and massive, gazed back at her.

Freija froze.

Skítja.

THE SIEGE-FIRE WAS horrifying, vaporising ice and snow and shattering rock, tearing up ancient outcrops of granite and dissolving them into clouds of scree. The superheavy guns had been dragged into range, and the Fang reeled under the dense volume of ordnance. Its flanks were wreathed in both smoke and steam as the snow was boiled away from the rock and the gun emplacements were picked off, one by one. The entire peak was clothed in raging tongues of flame, blazing as if the magma at the planet's core had been released and flung into the permafrost of Asaheim's summit.

The defenders waited within the walls, letting the fortress defences do their work for as long as possible. Static gun emplacements thundered with lethal force, chewing their way through whole loops of ammunition in moments, cutting down oncoming armour and leaving the tilting wrecks blocking the advance. Teams of kaerls worked ceaselessly to keep the death-dealers fed and operative.

It would not last forever. The Thousand Sons were advancing, claiming each metre of land in blood and fire. Only when the doors were broken would the Wolves take to the field again, welcoming the invaders with the embrace of Morkai.

Until then, there were other powers in play.

Odain Sturmhjart was angry. His habitual bluster had gone, shaken by his inability to predict the attack of the Thousand Sons, rocked by his failure to see the deception as it unfolded. He no longer laughed with the savage glee of the coming battle, but glowered under his arcane psychic hood, his eyes blazing. To make matters worse, he had failed to watch Wyrmblade as he had been commanded to do, and knew the Tempering was still proceeding behind closed blast-doors. He had failed in everything that mattered, and the trust the Great Wolf had placed in him had gone unrewarded.

So far.

Sturmhjart had worked with fanaticism since the revelation of failure, driving himself close to the limits of even his battle-hardened frame. The wards throughout the Aett had been reinforced. He had worked until his hands were raw, rubbing the stone figures with his own vital blood, instilling the power of the world-soul within them. Now that the enemy was here, the time for such preparation was passed.

He stood encased in his runic armour high up in an observation chamber of the Fang, watching as the fire rebounded from the void shields before him. No missile would survive passage through that curtain of immolation, but there were other weapons to wield.

Sturmhjart slammed his staff on the floor, and the iron shaft shivered from the impact. The soul of the storm began to quicken around him. He felt the air race, felt it grow colder and keener. His rage at himself fuelled the brewing tumult. He could use that anger, turn it into something of terrible, terrible potency.

The winds ran round the horned summit of the mountain, whining through the plasma-boiling air, whipping against the red-hot rocks. The sky, which had been pure blue and empty, began to pucker with clouds. A low rumble echoed between the encircling peaks.

Feel this. Feel the coming of the world-soul. This is power the like of which no witch will ever wield.

Sturmhjart screwed his eyes shut, clutching the staff tight. His second heart broke into a steady rhythm. The summoning was painful. He relished the pain. Like the searing irons, it cauterised the deeper pain within.

More clouds rolled into being, tumbling from the crown of the mountains to the north, their skirts flickering with lightning. In their shadow came the hail, a sweeping wall of ruin, slamming and bouncing into the ground below.

Raise your eyes to the heavens, Traitors.

He saw the sorcerers amid the hosts of the enemy like stars, their psychic essences standing out even through the noise and confusion. They were powerful, steeped in sickening energies. He could see their arrogance, their confidence. Some were physically corrupted, giving in to the terrible flesh-changes that blighted all their kind. One of them, the brightest star of all, was far down the roads of ruin.

You are many, and we are few. But this is our world, and we wield its power.

The storm spread, breaking across the summits, sweeping toward the Fang in a howling, screaming gale. The sky darkened, making the explosions around the mountain look like embers in a fire pit. The hail hammered down, cracking and bouncing on the stone.

You think you come to fight mortals, like yourselves.

The wind picked up speed and power, growing to a crescendo of whirling, horrific destruction. The pinions of the blizzard closed, fed by the surging energy of the storm. Tanks were upended, knocked from their tracks. Flanking columns of troops were swept away, dragged to the precipices at the edges of the causeways and thrown to their deaths.

You think we will succumb to witchery as you did.

Sturmhjart felt blood well in his mouth, trickling down to the mass of his slicked-down beard. He ignored it. The sharp pain was lost in the whirlwind of psychic power flooding his body. He was nothing more than the conduit, the vessel through which the untamed fury of the maelstrom passed. The raw howl of the wind became a bellowing roar. The flames around the Fang were lashed and pulled into dazzling flares of energy, ripped across the air by the scouring gales.

You are wrong.

The sorcerers responded, guarding what vehicles they could, sending flickering lightning and translucent kine-shields of their own to combat the danger from the skies. They were mighty, and there were dozens of them. Even so, they struggled against the elements, and the assault faltered. Gunships blazed to the ground like comets, torn apart by the electric sky. The screams of the dying and the terrified echoed through the rippling currents of the storm.

Sturmhjart relished the cries. They fed his power. They fed the planet's power. The invaders had brought maleficarum with them, and righteous punishment was the consequence.

Even as they bled and scrambled for cover, the witches were learning a lesson; the same lesson that had been learned by every Rune Priest since the Allfather had first brought the way of the wyrd to the frozen death world.

Sturmhjart knew it. He had known it for centuries, and took delight in making it as clear as the ice itself to those who dared defy him.

We do not defend Fenris. Fenris defends us. The world, the people, are one. We share a soul, a soul of hatred, and now it comes to you, dark on the wings of the storm.

Learn it well, for soon this truth will kill you.

* * *

THE SHADOW IN the dark reared, and the dreadful eyes disappeared. Freija scrambled backwards, snatching her rifle up clumsily, letting fly with a burst of eye-watering gunfire. *Skjoldtar* rounds did more damage than Imperial Guard autoguns when handled right, and a howl of inhuman pain echoed around the chamber.

'Huskaerl!' came a cry to her left.

There were fresh muzzle-flares from her left as her men ran forwards, firing from the waist and spraying rounds at the space recently occupied by the... *animal* that had been in front of her.

'Get back!' she roared, ceasing fire and trying to make sense of the signals on her visor display. There had been nothing on the proximity scan. Nothing.

Her troops withdrew alongside her, still firing. The bursts were poorly controlled, driven by fear.

Russ, where is our courage?

'Get a grip!' she shouted, cuffing the nearest trooper. 'Fire when you *have a target.*'

He kept firing, his finger clamped to the trigger. Beneath his mask, Freija could see a pair of eyes, wide with fear.

'It's coming!' he screamed. 'It's coming back!'

Then Freija saw it, a huge, bounding shape eating up the ground, bursting out of the gloom like a night-mare. The guns kept firing, lighting up its hunched, powerful body in a tracery of lightning-white. She only had time for impressions – yellow eyes, incred-ibly powerful shoulders, blood-red jaws – and then she was firing back too, retreating until she felt the metal limbs of the servitors at her back.

There were more of them, more terrible forms leaping out of the dark, slinking along the ground, limping into range. They were all different, all horrifying, like the dreams of fleshmakers taken apart and reassembled into jumbles of canine horror.

'Hold the line!' she bellowed, emptying her magazine and scrabbling to load a replacement. 'Keep them back!'

She saw one of the monsters recoil as multiple streams of gunfire slammed into it, knocking it into a pain-clenched crouch. It screamed in a mix of fury and pain, then made another lunge toward them.

Blood of Russ – it's still not dead.

Then another beast broke into the open, bursting through a torrent of fire, shrugging off the impacts like they were a light rain. It was gigantic, a hulking brute of muscle and thick, wiry fur. A long, grinning face leered up, lined with fangs and containing a glistening, lolling tongue. It went on four legs, but had reared on its huge haunches in a bizarre mockery of a man.

Freija whirled round with her reloaded weapon, got her shot and fired.

The gun coughed and jammed.

Cursing, she fumbled in the dark to fix it, hearing the screams of her men as the horror got among them. It picked one up and threw him across the chamber. There was a sloppy crunch as the trooper slammed into the rock wall and slithered down. As fast as thought, other creatures bounded over to him, slavering and wheezing.

Freija crouched low as she slammed the clip back in place, risking a quick look at the servitors. They were working as if nothing were going on around them, polishing and tending, bowing and chanting. The doors to the chamber beyond remained shut.

Curse him.

Then she was back on her feet, firing wildly. She heard another of her men being dragged back into the dark, and her fear dissolved in the face of impotent rage.

'Damn you!' she screamed, keeping the trigger depressed, hurling her abuse half at the creatures of the Underfang, half at the Iron Priest who'd dragged them down to their deaths.

Dead for nothing. I could have fought alongside my father.

One of the monsters, a gigantic brute looking like some tortured cross between a wolf and a grizzly bear, towered in front of her, bellowing a spittle-flailing blast of fury and challenge. The stink of animal breath washed over her, making her gag even over the rebreather.

She fired at point blank range, loosing everything she had left in a thudding stream of bullets. The beast recoiled, flinching from every hit, but did not withdraw. When the *skjoldtar* was empty, it came back at her, jaws open, eyes wide with alien hatred.

Freija shrunk back, more out of instinct than anything else, reaching for the knife strapped to her boot.

Look it in the eye.

She forced herself to keep her head up, the knife held shivering in her fists, as the horrific creature leapt at her.

Look it in the eye.

But the impact never came. It was only then that she

realised her eyes had screwed shut after all. She opened them.

The creature was hanging, suspended by the neck, writhing in some kind of lock under its jaws. The gunfire fell silent, plunging the chamber back into utter darkness.

Then, slowly, a red light bled into the shadow. From somewhere, illumination had come back. There were echoing yelps and growls. The creatures were all still there – they just weren't attacking.

Freija looked up at the beast in front of her, following the curve of its ribcage to the stretched sinews of its neck. A vast, clawed, metal fist held it tight between curving talons. Incredibly, something more powerful had emerged. She realised then that the doors had opened. Whatever was in the chamber beyond, the things Arfang had come to rouse, they had broken the threshold.

You disturb my slumber for this, Iron Priest?

The voice was resounding, a deep bass, and it came from over her shoulder. It reverberated through the rock around her, running down her spine and making her hair stand on end. It was far deeper than Jarl Greyloc's, far deeper than Ironhelm's. In that voice was an ancient dignity, a magisterial self-assurance, a profound melancholy edged with eternal bitterness. Even mediated by coils of inert machinery, it was the most powerful, most disturbing voice Freija had ever heard.

'You were long in the waking, lord,' came Arfang's reply. It was uncharacteristically apologetic.

Moving slowly, driven by the curiosity that was

always her undoing, Freija turned her head to look at what had come through the doors.

Long indeed, came the voice of Bjorn, called the Fell-Handed by the skjalds when declaiming the sagas, the last of the Chapter to have walked the ice with Russ, the mightiest of all the Wolves, a living link to the Time of Wonder.

The dead had been woken.

Bjorn cast the wolf-creature aside as if it were a pup, and the mass of fur and fang tumbled, yelping, into the shadows. With a grind of servos and a hiss of pneumatics, the huge mass of metal and weaponry took a single, heavy step into the chamber. Freija felt her jaw sagging, and snapped it shut.

But now that I am restored, I remember what my purpose has become.

The venerable Dreadnought strode past Freija, seemingly unaware she was there. Before his massive profile, the beasts withdrew, lowering their heads in submission. Even Arfang seemed little more than a whelp beside that figure of legend.

I am here to kill. Show me to the enemy.

PART III:
THE CLOSING
NOOSE

CHAPTER ELEVEN

APHAEL LOOKED UP. The storm-fury hammered at the kine-shield above him. The translucent barrier buckled, flexing like fabric under the repeated impacts. The power of the Dogs' priests was impressive, but then this was their world, and who knew what crude powers existed here, ready to be dragged up by the savages in half-understood rites. The maelstrom could cause the fringes of his army some harm, but it would do no more than slow the advance on the gates.

A fresh wave of burning hail slammed into the shield, stressing the protective sorcery further. Aphael glanced at the position locators on his helm display. His sorcerers were evenly spaced throughout the host, feeding power to the wards across the army. Hett, the most powerful of the Raptora, was nearby, working with calm expertise, maintaining the domes of warding magicks that kept the command clusters of troops safe as they crawled into range.

Aphael turned his attention to the tactical situation. He stood deep within the ranks of his Legion, surrounded by his Terminator retinue. On either side of him were Land Raiders, each with a full complement of Rubricae and grinding forwards at little more than a walking pace. Beyond them were the Chimera troop carriers, rocking from the impacts as Dog shells tore through the weaker parts of the barrier and exploded among them. Ahead were the mobile artillery pieces, still moving closer to the mountain. Larger units had settled into static ranks behind them, locking bracing arms to extend their reach and swinging their gigantic barrels into firing angles. They shuddered with every detonation, sending gouts of black smoke into the already darkening air.

Ahead of him, the pinnacle of the Fang filled his vision. After another day of heavy, grinding battery, the high cone was now entirely covered in fire, ripped into curling fronds of plasma by the racing winds. The defensive barrage had remained strong for longer than he'd expected, sending death in raking columns from a hundred gun positions around the towering gates, but now the torrent was finally thinning out as emplacements were destroyed.

The rest would follow, one by one. The damage they were doing had been allowed for, estimated by the Corvidae months ago and put into the battle ledgers. Tanks would burn, mortals would die, but the advance would not be halted. Within hours, the gate-breakers would be in range of their target and the portals, those graceless hunks of stone and ice, would be breached.

Then the real work would begin.

+What progress, brother?+ Aphael sent, knowing the inquiry would irritate Temekh, hundreds of kilometres above in the *Herumon*.

There was a long pause before a reply came.

+You have just set it back. I cannot remain in communication with you, not in this state.+

+My apologies. But you should know the assault on the gates is nigh.+

+What for? It means nothing until the wards are down.+

Aphael found himself stung by Temekh's tone. The Corvidae was safe from harm, surrounded by the comfort of the *Herumon's* vast hold. Out on the ice, things were rather less comfortable.

+They will be down shortly. I need to know that your work is proceeding with equal speed to mine.+

+I will send when I am ready. Until then, do not make contact again.+

The link between the sorcerers broke off. The severance was almost painful, causing Aphael's eyes to water.

Why is he so hostile?

He felt a prick of anger then, a tremor of frustration at the Corvidae's superior manner. As he did do, the itching in his neck broke out again, rippling across the skin.

He tensed, pausing in the march toward the gates. Soundlessly, his Terminators matched the altered pace.

The contagion was growing.

He knows.

Irritation was replaced by the cold vice of unease. Since Ahriman's rubric, the threat of mutation had become the ultimate stigma, the final taboo. In a Legion that had sacrificed everything to avoid the clutches of the Changer of Ways, any sign that the magicks had been less than totally successful was something akin to heresy.

'Increase speed,' he barked over the mission channel.

On either side of him, the Land Raiders gunned their engines and picked up the pace. More artillery pieces reached firing position and were dug into the steel-hard rock.

So why now? Why, when my hour of victory draws close, does this... flesh-change return?

He looked up at the gates, running his gaze over the burning stone. There were sigils carved into it, protective symbols designed to shun the mutating power of sorcery. Those were the things he had to destroy, to pave the way for the greater power to come.

For what reason am I damned to this?

As Aphael looked at the mighty runes carved across the towering cliffs ahead, his mood darkened further. The mystical shapes simply reminded him of what he already knew – that there was no escape from the pattern of fate. If there was salvation for him, it would not lie in the fortress of the Emperor's Dogs.

So be it. I will embrace it, and turn this corruption into strength.

He resumed his march, barely noticing the Terminators shadowing him. He could feel the mutation quicken within him, boiling under his skin like a swarm of trapped insects. For a while more, his armour would hide the effects.

Above him, fresh plasma explosions rippled across the kine-shields. A troop carrier was carved open by a hail of projectile fire, and its red-hot shell was toppled by the stormwind. Men were dying every moment, hundreds of them, all fuel for a fire that had been burning for centuries already. Their fates meant very little to him, and even less so now that his own prospects were narrowing.

'Lord, gate-breakers are coming into position before both targets,' came a Spireguard's voice over the comm. 'They await your orders.'

Aphael felt his lip curl, though the movement wasn't voluntary. The infection had reached his face.

'Tell them to fire when ready,' he replied, working hard to maintain his usual voice over the channel. Sweat broke out across his twitching skin. 'Get us in there fast, captain. This idleness plays badly with me, and I thirst to spill blood.'

BLACKWING STRODE DOWN the corridor with two dozen fully armoured kaerls marching in his wake. He was wearing his carapace armour and carried a bolt pistol out of its holster. His men went warily, their weapons poised to fire, their eyes wide behind their face-masks. Even after so many hours of searching, he still felt alert. Now that the task had moved from engine maintenance to a kill mission, his weariness had fallen from him.

Neiman had examined the corpse of the crewman in

the council chamber and told the rest of them what they knew already. The man had been a spy, altered to blend into the background, silently feeding information from his unnatural eyeballs to whomever or whatever was controlling him. Since then, Blackwing had ransacked the entire ship, moving through the decks with remorseless efficiency. Other spies had been found during the search, all with the same transplanted eyeballs. Now they were all dead, their bodies hurled into the fires of the enginarium.

Blackwing looked around him carefully. They were low in the ship, passing through regions where the light was bad and few crewmen had reason to go. The perfect place to hide.

The Wolf Scout knew how vulnerable he was. Whatever intelligence had controlled those puppets was a master of sorcery. Blackwing had no weapons to combat such powers and his crew were even less able to defend themselves. Even if he managed to find where the stowaway was hiding, the chances were that he'd come up against something he couldn't hope to kill.

The prospect didn't scare him, but it was definitely annoying. At the very least, he'd hoped to survive long enough to get his manoeuvre above Fenris into the sagas. The thought that it might all be for nothing was an irritant.

Of course, there was the matter of the Fang's survival. That was important too.

'Where the Hel are we?' he voxed, looking at the dirty, dark tunnels ahead with distaste.

'Beneath the aft fuel tanks, lord,' came the voice of Raekborn, the huskaerl. His voice sounded tight. Not scared either, but definitely stressed. Blackwing occasionally forgot that mortals required a few hours' sleep in every cycle. If they didn't strike gold soon, he'd have to tell them to stand down for a while.

So weak. So tediously weak.

He glanced at his helm display. Scouts rarely wore helms into combat, which was a habit Blackwing had never understood. Risking losing your head to a stray las-beam seemed less a case of bravado and more a case of stupidity. His clear-visored unit gave him a tactical display that showed up life signs within a range of thirty metres, as well as reporting on the status of his unit. Not as comprehensive as the Mk VII helm he'd worn as a Hunter, but not far off.

All his visor-runes showed at the present time were the increasingly disrespectful recall requests from Neiman. The Navigator had wanted him back on the bridge for the past six hours to sign off the course vectors before he retired to his observation chamber.

Blackwing grinned. There was no chance of him calling off the search for such mundanity. Even if the need to uncover the infiltrator hadn't been so pressing, he enjoyed irritating the three-eyed mutant by keeping him waiting.

'You getting anything down here?' he voxed to his squad, in the probably vain hope that his men's equipment had picked up a signal that his hadn't.

'Negative.'

Blackwing let his photo-reactive lenses do the visual work for him. Like all his kind, he had astonishing sensitivity to movement even in near pitch dark conditions. His nostrils could differentiate the subtlest aroma lingering under the fug of engine oil and general bilge-grime. His tactile senses could detect movement on the floor a hundred metres away and his hearing would pick up a kaerl coughing on the command bridge.

Still nothing.

'Let's move,' he growled, motioning forwards. Ahead of him the tunnel narrowed, sweeping around a damaged bulkhead draped in wiring. Lights flickered erratically in the distance, briefly illuminating the outline of meshed metal barriers.

Blackwing swerved around the bulkhead. The footfalls of the troops behind were stealthy for mortals, but still announced their presence to one who knew how to listen. The squad went forwards for about twenty metres before reaching a T-junction. The corridor running right-left was in a bad way. Clusters of cables hung from the ceiling like tufts of wild grass, fizzing and sparking. There were cracks in the floor where something had pushed the struts up, and the headroom was minimal. Even the kaerls had to duck, and Blackwing hunched down uncomfortably. The only remaining lighting was at floor-level. It seemed to be running at about quarter-intensity.

'Left, or right?' mused Blackwing, training his pistol at the shadows and sweeping it round. As he did so, he felt a slight pricking sensation in his palms. An indefinable sense of expectation caught hold of him, and he narrowed his eyes.

A few metres down the corridor to the left was an open service hatch, its covering grate swinging lazily from a single intact bearing.

There were times when the preternatural senses

Here the thread is severed
of Harek Eireik Eireiksson,
called Ironhelm by jarls,
and his debts reckoned

On the World Spine
the Father of Mountains

The humbled god comes
hands stretched open
one eye, fire-ringed

And let it be said, brothers
let this be recorded

The betrayer of old
cripple-son of the Allfather
extends his arm
his gaze Helwinter-cold

And Ironhelm
master of the Wolves of Fenris
with fangs bared
laughs like sunrise

Ironhelmssaga XXXIV a-f Cited *Prolegomena ex Fenris II*, attr. Inq. L. Darshiva Natarrji O.H.

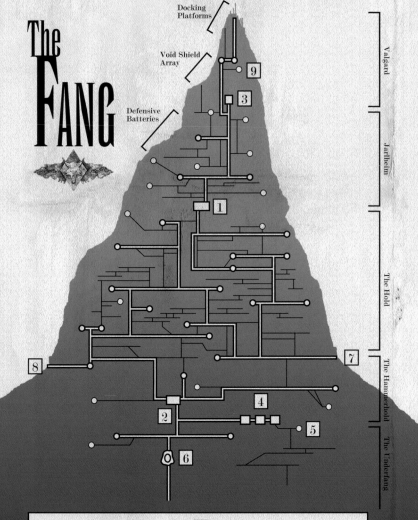

The FANG

Docking Platforms

Void Shield Array

Defensive Batteries

Valgard

Jarlheim

The Hold

The Hammerhold

The Underfang

═══	Arterial Route	
───	Major Route	
○	Major Chamber	
☐	Named Chamber	
1	The Fangthane	
2	Borek's Seal	

3	Chamber of the Annulus
4	Forges
5	Halls of the Revered Fallen
6	Geothermal Reactors
7	Sunrising Gate
8	Bloodfire Gate
9	Fleshmaker Laboratorium

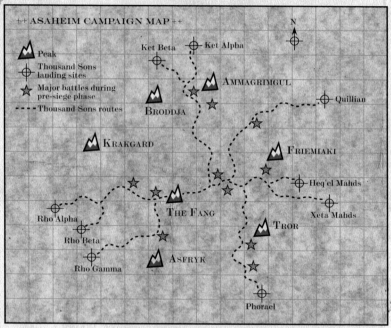

++ ASAHEIM CAMPAIGN MAP ++

N

Peak
Thousand Sons landing sites
Major battles during pre-siege phase
- - - Thousand Sons routes

Ket Beta
Ket Alpha
AMMAGRIMGUL
BRODDJA
Quillian
KRAKGARD
FRIEMIAKI
Heq'el Mahds
THE FANG
Xeta Mahds
Rho Alpha
TROR
Rho Beta
ASFRYK
Rho Gamma
Phorael

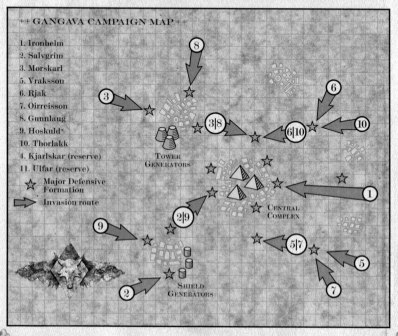

++ GANGAVA CAMPAIGN MAP ++

1. Ironhelm
2. Salvgrim
3. Morskarl
5. Vraksson
6. Rjak
7. Oirreisson
8. Gunnlaug
9. Hoskuld
10. Thorlakk
4. Kjarlskar (reserve)
11. Ulfar (reserve)

Major Defensive Formation
Invasion route

8
3
3|8
6
10
6|10
TOWER GENERATORS
1
2|9
CENTRAL COMPLEX
9
5|7
5
2
SHIELD GENERATORS
7

engendered by the Canis Helix trumped any technology. Blackwing looked at the hole and felt his muscles tense up of their own accord.

'On my mark,' he voxed, preparing to advance. 'Stay–'

That was the last word he got out before the wall exploded. A vast armoured figure with a sapphire battle-helm burst through whirling slivers of metal, its boltgun lowered and already firing.

Blackwing hurled himself face down to the floor, feeling the rounds whistle across his back and detonate amongst his men. The corridor behind was suddenly filled with screams, punctuated with erratic return volleys that zinged off his carapace plate.

Ignoring the projectiles, Blackwing rolled on to his back, trying to draw a bead while avoiding the hail of incoming bolt slugs. It was then that he saw the second figure loom up out of the shadows, limping under a cobra-hood crest and wheezing like a burst bladder.

'Oh, not good,' he growled, cursing his stupidity and scrabbling backwards. 'Not good *at all.*'

THE BOOM OF the detonations ran along the ground, shaking the roots of the mountains, shivering veins of rock that ran kilometres down. Gate-breakers, vast engines of destruction, settled into their firing formation. Single gun-barrels, mounted on immense armoured tracks, two hundred metres long, dark as the shadows of the Underfang and streaked with the smoking patina of war. They'd been hauled into position under the barrage of the lesser artillery and were now unleashed.

Each engine was a piece of tech-sorcery in itself, a

fusion of forbidden devices and proscribed mechanics from across a dozen lost worlds. Strange energies slewed across the surface of the barrels like quicksilver, shimmering with ghostly, half-seen witchlight. A low-pitched howling came from within the cavernous firing maws, a shadowy sound that echoed like the fractured sobs of great, nameless crowds. The muzzles of the cannons were ringed with the esoteric bronze shapes so favoured by their creators, each one different, each drawing on some significance long forgotten by the darkening mortal galaxy.

They had names, those monsters. When they'd been assembled over the centuries in daemon-stalked foundries deep within the Eye of Terror, the Thousand Sons had insisted on that. So there was *Pakhet*, and *Talamemnon*, and *Maahex*, and the damaged *Gnosis*, rocked by heavy fire from the defending batteries. That last one was smoking heavily, leaking rolling columns of death-black soot as it shuddered from incoming impacts.

They fired. They all kept firing. The detonations were tremendous, scattering the ranks of troops around them, scrambling auspex readings, overloading auditory feeds, atomising the very air as huge neon-yellow beams of energy lanced to their targets. The explosions of impact were like tidal waves – huge, thundering walls of rippling flame that sluiced down the already tortured flanks of the Fang.

Again and again the gate-breakers loosed their power, drowning out the sounds of all else, blocking the incessant rain of plasma from the orbital blockade, masking the screams of the dying and the wounded across the approaches to the gates.

They were not subtle weapons. They relied on vast numbers of supporting troops for protection, drank whole reservoirs of promethium in moments, and were operated by hundreds of shackled mortal crew, many hard-wired into the chassis in a grotesque fusion of man and weapon.

Their only purpose was to break the portals of the Fang, to disintegrate the protection over Russ's fortress and render it as broken as the scoured wastelands of Prospero. Thousands had died to create them, their souls welded into the structures to bind the infernal powers within. The Legion had exhausted itself on them, poured every resource it still had into them, knowing full well that they would only be used once.

They were statements, those devices.

We will ruin ourselves, starve ourselves, cripple our future viability and leave ourselves destitute, all so long as we can destroy the gates that guard your citadel.

So they fired again, vomiting beams of destructive essence like shards of a supernova, venting the hatred that had seethed for over a thousand years, focusing it on the gates.

Those massive arches, each carved from the cold rock by ancient machines no less powerful, began to glow red from the impact, wavering in the heat-shimmer. The void shields were strengthened by desperate kaerls, fed with more power from the inexhaustible wells below the Fang until the unseen barriers screamed. The stone cracked and buckled, rocked by the torrent of fire and energy.

Above the lintel of the Sunrising Gate, the rune

Gmorl had been graven. It signified Defiance.

When it was broken open at last, a vast sigh shuddered through the stone. There was a snap in the air, and a bow-wave of force rushed out from the citadel. Piers of granite and adamantium collapsed, breaking the symmetry of the buttresses. Cracks opened beneath the doors, running over the ground like rivulets of dark lava.

The remaining void shields shivered, and those at ground level went out. A hail of fire immediately poured through the gaps, slamming into the mountain beyond. The gate-breakers recalibrated, aiming for the weakest point. Their enormous barrels loosed columns of immolation, and Sunrising disappeared behind a wall of plasma.

When the fireballs cleared, the mighty doors were broken open, swinging crazily on hinges the size of Thunderhawks, buoyed by nothing more than the continuing explosions around them.

For a moment, no one moved. As if suddenly horrified by what they'd done, the entire Thousand Sons host held back, gazing up at the hole in the side of the mountain. The howl of the wind raced across the battlefield, its note of fury replaced by a whine of anguish.

Then the paralysis passed. Men began to run forwards, flanked by rows of tanks and troop carriers. The artillery resumed its crushing onslaught. The horde of vanguard warriors, thousands strong, rank upon rank of them, surged towards the gates, suddenly filled with the hope of victory.

Behind the climate-masks, they had all begun to realise what they'd done, what no one had done before them. In the face of that knowledge, even the fear of the Wolves shrank back slightly.

Every trooper, from the lowliest gun-servitor to the mightiest sorcerer knew the truth, a truth that would now never be erased from the annals of galactic history.

They had come to the Citadel of Russ, the mightiest human fortress outside Terra, and they had broken it.

BLACKWING DUCKED AND ran, weaving between the bolt-rounds that tore gashes in the tunnel walls. Electrical cables were ripped open, causing showers of sparks to sluice across the floor. His men had either been killed or were fleeing back down the corridor ahead of him. It was a shambles.

Blackwing veered around the T-junction corner and crouched down against the near wall, turning back to face his pursuers. The body of one of his kaerls was flung across his field of vision, limbs cartwheeling, before the Rubric Marine careered into view.

Blackwing opened fire, loosing a dozen rounds at point blank range before leaping back to his feet and hurtling down the corridor. From over his shoulder he could hear the crack of his bolts' detonation, and risked a glance back.

The Traitor Marine had been rocked, its armour dented and smoking, but was already recovering its feet. Its boltgun barked, and Blackwing slammed himself into the cover of the broken bulkhead. Six slugs thunked into the structure and exploded, obliterating it, forcing Blackwing to scramble further back, covered in a rain of broken metal.

+Just one of you,+ came a voice in his mind. Its sending was halting, as if the speaker was in terrible pain. +I didn't quite believe it until now.+

Blackwing had no way of replying, and concentrated on staying alive for a few moments longer. Leaping and ducking, relying on his gene-enhanced agility, he scampered away from the Rubric Marine, firing blindly behind him as he went.

The corridor opened out into a larger chamber, one he'd patrolled through just moments earlier. His men had set up a bulwark there, overturning tables and crates for barricades. They opened fire as Blackwing burst into the room, just managing to avoid hitting him as they aimed for the leviathan hard on his tail.

Blackwing pounced behind one of upturned tables. He drew his power sword, a short stabbing blade, and flicked on the disruptor field. A heartbeat later and the Rubric Marine had followed him in.

It shrugged off *skjoldtar* fire as if it were a hail of pebbles. The Traitor Marine moved incredibly quickly for its huge size, hurling barricades against the wall and pumping bolt-rounds into the exposed troops before whirling round to smash apart more flimsy pieces of cover.

+A mere Scout, too. It seems I am in luck.+

Blackwing pushed his barricade aside and launched a stream of bolts directly at the Rubric Marine. It evaded some of them, swaying back with astonishing agility. The rest hit, exploding against the armour and shattering the ornamentation from the helm and shoulder-guards.

Then Blackwing pounced, swinging his blade into

246

the contact zone and aiming for the cables at the neck. The Traitor's Mk IV armour only had a few weaknesses, but that was one of them. His blade whistled towards its destination.

It never arrived. The Traitor sidestepped the swipe, pulled its fist back and punched out. Blackwing jerked his head away but the gauntlet still connected, crunching under his jaw and throwing him into the air on the follow-through.

+Not much of a contest, is it?+

Blackwing swivelled in mid-flight and crashed face-down to the ground. His visor shattered on impact, turning his vision into a crazy patchwork of angular lens fractures.

That's why they don't wear helms.

Groggily, he dragged himself back around. He heard sporadic gunfire as the few remaining kaerls launched a desperate assault on the rampaging Rubric Marine.

Blood ran down his temple. The gilded monster was busy finishing off the kaerls, breaking limbs with casual flicks before blasting men apart with single shots.

And in the background, limping up the corridor beyond, was the sorcerer.

+We will take this ship when you are dead, Dog,+ the cobra-masked figure wheezed. +Right into the middle of your fleet.+

Blackwing cleared his head, curling his fist around the grip of his sword, judging the distance. The last of his kaerls was dispatched contemptuously, and the Rubric Marine turned back to him.

+Then I'll detonate the warp drive. What do you think of that?+

Blackwing sprang to his feet. Moving with all the explosive power he could muster, he fired his pistol straight at the Traitor Marine while simultaneously sending his power sword spinning towards the sorcerer. It glittered as it travelled, the biting edge whirling dead-eyed towards its target.

It was the most perfect manoeuvre Blackwing had ever executed, a stunning double-handed attack launched at unstoppable speed. The aim was perfect. His bolter rounds hammered home, thudding into the Rubric Marine's armoured shell and tearing off plates.

The cartwheeling blade flew to its target too, blazing with ceramite-cleaving energies as it span. Even in the midst of everything, poised to leap at the sorcerer to finish the job, Blackwing felt a burst of pride. Not many of his battle-brothers could have done what he'd just done. It was magnificent.

Then the blade hit the sorcerer's kine-shield and broke into fragments. The Rubric Marine reeled, its right arm blasted off, exposing a gaping hole at the shoulder. Then it righted itself, and started to advance again.

At that point, Blackwing knew he was dead. There was nothing further he could do to halt them.

I'll scar you, though, you bastards.

'Fenrys!' he roared, charging towards the sorcerer, emptying his clip at the hunched figure, feeling the weapon kick back against his palm as it unloaded its mass-reactive contents.

An explosion of wild, writhing, multi-coloured light boomed out from the sorcerer, followed by a deafening crash of something terrible breaking open. The stink of the immaterium bloomed out, and Blackwing was thrown on his back again, landing crushingly hard amid the ruined barricades and corpses. Something heavy hit his head, knocking open the damaged visor further. The world reeled around him, punched off its axis by the unholy release of warp-energy.

For a moment he lay still, stunned. There were more crashes, more blasts of eye-watering warp-power. They passed.

Then, slowly, something occurred to him.

I'm not dead.

He lifted his head painfully, feeling the compression in his neck. The Rubric Marine stood immobile three metres away, locked in a half-completed stride forwards. The sorcerer had crumpled to the floor, his robes burning with lurid flames and his armour prised open. The flesh within was... horrible.

'Do not look yet,' came a familiar voice.

Ignoring the advice, Blackwing craned his head round to see where it had come from.

Neiman was there, rebinding his warp-eye. The Navigator looked shaky, and his face was pale.

'I came to get you,' he said, furiously. 'And thank the bloody Emperor I did, you stupid bastard.'

GREYLOC SURGED TOWARDS the breach, his retinue a pace behind him, his twin claws shimmering in the dark from their disruption fields.

'For Russ!' he bellowed, and the sound echoed from the walls of the Fang's cavernous entrance chambers.

Ahead of him were the shattered gates, still burning from the explosions that had destroyed them.

Beyond the crushed pillars, partially masked by sheets of smoke and hammering hail, was the advancing enemy. The first lines of invaders were already closing on the opening, emboldened by the devastating power of the gate-breakers. Greyloc's helm display flickered with signals as his armour's machine-spirit rapidly made sense of the thousands of life signs ahead and prioritised them into target-runes.

Roaring with defiance, he burst out into the open, shrugging off the lines of incoming las-fire, revelling in the cold, sharp air of Fenris once more. Though polluted with engine oil and the acrid tang of spent ordnance, it was still better than being cooped up behind the walls.

We are predators. This is where we belong.

As he charged, his squad swept alongside him, their massive Terminator suits ploughing through clusters of smoking metal and ruined stonework. Volleys of armour-piercing fire streaked over their heads, sent by the Long Fangs still in the shadows of the mountain. Kaerls came out in their wake, mortals clad in carapace armour and loosing their heavy projectile guns in controlled bursts. They struggled to keep pace with the Wolves in the vanguard, but Greyloc knew they were just as eager to make contact. Many were knocked from their feet by the rain of las-fire spitting across the storm-whipped earth, but most made ground, rushing to secure terrain before it was seized by the oncoming horde.

Buoyed by Sturmhjart's ferocious storm whirling about him, Greyloc thundered into the first ranks of the invaders. They were mortals, decked out like his

own kaerls in environment suits and shouldering lasguns. He'd already killed hundreds of such warriors
since their drop-ships had first defiled his home world.
Before they could loose a massed shot at him, he was
amongst them, carving his way deeper into the ranks.

'Slay them!' he roared, feeling the kill-urge distort
his voice with its intensity. 'Slay them all!'

He barely heard the thud and crash of impact as his
retinue slammed into battle beside him, each bellowing his own oath of combat, each tearing a channel
through the Thousands Sons vanguard. Bodies were
hurled into the air, limbs severed, armour ripped
apart.

Grey Land Raiders lumbered from the ruined gates
then, grinding over the broken terrain, laying down
heavy bolter fire and sending lascannon beams scything into the sweeping tide of men and armour. More
Wolves loped alongside them, Grey Hunters and
Blood Claws, their armour draped with gruesome
totems of death and vengeance. In the face of their
sudden assault, the Thousand Sons' charge on the
gates faltered.

Greyloc remained at the spear-tip. The wolf within
him slavered, hungry for more killing, taking keen
pleasure from the men falling beneath his talons. He
kept bellowing oaths of hatred and damnation as he
slew, each syllable amplified by his armour into a crescendo of savage elation.

The roars of defiance and anger were not idly made.
They were part of the projection of intimidation, the
wall of sound that drove lesser men mad with fear.
Every blow was aimed to aching perfection, every

blade-plunge was judged with accuracy, every bolter discharge was aimed with exacting precision. These Wolves hunted the way their Jarl had taught them to – fast, deadly, efficient. At their head, the White Wolf cut his way through walls of living flesh, his claws drenched in the blood of his prey, energy sluicing from his claws and crackling with cold fury.

We must make them pay for the passage of the gates.

Greyloc punched a warrior aside, breaking him in two, before launching himself at the flanks of a troop carrier trying to turn in the churned-up slush and gravel. He was in constant motion, swivelling and scything like a whole pack of predators combined into a single, terrible amalgam. He felt Sturmhjart's powerful wards protect him as he went, a barrier against the flickering spells of the sorcerers. He knew the value of that protection: for this short time he was free to kill unimpeded, to bathe in the blood of those who had come to his domain to bring death.

He would use that time well.

Beneath the shadow of the gates, the two armies crunched together, one massive and ponderous, the other swift and feral. As the Fang burned, tortured by the remorseless volleys of long range fire, its slopes echoed from the sound of close combat killing at last. As men died and vehicles smouldered, as the gunships came in low for renewed attack runs, amid all the carnage of the ground assault, every warrior on the field knew the cold reality of the situation.

The noose had closed, and had begun to tighten.

CHAPTER TWELVE

Freija felt like she'd stumbled into some drug-induced trance. Her body ached from the brief firefight, and she could still feel blood trickling down her ribs. Coming down here had been insane. Three of her men had died, all to protect a bunch of scuttling half-breeds while their master did whatever he had to do in that vault. Even the awesome sight of Bjorn, a figure she'd never been quite sure was more than a myth, had only partially assuaged the sense of futility.

The Fell-Handed was just one of the Dreadnoughts roused by Arfang. Others had emerged in the time since then, marching in a procession of stately, grinding majesty. Hours had passed as more of the venerable warriors were awakened. All the while, the pack of beasts hung back in the shadows, growling and pacing. It was unclear how many there were – maybe a dozen, perhaps many more.

Freija didn't know which to be more wary of, the malshaped horrors of the Underfang or the grim, sepulchral structures of the walking dead. As the Dreadnoughts passed through the doors to the vault, they flexed giant fists and spooled up huge auto-cannon barrels. Even by the standards of a savage Chapter, they were fearsome in aspect. They hissed and steamed as they moved, throwing up clouds of smoke from exhausts mounted behind layers of thick armour. All were scored with old runes and draped in ancient skins, black from age and as dry as stone. As each one entered the chamber, the air vibrated a little more from the growling judder of their engines.

Bjorn had said nothing since his arrival, and brooded alone. Every so often he'd raise his vast lightning claw and rotate the blades, as if reminding himself of some-thing from the distant past. None of the mortals dared approach him, though the beasts did. They slunk up to him, heads low, jaws drooling. They were submissive before him, like whelps of the pack paying homage to the alpha predator.

As they crawled into the scant light of the open vault doors, Freija began to make out more of their out-lines. They were a motley assortment of bestial forms, all hunched and awkward. There were glints of metal amid the fur and sinew as they moved. One wolf-shape had no visible eyes in its sleek face at all, another had steel claws, and a third had an almost human smile on its tooth-crammed jaws. All of them were gigantic, as big as the Fenrisian wolves that stalked the high places, though with none of their savage grace.

Do not watch them. They take it as a challenge.

The voice rumbled from over her shoulder, almost as deep and machine-thick as Bjorn's. Freija spun round, seeing the profile of another Dreadnought in the dark. As far as she could see, it looked much the same as the others – hulking, angular, humming with coiled menace. Perhaps this one was a little less battle scarred, a little cleaner looking, but only slightly. She could make out the rune Jner, Pride, on its massive armoured leg.

'Thank you, lord,' she said humbly, keeping the bitterness out of her voice. It might have been better to have been told that before she'd been asked to guard this place. The Wolves' love of exuberant danger was maddening. Why, in the name of all the Hels, were such horrors tolerated within the Aett?

The Dreadnought clumped alongside her. It stood motionless for a moment, inscrutable behind its blank fascia of ceramite. It stank of oils and exhaust fumes.

You are mortal. Why are there no Sky Warriors here?

A good question.

'They are fully engaged, lord. The Aett is under assault.'

The Dreadnought didn't respond immediately. Its speech was sluggish and halting.

Under assault, it repeated, as if the concept were hard to understand.

The Dreadnought sank into contemplation. A row of lights flickered along its flanks. Perhaps they were some age-slowed systems finally coming online. Every movement it made was heavy, hesitant and cumber-some.

And I thought I was bad in the morning.

An Underfang beast slunk up to them then, belly low. Freija stiffened, bringing her sidearm up.

Leave it.

Freija kept the muzzle pointed at the mass of fur and tooth. It had pale amber eyes, shining in the dark. She felt her jaw tighten.

I said, leave it.

Slowly, she lowered her weapon. The beast paid her no attention, but performed the same abasement before the Dreadnought as the others had done before Bjorn.

'What are these things?' she asked, staring at the bizarre scene.

You are curious.

Freija winced inwardly.

'I am told so, lord. It is a weakness, and I will work to correct it.'

So you should.

The beast shot a single, unreadable glance at Freija, then crawled back into the gloom. As it went, she saw bands of dull metal around its foreleg. There were steel tendons there, pistons moving smoothly as the beast walked.

They are weapons, mortal. We are all weapons. Even you, in your own way, are a weapon. Let that be enough for you.

'Yes, lord,' said Freija, bowing. She could feel her cheeks flushing with irritation at the evasion.

My men have died for your damned mysteries!

I am called Aldr. In life I was a Blood Claw, though the Long Sleep has... changed that.

That admission came as a surprise. Freija didn't know what to say in reply. Making small talk with a Dreadnought was not something she'd been trained for. Russ, it was hard enough speaking to regular Space Marines.

This is my first awakening. The process is difficult. Tell me of the world of the living. That will help.

'What do you wish to know, lord?'

There was a pause. Deep in the vaults, Arfang was still busy. Freija had no idea how many of the Revered Fallen were kept down here, nor how many more he planned to awaken. The process might nearly be over, or there might be hours still to go.

Everything, said Aldr, his ponderous voice touched with a note of eagerness. Or perhaps it was desperation. The yearning was almost childlike.

Tell me everything.

'FENRYS HJAMMAR KOLDT!'

Odain Sturmhjart bellowed out the curses until his mighty lungs were raw. He stood before the ruined Bloodfire Gate, his staff clutched in both fists, marshalling the fury of the maelstrom. The battlefield was darkening as the Fenrisian sun, that old ball of blood that gave the portal its name, sank slowly to the sawtooth horizon. The sky was already a dark wine-red, streaked with trails of smoke and the flickering illumination of promethium fires. Hail continued to hammer down in a blur, whipped into deadly eddies by the mastery of the Rune Priest.

'*Hjolda!*' he roared, fangs bared, feeling the awesome power of his calling answer the summons. Lightning, ice-white and blazing with spectral energy, lanced down in the wake of the hail, ripping through enemy formations and tearing up whole columns of men and vehicles where it landed.

Ahead of him, the Wolves infantry had charged into the foremost formations of the invaders, hurling them back from the breach. Grey Hunters hacked and punched their way through whole regiments of Prosperine mortal troops, backed up by the ranged fire of the Long Fangs and the kaerl heavy weapon squads. Blood Claws raced into battle alongside them, howling in a frenzy of distilled kill-urge, flanked by growling Land Raider formations and whole rivens of kaerls. Protected and warded by Sturmhjart's peerless control of the storm, the Wolves had room to kill, and they did so eagerly. The magicks of the sorcerers in the Thousand Sons had failed to do anything to answer the Rune Priest's onslaught in the hours since the gates had gone down, tied up as it was defending their own troops from the elemental fury.

For all that, the Fenrisian position was precarious. The Wolves fought like the demigods they were, laying waste to whole companies of mortals, but there were thousands upon thousands of troops in the enemy vanguard alone. Every so often, a massed thicket of las-beams would down a Hunter in his tracks, or a tank shell would find its mark with armour-cracking force. Each time a Sky Warrior fell, a pang of frustrated anger swelled within Sturmhjart's breast, and the swirling majesty of the storm was raised to an ever higher level of lethality.

They were losing ground. They would lose ground through the night and they would lose ground for as long as they fought into the dawn. Traitor Marines had made their way to the front ranks and joined the battle. They were mirror opposites of the *Vlka Fenryka*, equal in deadliness but utterly different in method. Whereas the Wolves fought with an exuberant, flamboyant skill, exulting in their raw prowess, the Thousand Sons came to the battlefield silently, marching like strangely animated bronze-crested ghosts. There were already too many of them to hold back, dozens more than the defenders could bring to bear in response, and additional troops were coming into the contact zone with every hour.

Faced with such odds, the warriors of the Twelfth fought with a zeal that made Sturmhjart's hearts swell with savage pride. No quarter was given, asked for or contemplated. The Wolves hurled themselves into combat with an utter disregard for anything other than the pain they could inflict on a foe they hated more than there were words to express. As the sun finally sank below the horizon, Sturmhjart saw a lone Grey Hunter barrel into a whole squad of Rubric Marines, his power axe blazing in the dark before disappearing into a forest of sapphire amour. The manoeuvre cost him his life, but it gave an entire company of kaerls time to withdraw to higher ground and establish new firing positions.

It was bitter, as bitter as gall, to lose brother warriors in such a cause. Full retreat would come in time, and then the ground would be yielded to the enemy.

But they all knew the score. Every metre of stone, every rock, every patch of blackened ice, would be fought over until the blood of the enemy ran in rivers across it. Such was the way of Fenris, just as it had been since the dawn of the Imperium, just as it ever would be.

Sturmhjart stole a quick glance over his shoulder, back toward the gaping gate-ruins. The proud arches slumped into rubble, studded with gigantic fallen lintel-stones like megaliths. In the light of the fires he could see squads of kaerls hurrying to the front, many carrying fresh ammunition crates. Some of those contained boltgun magazines. Those carriers would sell their lives to get them to the Wolves on the frontline.

Sturmhjart saw the look of fierce determination in their mortal eyes.

No fear. Blood of Russ, they have no fear.

Further back, under the sagging arch of the Bloodfire portal, more kaerls were working furiously in the halls beyond. Sturmhjart knew what they were doing, and it chilled his heart.

It was worth it. The sacrifices were worth it. These were the fires in which faith was forged.

He turned his attention back to the battlefield. For as far as he could see, the vast causeway swarmed with the enemy. His entire visual field was filled with ranks of infantry, studded with the hulking formations of mobile armour.

Inexorably, inevitably, the enemy was driving them back to the gates.

'You're not here yet, you faithless bastards,' growled Sturmhjart, spinning his staff round and drawing down more power from the storm. Lightning arced through the air, tearing apart a column of lumbering troop carriers and throwing the vehicle shells high into the hail-wracked wind.

For the first time since the orbital war, Sturmhjart began to feel himself again. For too long, he'd been mired in guilt and the need to atone. The failure to predict the attack had hit him hard, driving his ebullient wolf-spirit into an unfamiliar realm of doubt.

Enough. My soul lives for this.

It was cathartic, this exercise of power. As he governed the elements in the cause of righteous murder, his blood ran as hot as *mjod*. He felt the avatar of the Helix, the grey-flanked beast that prowled the corridors of his mind, flex its claws in savage pleasure.

He looked up. From out of the darkening night, a formation of enemy gunships was swooping low, engines burning and weapons spooling up to fire. They'd failed to take him out by sorcery, and now more conventional weapons were being employed.

'Bring it on,' growled Sturmhjart, summoning up the inferno that would rip the squadron out of the skies. His staff erupted in wyrdfire, possessed by power of such raw savagery it made him grin just to feel it.

By the time the gunships were in range to fire, Odain Sturmhjart, High Rune Priest of the Space Wolves Chapter, was laughing with all his old, battle-tempered might.

TWELVE DREADNOUGHTS HAD emerged by the time Arfang had finished his rites. They lurked in the dark, their engines drumming. The servitors fussed around them, adjusting bearings and oiling exposed metalwork. The massive machines waited patiently, like giant plains-beasts tolerating the attentions of parasite-cleaners.

'I can do no more, lord,' announced Arfang, bowing to the mightiest profile of them all. 'Both gates are now broken and under attack. Jarl Greyloc summons me to the surface again.'

Bjorn turned his torso section to face the Iron Priest.

Greyloc? Your Great Wolf?

'Jarl of the Twelfth. Only a single company remains within the Aett. The Chapter has been called to Gangava, where Magnus the Red has been located.'

There was a low growl from Bjorn at that name, a rumbling mechanical noise that emanated from his very core.

Brief me as we ascend. Your tidings anger me, Iron Priest. I should have been consulted before this was done.

The venerable Dreadnought's voice had lost its undertow of sluggishness. Gradually, painfully, the ancient intelligence within was rising to a full pitch of awareness. There was an unfamiliarity in the accent it employed, even filtered through layers of vox-generators. Each syllable Bjorn uttered was somehow archaic, the embodiment of an age that had passed.

Freija found herself marvelling at that speech. It made her skin prickle with anticipation. It was irascible and severe, as hard as the granite roots of the mountain. But there was something else. The same quality Aldr's voice had.

They are crippled with grief. The darkness, the cold. It has entered their souls.

Arfang bowed to Bjorn in apology and took up his staff again. There was a faint click as something in his armour's mechanisms communicated a signal to the servitors. They fell into line. All of those half-human horrors had survived intact.

Not like Freija's troops. Three of them would lie in the dark at least until the surface battle was over, uncremated and without the rites being said.

Arfang shot a glance toward Freija then.

'We are heading back now, huskaerl,' he said. His voice was as metallic and clipped as ever, but there was an unhideable exhaustion there. Whatever he'd been doing in that vault, it had tested him to his limits. 'You have come through the deep dark. My servitors are intact.'

Freija felt a surge of bitterness at that bald statement. She was surrounded by warped monsters and ghosts from the past, all of whom were utterly indifferent to anything but their own arcane concerns. Looking for the right words, she almost replied too curtly, which would, of course, have been a big mistake.

Luckily for her, Arfang's next words stopped her in her tracks. He fixed her with a direct stare, though what thoughts passed behind that scarred helm-plate were, as ever, impossible to read.

'Thank you,' he rasped curtly.

Then he turned away and stalked across the antechamber toward the tunnels. In his wake, the procession of Dreadnoughts rocked on their servos and primed to march. With a grind of long-static gears, the giant armoured hulls swayed into line. The beasts of the Underfang, still cowed by their presence, remained in the shadows, watching the ungainly progress as it unfolded.

One of Freija's men came close to her.

'What now, huskaerl?' he whispered over the mission channel.

For a moment, Freija had no idea how to reply. Then she shook off her surprise at Arfang's brief concession to courtesy and snapped her *skjoldtar* into position.

'Stay close, kaerl,' she said. 'Keep away from the beasts, but do not hinder them if they follow.'

Freija grimaced as she recalled what they were capable of. This whole situation was too insane for words, but there was little to do but cope with it. Above all, her squad still needed leadership.

'They will march, as we all do,' she said, watching Aldr's angular bulk fall into line amongst the other Dreadnoughts. 'To war.'

THE BLOOD CLAWS swept back into the attack, leaping over boulders and tearing across the broken terrain. Brakk was in the forefront, his body low, weaving between incoming las-fire. Though dawn was close, it was still dark, and the slopes leading to the Sunrising Gate were lit only by the plasma fires still streaming across the shoulders of the Fang.

'Tired, brother?' inquired Helfist, coming into contact range and smashing a Prosperine soldier three metres back into his terrified comrades.

'Of you, yes,' replied Redpelt, swinging round to gun down a line of mortals before triggering his chain-sword into throaty life. 'Otherwise, fine.'

Helfist laughed, plunging through the wavering

ranks and laying about him with his crackling power fist.

'You'd miss me,' he said, seizing a retreating trooper and slamming him into the ground with spine-breaking momentum, 'if I wasn't here.'

'Like a bolt in the arse, brother,' grunted Redpelt, dragging his blade through the torso of one victim before whirling round to take the head off another.

Though neither would have admitted it, they were strung out. The battle had raged for hours, a terrible, meat-grinding conflict in which the Wolves had gone steadily backwards, forced towards their own ruined gates with a grim inevitability. Though the Claws had launched charge after charge, breaking the enemy with every surge, the ground could not be held. There were too many artillery columns laying down hammering curtains of fire, too many troops ready to fill the gaps.

And too many Rubric Marines. Even as Brakk's pack surged through their mortal opposition, more sapphire giants loomed up to meet them from the dark, their power weapons glistening in the shadows.

'Traitor filth!' roared Helfist, powering towards them as soon he saw the hated armour-profile, lacing his voice with the vitriol reserved only for fallen brothers.

Redpelt was at his shoulder in an instant, and the two warriors crunched into the lead Rubric Marine together, slamming him back and off-balance. There was a ripple of crashes and sharp cracks as more Blood Claws launched themselves into combat, bellowing their fury with a tidal wave of fervour.

Then Brakk was among them, heaving his power sword in huge, crushing curves. The Wolf Guard remained comm-silent as ever, but his presence was immense. He squared up to a Rubric Marine and their blades came together with a heavy, resounding clang. The twin lengths of metal danced, both of them blurred with speed, hacking and parrying with astonishing control and weight.

Helfist and Redpelt maintained their own attack, driving the Rubric Marine back another pace. Redpelt thrust his chainsword low even as Helfist lunged high with his disruptor-field. If their adversary had been mortal, he'd have been dead in an instant. As it was, the Traitor swung his sword down to knock aside the buzzing chainblade before veering expertly away from Helfist's heavy punch. Righting himself, the Rubric Marine then loosed a burst of bolter fire at Redpelt, hurling the Blood Claw back and out of combat.

Helfist suddenly stood alone. For a split second he saw the face of his foe lit up by the storm. The helm-mask was ancient. Pale green witchlight bled from the lenses.

The warrior within had fought for centuries, just as passionlessly, just as skilfully. There was something horrifying about that silent visage – the irreversible corruption of what had once been the apotheosis of humanity.

For an instant, Helfist froze, stricken by the vision of what the Adeptus Astartes could become. His own reflection was visible in those terrible lenses.

'Maleficarum!' came a voice from close by, urgent and desperate.

A new figure slammed into the Rubric Marine,

sending it tumbling out of contact. Helfist shook his head as he recovered, burning with shame.

It would have killed me.

He powered back into action. Brakk had been the one who'd saved him. Isolated and out of position, the Wolf Guard now took on three Rubric Marines single-handedly, including the one who'd frozen Helfist. The old warrior fought like a berserker of old, laying about him with the dread blade Dausvjer, his charred pelts flailing. His free fist punched out, shattering the snake-mask of a Traitor as his sword carved deep into another's armour.

'Blood of Russ!' yelled Helfist, rushing to his aid, feeling the force in his power fist explode again into roaring life.

He arrived in time to see Brakk cut apart, his helm-plate blasted into pieces by close-range bolter-fire as the third Rubric Marine stabbed his blade in deep below the breastplate. More Traitors piled in soundlessly, hacking and slicing like butchers, as impassive in victory as they were in defeat.

'Morkai!'

Helfist burst amongst them, overcome with a flood of horror and grief. The wolf within him screamed, its jaws wide and eyes rolling. His vision went red, ringed with black, spiked stars. He forgot his training, forgot his technique, forgot everything but madness. He only felt his limbs moving, striking out with horrible, unnatural speed. He saw Rubric Marines scatter under his blows, ripped into dust-blown husks by his crushing strikes.

Somewhere deep within, lips were pulled back from yellow teeth.

'Kyr!'

It might have been seconds, it might have been minutes. The combat claimed him, warping him into a maniacal engine of death. He killed, and killed, and killed.

'Kyr!'

The sounds of battle disappeared into a single roar of insanity, a continuum of bestial rage. He was the Wolf. The Wolf was him. The barrier had fallen.

'*Kyr!*'

A new opponent loomed up in front of him, vast as a mountain, its eyes blazing red. Helfist tensed to spring, ready to rip the monster's throat out with his teeth, to bathe in hot blood, to drink it down and quench the burning pain...

A vast gauntlet clamped on to his bolter-arm, holding it steady. For a second, Helfist still pressed forwards, consumed by kill-rage, lost in the frenzy of bloodletting.

'Kyr. Brother. Come back.'

The voice was firm, unyielding.

Helfist's vision cleared. He was restrained by a hulking Wolf Guard in gunmetal-grey Terminator plate. Tromm Rossek, his helm-lenses as red as heart-blood, his chainfist ready to end him. All around the pair of them were the destroyed shells of Rubric Marines. Their armour-plates were scattered as if a hurricane had cut through the squad.

Helfist's blood was still pumping. The horror was still raw. The Wolf still called him back, still beckoned him into the embrace of sweet madness.

'He is gone, Blood Claw. Now we withdraw. I will not see more warriors wasted under my watch.'

The voice was thick with grief. It brooked no defiance.

How much time had passed in that mad rage? Helfist glanced at his helm-display. His squad had been mauled. Even now, more enemy signals were closing on their position, drawn by the carnage.

'If you stay, the Wolf will claim you.'

Helfist knew it was true. He'd never been so close. Redpelt and he had laughed about the Wulfen before, cracked coarse jokes about the mad howlers when out of earshot of the Priests.

Now he'd seen it. Now he'd seen what he could become.

Helfist released the disruption field around his fist, and the energy crackled out. Brakk's body lay, broken, at his feet. He had stood over it, lost in a mania of kill-urge. The frenzy had passed now, and he felt drained.

Sick.

He stooped and retrieved the blade Dausvjer from the Wolf Guard's stiff grasp. It was bloodless, used only against the empty shells of Traitor Marines. This, at least, would be recovered.

Rossek nodded in approval, then stomped away, back to the gates. All around them, the Wolves were falling back. The causeways were lost.

Shakily, his soul harrowed with shock and misery, Helfist turned to follow the Wolf Guard. As he did so, Redpelt limped up to him. The Blood Claw's breastplate was cracked open and punched with bolter holes. His breath was wet and rattling, as if blood still bubbled up into his mouth.

He laid his gauntlet clumsily on Helfist's shoulder.

'Brother,' he said.

In the past, after conflict, the two Blood Claws had always made light of what they'd seen. It was their way, their homage to the vital energy that pulsed through their gene-enhanced veins.

Not this time. When Redpelt spoke, the only emotion there was awe – a horrified, wary awe.

THE RETREAT HAD been well planned, and there was no panic when it came. The kaerls broke first, streaming back to the uncertain shelter of the ruined gates, plagued by constant fire slamming into their backs. The Wolves came after them, faces turned to the enemy, firing from the waist and ready to punish any overeager attempt to rush them. Wyrmblade's Wolf Priests, only four in number including the old dog himself, lingered the longest, retrieving all the geneseed they could before falling back. Long Fang squads stepped up the volume of covering ordnance, but it was painfully insufficient. The emplacements on the cliffs around the gates had mostly gone, shot out by the volume of incoming shells and las-beams from enemy artillery positions.

Though the vanguard of the Thousand Sons had been badly mutilated by the ferocity of the disruptive sortie, sheer pressure of numbers meant it retained cohesion. As the approaches to the massive gates were finally overrun, troop carriers ground their way to the front, disgorging yet more companies of mortal soldiers into the battlezone. In their midst strode the Rubric Marines, now in their hundreds, guided by the hidden sorcerers at their backs. With Sturmhjart and Cloudbreaker's withdrawal, the field was clear for them once more, and glittering kine-shields arced over the advancing ranks. The storm that had done so much damage began to ebb and gust out.

Greyloc watched as the last of his forces made the cover of the Sunrising Gate and disappeared within the Fang. He stood on an outcrop of piled stone-work just under the lee of the breach. His claws still hummed with energy. Both hearts thumped, and his breath was ragged. He'd fought hard, perhaps more so than any of his warriors. As ever, the temptation had been to give in to the joy of it, to forget the strategic demands of the battle and glory in the immediate thrill of the hunt.

I am Jarl. Such things should be beneath me now.

Perhaps he overcompensated. He knew his reputation among the Blood Claws, and possibly strove too hard to correct the image of cold bloodedness. If so, that was unworthy too.

In any case, he'd given the order at last. The causeways had been emptied of his troops, and now the enemy swarmed toward the open doors of the Fang. The closest of them were only a few hundred metres distant. A price had been extracted for their assault up the slopes, but only fate would tell whether it had been enough.

'How stands Bloodfire?' Greyloc voxed calmly, watching the front ranks of the enemy sweep towards him.

'Clear, Jarl,' came Skrieya's reply from the far side of the mountain.

'Good. You have command there.'

With a final gesture of defiance, he withdrew at last

from his position and loped down into the vast maw of the gates.

Once in cover again, he went swiftly, running from the ruined areas into the vaulted spaces of the entrance halls. Massive statues passed by in the flickering dark, stern-faced warriors of old lining the passage into the mountain. Runes of intimidation and destruction had been carved deep into the living rock above them. Never had a living foe seen those figures, nor set foot on the hallowed portals. In moments, though, hundreds of the enemy would surge past the graven images, racing to complete what they'd started on the causeways.

No defenders would oppose them there. The halls were empty. No barricades had been raised, no fire pits dug, no gun-emplacements mounted. As Greyloc sped into the heart of the mountain, only his heavy treads resounded from the rough floor.

After a kilometre, the tunnel ended and Greyloc burst into a high vaulted chamber lit with roaring hearthfires. This was the division of the ways, where the single entry route running into the Fang branched off into other corridors and elevator shafts. The great seal of Russ hung from a gigantic chain in the centre of it.

Here the defenders waited. There were Rossek, Cloudbreaker, Rojk and Wyrmblade. All stood defiant, waiting for the arrival of their lord. The surviving Wolves were there too, reloading weapons and making hasty repairs to their armour. Further back, mortal troops bustled back and forth, doing their best to meet the expectations of the unforgiving huskaerls.

Stretcher-bearers went among them, hauling the wounded away from the front and deep into the heart of the citadel. Box-guns rotated into firing positions, their squat barrels locked on the arch Greyloc had just come through.

None of those things caught Greyloc's attention as he entered the chamber. One figure alone dominated the massive space, reducing even the Terminator-clad warriors around him to pale, childlike shadows. In the centre of the hall, directly under Russ's seal, was the legend.

As he laid eyes on Bjorn, Greyloc felt hope leap in his heart again.

With no thought of honour or entitlement, he fell to his knees.

'You answered the call, lord,' he said, and there was joy in that weary voice.

The Dreadnought lowered its claw and ponderously beckoned him to rise.

You are Jarl Greyloc?

'I am,' said the Wolf Lord, getting to his feet.

And you plan to make your stand here?

As Bjorn spoke, the first sounds of pursuit began to come down the corridor behind Greyloc, distorted by the echoing chambers beyond. There were thousands of footfalls in the distance, a crescendo of aggressive battle cries, all from troops intent on resuming the slaughter they'd been denied by the Wolves' retreat.

'I do not.'

Bjorn said nothing, but inclined his torso fractionally in an almost-human gesture of questioning. Greyloc smiled, and nodded to Wyrmblade.

'Now, Thar,' he said.

The Wolf Priest took up a detonator and depressed the control rune.

The explosions boomed out instantly. Fireballs erupted all along the kilometre-long tunnels, breaking the rock shells around them and caving them in. The sharp bang of detonation was quickly replaced by the rolling roar of the heavy roof sections falling in, burying any invaders that had made it inside.

A bow-wave of rubble flew into the chamber of the seal, carrying the last screams of the crushed on its wings. Outside the Fang, huge columns of black dust rose from the collapsed Bloodfire and Sunrising Gates. Loosened rocks around the portal entrances rolled down the slopes, causing havoc in the companies of soldiers preparing to follow their comrades in.

The flanks of the mountain shook. There were a few last, grudging booms from deep within. Then the dust-clouds drifted into the night, ripped into shreds by the dying stormwind.

The Fang was sealed.

Bjorn looked down at Greyloc. The Wolf Lord looked back.

Nicely done, said Bjorn.

CHAPTER THIRTEEN

GANGAVA PRIME. A dark world, far from its giant red star. As the solar terminator swept across the rust-red planetscape, the night-side sank deep into occlusion. There were pinpricks of artificial light all across the shadowed hemisphere, but they concentrated into a bright cluster towards the high northern latitude. Swirls of sulphur-yellow picked out a city. A vast, sprawling city.

From the bridge of the *Russvangum*, Ironhelm watched the lights wink on far below. The inhabitants of that place knew that the Wolves had arrived. They had detectors, sensor-arrays and void shields raised. The entire Chapter fleet, minus the few guard-ships left on Fenris, was now in high orbit. The firepower assembled there was immense, as great as anything pulled together during the Great Scouring. Gangava had no orbital defences, but they would have been an irrelevance anyway. Lean strike cruisers and plough-share-bowed destroyers now prowled across the void with impunity, poised to unleash Hel on the world below them.

The Great Wolf felt a mix of emotions, looking down on the city he was about to destroy. He'd slept badly during the twenty-one days in the warp. Magnus had come to him in his dreams regularly, goading him, taunting his failure to catch up with him over the decades. Ironhelm hadn't seen the face of the pri-march, just as he hadn't seen it over the many years of prior visitations.

But he had heard the voice. An unforgettable voice. Proud, powerful, cultivated, but with a touch of petulance that wasn't quite under control. For all his primarch's qualities, he now came across as a dimin-ished, querulous presence.

My gene-father broke your back, monster.

Magnus had smirked at such defiance, but there was a residue of pain there. Real, mortal pain.

Brooding over the realspace viewers in his private chambers, Ironhelm felt his fingers itch within their gauntlets. The journey had been too long. Only hours now remained before the drop-pods would begin to fall, accelerating into a hail of dark seeds from the void, all aimed beyond the cover of the city's shields.

Ironhelm saw the ingress routes in his mind's eye. They were available at any time from his helm-display, but he knew he'd not have to use that. He could visu-alise all aspects of the battle as it would unfold. If he closed his eyes, the tactical outline would still be there, a pattern of hololith lines and deployment runes overlaid on the streets of the vast city.

Many in the galaxy believed that the Space Wolves were simply feral barbarians, brutes who charged headlong into battle yelling incomprehensible curses. Only later, when they found their supply lines severed, their comms jammed and their allies breaking out in rebellion behind them did they discover the weakness of that interpretation. Planning was everything, the coordination of pack movements, the encirclement of the prey, the cleanliness of the kill.

The Wolves were savage, but not savages. Gangava would be destroyed swiftly and without indulgence. Primarch or no, Magnus would come to regret his decision to establish himself within strike distance of Fenris.

There was a chime from the wall-unit behind him.

'Come,' Ironhelm said, without turning.

He heard the heavy treads of Kjarlskar, together with the marginally lighter ones of Rune Priest Frei. The two armoured giants came to stand alongside the Great Wolf.

'All is prepared?' asked Ironhelm, his gaze still fixed on the planet below.

'As you commanded,' said Kjarlskar. 'Nine Great Companies are primed for first-wave assaults; the reserves are ready when needed.'

'And word from Fenris?'

'Scheduled astropathic updates,' said Frei. 'No news. I think they're bored.'

Ironhelm laughed harshly.

'Too bad. We'll bring back trophies for them.'

Kjarlskar took a step closer to the viewers. His forces had been in orbit above the city for twenty-eight days. Ironhelm knew the Wolf Lord had been desperate to launch an attack during that time, but he'd followed his orders to maintain the blockade. Until the entire fleet had been mustered, not so much as a single bolter had been fired in anger.

'You still sense him, Frei?' Kjarlskar asked.

The Rune Priest nodded.

'He's down there. Just as he has been for weeks.'

Kjarlskar frowned.

'Why so passive? This I will never understand.'

'It was the same on Prospero,' said Ironhelm calmly. 'He trusts in sorcery to protect him, that we'll be daunted by a few spells. It is inconceivable to him that anything, even the Rout, could threaten him in a citadel of his own making.'

'And can we?'

Ironhelm turned to face the Jarl of the Fourth.

'You sound doubtful, Arvek. I do not like that, not on the eve of battle.'

Kjarlskar wasn't intimidated by Ironhelm's tone. He was too old, too battle-wily, to care much about prestige or reputation.

'Don't intimate fear to me, lord, or even unwillingness – I would fight alongside you beyond the doors of Hel, and you know it. I just make explicit the question we all leave unsaid.' He returned his master's gaze evenly. 'Have mortals ever killed a primarch in battle? Can it even be done?'

Ironhelm didn't waver in his response.

'I do not know, my friend,' he replied. 'Though before this is done, one way or another, the question will be answered.'

ANOTHER DAY DAWNED across the frigid wastes of Asaheim. The exterior of the Fang presented a charred, diminished aspect. The barrage of plasma from orbit had ceased, its work done. The rain of offensive artillery had also given out, as no defensive batteries still remained on the surface of the mountain to trouble them.

Smoke rose in dreary columns from the blackened rock walls. With the passing of the wyrd-summoned storm, the full extent of the devastation was illuminated by crisp morning sunlight.

The Thousand Sons now controlled both causeways. Their troops moved at will across the wide expanses of stone. Broken companies recovered their shape. Supplies were brought up to the battlefront and casualties taken away from it. More tanks crawled up the slopes, now free of interference from the defenders. The mountain stood alone, surrounded by a carpet of besiegers, its inhabitants buried deep in its interior. Except for the landing platforms still visible at the very summit, it could have been any other peak of Asaheim, lifeless and desolate.

As the sun climbed into the sky, Aphael made his way to an observation platform a kilometre from the scorched citadel. The cold was getting to him. His constitution should have made him functionally immune to such climatic extremes, especially when sealed in his armour, but still he shivered.

He knew the cause of it. The flesh-change was gaining speed. Aphael doubted whether he could take his helm off now even if he wanted to. The muscles in his fingers pressed painfully against the inside of his gauntlets. He was being altered. The initial response – disbelief – had given way to a fearful kind of resignation.

There would be some purpose behind the transformation. There was always some purpose. He just didn't know what it was yet.

The platform was ringed by Rubric Marines. Few of them had died in the assault on the gates, though hundreds of mortals had perished. The savagery of the Wolves had been expected, and Aphael had used the vast forces at his command to blunt their peerless martial prowess. An individual Space Wolf was arguably the finest exponent of close combat in the galaxy, but even he could only kill a finite number of foes before being brought down.

Hett was waiting for him on the platform. His robes were ripped and charred from where his Rubric Marine squad had run into trouble. Aphael had heard stories of some of the Wolves descending into berserk rages and slaughtering dozens before they could be finished off. If so, that was all good. He had the troops to spare, and the lapses indicated the mental stress the Dogs were under.

'A good night's work, eh, Ramsez?'

The Raptora inclined his head in greeting.

'For you, perhaps. I lost my Rubricae. Some crazed boy-Dog, going mad at the death of his mentor.'

'Then you'll have to take responsibility for some more, my friend.'

Aphael cast his gaze over to the smoking mountain. The once pristine cliffs were now a dirty brown. Fires still burned across the causeways where promethium had ignited. The stunning vista had already been turned into a cauldron of devastation.

We have achieved so much already, Dogs. Now watch as we defile your world some more.

'It astonishes me,' mused Hett, looking at the same view, 'how quickly the Dogs are able to kill. I have never seen fighting like it. Any other force in the galaxy would have hidden behind those walls, waiting for us to come to them. Yet they met us in the open, fighting like daemons. What drives them? What makes them the way they are?'

Aphael shrugged.

'Do I detect admiration, brother?' he asked. 'If so, it is misplaced. They were made to do the dirty work no other Legion would do. They are the exterminators, the vermin control of the Imperium. They cannot change, and they cannot improve. Just like us, they are imprisoned in the image of their primarch.'

At the mention of Russ, Hett made a warding gesture. Aphael laughed harshly.

'Do not fear – he cannot come to their aid now, as you well know.'

Both sorcerers fell silent. Far below the platform, more heavily armoured vehicles were crawling their way through the ranks. They were of an ancient and obscure design, though a historian of the Imperial military would have been able to detect the faint emblem of the Legio Cybernetica on their flanks.

'So what now?' asked Hett.

'It is as I said before, brother,' replied Aphael, watching the vehicles with distracted interest. The feathers at his neck were irritating him. 'The Cataphracts will be deployed. The Dogs have chosen to go to ground.'

Aphael took a deep, combat weary breath then, feeling the sharpness of the air even through the filters.

'And we, my friend, have chosen to drill them out.'

BLACKWING HAD RESUMED his place on the command throne of the *Nauro*. Neiman was back navigating the ship in his isolated chambers, and the remaining kaerls were at their stations. The course had been maintained, still at full speed despite the engines haemorrhaging fuel and coolant.

A standard Terran day had passed since the encounter with the Thousand Sons sorcerer and his mute bodyguard. It was a meaningless period of time, neither corresponding to the Fenrisian diurnal cycle nor the natural rhythm of a starship, but the crewmen clung to it nonetheless, perhaps thinking that something of their essential humanity was reflected in it.

Whatever the reason, twenty-four hours had still not been long enough for the *Nauro* to recover its equilibrium. Blackwing's command reputation had taken a hit. All the kaerls he'd taken with him on the hunt had died, and the whole crew was aware that it had only been the fortuitous use of the Navigator's deadly warp eye that had saved his hide. In the normal run of things, perhaps even that wouldn't have damaged Blackwing's standing much with the ratings, but everyone was exhausted, run ragged by the endless demands placed on them. So it was that the muttering had begun, quiet enough for the whisperers to feel secure, but loud enough for Blackwing's animal-sharp hearing to catch what was being said.

The gossip and moaning didn't bother him. What did was the fact that he'd been so comprehensively out-fought by a badly wounded spellcaster and a single warrior in power armour. The encounter should have gone better. He had been in his element, stalking in the shadows like a Wolf Scout should. He should have detected the intruders sooner, laid some ambush for them and caught them just as he'd been caught.

The fact he'd stumbled into the firefight so brazenly was worse than sloppy. It was embarrassing.

At the least, Allfather be thanked, it had not ended worse for him. The Rubric Marine had been half-destroyed by the Navigator's baleful gaze. When the sorcerer had been killed in turn, the last of its animating genius had been removed and the lumbering warrior-drone had slumped into inaction. The engines had consumed their remains, turning the corrupted metal and broken flesh into just one more piece of fuel for the hungry furnaces.

Blackwing had spent a lot of time thinking about the two stowaways since then. The sorcerer's body, though crippled by a botched transport, was much the same as his – extended physiology, a broad, stocky frame with overdeveloped musculature and enhanced organs. In many ways, the sorcerer's corpse had been closer to the Adeptus Astartes ideal than Blackwing's own, with his rangy, loping frame and Helix-derived peculiarities.

But the Rubric Marine... that had been strange. Underneath the shattered armour, there was nothing. No flesh, no bones, just a smattering of grey dust. Blackwing had heard the stories, of course. The Wolf Priests had declaimed sagas of the bloodless remnants of Magnus's Legion, cursed by the dark sorcery of the faithless Ahriman to march to war forever with their souls destroyed, so he shouldn't have been surprised. He should have found it routine, just another quirk of the galaxy's tortuous, tragic history.

But he couldn't stop thinking about it. For some reason, the notion that Space Marines could mutilate themselves so completely, just to avoid an inexorable flaw in their constitution, was abhorrent to him. There were some things that just had to be dealt with. For the Sons of Russ, it was the Wulfen, the dark spectre of the Wolf that hunted in all of them.

Perhaps the Thousand Sons had suffered from some similar flaw. If so, they hadn't stood up to it like men, but had turned themselves into monsters. The longer Blackwing contemplated it, the more it horrified him.

That's the difference. We are all corrupted, the old Legions, but the Wolves didn't run away. We face it, every day. We keep the danger close to us, use it to make us strong. Whatever else we do, we must remember that.

'Lord.'

Blackwing shook himself out of his introspection. Georyth was standing before him on the command platform. Like all the ship's mortals, he looked terrible. His uniform was crumpled, and there were dark rings under his eyes.

'Speak,' drawled Blackwing, feeling hollow himself. He'd been awake for days.

'Secondary search has been completed. No further anomalies detected on any decks.'

'Good. And the engines?'

Georyth let out a long breath.

'I've got crews on triple rotation. We're keeping the worst of the fires back, but I don't know for how much longer.'

'We need six days.'

'I know. If we had more men...' he trailed off. 'But we don't.'

Was that a dig at him? Would Georyth have asked for those dead kaerls to be pressed into engine duty? Blackwing felt his hairs prickle with annoyance.

'That's right, Master,' he said. 'We don't have enough men. We don't have enough anti-flamm, we don't have enough parts for the damaged plasma drive, and we've got a cracking Geller generator. All these things I know, so I don't need to hear them repeated. I need you to tell me things I don't know. Have you anything further to say?'

The Master let a rare flash of belligerence pass across his face. In his state of fatigue, he was ready to lash out at almost anything.

'You know my advice, lord,' he said coldly.

So he was still advocating the void-flush. The fact he'd offered it up twice was itself proof of Blackwing's flagging authority.

Suddenly, Blackwing realised that the thralls manning the bridge below the command platform were listening intently. Georyth was speaking for all of them. This was something they'd planned.

A cold sensation passed through him. The implications of that were serious.

'I do know your advice,' he answered. He spoke clearly, knowing he could be heard all across the bridge, and let a low, snagging growl undercut the speech. He fixed his pin-pupil eyes on Georyth and pulled his scarred lips back to reveal his fangs. 'Perhaps my earlier guidance on the matter was not sufficiently clear. This ship has one purpose: to deliver the message to Wolf Lord Harek Ironhelm on Gangava and recall his forces to Fenris. I do not care whether it does so with all the daemons of Hel crawling through the pipework, or if we have to feed our thralls to the furnace to maintain the current speed. Hel, I don't even care anymore if it's me that hands over the message. But we will get there, and we will get there on time.'

Blackwing leaned forwards in his throne, raising a claw to point directly at Georyth. The look of menace on the Scout's face made the Master visibly blench.

'And know this. I am lord of this vessel. It exists by my will. Its wyrd is in my hands, as are all of yours. If I detect any effort to subvert that will, to turn this ship against its ordained purpose, then I will not hesitate to bring down the full quotient of pain upon you. We will maintain speed. We will maintain the repair programme. We will not fall out of the warp. Is that clear?'

The Master nodded hurriedly, his face white with fear. The tentative measures he'd taken to transmit some indication of crew dissatisfaction had backfired badly.

Blackwing smiled, but it was not a kindly gesture.

'Good,' he said, letting his voice fall to a level only the two of them could hear. The growl of threat still reverberated in his voice, a mere echo of the savagery he could bring to bear if he chose. 'Between the two of us, we may speak even more plainly. Perhaps you will pass the sentiment on to the rest of the crew. The first mortal to consider mutiny on this ship will find a close welcome under my claws. I will tear his skin from his body and use the hide to plug the gaps in our hull. It won't help our integrity much, but it will make me feel better.'

He leaned back against the hard steel of the throne.

'Now go,' he snarled, 'and find a way to keep us alive for another six days.'

A FIGURE HAD formed over the altar. It was not entirely substantial; Temekh could see the far side of the summoning chamber through translucent skin. More troublingly, it was not quite what he'd been anticipating. It was not the icon of a flaming eye that his dreams had promised, nor was it the mammoth profile of a primarch, clad in red and gold with a towering helm.

It was a child. A red-haired boy, wearing a white shift, looking painfully immature.

'Lord,' said Temekh, descending through the Enumerations gracefully.

His work was not over, and there were many days of trial still to come, but the hardest part was over. In the absence of Aphael's interruptions, much progress had been made.

'My son,' replied the child.

'You do not look quite as I expected.'

'How did you expect me to look?'

Temekh found comfort in the familiar dialectical speech. He'd learned a long time ago not to place much faith in visual appearances. The way a man spoke, however, was hard to imitate.

'Much like you appear in the Tower. I'm not sure the Wolves will find this aspect... threatening.'

The boy smiled, and the skin around his closed eye creased.

'And what makes you think my image on the Planet of Sorcerers has any special veridicality? You are Corvidae, Ahmuz. You know that what we see depends, in large part, on what we want to see.'

'Maybe. In that case, I wanted to see some reflection of your true power.'

'Look harder.'

Temekh concentrated. Perhaps this was some kind of test. If it was, he didn't understand it. The child looked as unassuming as milk, though the steady, single eye and adult mode of expression were disconcerting.

'I think you are only a fragment, lord,' he said at last. 'A possibility. Despite my work, you represent only the first steps on a journey.'

'Very good,' said the child. 'Much of me remains on Gangava. It must be so, or the illusion will fracture.'

Temekh frowned.

'I do not understand this, lord. I have tried, but the fundamentals elude me.'

The child didn't look perturbed by that.

'Ahriman was the same. For all his gifts, he chose the wrong solution. There is no succour in remaining static, in trying to fight the power of the Ocean with spells. What has he brought us? Empty husks, slaved to sorcerers. There is a higher truth about our transformation, one that we need to learn to embrace.'

'To be everywhere, and nowhere.'

'I'm glad you remember.'

'I remember the terms you use. I still don't understand them.'

The child shrugged.

'There is time for you to learn, and for Hett, and Czamine, and the others. Once the distractions of this episode are over, we shall have the leisure to begin again.'

Temekh paused then, struck by an unwelcome thought.

'You do not mention Aphael.'

'Why should I?'

'He is the greatest of us, the most powerful of those who refused Ahriman.'

'And he will become more powerful still, more than he can possibly imagine, but I did not reach this level of emergence to discuss his fate.'

'No. I didn't think so.'

'I came to encourage you. I have invested much in you, Ahmuz Temekh. The fleet and army we have assembled will wither away soon enough – this is its only purpose, and after that our goals will be different.'

The child smiled. The gesture was simple, but it conveyed a whole host of subtle emotion. Pride, perhaps, and recrimination, but mostly regret.

'Do not fail me, Ahmuz,' said Magnus softly. 'It is a grave matter, for a son to fail the father.'

'I will not, lord,' said Temekh, knowing to what his primarch referred and speaking earnestly in his turn. 'That lesson, at least, has been well learned.'

OVER GANGAVA, THE hour finally came, and comm-signals were sent throughout the fleet. Seamlessly, without fuss or fanfare, the shields over the launch portals of the warships flickered out. Waves of drop-pods flew out of the launch tubes, hurtling down into the atmosphere and blazing like comets. Thunder-hawk gunships followed in arrow-shaped squadrons, spiralling down at phenomenal speeds, their angular prows dipped steeply as they plunged through the ever-thickening air. Behind them came heavier drop-ships, falling fast and manoeuvring with the aid of jetting thrusters. All were decked in the grey of the Space Wolves, bearing black-and-yellow banding and the crest of the snarling muzzle on their flanks.

There were dozens of deployment zones, all beyond the shielded perimeter of the city. Ironhelm had over-whelming force at his command and had allocated his troops accordingly. There were three principal targets. Massive power generating facilities had been detected in the north-west quarter of the urban sprawl, and two Great Companies had been assigned to their destruc-tion. Another two Companies had been deployed to strike at the city's void shield projectors, situated in the south-west and surrounded by heavy defensive formations.

The centre of the giant city, though, was the main prize. A whole district, many tens of kilometres across, had been constructed in the image of Tizca, with pyramids rising high into the dust-thick air. They weren't the gleaming silver edifices that had glittered under the pale skies of Prospero, though. On Gangava, the industrial filth clung to their sides, turning the surfaces the same dirty red as the rest of the planet. From space they looked almost organic, like strangely geometric mountains looming above the chaotic tangle of hab-blocks and manufactoria around them.

Magnus was in those pyramids. Frei had confirmed it again. All the Chapter's Rune Priests could sense it, could feel the terrible presence lurking under the greatest of the structures, polluting the wyrd like a slick of oil on water. Ironhelm led the assault on that central target, taking five whole Great Companies and the majority of the Chapter's Rune Priests in a spearhead of colossal firepower. Their landfall was directly to the east of the void shield fringes, a hundred-kilometre slog away from the heavily defended heart of the city.

The fleet Tacticae had estimated that hundreds of thousands of troops, possibly millions if the civilians had all been armed, were hunkered down behind extensive fortifications and protected by gun emplacements. Augurs had picked up the movement of mobile artillery pieces moving through the streets in convoy, clogging choke-points and blocking passage along the main highways. Whatever forces Magnus had been assembling were clearly well-armed and ready for action, despite their lack of orbital cover.

Intercepted comms traffic had given some idea of the defensive strategy. The orders had been encoded, but many of the ciphers had been cracked during Kjarlskar's blockade and little remained unknown to the attacking commanders. From the interceptions, it was clear that the Gangavans knew full well the fury that awaited them. Their only response lay in numbers. Huge numbers. They couldn't hope to take on the Wolves in combat, but instead planned to wear the invaders down through sheer inertia, dragging them into tar-pits where thousands of dug-in mortars and lasguns would present – so they hoped – a whole series of killing-zones.

The Gangavans also talked, in hushed tones of horror and fear, of what was in the pyramids. Over and over again, the vox-chatter had referred to the Bane of the Wolves. The expression had brought a wry grin to Ironhelm's battered face the first time he'd heard it.

'Bane of the Wolves? He's gone in for melodrama in his old age.'

That had brought a laugh when he'd said it, up on the command bridge of the *Russvangum* surrounded by his Jarls, but the time for laughing had now passed. Every warrior in the first wave had gone about his purpose with a cold, clear attention to detail. Rites of hatred were performed with close attention, manes of unruly hair were lacquered down ready to take battle-helms, bolters were carefully checked and reverently stowed. There were no smiles, no raucous banter from the Blood Claws, no casual joking from the Long Fangs. All of them knew what this prey was worth.

Then the drop-pods had begun to fall, scything down through atmospheric turbulence and sporadic anti-aircraft fire from the glittering suburbs beneath.

Ironhelm's own drop-pod, christened *Hekjarr*, was one of the first to come down in the eastern landing zone. It threw up a giant cloud of red muck as it made planetfall, the adamantium structure still furnace-hot from the atmospheric descent. With a hiss, the hatch bolts blew, sending the outer shell-segments slamming down against the impact-crater sides. Bolters descended from the roof-space and barked into action even as the restraint harnesses flew up and cracked back into their cradles.

As the bands of metal that held Ironhelm were withdrawn, the Great Wolf thundered down the ramp and on to the soil of Gangava. The night sky was the colour of old blood, striated with the dark tracks of his Chapter's vehicles plummeting into range. There were buildings all around him, huge black spires of iron that jutted upwards, linked with bridges and mass transit tubes. Spotter lights whirled, trying valiantly to give the defensive gunners something to aim at, and there were wailing klaxons somewhere far off. Already the broken hammering of heavy weapons fire had started up close to his position, echoing from the precipitous flanks of the structures around him.

Ironhelm breathed deeply, enjoying the familiar sounds and aromas of war as they filtered through his helm. Kill-urge was already pumping around his system, priming him for the extreme and sustained violence to come.

'So we come to it at last, brothers,' he growled, hefting his frostblade and thumbing the energy field into life. 'Let the killing begin.'

CHAPTER FOURTEEN

THE FANGTHANE RANG with activity. The sacred space was filled with the hoarse cries of thralls as they hurried to do their masters' bidding. Ever more crates of armour-piercing shells were unloaded from rattling transports and stacked neatly behind the heavy bolter turrets and box-guns. The barricade across the western end of the gigantic hall edged closer to completion.

Morek looked at it grimly. He'd heard the reports of the enemy, and had a rough idea of their powers. Such barricades and gun-lines would do little but slow them down. In the past he'd have trusted the Sky Warriors to hold almost anything back, but they'd already been bloodied twice. In the light of that, he wasn't sure what he knew any more.

Morek shook his head, trying to rid himself of the

depressive emotions that had clutched at him since the journey to the fleshmakers. All around him, a makeshift field hospital had been organised. At the east end of the hall, under the gaze of the huge statue of Russ, lines of metal beds had been laid out in rows.

Just like the vials on Wyrmblade's table.

The beds were reserved for mortals; the Space Marines were taken into the dedicated surgeries high up in the Jarlheim. As he walked down the aisles, Morek saw the twisted expressions of agony on the faces of the wounded. Fleshmaker thralls worked quickly and expertly, stitching and cauterising. Their methods were effective, but made few concessions to pain relief. Morek saw ice-tough Fenrisians, hardened to trial and deprivation, weeping in agony as they were carved open by the steel blades.

One man was in the process of losing a leg just below the hip. If he survived it he'd have a basic augmetic limb attached in time, but he'd play no further part in the battle. Morek watched the man grimace as the knives went in. The patient was groggy with numbing agents, but still conscious enough to know what was happening. His jaw was clenched tight, the muscles strung out. As the fleshmakers did their work, he gripped the sides of the bed, knuckles bone-white and shivering.

Morek looked away. There were moans and low, wracking sobs everywhere. Hundreds had been prepped for the knives. Hundreds more still lay out on the causeways, their bodies already frozen. For the first time since the battle had started, Morek found himself glad that Freija had been taken down into the

Underfang by the Iron Priest rather than thrown into the first rank of the battlefront

The two of them had only spoken once since her return from the lower levels. Duty had called them both away after that, so the time together was short.

Morek recalled the embrace they'd shared. He'd clutched her tight, feeling her stocky body safe in his arms again. He'd been unwilling to let her go.

Did she need me then? Or did I need her?

'Are you well, father?' she'd asked, looking into his eyes with concern.

'As ever, daughter,' he'd replied.

'Something has happened?'

Morek laughed.

'War has happened.'

They'd exchanged a few words after that, a mere handful before she was called back by the Dreadnought that shadowed her.

'I'm assigned to him now, father.'

It almost sounded like she was proud of that. She'd never been proud before, not to work for a Sky Warrior.

'What need can he have of mortals?'

Freija shook her head.

'I don't know. But he does. They are strange. Some things they remember like a skjald does. Other things they forget. I help him with those.'

Morek looked into her earnest, blunt face. Her blonde hair had fallen over her eyes, just as it used to do when she was a girl. He had to stop himself smoothing it back. Her mother had always told him not to. He found words tumbling, unbidden, into his mind.

You are all I have now! My only link to her, who was so

beautiful and fierce. Be careful, my daughter – watch what you say, watch what you do. Preserve yourself. Let the Aett and all its chambers be consumed by fire, if only you are preserved!

But he didn't say that. He kissed her on the forehead.

'Stay in vox-contact, when you can.'

'I will, father. The Hand of Russ ward you.'

'May it ward us all.'

Then she'd gone, trotting after that Dreadnought, the one they called Aldr Forkblade.

Morek sighed and looked up at the statue rearing above him, trying to banish the memory. The massive image of Russ was there as it had been before, feet braced, face contorted into a snarl. His features were those of a true wolf – distended jawline, pronounced fangs, pinned pupils.

It had been ten days since Jarl Greyloc had stood beneath that mighty frame and roused the Aett into defiant fury. Above it all, Leman Russ had stood, his spirit watching over them.

Do you know? Do you know, lord, what is being done here to your sons? Does your gaze penetrate to the halls of the Priests? And do you condone it?

The stone gave no answer. There was nothing but a grimace of kill-urge on those immobile features.

Then, from the far end of the hospital, a commotion. A huge warrior in coal-black plate had returned from the front. His armour was scorched and dented, the pelts ripped from it. He stormed past the rows of beds, and a gaggle of thralls struggled to keep pace with him.

Wyrmblade had returned. He was bare-headed, and his golden eyes blazed in their sunken sockets. He strode toward the elevator shafts, back to his lair in the Valgard, the place where his work was done.

Morek's eyes followed him. He didn't dare move. He didn't know whether he was looking at the guardian of all he held dear or the destroyer of it.

Suddenly, Wyrmblade seemed to sense something. He stiffened, and stopped walking. His mournful face, marked by that severe, hooked nose, swept round.

The eyes, those predator's eyes, locked on Morek. For a moment the two men were looking at one another.

Morek felt his heart hammering. He couldn't turn away.

He knows! How can he know?

Then Wyrmblade grunted, and resumed his course. His retinue swept after him.

Morek felt light-headed, and leaned against a bed. He stared around him guiltily. The hospital orderlies carried on working as if nothing had happened. No one had noticed. Why should they have done? He was just a kaerl, a mortal, an expendable.

He took a deep, shuddering breath. He was beginning to jump at shadows. Morek pushed himself away from the metal frame and resumed his patrol. There was much work to do, and he had a whole riven of kaerls to keep in line. Trying to ignore the screams and moans, he picked up the pace.

He needed to keep busy.

It was then that he found himself wishing the invaders would breach the defences and come quickly. At least they were enemies he knew how to fight.

* * *

TWENTY-FOUR DAYS AFTER Ironhelm had called the Council of War that had authorised the mission to Gangava, the Chamber of the Annulus was opened once again. It was as grim and shadowy as ever, though the torches burned a little lower in their iron grates this time, and the mood of the gathered commanders was sombre rather than anticipatory.

Only seven figures stood around the huge stone circle, heads bare but otherwise in full armour. Greyloc was there, as were Sturmhjart, Arfang and Wyrmblade. Of the Wolf Guard, Skrieya and Rossek were present. The flame-haired warrior looked half-wild still, and his mane was tangled and unkempt.

At the head of the circle, the position of honour, stood Bjorn. When he'd entered the hallowed place nearly an hour ago, he had remained unmoving for a long time, staring at the floor-mounted stone plaques in silence. None had dared disturb him while he reminisced on the past, and none had taken their place until he had recovered himself.

As the Council got underway, Greyloc looked up at the massive facade of the Dreadnought carefully. The ceramite sarcophagus was decorated with extraordinary care. Gold-plated images of wolves and snarling beasts' heads were embossed on the heavy front panels. An iron skull with crossed bones had been mounted on the long face-plate. Runes had been engraved everywhere, each of them placed in the proper position by long-dead Rune Priests and bound with complex rites of warding.

Bjorn was magnificent, more so than any living Space Wolf, and more so than most of those who had died.

Do you know how much care has been lavished on your living coffin? Do you care?

Bjorn stirred himself then, as if Greyloc's thoughts had somehow transmitted themselves to him.

So now we plan our survival. Jarl, your assessment.

'All accessible entrances to the Aett have been collapsed,' reported Greyloc. 'The explosives were a mix of melta and fragmentation devices. Some were placed to remain intact, ready to detonate when further disturbed. Allfather willing, that will slow the excavators.'

'How long have we got?' asked Skrieya.

Greyloc shook his head.

'Depends on what toys they have. A week. Perhaps less.'

A low, grinding noise came from Bjorn's innards.

Sealed in, he growled. **Not a noble way to conduct war.**

Greyloc bristled a little. He had made the choices he'd had to, faced with an invading army over twenty times the size of his defending force.

'You are right, lord,' said Greyloc. 'It is not noble. But the portents are against us. We have eighty-seven brothers of my company still capable of fighting, not counting the twelve Revered Fallen. We have a few thousand kaerls – enough to man the defences, but little more. We need a period of time to recover what strength we can. When the enemy enters the Aett again, we will have to fight continuously until completion, however long that takes.'

Bjorn grunted again. Even the smallest of his gestures produced some rumbling sound from deep within the arcane machine-body.

What strength does the enemy possess?

'Many Traitor Marines. Perhaps six hundred, although we killed several squads during the first landings and the approaches. Their mortal troops are, to all intents and purposes, inexhaustible. The armoured divisions far exceed anything we can field, though that will not avail them in the tunnels.'

And there is no communication beyond Fenris?

'None, lord,' said Sturmhjart. 'Our astropaths were killed by remote means. Local space comms are jammed, and attempts to penetrate the barrier above us have failed.'

What could do that?

Sturmhjart looked uncomfortable.

'The witches have many dark powers, lord,' he said, unconvincingly. 'Whatever the cause of it, we do not have the power to defeat it. Anything short of a full battle fleet would be annihilated by the blockade above us. We are alone.'

And the Great Wolf?

'His thoughts are concentrated on Magnus, lord,' said Wyrmblade. 'If it occurs to him to make contact, it will not be beyond the powers of our enemy to make it seem as if all is well here. They drew him away by design, and would not have neglected to consider all the ways of keeping him away.'

At that, Bjorn sank into thought. The Chamber fell silent, save for the distant, muffled sounds of clanging from far below. In the Jarlheim, preparations for invasion continued unabated.

All eyes remained fixed on the Dreadnought. The veneration he was held in remained absolute, and none would speak until he did.

They will make for the reactors, Bjorn said at last. **The greater number of troops must be stationed at Borek's Seal.**

'And what of the Hould?' asked Wyrmblade.

It cannot be defended. Too many tunnels. The Jarlheim must be held from the Fangthane.

'That means dividing our forces,' said Greyloc.

Indeed. But we can cede neither objective. If the reactors are taken, then the Aett will be destroyed. If the Fangthane is breached, then no other part of the upper citadel can be defended. They are the two choke-points, the two places where a small army can stand against a larger one.

'There are other considerations, lord,' said Sturmhjart. 'There are wards across this place. The mightiest were at the gates, but they are gone. For as long as even the lesser runes are defended, the power of the sorcerers within the mountain will be limited. If the sacred places are defiled, then their power will wax.'

You need not instruct me on their power, said Bjorn, and there was a sudden note of fervour in his rumbling voice. His claw twitched as if in memory of some ancient pain. **The wards will be protected where we can. But there must be sacrifices. If we attempt to salvage everything, we will lose everything.**

'It will be as you command,' said Greyloc, bowing his head. 'We will make the bulwarks into killing-grounds. But there will be resistance at the places where they must emerge. I would not have their first steps inside the Aett to be blood-free.'

Bjorn gave a cumbersome nod of approval.

Then we are agreed. I will stand at Borek's Seal with my Fallen brothers. Combat will come there the swiftest, and it has been too long since I felt the kill-urge in anything other than dreams.

The Dreadnought inclined his massive profile to gaze at the central device on the Annulus, the rearing wolf amid a field of stars.

I was on Prospero, brothers, he said. **I was there when we burned their heresy from the galaxy. I saw Leman Russ lay waste to their cherished places. I saw Traitors weep from corrupted eyes as we turned their pyramids of glass into barren wasteland.**

The council listened intently. Bjorn's fragmentary accounts of distant days were seized on whenever he chose to offer them.

That will not happen here. They were made weak by the knowledge of their treachery. We are made strong by the knowledge of our fidelity. Where Tizca fell, the Aett will stand.

The Dreadnought's voice was growing stronger. As the days passed, he was remembering himself, becoming once more the god of war the skjalds spoke of in their hushed voices. Amid all the desperation, that was cause for hope.

Though it may cost the lives of us all, Bjorn growled, the words made machine-harsh by the vox-generators within him, **the Aett *will* stand.**

AFTER THE COUNCIL had ended, Rossek watched Bjorn clump down the corridor outside the Annulus with Greyloc and the other senior commanders in tow. He hung back, staying in the shadows, eager to avoid contact. He hadn't spoken during the deliberations. Indeed, he'd barely shared two words with Greyloc since the withdrawal from the landing sites. Several times he'd tried to approach his old friend, but the Jarl had avoided anything other than routine exchanges.

Perhaps that was for the best. Rossek didn't even know what he'd say if he had the chance.

That he was sorry? Apologies were not for the Wolf Guard.

That he saw the faces of the warriors he'd killed every night in his tortured dreams? That was true, but would change nothing.

Contrition did not come easily to a son of Russ. For a few blessed moments, while Rossek had had the blood of enemies flowing across his claws, he'd shaken off the cloud of torpor and remembered his savage inheritance. He'd willed the assault on the gates to last for much, much longer. For as long as he fought, the guilt was less acute.

But it always came back.

'Wolf Guard Rossek.'

The voice was iron-dry and sardonic. Rossek knew who it was without having to turn. Wyrmblade must have stayed behind, waiting for the rest to leave.

'Lord Hraldir,' acknowledged Rossek. His voice sounded surly, even to him.

Wyrmblade emerged from the gloom of the Chamber's apse and into a pool of firelight. His black armour was perfect for blending into the shadows of the sparsely-lit places. The bone devices across his battle-plate were chipped and scarred by plasma-burns, and the ragged pelts he'd once draped over the ceramite had been ripped away. His golden eyes still glowed as they ever had done, locked within that desiccated old face like amber jewels beaten into leather.

'You are not yourself, Tromm,' said the Wolf Priest, his mouth breaking into a crooked, mirthless smile.

Rossek towered over Wyrmblade in his Terminator plate, but somehow still seemed the lesser figure of the two. That was always the way. The Wolf Priests had a grip of authority over the entire Chapter, one that transcended the normal patterns of command.

'I long for combat,' replied Rossek, which was truthful enough.

'So do we all,' said Wyrmblade. 'There isn't a Blood Claw in the Aett who doesn't. What makes your mood special, Wolf Guard?'

Rossek narrowed his eyes. Was the old man goading him? Trying to provoke some kind of furious response?

'I claim no special privilege. Just a desire to do what I was bred for.'

Wyrmblade nodded.

'So it has ever been with you. I remember when I brought you off the ice. You were a monster back then, a bear of a man. We marked you for greatness from the beginning.'

Rossek listened wearily. He wasn't in the mood for a prepared homily. Any reference to his potential, to his destiny within the Chapter, had become loathsome to hear. He'd coveted the Wolf Lord position for years, however much he'd tried not to, and had always resented Greyloc's elevation at his expense, but now the proof of his inadequacy had been painfully exposed.

'Well, perhaps you were wrong,' he said, casually.

Wyrmblade shot him a look of contempt.

'Do I hear self-pity? That's for mortals. Whatever guilt you're carrying with you, shed it. You cannot bring your brothers back, but you can remember how to fight.'

Rossek started to reply, so missed the uppercut.

Sharp as a jaw-snap, Wyrmblade had let fly with his left fist, connecting cleanly and sending the Wolf Guard crashing to the floor. An instant later and the Wolf Priest had him pinned, his gauntlet fixed on the exposed flesh of Rossek's neck, his curved fangs bared.

'I wanted to have you disciplined for what you did,' hissed Wyrmblade, his face only centimetres from Rossek's. 'Greyloc prevented it. He said your blades would be needed. Blood of Russ, you'd better prove him right about that.'

By instinct, Rossek primed himself to throw the Priest off. He was capable of doing it. His armour was more than twice as powerful as Wyrmblade's, and the Wolf Priest was old.

Even so, he couldn't do it. The sacred power of the Priesthood was too strong. Wyrmblade's face had been the first one he'd seen on entering the Aett as a daunted aspirant. It was likely to be the last face he saw before leaving for the Halls of Morkai, too.

'So what do you want, lord?' Rossek growled, tasting his own blood in his mouth. 'For me to fight you? You would not like the result.'

Wyrmblade shook his ragged head in disgust, and released his grip. He hauled himself to his feet, leaving Rossek slumped against the wall.

'I wanted to kindle some *spirit* in you, lad,' he muttered. 'To remind you of the fire you've had in your blood since you first came here. Maybe I'm too late for that. Maybe you have let failure quench it.'

Rossek clambered to his feet, feeling the stressed servos in his battered suit whine.

'This melancholy makes you useless to us,' said Wyrmblade. 'You think you're the first Wolf Guard to lead a squad to defeat?'

'I am coming to terms with that.'

'I see no sign of it.'

'Then maybe you should look harder.'

'At what?'

'At the warriors I saved,' snarled Rossek, feeling anger surge up at last. 'At the Blood Claws I pulled from under the hammer when Brakk was felled. At the Traitors I killed then and after. At the whelp who was taken by the Wolf, who I brought back from the edge.'

Wyrmblade hesitated, and looked at him carefully.

'You did that? Without a Priest?'

'I did. And now, with Brakk gone, I will lead the remains of his pack. They need guidance.' The haunted look returned to his eyes briefly. 'From one who has learned a lesson in command.'

Wyrmblade still watched Rossek's face intently.

'Do so, then,' he said at last, and his voice had lost its edge of condemnation. 'But snap out of this melancholy. At the end of all this, I would have Greyloc's verdict on you proved right.'

Rossek grunted, eager to push past the Wolf Priest and end the lesson. The practice cages beckoned, and he had frustrations to work out in them.

'One final thing,' said Wyrmblade, clamping a gauntlet on Rossek's breastplate to prevent him walking away. 'The Hunter who lies in my chambers. Aunir Frar. He will live.'

Despite himself, Rossek felt relief flood through his body at that, and had to struggle not to show it. 'Thank you for telling me.'

'But you did not bring him to the fleshmakers.'

Rossek shook his head. 'A rivenmaster brought him.'

'So I gather. What was his name?'

Rossek recalled it instantly. The mortal in the Fangthane, the one with the honest, tired face.

'Morek. Morek Karekborn. Why do you wish to know?'

Wyrmblade looked evasive then.

'For completeness,' said the Wolf Priest, letting his hand fall to allow Rossek to pass. 'It's nothing important. Go now. Remember my words. The Hand of Russ be with you, Tromm.'

'And with us all,' replied Rossek, before lumbering off into the dark, back into the Jarlheim, back to where the Wolves were preparing for war.

THE BEASTS PROWLED in the recessed darkness of Borek's Seal, hugging the pools of obscurity behind the vast pillars. They went silently, slinking on huge pads and keeping their distorted muzzles low to the ground. Only when they wished to announce their presence did they break cover, with a sudden flash of wide, liquid eyes, or a deep, rumbling growl from within those massive ribcages.

It was impossible to know how many had gathered

there. At times it seemed like only a few dozen had emerged from the Underfang; at others, like there were hundreds. Something had attracted them to the living sections of the Aett, and whatever it was, it continued to work its magic. Since Bjorn himself had emerged from the Hammerhold with the retinue of snarling horrors in tow, none could deny that they had some kind of bizarre claim to be there. But that didn't mean that the kaerls liked seeing them, nor that they didn't make the sign of the spear whenever they were forced to go anywhere near them.

So the mortal troops stayed far away at the fire-lit end of the cavernous chamber as much as possible. The stairways and elevator shafts leading both up and down were all placed at the western extremity of that space, and so the defences were built there, lit by roaring blazes. As at the Fangthane, gun-lines had been drawn up and barricades erected across the access points. More ammunition, building supplies and armour were delivered with every passing hour, some freshly forged in the angry red depths of the Hammerhold and still hot to the touch.

Freija did her part in the carrying and lifting, though she spent most of her time with Aldr. Like most of the Dreadnoughts, he'd been stationed at Borek's Seal and now waited grumpily for action. When the enemy came, his guns would be at the forefront, thrust into the inferno again with those of his battle-brothers.

The Dreadnought had become steadily less strange as the memory of his incarceration faded. The maudlin expressions of discomfort and loss had been replaced by a more reassuring resolve. Freija could tell he was looking forward to the combat. To be awakened from the Long Dark only to face days of preparation and waiting was difficult for him – he'd have preferred to have walked out of the vault straight into a firestorm. Instead, he'd had to wait patiently as servitor-thralls had fussed over him, conducting impenetrable rites and preparing his adamantium sarcophagus for war.

'So what's it like?' Freija asked him, chewing on a tough ribbon of dried meat during a rest period.

What's what like?

'Having your armour fussed over,' she said. 'Can you feel a touch on it, like skin?'

Freija could sense when she'd irritated him. She didn't know how – there were no facial cues, after all – but the impression was definite enough.

This curiosity. This lack of respect. Where does it come from?

Freija grinned at the Dreadnought's annoyance. She felt no aura of intimidation from Aldr. Despite his vast killing potential, far in excess of even the Jarl, his moods were strangely immature, and she'd become intrigued by him in a way that she could never have done with a living Blood Claw.

'My mother. She came from the ice, and passed on its crude ways.'

As she spoke, Freija recalled her face. Heavy-set like hers, blonde hair in messy curls, a tight mouth that rarely smiled, features made harsh by unremitting labour and hardship. But the eyes, the dark, sparkling eyes – they had exposed the bright intellect within, the questioning, rebellious soul that had never quite been ground down. Even at the end, when the punishing

311

demands of the Sky Warriors had exacerbated the ill-
ness that would kill her, those eyes had remained alive
and inquiring.

You should learn to control it.

'I know,' she said wearily. 'It leads to damnation.'

Indeed it does.

Freija shook her head resignedly, and fell silent.
The Wolves' obsession with ritual, tradition, saga and
secrecy was something she'd never understand. It was
as if the world they inhabited was frozen in some half-
forgotten moment, when all the forces of progress and
enlightenment had suddenly been snuffed out and
replaced by a numb rehearsal of old, tired routines.

After a while, Aldr shifted heavily on his central
drive-column.

**It feels like being alive, and yet not alive. When
something touches my armour, I sense it more
closely than I could when a living warrior. My eyesight is sharper, my hearing more acute, my muscles
more powerful for being plasfibre and ceramite.
Everything is more immediate. And yet...**

Freija looked at the Dreadnought's face-plate. The
slit in the armour was dark, an opaque well into the
ruined corpse within. Though there were no visual signals, no possibility of facial expression, she could feel
his misery as acutely as if he'd been weeping. For an
instant, she caught the image of a Blood Claw racing
across the wind-blasted ice, his blades whirling, long
hair streaming, caught up in the feral joy of his calling.

It will never be like that again.

'I'm sorr–'

Enough questions. There is work to be done.

Freija dutifully shut up. Already she could see a new delivery of medical supplies and field-rations arriving on the back of a transport, all of which would need to be stowed somewhere. She bowed to the Dreadnought and made her way toward the huskaerl in charge of the consignment. As she did so, she stole a look back at the hulking shape of Aldr, motionless in the shadows.

She didn't look long. She felt like she'd violated his privacy enough. In any case, she didn't like the emotions their conversations were engendering in her. For years, stung by what had happened to her blood-family under the harsh regime of the Aett, she had resented the Sky Warriors almost as much as she had been awed by them. Now that war had come to Fenris, those old feelings were being tested, and in ways that she found surprising.

She had learned to live with disliking them. She could, perhaps, have learned to live with loving them, as Morek did, or even despising them, as did the Thousand Sons. What she couldn't resign herself to was the way she felt then. She knew she had to shake those feelings off, or they would compromise her role in the fighting to come. They were alien to her, un-Fenrisian, weak and foolish.

But it was no good. Try as she might, Freija couldn't help it.

Now I see into their souls, see what lives they lead, what choices they've made... This is what I have come to.

Blood of Russ, I pity them.

CHAPTER FIFTEEN

'Fenrys hjolda!'

Harek Ironhelm charged down the ruined street, uncaring of the small arms fire clattering off his battle-plate. His retinue came with him, a whole score of elite warriors in Terminator armour. As they thundered onwards, their huge footfalls cracked the rockcrete under them. Their pauldrons had been slathered in blood; some of it ritually applied before combat, some of it the result of the heavy killing over the past four local days. None of them had slept during that time; indeed, they'd barely paused in the slaughter. Inexorably, irresistibly, the Wolves' spearhead had crunched, sliced, shot and hammered its way into the heart of the city.

Ironhelm had fought with all the vigour of his

youth during that time, swinging his frostblade two-handed in massive, body-breaking arcs. He'd not even bothered to mag-lock a ranged weapon, preferring to keep the fighting at close range. Most of his guard went similarly, kitted out with claws, blades and axes, whooping and baying as they used the killing edges against the fragile armour of those who dared to stand against them.

'The tower,' Ironhelm snarled, nodding to his right as he tore down the roadway. Instantly, his pack adjusted trajectory. 'Incoming, high up.'

The hunting pack had broken out on to a long, straight highway overlooked by rows of towering hab-blocks. Once there had been mass-transit rails running down the central reservation and elevated walkways criss-crossing the road below. Now, thanks to heavy aerial bombardment, the entire street had been turned into a smouldering valley of tortured metal struts and melted plascrete craters. Rolling clouds of smoke obscured everything, acrid and tart from heavy bolter-round discharge. The precipitous walls on either side of the burning chasm were eyeless, the windows having been smashed even before the current assault had properly launched. Huge swathes of the city were like this now, a wasteland of broken hopes and balustrades, all after just four days' intense, brutal activity by the Wolves.

The highway ran straight towards the central pyramid cluster. The huge multi-laned arterial conduit had once reverberated with civilian transports and semi-grav flyers, though now only echoed to the crackle of flames and the distant rumble of tank tracks. The

Wolves tore across the broken terrain like molten metal, swaying fluidly around obstacles, disdaining cover and relying on speed and agility to evade incoming fire.

Ahead of them, on the right-hand side of the highway, a single blunt-faced tower was still occupied by defenders. As the pack neared it, heavy projectile rounds slammed into the rockcrete around them, tearing up what remained of the road surface and ripping it to spinning shreds. There were deeper explosions amongst the barking chatter of the man-mounted cannons – artillery pieces were clearly lodged there, all aimed at the fleeting wolf shapes tearing towards the tower.

The rate of fire was high. Too high. They were squeezing their triggers in a panic, terrified of what the Wolves would do when they reached them.

You are right to be terrified, traitors. And we are thankful for it – your fear draws us to you quickly.

'Time to silence those guns,' growled Ironhelm, loping fast toward the tower's base. Acting purely on instinct, he bounded to one side. A second later, the ground he'd been occupying disappeared in a blast of cordite and promethium. 'Level Six.'

The Wolves sped up to the base without hesitating, all at full speed. The entrance level must once have been grand, clad in glass and steel and adorned with the Eye emblem that had been daubed all across Gangava Prime. Now it was just a shell, a gaping hole laced with broken panes and charred plascrete pillars.

The Wolves broke inside, racing around piles of rubble and still-burning heaps of refuse. Ironhelm remained at the blade-tip, crashing his way toward the elevator shafts clustered at the centre of the structure.

'Can we use these?' he barked over the mission channel.

A Wolf Guard named Rangr snapped open a remote auspex, took a look at it and shook his head.

'Rigged to blow.'

'Then take them out,' commanded Ironhelm, gesturing to Brother Aesgrek, who carried a heavy bolter in his gigantic armoured fists.

The mammoth weapon thundered out, spraying shells into the waiting elevator cages. They exploded in a hail of crashing, tumbling beams and plates. Aesgrek destroyed them all, sending six cages plummeting down the shafts and into oblivion below. By the time he was finished, the rectangular wells gaped like wounds, black and naked.

Without waiting for the flames to die away, Ironhelm ran and launched himself across the nearest shaft, clutching the metalwork on the far side of it and clinging on. The steel beams bowed under his weight and began to peel away from the plascrete walls, but he was already moving, clambering up the levels like a giant armoured insect.

The rest of the pack did likewise, throwing themselves into the gaping pits, latching on to other parts of the steel struts and braces, using all the remaining five shafts to distribute the weight better across the damaged structure. Like sewer rats, the Wolves raced up the elevator columns, clamping their gauntlets unerringly to the metal handholds, powering up the sheer paths with contemptuous ease.

As they rose, gunfire began to strafe down from above. The defenders, realising the destruction of the elevator cages had done nothing to slow the closing assault, were belatedly trying to prevent the pack from reaching their position.

Ironhelm laughed rakishly as the first las-beams hit his armoured shoulders.

'This is warming my arms!' he cackled, hauling himself over a protruding ledge and thrusting ever higher.

'Multiple signals approaching,' voxed Rangr, betraying urgent kill-urge in his voice. 'Next level is Six.'

The Wolf Guard's eagerness infected the entire squad, and they tore upwards even faster, gouging huge rents in the walls of the shaft in their determination to reach the murder-ground first.

For all his age, for all his ancient war-tempering, the Great Wolf got there in front, hurling himself over the lip of the floor platform and crashing through the outer doors of the elevator shaft. The ruined panels were shouldered aside, and he waded straight into a torrent of las-fire. The beams cracked against his armour and burned off harmlessly. A whole level of the tower beckoned, open-plan, stripped of civilian trappings and with nowhere to hide.

'Feel the wrath of the Wolves, traitors!' Ironhelm bellowed, spittle flying against his vox-grille, plunging straight into the ranks of horrified troopers beyond the broken doors. The booming echo of his challenge shattered what was left of the glass in the windows around the edges of the tower-level. More Wolves emerged from the shafts and charged into the contact zone, smoothly withdrawing power weapons from where they'd been mag-locked and gunning them into life.

The fight was short, brutal, terrifying. There were a few hundred mortal troopers deployed on the level, many with heavy weapons. Some were refugees from earlier fighting who'd survived and fallen back; others were fresh troops from the centre with gleaming armour and fresh lasguns. There were emplacements among them, including the artillery pieces the Gangavans had been using to snipe at the hunting packs' approach. They were busy turning them inwards in an attempt to halt the advance of the horrors coming to kill them.

It did them no good. As Ironhelm crashed in among them, his blade whistling, he began to laugh again. Still amplified by the vox-units in his armour, the horrific sound echoed around the entire level. Rangr joined in, chuckling in a strange, chilling fashion as he mowed down whole swathes of wavering enemy soldiers.

'Face me, filth!' roared Ironhelm, ripping a man open with the backswing of his blade even as his free hand punched the chest in of another. 'Fight like the men you once were!'

At the far side of the level, open to the elements where the shattered windows had once been, an auto-cannon crew were trying to swing their weapon round to target the rampaging Wolves. Ironhelm caught sight of that, and roared with pleasure.

'Well done, lads!' he bellowed, hurling the broken-backed corpse of a Gangavan defender into a pillar and lurching towards the gun-crew. 'Now try to get a shot!'

The frantic troopers almost did it. The heavy barrel

swung round on its cumbersome pintle-mount, swaying into range and spooling up to fire. The ammo belt was sucked into the slot and the safety indicator blinked off. With an agonised look on his face, the gunner pulled the trigger, wincing as the gigantic form of the Wolf Lord thundered into swing range.

As fast as death on the ice, Ironhelm hammered into them, ripping the autocannon barrel from its mount one-handed. He swung it round like a club, knocking three of the crew clean through the empty window-frames. Even before their trailing screams had died away, he'd cut open the rest of them with the frostblade. Then, with a savage kick, he sent the autocannon mount plunging into the chasm of the highway below.

'*Hjolda!*' he roared, throwing his arms into the air, frostblade in one fist, autocannon barrel in the other.

From that high vantage, right on the edge of the tower, Ironhelm could see out across the city. In every direction, fires were burning out of control. He saw other towers reel on their foundations, stricken with explosions. The sky was tattooed with the contrails of his gunships. The boom of ordnance made the ground drum, punctuated by the unmistakeable growl of advancing Land Raiders.

The city was being destroyed, block by block, district by district. No matter how many troops were thrown into the meat-grinder, the end was coming swiftly now.

He glanced at the mission schematic overlay on his helm display. Objectives were being captured in every theatre. Like a giant pair of claws, the Wolves were closing in on the principal targets. The void shield generators would be down before dawn, and the power stations wouldn't be far behind.

His brothers had excelled themselves. Never had their perfection in war been quite so brazenly on display. Ironhelm grinned, feeling his curved fangs scrape the inside of his helm.

It was then that the curtains of smog and fuel-smoke cleared to the west, exposing the vast, hunched outlines of the pyramids on the horizon. They were much closer now, dark and massive, ringed by the heaviest defences left in the city.

'They won't help you,' growled Ironhelm, lowering his frostblade in the direction he knew he must travel. 'Nothing can help you now, faithless ones. You have played fire with the Wolves of Fenris.'

His lupine grin returned. Kill-pleasure surged through his body.

'And now they are biting at your heels.'

THE CATAPHRACTS WERE awesome machines, fusions of cybernetic technology and weapons research from a more capable age. The huge figures, vaguely humanoid but far broader and heavier, worked tirelessly, hacking and drilling at the rockface of the tunnels, hammering away with their enormous drill-arms without pause or complaint. Their heavy segmented legs braced against the recoil, shrugging off the storm of emerging rock-fragments and wading through the piles of rubble created. In their wake came hundreds of Prosperine engineers, hauling away the broken stone, shoring up the tunnel roof, adding bracing pillars and knocking the jagged stone walls smooth. The work progressed like everything else did in the Thousand Sons fleet – calmly, efficiently, expertly.

It wasn't fast enough. Aphael found himself increasingly unable to control his frustration at the pace of excavation. Already days had passed, days he could not afford to lose. The tunnels had not just been filled with loose rockfall, but had been cemented closed with melta blasts. At times the residue was as hard to dig out as the living rock would have been. The crust of Fenris, as might have been expected, was as unyielding as iron. To make matters worse, the Dogs had placed mines and unexploded fragmentation bombs within the fused stone, and several priceless Cataphracts had been lost as their drill-arms had set off the residual traps.

The delays infuriated him. Aphael knew that Temekh was drawing closer to his goal. If the Fang was not compromised and its wards of aversion destroyed by the time he did so, then Aphael's position as commander of the army would be under threat. All of them, the sorcerers in charge of the invasion fleet, knew the stakes.

From his position inside the tunnel, Aphael watched as a trio of Cataphracts carved their way further into the heart of the mountain. Glowglobes hovered around them, bathing the robots in a dull orange light. The roof of the tunnel was barely above their massive shoulders as they worked. They were already knee-deep in broken stone, and the scurrying lines of mortal workers struggled to keep up with the task of removing it.

Aphael's neck began to itch again. The sensation was maddening, as if tiny clawed hands had lodged themselves under his skin and were scraping to get out. When he turned his head, he could feel the fingers and spurs of the feathers rustle against the inside of his armour. Something else had been growing on his face for some time, pressing against the plate of his helm. Soon, he knew, the cracks would begin to show. Already his right gauntlet wouldn't close.

Aphael turned away from the rockface and stalked back the way he'd come, past the waiting rows of haulage transports, their hopper doors open and load-cranes extended. As he went, the men in the tunnels were quick to get out of his way. They'd grown wary of his erratic moods since the assault had ground into the sand.

He ignored them. As he got nearer the tunnel exit, the marks of excavation gave way to a rough roadway and permanent lighting. The tunnel roof and walls had been carved wide enough to allow Rhinos and Land Raiders to enter, which was one of the reasons hollowing it out had taken so long. Light armaments were already being shipped into the enclosed space. As the Cataphracts drew closer to their goal, they would be augmented with heavier weaponry. By the time the final walls were breached, whole companies of Rubricae would be waiting to pile in.

Aphael reached the tunnel entrance and stepped into the bright, harsh light of the Fenris morning. His eyes seemed to have lost their usual photo-reactive speed, and for a moment he was half-blinded by the glare. Fresh snowfalls had covered over much of the devastation, but the causeways were still jammed with men and materiel. Plumes of smoke were everywhere, either from labouring vehicle engines or from fires lit by the troops to banish the worst of the chill.

A Prosperine captain hurried up to him. The man's face was hidden behind his environment mask, but Aphael could already sense his fear. This would not be good news.

'Lord,' the man said, bowing clumsily.

'Make it quick,' snapped Aphael, wishing he could scratch his flesh for just a moment.

'Captain Eirreq has voxed from the flagship.'

'If the Lord Temekh wishes to speak to me, then he can do so himself.'

'It's not that.' The man swallowed. 'Lord Fuerza. His life-signature has departed from the aether.'

Aphael felt his primary heart jump a beat.

'Out of range?'

'I do not believe so, lord. I was told to inform you that, as far as the scryers can ascertain, he is dead.'

Aphael felt the dam of his pent-up fury break then. The frustration, the irritation, the fear of what he was becoming, all came to a head. Without thinking, he grabbed the warrior by his chestplate, holding him aloft in one hand.

'Dead!' he roared, uncaring who heard him. At the edge of his vision, he could see soldiers putting down their weapons and staring. 'Dead!'

Let them stare.

'Lord!' cried the captain, struggling ineffectively against the power-armoured grip. 'I–'

He never had the chance to finish. Aphael swung

round, hurling the fragile body against the near wall of the tunnel entrance. It impacted with a thick, sickening thud, and slid down into the slush. Once there, it didn't move again.

Aphael whirled round to face the rest of his men. There were hundreds of them close by, all staring at him. For a moment, a single, terrible moment, Aphael felt like launching into them too. His gauntlets crackled with the first sparks of his sorcerous fire, the deadly trade of the Pyrae.

Slowly, with difficulty, he reined himself in.

What is happening to me?

He knew the answer. Every sorcerer in the Legion was schooled to know the answer to that. In time, the Changer of Ways always extracted the price for the gifts he bestowed, and even the Rubric was no guarantee of escaping it.

I am being turned into the thing that I hate.

'Get back to work!' he bellowed at the men.

They hurried to comply. None of them made any move towards the prone body of the captain. Perhaps they would later, when Aphael was gone, moving furtively and in fear of what the Masters would do to them.

Aphael looked up. Far, far into the hazy distance, the pinnacle of the Fang soared into the icy air. Even after being blackened by days of bombardment, it was still magnificent. It rose defiant, as immovable and gigantic as the Obsidian Tower on the Planet of the Sorcerers. For the first time, Aphael noticed the similarities in the structures. It was just one more mockery.

'I *will* break it,' he muttered, uncaring that he spoke

out loud. His left hand clenched into a fist, and he hammered it against his helm. The pain of the impact helped to dull the incessant itching.

So he did it again. And again.

It was only when he felt the warm trickle of blood down his neck that he stopped. The sensation was strangely calming, as if the crude medicines of the old leeches had been applied, relieving the pressure within his tortured body.

The respite was fleeting. Even as he turned away from the mountain, ready to walk back to the command platform above the causeway, he could feel the burning start to return. It would never leave him alone. It would plague him, torment him and goad him until it got what it wanted.

'I *will* break it,' he mumbled again, hanging on to the thought as he limped away from the Fang.

As he passed from the front, the mortal soldiers looked at one another, startled. Then, slowly, they returned to their duties, readying the army for the assault to come, trying not to think too hard about the behaviour of the warrior they had been taught to revere as a god.

CHAPTER SIXTEEN

THE PYRAMID REARED, vast and dark, into the fire-torn sky. Its flanks were dull, caked in the red dust that covered all of Gangava. Huge holes had been punched in its sides by heavy weapons, and the edges of the rents were still licked with flame.

What resistance there was had been swept aside by the Wolves, wiped out with sharp-edged disdain. The entire city was burning, and those few defenders who had not perished in the assault now faced a lingering death by fire. The scale of the violence was overwhelming. There had been no respite, no quarter, no mercy. Another Chapter, the Salamanders perhaps, might have made some provision for civilian evacuation, or paused in the attack to assess the possibility of asset recovery for the greater good of the Imperium.

Not the Wolves of Fenris. The task had been set before them, and they had brought it to completion. Gangava was destroyed, rendered down to ash and molten iron. Nothing was left to preserve, nothing to remember. The city had been scoured from the face of the galaxy as completely as Prospero had been.

Almost.

The pyramids still remained, insolently defiant, still free of the horrifying presence of the *Vlka Fenryka*. Ironhelm had insisted on that. No battle-brother would assault the central bastions until the ruin of the city had been compassed.

I want you to see the failure of your dreams, Traitor, before I come for you. I want to hear you weep, just as you wept before.

Now the time had come. The spearhead had assembled in a huge courtyard before the main pyramid, out in the open, careless of the lack of cover, bristling with desire to go for the throat. Fully three hundred battle-brothers were there: all of Harek Ironhelm's Great Company, other packs who'd arrived at the muster ahead of their brothers, plus the twelve Rune Priests who'd accompanied the forward assault squads. The wyrd-masters stood with Ironhelm's command brotherhood, their glyph-inscribed armour blazing arterial red.

Ironhelm turned to Frei, the one who'd brought them to Gangava in the first place.

'There is no doubt?' he asked a final time.

By way of answer, the Rune Priest drew a bag of bone-fragments from a capsule at his belt. The pieces looked insignificantly small as he tipped the contents into the palm of his gauntlet. Reverently, he cast them on the ground, and they clattered against the broken stone.

For a moment, Frei said nothing, gazing at the patterns on the bones. Each piece was inscribed with a single rune. Trysk, Gmorl, Adjarr, Ragnarok, Ymir. The sigils had an individual meaning – Ice, Fate, Blood, Ending – as well as a collective one. For a master of scrying the mysterious power of Fenris, they could reveal hidden facets of the present, or secrets of the past, or portents of the future. In their presence, all brutal laughter was silenced, all weapons lowered. The Wolves venerated the runes, just as their gene-father had done.

It was long before Frei spoke. When he did, his voice was hoarse from days of shouted orders and storm-summoning.

'The runes tell me he is in there,' Frei said. 'His spoor reeks, trapped in the heart of the pyramid. But there is something else.'

Ironhelm waited patiently. All around him, his battle-brothers did the same.

'I see another presence. The Bane of the Wolves.'

Ironhelm snorted.

'That's what he's calling himself. This we already know.'

Frei shook his head.

'No, lord. That is not his name. It is another power, locked in the walls with him. If we enter, we will face it.'

'And that troubles you, priest? You think any power in the galaxy can face our fury? Even a primarch cannot stand against our combined blades.'

Frei stooped to collect the bone fragments. As his fingers reached for the oldest device – Fengr, the Wolf Within – the piece broke cleanly, separating into two down the middle.

Frei froze for a second, staring at the broken rune. Ironhelm could sense his shock. He hadn't touched the bone fragment – it had just shattered.

From the pyramid ahead of them, a faint boom like distant rolling thunder rocked the ground. The sky above them shuddered, and the flames around them guttered.

Then the moment passed. Ironhelm shook his head, shaking off the flicker of dread that had briefly latched on to his soul. Uncertainty was replaced by anger.

Still you taunt me. Even now, you cannot resist the cheap trick.

'Arvek,' he voxed. 'Are the voids down?'

'They are, lord,' came the rolling voice of Kjarlskar over the comm. 'The fleet has a firing solution and awaits your orders.'

Ironhelm looked up at the pyramid before him. Its very vastness was like an invitation. It could be atomised from orbit whenever he chose.

The retinue around him waited for his response. He sensed their eagerness. Like hounds straining at the leash, their kill-urge tugged at them. From all over the city, more Wolves were arriving every moment, their claws dripping with the blood of recent slaying, ready to make the push to completion.

'Lord...' came the voice of Frei, oddly shaken.

Ironhelm gestured for him to remain silent.

'This is the moment the wyrd turns, brothers,' he announced, speaking softly but firmly over the mission channel. 'This is what we came to do. There will be no bombardment from orbit. We will enter the den of the Traitor, and kill him as we look into his eye.'

He unlocked his frostblade and thumbed the power weapon into activation.

'That is the way of us. We keep the danger close. Take up your weapons, and stay hard on my heels.'

THE FIRES HAD reached the service levels below the command bridge of the *Nauro*. They now raged out of control across eighty per cent of the ship, and had long since made the task of salvaging her impossible. Georyth had given up trying to fight the blaze conventionally and had resorted to constructing two-metre-thick firebreaks at the major intersections, surrendering huge areas of the warship to immolation.

Now those bulwarks had failed. The temperature on the habitable levels had reached the upper limits of survivability, even in the environment suits that all the remaining crew now wore. The ship was in the final stages of collapse, its engines ready to explode, its Geller field near cracking, its void shields unable to activate.

We did well to get this far. Russ's teeth, just a little further.

Blackwing sat on the command throne, overlooking the bustling bridge below impassively. All the survivors, two hundred or so, milled about on the platforms and gantries, getting in each others' way and gumming up the necessary business of running the ship's few remaining functions.

They had nowhere else to go. Barely three hundred metres down, the corridors were red-hot from the fires and the air was unbreathable. Only the bridge and some other ancillary chambers remained, pockets of habitation amid a hurtling mountain of burning space junk. How long those pockets would remain intact was hard to predict. Minutes, certainly. Hours, hopefully.

'In range yet, Navigator?' Blackwing asked over the comm.

Neiman was a dead man. His observatory cell was cut off, separated from the command bridge by corridors of slowly melting metal. He'd had the chance to withdraw to safety but had chosen not to take it. That action alone had given the *Nauro* her best chance of reaching its destination, since the Navigator could only make the difficult transition to realspace accurately from within his sanctum.

'The more you keep asking, lord,' he replied irritably, 'the longer it will take to make the calculations.'

For someone doomed to an agonising death under the flames, Neiman sounded remarkably phlegmatic. Blackwing had noticed this trait in Navigators before. Something in their mutant genetic makeup seemed to invoke a kind of fatalism. Perhaps they saw things in the warp, things that made them somehow less concerned about their own particular fate. Or maybe they were just cold fish.

'We don't have long, Djulian,' Blackwing replied, watching on the auspex read-out as another bulkhead failed. He used the Navigator's first name as a courtesy, which seemed the least he could do. 'Give me an estimate.'

'An hour, perhaps. Less, if you let me get on with things.'

'Thank you. Report as soon as you can.'

Blackwing shut off the comm-link. There was a commotion ahead of him. One of the realspace viewers over the command bridge, a huge dome of plexiglass a metre thick and several wide, was cracking. The line of stress snaked its way from the adamantium frame, breaking into rivulets at it reached the centre of the curve.

There were no void shields active. When the physical hull went, the whole bridge would be open to space.

Blackwing stood up.

'That's enough,' he announced over the ship's open channel. 'We've done all we can. To the saviour pods. Now.'

Some of the crew looked up at him, hope suddenly kindling on their faces. Others, the kaerls mostly, looked appalled.

'We have not yet translated, lord,' came Georyth's voice.

The Master was standing on the stairway immediately below Blackwing, slumped with fatigue. His voice was thick and slow, betraying the liberal use of stimms to keep him on his feet.

Blackwing had to smile. Georyth had been a pain in the arse – a pernickety, officious pain in the arse – but he'd also been a fine Master and had earned himself a place in any sagas that came out of this sorry episode.

'I had noticed that, Master,' said Blackwing. 'Our trajectory is fixed, and only Neiman can pull us out of the warp. As soon as the Geller field's down, I've triggered the saviour pods to eject. Much as I find each and every one of you personally objectionable, it seems a waste to let them go empty.'

Georyth swallowed.

'And you, lord?'

Blackwing picked up a helm from the floor beside him. He was in Scout-pattern void-armour, the last suit he'd managed to salvage from the ship's armoury before the fires had engulfed it. An extension of his usual carapace plate, it did little more than keep the vacuum out and the temperature at survivable levels. Not for the first time on this mission, he missed his old Hunter plate.

'Your concern is touching,' he said, clamping the helm in place and feeling the seals hiss closed. 'Patronise me with it again and I'll shoot your pod down myself.'

Georyth nodded, responding to the sarcasm with a weary resignation. He'd learned how to cope with it over the past seventeen days.

Seventeen days. Four fewer than the estimate. Blood of Russ, I love this ship. When she's gone, I shall weep for her.

'Very well, lord,' said Georyth, clenching his fist against his breastplate in the Fenrisian style and making to leave. 'The hand of Russ ward you.'

'That would be nice,' agreed Blackwing.

Already, the mortals were streaming down from their stations and making for the service corridors leading to the saviour pod bays. The bridge emptied quickly.

All the crew knew how precarious the situation was, and getting out of the path of the breaking realspace viewer was simply good sense.

With their departure, the bridge looked huge. Huge and fragile. The cracks in the viewers continued to grow. They looked out on to nothing but blackness, but it wasn't the dark of the void. If the chromo filters were removed from the plexiglass, the view would be of the immaterium, a mad whirl of colour and movement. No human wished to look out onto that, and so the viewers were made permanently blank while in warp-transit.

For a moment, Blackwing pondered opening them, revealing the true substance of the matter through which the doomed ship plunged. It was a tempting prospect, and one he'd never indulged before. Would he go mad, just by looking at it? Or would it leave him indifferent, just as so much else in the galaxy did?

His thoughts were interrupted by a crack far below him. Something big and heavy had given way. Despite himself, despite all his conditioning, Blackwing felt a tremor of alarm pass through him. Standing on the bridge of a ship that was literally falling to pieces as it hurtled out of the warp and into a planetary war-zone was about as insane as it got.

And once he thought about it in those terms, the situation made a whole lot more sense.

I am a son of Russ. Not a good example, to be sure, but one of his mad progeny nonetheless, and this is the kind of thing the Blood Claws dream of doing.

He strode forwards to the railing around the command platform, as if by getting closer to the prow he could ride the coming inferno better.

Something else broke then, a strut or a bracing rod, far back in the spine of the vessel. The echoes of its demise filtered through the burning corridors, prompting more muffled crashes from down below.

The *Nauro* was dying under his feet, component by component, rivet by rivet.

'Come on, Neiman,' Blackwing hissed, his pulse pumping, watching the cracks in the plexiglass above him grow. '*Come on...*'

THE LONG FANGS unleashed their cargo of destruction and the gates to the pyramid dissolved into piles of smoking slag. Huge bronze lintels crashed to the ground, brought down by toppling pillars. Images of zodiacal beasts were blasted apart, masterpieces of depiction destroyed in a few moments of concentrated fire.

The Eye was the last to go. The beaten metal, hung over the main entrance gates, took more punishment than the rest before it finally caved in, raining broken chunks on to the burning detritus below. As it broke open, a sigh seemed to pass through the air, as if some warding presence had been withdrawn. The giant pyramid shuddered, and fragments of iron and stone tumbled down its sheer sides. The mighty gates had been reduced to a gaping, jagged-edged mouth, utterly dark and forbidding.

Ironhelm didn't hesitate. He was first in, leaping over the tangled ruins at the base of the breach and barging aside metal struts the size of a Rhino's flank. The Wolf Guard came with him, crashing through the devastation in their Terminator plate, loping fast and low across the uneven terrain. In their wake came the rest of the Great Company, a whole host of gunmetal-grey warriors thirsting for combat.

'The vengeance of Russ,' hissed Ironhelm over the mission channel.

Every pore in his body oozed with kill-urge. He could feel the Wolf within uncurl again, stretching its limbs in the dark, stirred by the prospect of fresh blood. Yellow eyes opened in his mind, red-rimmed and intense.

The breach opened out into an inner hall. Its roof disappeared into the gloom above, supported by gigantic pillars of obsidian. The air was hot and dusty, thick with red motes thrown up by the explosions. Giant sigils of the Thousand Sons had been engraved into the stone, dim and half-seen in the shadows. The place was thick with the sweet smell of corruption, as if some ancient wrong had sunk into the stone and remained there, dormant and deadly.

The Wolves swept onwards, surging through the echoing hall, their armour black in the darkness and their helm lenses glowing. All carried their weapons ready, some with bolters, others with blades. There was no whooping or bellowing, just a low, murmured snarling. The Great Company had been unleashed on the pursuit, and every mind within it was focused with remorseless purpose on the task at hand. Like blood running down an axe-edge, the Wolves raced straight into the heart of the pyramid.

They were met by no enemies. The first hall led to another, even vaster, laid out in the same fashion. The

Wolves' footfalls echoed into the shadows, rebounding back from the dark.

Ironhelm felt no lessening of his vengeful fury in the eerie silence. Mortal enemies would have been an irrelevance in such a place – they would simply have delayed the encounter that he yearned for, the one that he'd yearned for ever since the dreams had started.

As he ran, he found he recognised the stonework around him. He recalled the sigils, looming out of the gloom and passing in the shadows. Their patterns had walked in his mind for decades. He had run this path before, over and over again.

I am meant to be here. This place, this kill, has been ordained for me, locked in the wyrd. I am ready for it. By the Allfather, I am ready for it.

The second hall gave way to a third, then a fourth, each one larger than the last. The sheer scale of the pyramid began to become apparent. In its sullen, shrouded majesty it was the equal at least of those glass-faced edifices destroyed in Tizca. There were no libraries here, though, no repositories of learning and scholarship. This was a poor imitation, an empty copy of that which had once existed, for the original was impossible to replicate. What was destroyed by the Wolves remained destroyed.

The packs passed through a final gateway, soaring high beyond imagining. A central chamber yawned away from them in all directions, gigantic under the apex of the pyramid. The air felt even thicker, as if something massive pressed down heavily on it. Great braziers, each the size of Imperial Guard Sentinel walkers, sent sapphire light bleeding across the marble floor. Banners, hundreds of metres long, hung heavily from chains suspended in the distant roof, all inscribed with dimly-lit devices.

They were company emblems. Ironhelm didn't look at them. He had no wish to be reminded of what the Thousand Sons had once been.

In the centre of the chamber was a raised platform reached by steep stairways extending in four directions. It was the pyramid in miniature, crowned by a flat space little more than a hundred metres across.

On the platform was an altar.

Before the altar stood a man.

Ironhelm increased his pace as he saw his target. His helm display didn't pick up anything, but his eyes didn't deceive him. A hunched figure was there, slightly under standard mortal human height, waiting for them. Even from far away, Ironhelm's keen vision picked out the details on the man's face.

The skin was lined and ancient, puckered like leather and festooned with age-spots. He wore wine-red robes that clung to a slender frame, and leaned against a long wooden staff. His hands were like claws, scrawny with uncut nails. His hair must once have been long and full, but now hung from a balding pate in silvery straggles.

As the Wolves closed in, the figure looked up to watch them approach. The man saw Ironhelm approach, and shot the Great Wolf a strange look. It was a mixture of many things.

Contempt. Pity. Pride. Sorrow. Self-hatred. Hatred for them.

Perhaps the expression was hard to read because the

man's face was unusual in one important respect.

Ironhelm bounded up the steps, leaving his retinue a few paces behind as ever, letting the disruption field across the frostblade flare into life.

'Now let the galaxy witness your second death!' he roared, hauling his blade back as he crested the final steps, tensing to leap into contact.

The man lifted a withered finger.

Ironhelm froze in mid-stride. Behind him, his pack was similarly locked into stasis. The entire Great Company ground to a halt, imprisoned in their gestures of impending murder.

Ironhelm roared soundlessly with frustration, flexing his steel-hard muscle-bundles against the maleficarum. His power-armour servos whined, straining at the unnatural bonds that constrained them. He felt sweat burst out across his brow, trickling down his temples. The vice remained, though it yielded a little.

I can fight this.

The Great Wolf clenched his jaw, feeling his fangs scrape across his flesh, battling the sorcery that clamped down on his limbs with every sinew.

'You are powerful, Harek Eireik Eireiksson,' said the old man. His voice was thin, dry, and tinged with an oddly paternal-sounding regret. 'That should not surprise me. I have watched you grow over many centuries.'

Ironhelm felt his lungs labouring, his hearts pumping. If he could have shouted, he would have screamed his defiance. One of his arms shifted a fraction. The deadening power over his body trembled.

'All that you wish for is to kill me,' remarked the old

man, looking through a single rheumy eye at his assassin. 'You may succeed. Even now I feel your vital spirit overcoming the bonds I have placed on it.'

He shook his head in grudging respect.

'So strong! You Wolves were always my father's most potent weapons. What could I ever do to withstand that? Even at the height of my powers, what could I ever have done?'

Ironhelm felt his lips pull back in a snarl. Control over his muscles was returning. He sensed his warriors all doing the same thing. The frostblade inched closer to its target.

The man made no effort to get out of the way.

'Time is short,' he said. 'So let me tell you why I brought you to Gangava. It was to give you a choice. That is the way of my kind. You think us without honour or scruple, but that verdict obscures many truths. We have standards of conduct, though they differ from the ones you still cherish. I myself make a point of observing them.'

Ironhelm felt the bonds crack further. His arms moved a whole centimetre before the restraining clamps reasserted themselves. If he could have smiled, he would have broken into a wolfish grin.

Your sorcery will fail you soon. Then my blade will finish your babbling.

'I was once told the truth, and failed to heed it. Mindful of that, I offer you the truth now. I have passed beyond your comprehension, son of Russ. Even now, my soul is split. Only a fragment remains here. It was enough to bring you, to keep you from the greater battle as it unfolds. If you kill me, I shall be free to go to the other place, and my presence there will be terrible. But if you stay your hand, your future may yet be different. That is the choice.'

The old man looked at Ironhelm keenly, his single eye unwavering.

'Consider this the honour of my calling. A path of ruin awaits you, and I show you the way to avoid it. If you do what your primarch could not, and stay your hand, then the Bane of the Wolves will never come to light.'

Ironhelm managed to grind out a guttural snarl, though static flecks of blood burst from his lips with the effort. His arms shifted again. The bounds set on his limbs felt suddenly fragile, as if one more push would shatter them.

I feel you weakening now.

The old man remained rigidly in place, though he winced. His wasted hands clutched the staff more tightly, and he leaned against it with effort. His control was being dragged to its limits.

'And so the moment comes. I can hold you no longer. This is the choice, Harek Eireik Eireiksson. You can walk away, and you will never see me again.'

Then he lowered his voice, and the wizened face took on an expression of dreadful warning.

'But slay me, Dog of the Emperor, and we shall meet again very soon.'

THE REALSPACE VIEWER buckled outwards, torn between the forces raging against it. It had been well designed and made, a peerless example of Imperial craftsman-ship from the era when mankind had truly aspired to

unmatched mastery of the stars. Blackwing watched
the material flex horribly, trying to hold itself together.
It had lasted longer than he'd expected, but still looked
ready to blow at any moment.

'Neiman...' he voxed, bracing himself for whatever
came next.

'Calm yourself,' grunted the Navigator over the
comm. 'We're coming out now.'

The mutant's voice was cracked and gasping. Flames
crackled in the background.

Blackwing felt a surge of relief. Below him, fires were
now running riot through the servitor pits. The semi-
human automata just kept working, even as their skin
flaked and rolled back. From far back in the bowels of
the ship, Blackwing heard massive warp-coils begin to
wind down. They made a strange grinding noise, as if
huge iron bearings had been placed out of sync with
one another and were trying to negotiate some kind
of priority.

'That's what I wanted to hear. You've done well.'

'You have no idea, Space Wolf.'

Blackwing bristled at the term. It was what off-
worlders called the *Vlka Fenryka*, ignorant of the ways
and language of Fenris. Like all his breed, he thought
it was a stupid name.

But Neiman was hardly ignorant of any of their ways.
He spoke with all the precision of his profession, and
now he was dying. So Blackwing replied carefully too,
honouring him as he would a pack-brother.

'Until next winter, Djulian,' he said.

There was no further response from the comm, just a
snap and a hail of static. Blackwing tried it again, with

the same result. The Navigator had gone.

Then the floor of the bridge buckled, as if the ship had hit a sudden burst of turbulence. Blackwing braced himself awkwardly in his void-suit, clambering back toward the throne. A gantry collapsed close to where he'd just been, hitting the rail around the command platform and crashing into the pits below. The rest of the bridge groaned as the metal was twisted and stressed by the forces of realspace re-entry.

Blackwing achieved the throne again and sat heavily on the burnished seat. There was a shudder, and more explosions. Klaxons began to blare out across the upper decks.

No one is left to hear you. No one but me.

Blackwing felt the effects of translation before the instruments reported it. His whole body lurched, as if his organs had been sucked out into the open, re-arranged and put back again. The fabric of reality seemed to slur, to drag, before reasserting itself. A powerful wave of nausea rushed across him, nearly blinding him with its intensity.

Then it passed. The *Nauro* had dropped out of the warp.

Blackwing depressed a control rune, and the snapping sound of saviour pods blasting free of their support cages echoed up through the burning corridors. Then he withdrew the chromo on the realspace viewers. The true black of space replaced the false black of the warp-guards. The long range augurs picked up signals. Ship-signs. Dozens of them.

And far off, past the cordon of battleships, was the

planetary signature he'd keyed into the cogitators himself seventeen days ago.

Gangava Prime.

The floor began to ripple like breaking pack-ice. The cracked realspace lenses trembled, spawning new snaking hairlines. More booming explosions ran through the ship, shaking the backbone of it. Every warning rune on the tactical console was red and flashing.

Blackwing got up from the throne, running his gauntlet finger across the armrest as he did so.

'Glad I insisted on getting you, girl,' he said aloud, watching as the structure of the bridge began to fold in on itself. 'Arfang was right. Oirreisson is a man of poor taste.'

Then he tensed, watching for the first viewer to erupt outwards. There was no hope of getting to the saviour pods now, much less the shuttle hangars. What remained was luck.

Or, as the Rune Priests had it, *wyrd*.

The first dome shattered, blowing up in a coronet of twinkling points. The gale of atmospheric expulsion clutched at him, and a maelstrom of debris flew out of the breach in the hull, whirling into space. Then another one went, pulling more loose matter into the void. As more viewers exploded open, Blackwing saw a servitor pulled free of its harness, tumbling out through the open viewers, still on fire until the frigid void extinguished it.

Blackwing hung on to the throne, making full use of his enhanced strength to pick his moment, watching the lattice of transparent lenses above him disintegrate.

Now.

He pushed himself away from the throne and swept upwards.

As soon as he left the floor of the bridge, he lost control, spinning like the rest of the jetsam toward the void-sucked realspace viewers. He had an impression of whirling chaos, of the whole ruined bridge sliding in front of his eyes, before he was sucked out, ripped into the void, and everything got very, very cold.

His breath became deafening in the enclosed space of his helm, ragged and quick. For a moment, his disorientation was almost complete. Stars, as vivid as he'd ever seen them, swept by as he rotated, out of control and flailing.

As he spun round again he saw the broken flanks of the *Nauro* drift across his vision, retreating fast into the distance. The damage was worse than he'd dared to imagine. The entire engine level was open to space, blazing away in defiance of the vacuum around it, shedding components in a spinning cloud of burn-black metal. It was a shadow of the ship he'd commandeered on Fenris, a shattered, hopeless wreck. Saviour pods spiralled away from it like seeds falling from an *ekka* pine.

Something about the silence of space made everything seem to take place in a weird kind of silent slow motion. Blackwing actually saw the plasma drives explode before he felt anything of it. Bright yellow light flowered out from the darkened hull-carcass, rushing into the void in an utterly gorgeous sphere of monumentally impressive destruction. The vessel snapped clean in two, its components flying apart like a snapped femur, each spur lit up by subsidiary detonations.

Then the impact caught up. Blackwing went from spinning aimlessly in space to being tossed around like an ice-skiff in a Hel-gale. He felt a sharp blow as something hard and metal hit his void-armour shell, then another, then many more.

He tried, fruitlessly, to right himself, or at least to cradle himself against the rain of debris, all of it moving with incredible speed through the friction-less void. It was as he was doing this that an ancillary drive-shaft, a piece of solid metal the length of a Thunderhawk, rushed up to meet him with the remorseless inevitability of basic physics.

Blackwing had time for three thoughts. The first was that, after all he'd survived over the past two weeks, this was a poor way to go. The second was that, when it hit, it was going to really, *really* hurt.

Then the shaft slammed into him at full speed, cracking against his armour with the full momentum of the plasma-drive explosion, shattering his helm-visor and bursting the shell of his breastplate open. The void raced in, sucking both air and consciousness out.

As he tumbled away from the impact, trailing droplets of blood and oxygen from his wounds, his eyesight blurred and slipping away, he had the third thought. A familiar shape had intruded on to the edge of his waning awareness, grey and blunt-edged, bigger by far than the *Nauro* and in much better shape.

Blessed Allfather, he realised, before blood ran across his eyes and blinded him. *That's the* Gotthammar.

* * *

THE BONDS SNAPPED. The old man staggered back, his staff falling from his grasp and clattering on the floor.

Fast as a throat-cut, Ironhelm was on him. The frost-blade whistled through the air, resuming its course as if no interruption had taken place. The Great Wolf adjusted the trajectory subtly, compensating instantly for the movement of his target.

The man made no attempt to protect himself, nor to run from the blade. Freed from the crushing weight on them, Ironhelm's muscles sprang back to life instantly, propelling the crackling edge into the kill-zone. The frostblade bit true, cleaving the man's chest open diagonally from shoulder to waist.

The old man looked at Ironhelm a final time, somehow hanging on to a sliver of life. His single eye remained open, staring inscrutably.

Then he was down, his blood running across the stone freely. Ironhelm towered over him, poised to strike again, mindful of the ways of the Traitor. His newly released Wolf Guard leapt up to join him on the platform, all eager to defend their master against the awesome power of the fallen primarch and his daemonic allies.

But none appeared. A sigh passed through the heavy air of the chamber, making the banners rustle. The only sound was the heavy thud of power-armoured boots on the stairs, and the constant, thrumming growl of the packs.

The man was dead. He stayed dead.

Ironhelm looked down at the corpse, still panting from his exertion against the maleficarum. He knew he should feel elation. He knew should feel something.

Instead, his entire frame felt hollow. Within him, he could sense a thin, mournful howling.

Frei drew alongside. Like the Great Wolf, the Rune Priest emanated none of the feral exuberance he ought to have done.

'What just happened?' asked Ironhelm, as bewildered as a child. He began to feel a sickness well up within him. The quest of decades had been achieved, and there was nothing but a faint confusion and nausea to show for it.

'The primarch was here,' confirmed Frei, looking down at the body before the altar. 'Now, he is not.'

'Then I have killed him?'

Ironhelm's voice betrayed his desperation. He knew he hadn't.

'Something died,' said Frei. Like his master, his voice had none of the earthy certainty it normally carried. 'But I do not under–'

'Lord!'

The voice was Rangr's, and it was full of alarm.

The braziers were growing in intensity. The sapphire flames lashed up, creating columns of writhing, fluorescent energy. The light was powerful, throwing back even the darkest of the shadows in the chamber's recesses. The banners were illuminated fully, exposing the company emblems. Ironhelm turned to look at them, finally sensing their importance. He had been wrong. They were not Thousand Sons devices. They never had been.

'Adgr's pack,' he muttered, recognising the crossed fangs over the sickle moon. 'And Gramm's. And Beor's...'

Frei's gaze swept across the newly lit-up emblems. Beyond them, carved into the walls of the chamber, were stone reliefs. They depicted familiar events in an angular, stylised fashion. On one frieze there were pyramids within a city, the exact dimensions of those on Gangava. The *Gotthammar* arriving in orbit was on another. The reinforcements from Fenris translating in-system, the destruction of the void shield generator, all the events were there. There was even a depiction of the Great Wolf hurling an autocannon mount from a burning tower.

This has all been foreseen.

Rangr kept his chainsword poised in the attack position. Like all the Wolves in the chamber, he was on high alert, his hackles high and his hearts beating solidly.

'What is the meaning of those emblems, lord?' the Wolf Guard asked. 'They're *Fenryka*, but no Great Companies that I know.'

Ironhelm began to move away from the platform, lumbering down the steps heavily. Like his troops, he kept his frostblade activated. The worst of the nausea subsided, to be replaced by the cold hand of dread.

'They are our cousins,' he growled, his voice shot through with loathing. 'The Wolf Brothers. The lost ones.'

Frei joined the Great Wolf, and the pair of them descended the last steps from the pyramid quickly. The retinue followed in their wake.

'The Brothers have been disbanded for over two hundred years,' said Frei. 'I do not understand–'

'So you have already said, Rune Priest,' snarled

Ironhelm, losing patience. All his fury, all his kill-urge, had been suddenly blunted, and the result was an almost physical pain. 'Enough uncertainty. This place is a mockery of us. We will return to the fleet and destroy it from orbit.'

As he neared the far side of the chamber, close to where a gilded archway marked the exit out to the halls beyond, the braziers suddenly changed colour. From blazing sapphire they switched to a sickly green, intense and overbearing. The Wolf Brothers emblems became distorted and grotesque in the shifting light.

With the sharp sound of metal grating against metal, massive blast-doors withdrew from the walls of the chamber. In every direction, huge vaults opened up, each of them bleeding more emerald sickness into the central chamber. Dark shapes emerged from the fog of green, twisted and diseased. They were Space Marine in profile, but horribly altered. Some had trailing tentacles in place of limbs, others had misshapen heads crowned with thorns. Their armour was warped and uprooted, the plate ripped by growths from below and fused with unholy flesh where it spilled into the open. Helm-lenses glowed with more sickly witchlight, piercing even the shifting miasma roiling from the vaults. They didn't march cleanly, but limped, dragged or scuttled, hauling their broken bodies into the open, tottering on cloven hooves and clawed crow's feet.

As they emerged into the light of the braziers, their origins became clearer. Their battle-plate had once been grey, adorned with the totems and fetishes of the hunt. There were pelts still clinging to the corrupted ceramite, as botched and altered as the armour beneath. Images of fangs and runes were still graven into breastplates and greaves, though stretched into new and blasphemous patterns by some dark and subtle artistry. As they lumbered into view, the mutated warriors began to howl in a mockery of the battle cries they had once roared so proudly. The sound was horrific, a chorus of fluted misery and distortion that resounded from the high walls around them and filled the chamber with perverted hatred.

'The Bane of the Wolves,' breathed Frei, finally understanding. 'Not him. Not us. *Them.*'

Rangr and the other Wolf Guard hesitated. Normally they'd have rushed into combat at the first sight of such corruption, but this time none of them moved. They could all see the runes on the armour, the withered pelts and the beast-mask helms.

They all knew, without needing to be told, that the gene-seed in each one of those horrors was the same as the Helix that animated them.

'Orders, lord?' asked Frei, seizing his staff in both hands, as riven by indecision as those about him.

Ironhelm raised himself to his full, terrible height then, watching the oncoming mutants with a grim horror. They were brothers in more than name. They were the only successors the Space Wolves had ever permitted to be made, the only other scions of the primarch Leman Russ that remained in the galaxy.

They shared blood. They shared gene-memory. They shared everything.

'Remember yourself, priest,' Ironhelm growled, picking out the first of his targets from the hundreds that presented themselves. 'These are no longer Wolf

Brothers. Kill them. Kill them all, and do not cease until their abomination has been cleansed from the universe forever.'

JARL ARVEK KJARLSKAR turned away from the slab in the *Gotthammar's* medi-bay. The Wolf Scout he'd dragged out of the void, Blackwing, lay on the metal, more dead than alive, though somehow still capable of disagreeable amounts of sarcasm. The ship he'd arrived in was now nothing more than a ball of spinning ash, though the *Gotthammar's* reclamators were still picking up saviour pods.

'Do we have a comm-link?' Kjarlskar asked. The great voice was as deep and resonant as ever, though there was a note of unusual urgency in it.

'Not yet, lord,' replied Anjarm, the ship's Iron Priest. 'Ironhelm is in the central pyramid, heavily engaged. There's jamming down there.'

Kjarlskar's eyes blazed dangerously.

'How can there be jamming? We destroyed everything.'

He clenched his giant fists, bunching them as if he wanted to punch his way through the tiled walls of the apothecarium. Controlling his rage with difficulty, he whirled back to face Blackwing.

'You're *sure*, Wolf Scout?' he asked. 'We've had comms from Fenris – all of them routine.'

Blackwing managed a weak, hacking laugh. More blood bubbled up from his throat.

'Sure? No, not really, Jarl. Maybe the *Skraemar* wasn't torn apart by a battleship twice its size. Maybe we didn't lose our orbital batteries in a few hours. And maybe Jarl Greyloc didn't really order me out here, at the expense of my ship and most of my crew. I just *can't be sure...*'

Kjarlskar swooped down on Blackwing, grabbing him by his broken void-armour and hauling him up to his face.

'No more games,' he hissed, his fangs fully exposed. 'You ask for the recall of the entire Chapter. This is Ironhelm's moment of triumph.'

Blackwing's head lolled as the Wolf Lord shook him. His eyes went glassy, and the sardonic smile left his lips.

'I nearly died to bring you this message, lord,' he drawled, on the edge of consciousness and loquacious from medication. 'In itself, that matters not. But the fact you're hesitating over this is now massively pissing me off. There are Thousand Sons on Fenris, a whole bloody Legion of them. Even if the fleet returns now, the odds are the Aett will still fall. So what else do you want me to say? *Please?*'

Kjarlskar glared at him for another moment, as if his eyes could somehow bore into the Scout's soul and uncover the truth. Then, with as much disgust as despair, he threw Blackwing back against the hard metal slab.

'Get me a comm-link,' he snarled to the Iron Priest. 'Get it now. Then organise landers, and send a message to the other ships to prepare for re-translation. We're going back.'

Anjarm nodded.

'It will be done. But we've had reports of Traitor Marines in the pyramid – Ironhelm will not come away from that fight easily.'

Kjarlskar spat on the floor.

'That is why they're there. Blood of Russ, how easily we've been led.' He started to stride across the medi-bay, thrusting aside the fleshmaker-thralls who got in his way. 'I'll make planetfall myself. By the Allfather, he'll listen to *me*.'

It was as the massive Wolf Lord neared the exit that Blackwing lifted his battered head a final time. The encounter with the drive-shaft had left him uglier and more misshapen than ever. His nose and cheekbones had been shattered, his chest driven in and both arms badly broken. Even for a Space Marine, those were serious wounds. The huge amounts of sedative in his bloodstream seemed to have finally got to him, and his bruised eyelids drooped half-closed.

'You do that, Jarl,' he slurred, drifting back into forgetfulness. 'And don't think I'll hold any of this against you. I'm a generous sort, so you can thank me properly when we get back.'

PART IV:
THE CRIMSON KING

CHAPTER SEVENTEEN

THE LIGHTS WERE low in Greyloc's chamber. None of the Jarls had ostentatious private quarters, and they were all arranged in much the same way: bare rock walls, racks of weapons taken from past encounters, totems gifted by the Wolf Priests, a hard bed layered with tough hides. Greyloc's was perhaps a little more sparse than most, but not by much. The only item that marked his territory was the old axe Frengir, hanging over the whetstone like an amulet.

The Wolf Lord was seated on a low three-legged wooden stool, the kind the men of the ice used for tribal councils. It was built to mortal scale, and even out of armour Greyloc looked awkward on it, all limbs and hands.

His eyes were closed, the pale skin of his face

relaxed. The sounds of the Aett – the hammering, the shouting, the grind of machinery – were muted. A fire glowed in the corner of the chamber, now little more than embers. A mortal would have struggled to see much in the gloom and would have found the cold crushing. The extremity of the chamber's conditions were testament to the majesty of the Adeptus Astartes, even if the contents were not.

Alone with his thoughts, Greyloc let his mind wander across possibilities, soaring like a *gyrhawk* across an open sky. He could sense the vast tide of hatred closing in on his citadel, pressing against the stone, burrowing into its roots, determined to break inside and destroy the life within. A lesser warrior might have been intimidated by that. Even a great leader might have felt a tremor of frustration, a burning sense of injustice that his time in command had been rendered so cruelly short.

Greyloc felt none of that. His humours were balanced, and the inner wolf was at ease. It was unusual for one of his kin to be in such a state prior to the outbreak of battle, and it was a trait he never revealed. There were times, he knew, when his battle-brothers felt he had lost something essential, that he had become too much like a mortal, and there was no point in fuelling the rumours further.

He understood why they thought such things. Greyloc was as much a gene-child of Russ as they were, but he had command of a quality that they often lacked, for all their bluster and outward confidence.

Certainty.

That had never wavered, not since the first implants

had taken, not since he'd learned to use the new, powerful body given to him by the Helix, not since he'd risen through the orders to become Hunter, then Guard, then Lord. At every stage, he'd known what his destiny was.

In another soul, that might have constituted arrogance. Greyloc, though, had never gloried in it, or even taken satisfaction. It was merely the way of the universe, as sacred as the balance between hunter and prey, between cause and effect.

At every stage, I chose the path I had to. Every note of the wyrd then was true. It will be no different now. The runes guide, and they never lie.

By the doorway, a red light briefly winked on. Greyloc's eyelids flickered open. His pin-pupils were dilated, as if he'd been hunting. They shrunk quickly, returning to their normal state.

'Come,' he said quietly.

The iron doors to his chamber slid open, and a hunched figure strode in. Wyrmblade was in his armour, as ever. As he walked, it hummed arhythmically, breaking the peace of the chamber. The doors slid closed again, sealing the two of them in.

Greyloc did not rise. Seated, he looked diminished. More so than most of his battle-brothers, he could control his aura of intimidation. A warrior like Rossek would always be terrifying; Greyloc was only terrifying when he chose to be.

'I'm sorry, lord,' said Wyrmblade, looking at the embers, the axe, and the simple robes worn by the Jarl. 'I can come another time.'

Greyloc waved a hand dismissively.

'You may come and go when you please,' he said. 'Or have the Wolf Priests given up that right?'

'Not yet,' Wyrmblade acknowledged. 'And not likely to.'

He did not sit. His armoured weight would have crushed a stool like Greyloc's, and there were no other chairs.

'You've been in seclusion long,' he said, leaning against the stone walls.

'There's been much to reflect on,' said Greyloc. 'Much to plan.'

'You're content with what has been done?'

Greyloc snorted.

'I'd be content if we had another three Companies and a battle-fleet. But, as we haven't, then yes. I am. The tunnel collapse has given us precious days. They'll break through soon, and we'll be ready. Bjorn is with us, so they'll get a fight.'

Wyrmblade looked at the Jarl cryptically. 'One we can win?'

Greyloc shrugged. 'What use is that thought, Thar? We'll do what we're bred to. After that, it's in the lap of the Allfather.'

'You know why I ask. There are things... *secrets* within the Aett. There is knowledge here that must never leave. Ironhelm knows it, and a handful of others, but no more. If we are defeated, then...'

Wyrmblade left the sentence hanging.

'You speak as if you were the only one who's thought about such things,' said Greyloc. 'It's been in my mind too. But what do you propose? That we destroy the Tempering? Ironhelm would have to sanction it.'

'He's not, as you may have noticed, here.'

'So is that what you want?'

Wyrmblade looked pained.

'You know it isn't. My life has been devoted to it. Yours too, since you were taken into confidence. But we must have a plan. This battle has already made it hard to retain the secrecy we need, and it will only get worse. If the time comes, I need to know I have your authority to act.'

Greyloc met Wyrmblade's gaze. The two of them were so physically different – one cold, white and vital, the other battered, dark and cynical – and yet there was a kinship there, a shared understanding.

For several heartbeats they remained silent.

'You do,' said Greyloc at last. 'But do not act until the very last moment, and then only if the Aett must be lost beyond recovery. Until then, preserve what you have. Lives may be sacrificed. Relics may be lost. But I would not see the work ended here, unless all else must be ended.'

As he spoke, his pale hands closed into fists.

'This is our future, Thar,' he said. 'This is our chance to grow. Should we lose it now, it will never come again.'

Wyrmblade nodded.

'Then you feel as I do,' he said. 'I'm glad, and it will be as you command. But I make one more request: keep Sturmhjart away from the Valgard. He has been given orders to interfere, and would not understand the need for further secrecy.'

'Sturmhjart is already taken care of. He will stand beside Bjorn and me at Borek's Seal. You will have the services of Cloudbreaker at the Fangthane. So do not worry – the need to divide our forces has rid you of your gadfly.'

The old Wolf Priest smiled.

'You would have made a formidable Great Wolf, Vaer,' he said, and his crooked smile was wistful.

'*Would* have?' replied Greyloc. 'You have so little faith in our chances?'

Wyrmblade shrugged, and looked down.

'It's in the lap of the Allfather,' he repeated, though the words sounded empty a second time.

TWO DAYS LATER, and the Fangthane was finally made ready. All clustered there knew that the tunnels would be breached imminently. Their demolition had given the Aett a much needed respite from assault, and it had been now been a full ten days since the gates had been lost. Now the fighting would begin again. There would be further retreats, further fighting withdrawals, all aimed at inflicting the maximum pain for the minimum of ground. But now the space to shrink into was finite. The Aett was massive, but even its network of tunnels ran out eventually.

Redpelt knelt low on the stone steps leading up to the Fangthane. His helm lay beside him as he carefully lacquered his russet hair down, ready to put it on. As ever, his armour was covered in layers of blood, and the lower jaw of his helm had its row of teeth embedded. Many of them had been knocked out, but enough remained to mark him. His breastplate was new, a replacement for the one cracked apart by the Rubric Marine's bolter rounds. Despite several days of acclimatisation, it felt awkward against his black carapace interface, and the input nodes still chafed.

His work done, he looked up. His pack-brothers were arranged around him, all fourteen of them. The combat squad was an amalgam of other Blood Claw packs, cobbled together from those who'd survived the gate assaults. As ever, the Claws' casualties had been high during the fighting, a testament to their head-strong way of war.

Brokentooth had been killed on the retreat, his back punched open by a lascannon beam even as he raced for the cover of the gates. A terrible way to cut the thread, that.

Of course, Brakk was gone too. The one who'd trained them for so long, who'd knocked as much fight-sense into them as had been possible, and who'd led them with such calm, controlled skill. The Wolf Guard had never said much, and almost nothing at all when in the thick of the fighting, but now he was dead the Aett somehow seemed a quieter, emptier place.

His replacement, the glowering giant Rossek, had changed the nature of the pack more than the arrivals from other squads. Whereas Brakk had been gruff and direct, Rossek looked like he'd been teetering on the edge of some bout of madness and barely survived. He too said very little, but Redpelt guessed the reasons for that were different. Brakk had always had the self-confident gait of a predator – controlled, taut, efficient. Rossek, by contrast, massive in his Terminator plate, looked haunted and grim. Something had got to him, had driven out the ebullient, belligerent spirit that had once made him the favourite to lead the Twelfth.

In his torporific presence much of the old banter that had once animated the Claws was gone, replaced with a grim sense of expectation.

And then there was Helfist. He crouched a few paces away from Redpelt, his horsehair crest hanging from his helm, his plate still adorned with the figures of Ymir and Gann. On the surface, he'd not changed at all. Despite his brush with the Wolf, he'd retained his juvenile humour and coarse love of the hunt. Alone in the pack, Helfist generated that sense of unpredictable energy that made the Wolves what they were.

Helfist sensed he was being looked at, and his blood-eyed visage turned to Redpelt.

'Put your damn helm on, brother,' he voxed. 'Using that face against them really isn't fair.'

Redpelt would have grinned at that in the past. Not now. Helfist's levity was too forced, too conscious. The young Blood Claw had been deeply wounded by the death of Brakk and his brush with the Wolf; he just didn't have the tools to deal with it.

Redpelt twisted his helm round and lowered it over his slicked-down scalp, slotting the bearings in place and hearing the faint lock of the atmospheric seals as they clamped down. Battle-runes flashed up across the display, indicating defensive formations throughout the Aett.

The principal Fangthane fortifications had been constructed on the broad, two hundred-metre long stairway leading up from the tunnels of the Aett into the main chamber at the top. The defences were arranged in a series of storied barricades, running from the base of the stairs to the summit where Freki and

Geri stood guard. The forty-seven Wolves assigned to the Fangthane stairs were reinforced by hundreds of kaerls, all protected by heavy adamantium bunkers and barricade walls. The Sky Warriors were led by Wyrmblade; the mortals by a rivenmaster with an honest-looking face and hollow eyes.

In the very centre of the defensive perimeter, half-way up the stairway, were the mightiest death-machines of all: six Dreadnoughts. The Revered Fallen were huge, towering over Wyrmblade and Cloudbreaker as the commanders stood alongside them. Skrieya led the three packs of Grey Hunters at the base of the slope, lined up with Rossek's Blood Claws, and Rojk stood with his Long Fangs near the top of the stairway, exuding calm solidity as always.

There were more fortifications beyond at the summit, dug into the floor and walls of the chamber itself, refuges where the defenders could retreat to in stages if needed. All along the gigantic flanks of the Fangthane chamber, fixed guns had been mounted, each capable of throwing bolt-rounds at the enemy far faster than even the Long Fangs could.

It was a devastating collection of firepower, all looked over by the distant statue of Russ himself. The field hospital at his feet had been cleared days ago, moved higher up into the Hould. Now there was only room for the tools of war in the Fangthane. All barrels, muzzles and blades pointed toward the huge, silent gates at the very base of the stairway, the portals through which the enemy would have to come.

It was a space less than a hundred metres wide. The killing ground.

'Watch yourself, when they're here,' said Redpelt, speaking over a closed channel to Helfist.

Helfist laughed.

'Going soft on me, Ogrim?' he asked.

'The Wolf is close behind you.'

'He's close behind us all, brother.'

Helfist drew his bolt pistol and checked the magazine for the twelfth time. As the wait dragged on, they all looked for displacement activity.

'And you shouldn't worry about me,' he added casually. 'Worry about yourself. Being so damn slow, and all.'

Redpelt tried to think of a reply, some suitable put-down. Nothing came to mind.

Then, from far below, came the sound of huge, resonating crashes. There were stronger booms after that, echoing up the tunnels. They were distant, clouded by kilometres of snaking corridors, but distinct enough. They didn't stop.

'Warriors of the Aett!' came Wyrmblade's dry old voice. He'd drawn the mighty power sword with the dragon device on its blade, and the energy field shimmered in the semi-dark. 'Now fate falls a final time! The tunnels are opened. Steel yourselves, stand firm, and kindle your hate!'

He took a great stride forwards, raising the glowing edge of his weapon high.

'For Russ! For the Allfather! For Fenris!'

The defenders replied as one.

'For Fenris!'

The echo of the massed roar ran around the empty shell of the Fangthane approaches, gradually sinking into the stone.

Redpelt drew his own pistol, gripping his chainsword in his other hand. The kill-urge began to cradle in him. As soon as the first of the Traitors came through the gates, he'd become the snarling, slavering exemplar of war he'd been bred to be.

'Russ be with you, brother,' he said to Helfist.

'And with you,' replied Helfist, a little too quickly.

And it was then, for the first time ever, that Redpelt heard trepidation in his comrade's voice. The bravado, as impressive as it seemed, was only armour-deep.

Helfist was deeply troubled by something, and it wasn't the coming enemy.

THE ROCK WALL glowed red, then orange, then harsh white. On the far side of the collapsed tunnel, enormous energies were being applied. The barrier held for a little longer, bowed out, then exploded.

Huge chunks of semi-molten stone were hurled across the Chamber of the Seal, smashing into the far wall a hundred metres distant. In their wake, lasbeams the width of a man's arm lanced through the air. Massive shapes lumbered through the gap, hacking at the edges of the breach with steaming drill-arms.

More cracks appeared, and a huge section of melta-fused stone toppled, crashing to the ground and sending rubble skidding across the floor. More las-fire flickered through the clouds of dust, flying harmlessly into the far walls of the chamber, hitting nothing.

There was nothing to hit. When the Thousand Sons broke into the heart of the Fang, there were no gun-lines to meet them, no ranks of kaerls ready to sell their lives in a desperate defence. The Cataphracts, still operating according to their simple machine-spirit instructions, lumbered into the open, shaking off their mantles of dust and charging up plasma cannon arms to fire.

'Cease!' roared a voice from the tunnel beyond.

Flanked by Terminator Rubricae, Aphael clambered through the breach. Kine-shields shimmered around him, distorting his image behind shifting curtains of warp-energy.

More Rubricae emerged, striding out into the chamber and hefting boltguns. Among them was Hett, flanked by his own retinue and similarly cocooned in heavy shielding.

'Send them forwards!' he urged, letting his sorcerer's staff blaze with eldritch power.

Aphael shook his head.

'They know we're coming,' he said, looking out across the chamber warily.

He crouched down and picked up a chunk of rock the size of a man's head. Lifting it as easily as a mortal might lift a pebble, he threw it across the chamber towards the tunnel on the far side. As it sailed into the dark, the space was rocked by massive explosions. The rock was blasted apart in an instant. From somewhere hidden deep in the recesses of the tunnels, autoguns thundered, sending a storm of ammunition screaming toward the Thousand Sons vanguard.

Aphael flicked a finger and the kine-shield bloomed outwards, enclosing the Cataphracts in a web of energy. The autogun assault detonated against the barrier in a rippling wave of fire.

'They'll need to do better than that, though,' he said, lifting his staff aloft.

With a single word, the kine-barrier suddenly hurtled forwards, sweeping across the chamber and transmuting into a wall of consuming electricity. Lightning flared out and snaked into the shadows, tearing up stone and blasting it open. The surge of energy slammed into the fixed guns, knocking them from their positions in a series of thumping detonations.

The explosions gradually gave out, and the lightning crackled into nothing, leaving a score of burned-out gun carcasses. Smoke drifted across the tunnels.

'Now we advance,' said Aphael coolly.

The Rubricae began to march. In silence, their eyes glowing softly in the dark, the last warriors of the XV Legion stalked forwards, clad in lash-curling trails of aetheric protection. In their wake came the Cataphracts, their massive claws cracking the stone beneath them as they moved.

From behind the vanguard, still in the tunnel leading to the gates, there was a vast, nebulous sound. It was the thud of thousands of boots striking the earth in unison, the sound of thousands of weapons being made ready, the sound of thousands of whispered prayers to the Masters of Sorcery.

It was the sound of the doom of Fenris drawing closer.

FROM THE CHAMBER of Borek's Seal, dozens of corridors branched off into the interior of the mountain. All were as dark as oil, kept in shadow, their hearth-fires long since kicked over. They curved and doubled back, leading the unwary a dance into choked dead-ends or taking them directly to the vast shafts that led to other levels. Even the kaerls didn't know all the myriad ways of travel through the Aett, and stuck to the ancient paths, hugging the light of the fires and avoiding the deeper dark. They knew, as all knew, that the Fang would kill you quicker than a crevasse if you crossed it.

The Rubricae swept through the shadowed paths, their preternatural sight guiding them in the utter occlusion. They moved fluidly, sweeping gun muzzles across junctions with a calm, focused efficiency. The sorcerers came behind them, many metres back, herding them like distant, bronze-armoured shepherds.

They didn't go unwarily. They knew the extreme danger. But they also knew they were the elite servants of the Red Primarch, warriors almost without peer. They were stealthy, whisper-quiet and eerie. Many a mortal force had been taken by surprise by them before, expecting raving hordes of fanatics only to be ambushed by the terrifying, dust-dry approach of the soulless ones.

But the defenders were no mortals.

Crouched against the stone of the corridor wall, his Helix-enhanced senses making him sensitive to the slightest variation in air-density, Greyloc heard the first squad coming from hundreds of metres away. He narrowed his eyes, gauging their numbers and formation, pressing his fingers against the sheaths of his wolfclaws, feeling the ancient devices respond to his touch. The talons were dormant, invisible in the gloom, but would ignite with a thought.

Behind him, his troops did the same. Four warriors, all that was left of his original Terminator retinue, all equipped with close combat weapons, their armour powered down and as black as the air around them. In their midst was Sturmhjart, his head bowed. Though his helm masked his features, Greyloc could sense the Rune Priest's concentration. Sturmhjart kept the whole pack shrouded, safe from the prying psychic eyes of the sorcerers. The runes on his armour were sunken and dull, like lines of onyx set in the ceramite, but they were burning inside.

The long corridor ahead of them was empty, free of the booby traps and fire pits that rigged the higher levels. Greyloc watched intently, hearing the muted boot impacts of the Rubric Marine squads grow closer, waiting for the first sight of the enemy.

When it came, it was like a vision of a mortal's nightmare. Lime-green points of light bobbed into view at the end of the tunnel, the gleam of the Rubricae's unholy helm lenses. There were many of them, marching in close formation, coming confidently but carefully.

Greyloc felt the first stabs of hatred spike into his hearts.

You come here. To my realm. To despoil my people.

More green lights emerged. The squad was drawing closer, completely unaware of the welcome that awaited them at the far end of the corridor. Sturmhjart gave out a low growl, below the hearing of any but the Wolves, working hard to maintain the protective shroud about them.

I will shatter you. I will drive your corrupted souls into damnation. I will break you open and throw the dust of your souls to the dirt.

The last of the Rubricae entered the tunnel. Greyloc's

helm-display indicated eighteen targets, plus a slower-moving signal at the rear. That was the sorcerer, the one Sturmhjart would have to deal with.

Because to me you are one thing, and one thing only.

Behind him, he could sense the power weapons of his battle-brothers pre-spike. Their pheromone kill-urge became apparent, thick and pungent. After days of inactivity and sparring, the glory of war had come to them again. Greyloc felt a fierce surge of elation as the endorphins rushed into his bloodstream.

Prey.

The moment came.

'For Russ!'

His wolfclaws blazed, sending harsh shadows leaping back along the corridor, and then he was charging, hurtling towards the lead Rubric Marine, bathed in streams of storm-fury kindled by Sturmhjart. His guard tore into battle beside him, bellowing with feral abandon, the very image of the maelstrom itself. Sturmhjart was with them too, his armour-runes exploding into angry red life, drenching the tunnel walls with the glowing stain of blood.

'*Hjolda!*' roared Greyloc, slamming into contact, scything his claws through the armour of his first victim, watching the empty plate buckle as the talons bit deep. The corridor was soon filled with the sharp crack, thud and crunch of close combat.

It had begun. The final assault. From that point on, they all knew, the fighting would not cease until the last of the Thousand Sons were killed, or the Fang was taken in flames.

* * *

FIRST, THE FIRESTORM.

From behind his barricade, Morek watched through a handheld augur as the Thousand Sons' attack arrived at the Fangthane stair. The volume of fire was both blinding and deafening, a mix of plasma and solid-round weaponry that leapt out of the approach tunnels and slammed into the heavy buttresses at the base of the stairway. He couldn't see the source of it, as the invaders were still hidden by the low ceiling and curving walls of the tunnel beyond the stairs. They stayed back, remaining in cover, hurling ranged fire at the barricades from afar.

Morek slid down against the cool bulk of the three metre-high, four metre-thick adamantium bulwark he'd been stationed to hold, final-checking his *skjoldtar*. Around him, crouching low in cover, were the men of his riven. All of them had seen action before, and none had any problem dealing with the barrage of incoming fire. The shielding warding them had been erected over many days, constructed out of siege-grade materials, and was capable of absorbing huge amounts of punishment before failing.

But this was just the prelude, and there was a long way to go before the real fighting took place.

'Heads down,' he voxed automatically. It was a superfluous command – his men mostly had their helmets between their knees and were hunched at the base of the giant barricades. The rain of plasma and bolt-shells either slammed into the barriers or flew harmlessly over their heads, impacting against the roof of the huge tunnel.

The noise was the worst thing – a disorientating,

devastating chorus of hammering and burning that echoed out of the enclosed corridors and bounced off into the massive space beyond. It made thinking difficult, let alone hearing orders over the vox.

Morek blink-clicked a rune on his helm display to augment his auditory feed and compensate for the thundering noise outside. It improved the situation, but only by a little.

From his tactical display, he could see the Wolves crouching down in forward positions, also using the cover of the barricades at the base of the stairway. They were the best equipped troops to deal with the volume of devastation, but even they didn't just walk blindly out into the torrent. Wyrmblade held them back, keeping the leash on the Blood Claws short, waiting until there were targets suited to their close combat mastery.

Rojk and the Long Fangs remained similarly unused, perched high up at the rear of the defensive lines, surrounded by heavy shielding. They endured the firestorm, letting the barriers take the strain, waiting for the real enemy to emerge.

Only Cloudbreaker was fully active. The Rune Priest, the most potent of Sturmhjart's acolytes, had summoned up a swirling, missile-devouring storm of turbulence over the portals, using it to misdirect incoming projectiles and explode shells before they hit their target. It was far from perfect, but it spared the barricades from the full, unadulterated force of the enemy's bombardment.

Morek took a deep breath, tasting the metallic edge of his rebreather filter, letting his heart-rate fall as the initial aural shock of the assault wore off. He'd seen action many times, and knew how to handle himself on a battlefield. Even so, there was no escaping the initial, stomach-twisting lurch of adrenaline when the shooting started.

Then, as he always did, he saw Freija in his mind. He knew she was stationed in Borek's Seal with the other defensive forces. It was better that way. If they'd been placed together, he'd have been distracted by the need to keep half an eye on her. As it was, he didn't even have vox-contact. The two theatres of war were almost entirely separated, blocked by kilometres of solid rock and the comm-jamming devices of the enemy.

'The Hand of Russ, daughter,' he breathed, forgetting his helm-vox was still active.

'What?' asked the kaerl nearest him, raising his head as if he expected to be ordered over the top.

Morek smiled bleakly.

'Not yet, lad,' he said, feeling the tremors against the barricade as it absorbed a staccato run of heavy bolter-rounds. 'But soon enough.'

GREYLOC SPUN ON the ball of his foot, smashing aside the Rubric Marine and jarring its sapphire armour against the tunnel wall. The Traitor slumped down the stone and the witchlight in its eyes flickered out.

Greyloc turned to his retinue, knowing the pack needed to fall back. The approach tunnels were crawling with the enemy now, and his squad had to withdraw to Borek's Seal before it was cut off.

'Broth–' he started, before feeling a sharp pain in his right leg.

The Rubric Marine hadn't been finished off. It had

dragged itself to its knees and stabbed its short combat blade into Greyloc's greaves.

Still not dead! Skítja – what do I have to do?

He raised both wolfclaws and rammed them point-down, shredding the prone Rubric Marine from shoulder to waist. The disruptor-charged talons sliced through the empty battle-plate, breaking open the carapace and exposing the empty space inside. There was a sharp hiss, like air escaping from a void-lock, and the components rocked apart. The Traitor's helm dropped heavily on to the floor, lenses dark, and stayed motionless.

That was enough.

'Now,' Greyloc snarled over the mission channel, angered by the wound he'd taken, angered that his guard hadn't been tighter. 'Back to the Seal.'

His retinue turned instantly, cutting their way out of combat and bludgeoning their way free. The six of them, Sturmhjart included, broke out of the melee and tore down the winding corridors, leaving a brace of disabled or destroyed Traitors in their wake. As he went, Greyloc felt a dragging sensation on his limbs. For a moment, he thought it was the wound. Then he recognised the true source.

'Rune Priest,' he ordered, giving the hand signal for maleficarum.

Sturmhjart nodded, still running, and clenched his fist tight. The runes on his armour suddenly blazed crimson. There was a thin cry of anguish from further up the tunnels, and the dragging ceased. The Wolves sped on, running hard through the utter darkness of the corridors, flawlessly negotiating the uneven ground, navigating as much by memory as by the senses.

They went down sharply, easily leaving behind the slower moving Rubric Marines. Streams of bolter fire followed them while the pursuers were in range, but it was either evaded or flew off the heavy Terminator armour and soon died out. Greyloc's leg muscles had begun to knit before he'd gone more than a few hundred metres, testament to the astonishing recuperative power of his gene-heritage.

'Signals ahead,' voxed Sturmhjart as they headed toward a junction in the tunnels where several routes coincided.

'Mortals,' spat Greyloc contemptuously. His kill-urge hadn't abated, and such easy targets would do nothing to assuage it. 'Make this quick.'

Seconds later, and a hapless Prosperine assault squad, ranging ahead of the slower moving Rubricae vanguard, blundered into the vengeful Wolves. Greyloc tore through them like a tornado, throwing bodies against the stone with spine-ripping force before carving them open and moving on. Las-beams and screams flickered in the eternal night of the underground, utterly hopeless against Greyloc's momentum and fury.

'We need to move,' warned Sturmhjart, grabbing a panicked trooper and breaking his neck with a single shake of his wrist. 'More signals closing in.'

Greyloc growled in annoyance, plunging into a fresh cluster of retreating bodies and laying about them with his whip-crackling claws.

'Let them,' he snapped, impaling two mortals at

once, one on each claw, before hurling them loose in a spray of blood. 'I'm just getting started.'

'There'll be plenty of fighting at the Seal,' insisted the Rune Priest, backhanding a mortal into the roof of the tunnel and unloading a single bolter round into the stomach of his terrified comrade. 'Jarl, we need to *move*.'

Then came the familiar barking snap of bolter rounds from further up the tunnels. Only Space Marines used such weapons, and they were very close.

'Damn them,' cursed Greyloc, watching the few surviving mortals limp and scamper back up the way they'd come, heading for the protection of the closing Rubric Marine squads. His voice was ragged and panting, not from exhaustion, but from the fearful, murderous energy only the Wolves of Fenris could unleash.

He stayed standing for a moment longer, unwilling to cede more ground. His pack stayed with him, their massive armour humming with a latent menace. They would stand and fight, if he ordered them to.

Teeth of Russ, they'd stand against Magnus himself if I ordered them to.

'Let's go,' he snarled, hearing the heavy tread of a hundred boots on the tunnel floors above. If they stayed, they'd be overwhelmed, just as Rossek had been.

The pack swept downwards again, following the swiftest route towards Borek's Seal. As they went, they passed wards against sorcery, freshly consecrated by the Rune Priests only days earlier. There were thousands of them in the warrens of the Aett, all serving to damp down and dilute the powers of the Sons' sorcerers. Until they were dismantled, the Fang would be a hostile, draining place for them.

As it should be, faithless witches.

The pack thundered down a long, shallow incline. Greyloc recognised the approach tunnels to the Seal as they widened. They were nearing the final chamber before the bulwark itself, a junction of several other routes running down through the mountain. As the walls opened out, he heard noises from the space ahead.

'Targets,' he snarled, torn between irritation at the delay and pleasure at the chance to resume killing. 'Lots of them.'

'What in Hel are these signals?' asked Sturmhjart, before the pack burst out from the tunnel and into the chamber.

The space was huge after the confines of the mountain routes, a hundred metres wide and roughly circular. Fires burned, but they were not the wholesome flames of hearth fires. Prosperine troops were there ahead of them, dozens preparing for the assault on Borek's Seal – the bulwark itself was now only a few hundred metres away, down another long, straight corridor carved into the rock.

For a moment Greyloc couldn't see any reason for the Rune Priest's confusion.

Then he did.

Among the mortal troops hurrying away from them, desperately trying to organise some kind of defence against the Terminators suddenly arriving in their midst, were two gigantic war machines. They had the

look of ancient, proscribed tech-sorcery and stood
more than a head higher than even Sturmhjart. They
had fearsome drills mounted on one arm and plasma
cannons affixed to the other. Their movements were
deliberate and methodical, yet nearly as fast as his.

As Greyloc tore into the chamber, a bolt of plasma
arced toward him from one of the machines. He
ducked left, evading the worst of it, though the ball of
energy still caught his right arm and hurled him back
against the stone.

'*Fenrys!*' roared Sturmhjart, kindling energy along the
length of his staff, whirling it round and throwing ball-
lightning of his own into the face of the machine.

'*Hjolda!*' answered the rest of the pack, charging
headlong against the other war-engine. The Prosperine
mortals began to lay down a curtain of las-fire, but
the flickering beams were more an annoyance than a
threat.

The machines, though, were serious opponents. Greyloc, leaping back to his feet, saw one of his warriors
torn apart by a plasma blast and another one thrown
bodily to the ground by a punch from the drill-arm.

Thrown to the ground. In Tactical Dreadnought Armour.

Greyloc powered back towards the nearest leviathan,
ignoring the second machine, now swathed in Sturmhjart's lightning strands.

'Cataphracts,' growled the Rune Priest over the vox,
understanding what the signals had been telling him.
'Soulless machines.'

Greyloc leapt into contact, evading another plasma
bolt in mid-air and sweeping his claws into the Cataphract's bronze shoulder-guards.

'They all fall the same way,' he grunted, jabbing the talons into metal, using his falling weight to drag the Cataphract off balance.

The massive war-engine staggered, pulled away from centre by Greyloc's weight. As it tottered, the Wolf Lord punched up with his claws, tearing the armour-plating open and revealing intricate circuitry within. His arm reached back, ready to rip out the wiring, when a colossal blow from the drill-arm floored him.

Greyloc hit the stone hard and sprawled on his back. The Cataphract loomed over him and levelled the plasma cannon at his head. Greyloc rolled away as the sunburst blazed out, shattering the rock below.

Then he was back on his feet with a fluid, twisting movement, already anticipating the next blow from the Cataphract. He veered away, dodging a crushing blow from the drill-arm, before plunging back in close, his talons shimmering from the disruptors.

'Bite on this,' he hissed, jabbing the edges up toward the exposed rent in the Cataphract's armour.

As the talons connected, the war machine was lifted high and thrown through the air, its massive limbs flailing. It crashed down amid a cluster of mortal troops. Its entire breastplate had been driven in, and the ancient metal was broken and smoking.

Greyloc spun round, perfectly aware he hadn't hit it that hard.

Bjorn was there.

The gigantic Dreadnought rose up in front of him, dominating the chamber as he dominated every chamber he entered, his massive plasma cannon arm still radiating heat from the discharge.

Feel the wrath of the ancients, abomination.

The aura of intimidation was astonishing. Even Greyloc, hardened by centuries of combat against the direst enemies of mankind, found himself awestruck in the face of that hatred. It was as if a fragment of Russ's own destructive power had been dragged back into the world of the living, as all-consuming and devastating as it had been when first unleashed on the galaxy two thousand years ago.

The Fell-Handed is among us! Blood of Russ, I would have faced a hundred deaths just to see this.

More Rubric Marines were entering the chamber by then, lumbering down the many tunnels and opening fire as they did so. Cataphracts were among them, and sorcerers, and mortal assault squads wearing heavy blast-armour.

Bjorn waded into battle, as imperious and uncaring of the odds as he'd ever been. His lightning claw blazed with thrashing, curling energy, trailing electrostatic barbs along the stone as it flexed open. His plasma cannon pounded a stream of bolts into the reeling enemy, hurling even the Rubricae aside as the blazing energy pulses exploded into them.

Be unleashed! boomed the venerable Dreadnought, his growling, resonant voice rising above the growing tide of explosions and war cries.

And in his wake came the beasts. Like a rolling wave, they leapt from his shadow and into the open. Huge, loping monsters, yellow-eyed, ribbed with metal plates and carrying outsized jaws lined with needle-sharp fangs, they tore forwards, devouring the ground between them and the enemy.

If the mortal invaders had been scared before, they panicked then. Thin pitched screams echoed from the chamber roof as the horrors of the Underfang pounced, slamming into the enemy lines and rolling across the stone with their prey.

More Dreadnoughts strode into the chamber, their autocannons spooling up to fire. In their wake came more racing bands of Underfang creatures, and squads of Grey Hunters, their war cries massive and echoing, and ravening packs of Blood Claws. Bolters barked out in response, and power-blades were kindled. The dark of the mountain was banished, replaced by the whirling, flashing light of muzzle-flares and plasma-bolts.

All this Greyloc saw in a single sweep of his helm. It was all the time he needed. He leapt to his feet, his claws still incandescent with killing energy.

'For Russ!' he roared, and the sound of the challenge shook the earth beneath his feet.

'For Russ!' roared the Wolves of the Fang, sweeping into combat, glorying in the savage thrust of arms.

For Russ! thundered Bjorn, the words amplified by his war-vox relays, drowning out all other sounds, rocking the walls of the chamber and cracking the stone under which he trod.

CHAPTER EIGHTEEN

TEMEKH HAD TO work hard not to give in to an unseemly excitement. He knew, as all the sorcerers did, that his emotions were entirely transparent to his gene-father. Just as they'd always been.

'Welcome to Fenris, lord,' he said, bowing low.

'None of that,' remonstrated the newcomer, waving away the ceremonial gesture. 'You're being misled by appearance. As I've surely demonstrated to you by now, that is the least important aspect of my presence here.'

Temekh let his head rise, and smiled.

'Perhaps,' he said. 'But it makes my hearts glad to see you restored.'

The two figures stood in Temekh's sanctum aboard the *Herumon*. The Corvidae sorcerer-lord was wearing his usual robes, helmless and with his violet eyes shining.

Before him stood a primarch, one of the Emperor's twenty favoured sons, the forgemasters of the Imperium, the demigods who had carved out the realms of men from the uncaring vastness of the void. He no longer wore the image of a child, or of an old man, but had unveiled the form that he'd taken during the long years of the Great Crusade. Tall, broad-shouldered, bronze-skinned and bronze-armoured, draped in a golden mantle stitched from shimmering feathers. He wore a golden helm crested with crimson horsehair. His own hair was thick and long, stained the deep red of cochineal. One hand rested on a leather-bound tome at his waist, chained to his immense frame by an iron chain, though not the one he'd carried before the Heresy. The other clasped the hilt of his sheathed sword.

Magnus the Red, the Crimson King, the Cyclops of Prospero.

The blessed, he was called, and the learned.

The cursed, he was called, and the fool.

Now he stood again within the ambit of realspace, fully embodied, glittering in the diffuse candlelight of the sanctum. For the coming battle he had assumed the appearance he had once worn by default, just another part of the symmetry of revenge. There was a weary, thin smile on his flawed face.

'How does it feel?' asked Temekh, emboldened by the humour his master seemed to be in.

'To wear physical form again? Different to last time I did so. I will never be truly flesh and bone again. But it is good, nonetheless.' The primarch raised a giant hand and flexed the fingers, one by one. 'Very good.'

'And do you have orders for me, lord?'

Magnus turned away from admiring his own presence and gazed fondly at Temekh.

'You have done all that has been asked, my son. The Wolves' lair is not for you. Only I will descend, though I will hold my nose as I do so.'

'Lord Aphael has penetrated the lower levels. His troops are removing the wards to allow your translation, and have penned the Dogs back to separate bulwarks within the Fang. It may still be several days before conditions permit you to enter.'

'They're still fighting? Impressive. Though perhaps I should not be surprised. It is their expertise, after all.'

'They are desperate, and as savage as beasts.'

Magnus lost his smile.

'I no longer think of them as animals, Ahmuz, though I once did. I now think of them as the purest of us all. Incorruptible. Single-minded. The perfection of my father's vision.'

Temekh looked up at his primarch, taken aback.

'You admire them.'

'Admire them? Of course I do. They are unique. And even in an infinite universe, that quality is rarer than you might suppose.'

Temekh paused before replying, weighing up whether he still risked saying something capable of damning him.

'If that is so, lord, then why are we pursuing this war? The others – the Raptora, the Pyrae – they prosecute it for vengeance, to inflict the hurt that they inflicted on us. I cannot share that sentiment. It seems... unworthy of us. We are better than that.'

Magnus walked up to the sorcerer-lord and placed a heavy hand on Temekh's shoulder.

'We are,' he said. 'We are much better than that. Let the drive for vengeance motivate the others – it will make them fight harder. This battle is about far more than the settling of scores.'

His single eye was unwavering then, a circle of gold flecked with the full spectrum of visible light. Temekh found it impossible to look into, impossible to look away from.

'We fight to prevent a possible future. A future that, even now, gestates within the mountain below us. If we succeed, the hurt we will inflict on the Wolves of Fenris will rival what they did to us. If we fail, then all we have accomplished since our arrival on the Planet of the Sorcerers will be as nothing.'

THE INTENSITY OF the first ranged attack was absorbed, contained, and blunted. There was an ebb in the pattern of gunfire from the tunnels below the Fangthane, and then the Rubric Marines stormed the lower slopes of the stairway. The Wolves leapt out to meet them, and the narrow killing ground was instantly clogged. Taking advantage of the higher ground and more established heavy fire support, the defenders initially had the better of it. The Blood Claws fought with all their customary abandon, only barely reined in by the monstrous form of Rossek. They were complemented by the more methodical Hunters under Skrieya, who'd learned over many years how to make the most of the confined spaces under the mountain.

Even so, there were casualties. The Traitor Marines doled out pain with both hands, their killing no less effective for all its unsettling silence. When the attackers broke away at last, pulling back to regroup from their mauling on the stairway approaches, there were grey-armoured bodies lying on the stone too, shattered and bleeding.

And so it went on. There was no sudden breakthrough, no decisive shift in the balance of power. The attacks came in waves, the Traitor Marines in the vanguard, each time attempting to bludgeon the Wolves higher up the stairway and seize the barricades. Every assault got slightly further before the unseen sorcerers called their soul-slaves back, leaving heat-reddened rock and cooling blood behind them.

Hours passed, punctuated by an unreliable rhythm of attack and repulsion. Mortal troops were rotated from the barricades, replaced with fresh kaerls held in reserve. Magazines were replaced, armour patched up, blast-walls repaired, fresh supplies brought down from the Fangthane. Bodies were hauled away from the frontline. The mortals were taken one way, the Wolves another. The Sky Warriors didn't die easily, but with every attack from the Thousand Sons, another brace of corpses were retrieved, every one a testament to some heroic stand against the overwhelming numbers of the attacking host.

At the forefront of every assault, and the last to withdraw to the barricades at the end of every action, was Tromm Rossek. He'd lost none of his brooding, terrifying intensity. With every defender's death, he seemed to withdraw further inside himself, transmuting deeper into a grim leviathan of the murder-make rather than the laughing, ebullient warrior-god he'd been of old. His movements were tighter, his orders sharper, his blows heavier when they hit. The loss of his pack had done more than drive the old fire from his soul; it had made him darker, and it had made him deadlier.

His new pack, the battle-ravaged dregs of others' commands, had responded to that new spirit. They'd lost some of their swagger too, and there was less chat over the vox as they indulged their raw-edge talent for killing, but they hadn't forgotten how to do it. The Blood Claws spun, kicked, punched and blasted their way into contact with their more orthodox opposite numbers, taking their lead from the glowering giant in their midst, feeding off the raw loathing that hung over him like the stench of death.

They still died. The Claws always died, thrust as they were into the jaws of Morkai by their reckless, selfless way of war. But when they fell, there were always more broken armour-shells around them, more sighing corpses of soulless, shattered Rubric Marines, freed from their unknowable life of emptiness. Brakk would have been proud, seeing the seeds he'd planted bearing fruit at last.

So the attacks continued, growing in ferocity as the hours, then days, blurred into one another. The Thousand Sons had the troops, and the time, and the patience. The Hunters would take over the burden, giving the Blood Claws a few hours' rest. Then the process was reversed. And again, over and over until the blood-drenched stairway looked like a vision of Hel's gateway.

The line held. Every assault was repulsed at enormous cost and with terrible sacrifice, but for as long as the barricades remained intact and the Wolves remained on their feet, the Fangthane remained unconquered.

BJORN WADED FURTHER into combat, watching through banks of optical implants as his enemies were cut down under his blades. He barely registered the steady rain of projectiles against his armoured outline. His visual field was thick with targets, blinking red runes set against a flickering backdrop.

He ignored them. He fought then as he always had done – on instinct. The animal-sharp reflexes he'd once enjoyed were gone, as distant a memory as his natural limbs, but he still moved far faster than looked possible from his heavy, blocky shell.

There were privileges to being the oldest Dreadnought in the Underfang. His chassis was of incredibly ancient design, incorporating technologies that had been rare even before the conflagration of the Heresy. The centuries since then had seen further refinements by successive Iron Priests, each desperate to outdo one another in the glory they could add to the sarcophagus of the Fell-Handed.

They think I do not know what they have done to my tomb.

Bjorn cared nothing for the finery. He would happily have lost all the gold emblems embossed on his living coffin, would have lost every silver rune-pattern traced across the ceramite, just for the chance to come *face to face* with his prey again.

He would never feel the hot splash of blood across his flesh again, the moment the blade went in and cut the thread of his prey. His nerve-lattice relays were good – much better than those fitted to any other Dreadnought in the Imperium – but they would never get the sensation quite right.

So, to assuage their guilt, they drape my tomb with skulls and totems. Trinkets. I loathe them.

He lowered his plasma cannon, barely registering as the orbs of sunburst-energy punched off into the dark. The screams of those he downed were just so much background static. Bjorn alone had terminated the life-signs of more enemies than some whole Chapters. With such a record, death had ceased to have much meaning. The pleasure had long gone. All that remained was the need.

And I need to kill. By Russ, I need to share my pain.

It had always been painful, ever since Russ had gone. There had been no explanation, no words of comfort.

One night, one midwinter's night of storm-fury, the primarch had gone.

Leman Russ had left without saying why, charging into the void as he always did, heedless of the danger, heedless of those he left behind.

Bjorn whirled on his axis, crunching a Rubric Marine in his claw and throwing it into the air. When the body landed the beasts got to work, slicing into the hollow armour with their rending claws. By then Bjorn had taken on another two targets, blasting holes in ceramite and slicing through ribs of banded steel.

Did you know how angry that made me, that you never said why?

He had fought differently when he'd been alive. Back then, many lifetimes ago, he'd raced into battle with Godsmote, and Oje, and Two-Blade, and their wyrds had been coiled together tighter than throttle-twine. The Wolves around him now cut threads with the same peerless majesty as those of old, but it wasn't the same. Bjorn knew the galaxy had aged, and he had not. He had no place here, not with the hot-blooded whelps who had inherited the mantle of the Aett.

I think you knew. You knew I would hate this. You knew every moment would be torture for me.

A sorcerer came into cast-range, half-obscured by ranks of Traitor Marines. He began to kindle maleficarum in the palms of his hands, conjuring balls of flame, ready to hurl into combat.

Bjorn registered the witch with contempt. Or, at least, his mind felt contempt. It was possible that the emotion translated into some physical pattern on his ruined face, submerged in fluid and withered by the pitiless weight of ages, but such subtlety certainly didn't register on his face-guard.

And that, above all, makes me believe you kept the truth from me for a reason.

He took a single, bracing stride, rocked back and detonated his cannon. The sorcerer disappeared beneath a tidal wave of explosions, burning and ripping up. Bjorn kept firing, kept funnelling all his hatred and weariness and anguish at the crippled Traitor. When he finally stopped, finally turning to find more prey, his victim's armour was little more than a super-hot puddle of sizzling hydrocarbons.

This anger, this betrayal. It keeps me alive.

The beasts stayed at his heels, tearing the head off any enemy who got too near, but allowing Bjorn to bring his close combat weapon to bear if needed. They darted and raced through the melee as they'd been designed to, matching the supernatural agility of the Wolves beside them. Bjorn knew how they were capable of such things, and why they'd been made. Very few others did.

I loved you as none of your sons loved you. You knew this.

Absently, Bjorn noticed one of his fellow Dreadnoughts, Hrothgar, suffering under a concerted onslaught from a whole squad of Rubric Marines, backed up by the indomitable presence of a Cataphract. Irritated by the distraction, he spun round, got a firing solution and took the war machine's head off. Even before the bronze skull had hit the ground he was back into the attack, plunging his claw-blades into fresh meat.

My thanks, lord, voxed Hrothgar.

Bjorn didn't reply. He was busy killing. That was all he ever did. It was either stasis, or killing. Unconsciousness, or fury.

You knew I would hate you. You, who left me to this fate. I would have pierced the veils of reality with you, marched with you to destiny, stood beside you against the enemy you knew was waiting.

His cannon bellowed out, laying waste to rows of the enemy. He was invincible, titanic, massive, far superior to any foe before him. Nothing the Thousand Sons had brought to face him had even remotely troubled him. Just as on Prospero, Bjorn was unmatched.

Perhaps – *perhaps* – this was how a primarch felt in combat.

And I know what you were doing. You birthed this hate in me, as potent as the love I still cannot shake.

If he'd possessed tear-glands, he would have wept. If he'd possessed a jawline, it would have been clenched into an eternal grimace of horror. If he'd possessed vocal cords, they would have trembled in a howl of utter, soul-burning anguish.

For hate is the most powerful drive in the universe, and you needed to give me such power that the Wolves would never be without a defender.

But Bjorn had none of these things. All he had was the fury of the favoured son rejected by his father. And, as the galaxy knew from bitter experience, that fury held nothing but the promise of death, and devastation, and a rain of blood.

ANOTHER ATTACK HAD been repelled. Wearily, the defenders at the Fangthane let their guns fall silent, preparing to count the dead and wounded and haul them from the frontline. Though the fighting had stopped for a short while, there was no pause in their labour. Squads of kaerls were rotated in the brief respite, with those having taken the brunt of the assault for longest being withdrawn and replaced by fresher troops. As the assault had ground on, a murderous procession of attack and counter-attack, all the mortals had gone without sleep, and even those being newly drafted to take up position had the heavy-limbed gaits of weary men. The habitual swagger of the Fenrisian kaerls had long gone, replaced with a blank, dogged defiance.

Morek had been on shift for thirteen hours by the time he was called back. A Wolf Guard gave him his orders. His armour was dented and scorched as if he'd waded through a lake of magma.

'Rivenmaster,' he'd barked, his booming voice distorted by a broken vox-unit. 'What are you still doing on station?'

'My duty,' Morek had said, his voice trembling with fatigue, unable to think of anything else to say.

Then the Wolf Guard had pushed him roughly up the slope of the stairway toward the rear positions, past the lines of barricades and gun emplacements towards the open hall of the Fangthane.

'Your duty is to obey the rotation patterns,' he snarled. 'Ensure your replacement is here before the next wave hits.'

So Morek had stumbled away from the frontlines at last, hardly able to lift his head from his armour's neck-guard, hardly able to hold his rifle in his hands.

He'd lost any awareness of how long the carnage had been going on for. The hours had bled into days, which had extended into a long train of horrifyingly brutal engagements and tense, exhausting waiting periods. He'd snatched some sleep where he could, but it had never been enough. He'd woken abruptly at one point during a lull in the fighting, screaming something about a horror lurking in the fleshmakers' labs. Thankfully, fighting broke out almost immediately afterwards, dragging the exhausted kaerls' attention to more pressing matters. Despite the lucky escape, his lack of control scared him.

As Morek passed through the rear defences, walking in the shadow of four massive gun turrets, he was only dimly aware of the movement all around him. Kaerls were everywhere, hauling crates of ammunition, armour or rations, dragging themselves back from the front like him or preparing to take up their positions in his place. Some still moved with a steady, dependable resolve. Others staggered as they marched, exhaustion evident in their movements.

None of them looked remotely likely to shirk their duty and seek a less dangerous station. Fenrisian rivens had no equivalent of the Imperial Guard Commissars. They weren't needed. The very idea of trying to evade combat in order to achieve some short lived safety was as alien to the death world's psyche as charity.

As Morek emerged from the gun-lines and into the greater space of the hall beyond, he nearly stumbled into a heavy weapons squad hurrying to the front. Mumbling a curt apology, he backpedalled away from them, only to crash into a stack of dried meat cases waiting to be doled out to the defenders. He fell clumsily to the floor, his legs giving out just as he tried to right himself.

For a moment, he stayed there, feeling the hard stone beneath his back, letting the temptation to rest – for a moment – sink into his bones.

Just for a minute. Just for two minutes. Then back on my feet.

The world reeled around him, losing focus, and he felt his tired lids flicker towards closing.

Then there was a massive presence looming over him. Some instinct told him that giving in to unconsciousness in front of it would be a terrible mistake, and he forced himself up on to his knees.

'Your pardon, lord,' he mumbled, trying not to scatter the cases around him any further as he rose.

To his astonishment, the giant before him extended a massive gauntlet. As he considered grasping it to haul himself up, Morek noticed that the ceramite wasn't grey, but black.

His eyes lifted, passing over a scarred breastplate, festooned with the bones of animals. The helm face-mask was a skull, cracked open by a blade-impact and as coal-black as the rest of the battle-plate. The lenses glowed angrily, staining the cheek-guards like bloody tears.

'Morek Karekborn?' came the dry, age-tempered voice of Thar Ariak Hraldir, the one they called Wyrm-blade, the fleshmaker. 'It is time, I think, that we spoke together.'

Morek gazed up into the skull-visage of the Wolf Priest. His fatigue seemed to fall away from him then. It was replaced, as he'd known it would be for so long, with the cold grip of fear.

'As you command, lord,' he replied, but his voice was as dry as embers.

APHAEL STALKED THROUGH the empty tunnels of the Hould. The battles at the two choke-points had been raging for days already, with no immediate sign of a breakthrough. He expected them to burn for many more days to come. The Dogs would be tenacious in defence. They had to be – there was nowhere for them to go.

That suited him fine. The purpose of the first wave assault was not just to inflict pain, but to clear the defenders from the heart of the Fang for long enough to destroy more of the wards against sorcery. That work was difficult and tiring, especially in his fevered state.

Aphael had continued to suffer from the flesh-change. Combat was only a partial release. In its absence, he'd become erratic, prone to violent mood swings, incapable of making decisions calmly. He knew it was happening. As if observing himself from afar, he could see his mental processes disintegrating with every passing hour.

And now, a new presence had started to press on him, crowding out what control he still possessed. Something conscious was stirring, deep within his own mind. A sentience not his own had taken root within his thoughts and was gradually accruing more strength. Even as his body rebelled against him, his mind had begun to slip away too.

Once the inevitability of his destruction became clear, Aphael had passed through the familiar response pattern. Disbelief. Rage. Misery. Now he'd ended up in a dull kind of acceptance. There was nothing he could do to fight the process. Already his body and armour were intimately fused together, such that he knew he'd never be able to remove it. The only task remaining was to carry out his duties for as long as he could.

I will see the Dogs burn. After that, do whatever you wish with me. But I will not pass into oblivion until our retribution is complete. I will not.

Such bravado, he knew, was pointless. The Changer of Ways was not a power to be threatened or cajoled.

And yet, the words brought a grain of comfort to him. He was still capable of defiance, at least verbally.

Aphael came to stand before another one of the wards. It had been placed at the intersection of four tunnels. The junction was a circular chamber with an empty fire pit in the centre of it. The ward had been created on a stone pillar that rose from next to the pit. It was in the shape of an eye, scratched into the stone, with a jagged incision scored across it. There was human blood in the scratch, and a few runes carved underneath.

So simple. A child could have made something similar. Yet the raw power bleeding from the symbols clamped down on his sorcery like a fist locked over a mouth. The Rune Priests, for all their clumsy misunderstanding of the warp, were adept at manipulating its signs. Somehow, as untutored and ignorant as they were, they had learned how to focus the parallel energies of the aether through the use of names, sigils and gestures. Created in such numbers, the wards of the Fang acted as a powerful dampener of sorcerous energy, such that even summoning the mildest of magicks was difficult and dangerous.

That had to end.

Aphael stood before the ward, wearily preparing for the rite that would destroy it. Around him, his guard of six Rubricae took up stations in the chamber. The last slivers of flame in the fire pit rippled out, plunging the space into complete darkness. Absently, Aphael blinked to adjust his helm lens filters.

It was only then that he saw the children. There were seven of them, huddled in the dark, rubbing up against one another like rats.

Despite everything, despite all his inner turmoil, despite the need for swift clearance of the wards, Aphael smiled.

He turned his bronze head toward them. In the perfect dark, his helm picked out the childrens' outlines in the fuzzy green of night-vision. He saw their terrified faces, their tiny fingers scrabbling at the rock walls.

How had they been left behind in the Hould? Did the barbarians of Fenris care so little for their own young that they abandoned them to the enemy? Or had some terrible mistake been made?

In either case, it gave Aphael a rare chance to exercise his skills in the cause of genuine pleasure. Their deaths would be lingering, a fitting punishment for all the hurt inflicted on his Legion by the Dogs of Fenris.

'Feel free to scream, little ones,' purred Aphael, withdrawing his blade and picking his first victim. 'There's plenty of ti–'

Something hit him hard in the helmet, thrown with astonishing accuracy and poise. Then it exploded, rocking him back on his heels.

'*Fekke-hofud!*' yelled one of the whelps, darting past him and scampering into the dark.

Aphael roared with rage, and swung his sword down quickly, aiming to scythe the little horror down as he ran. The stroke was knocked off-course by another grenade going off, this time hurled at his midriff.

They're armed! They were left here – with weapons!

'Kill them all!' shouted Aphael, whirling round and

405

reaching to grasp one of the fast-moving brats. He grabbed the bolt pistol at his waist and pulled it free. By then the Rubricae had swung into action, grasping for the children as ineffectually as he did.

They were as fast as rats, and just as at home in the tunnels. More grenades were discharged, including one that actually took down a Rubric Marine, detonating a flurry of frag-discharge into his face and dumping him on to the ground.

Then they were gone, darting down the corridor beyond like whelp-ghosts, leaping and laughing into the echoing dark.

Aphael swept his pistol up and released a torrent of rounds into the tunnel entrance. None of them connected. The urchins of the Fang, bred to a lifetime of darkness and survival expertise, were too fast, too wily, and too well prepared.

The laughter died away. The downed Rubricae regained its feet, looking all the more ridiculous for its very lack of embarrassment. It took up position again, as silent and serious as before.

There was no real harm done. For all their stealth and speed, the tunnel-rats had no means of hurting a Space Marine.

But it was humiliating. Deeply humiliating.

'I *loathe* this world!' roared Aphael, whirling round to the ward-pillar and letting his anger ignite his staff.

The shaft of iron exploded into ruinous, terrible light, banishing the darkness and sending flickering beams of aetheric electricity shooting in all directions. The blazing inferno crackled against the ward, sucked towards it as if by magnetism. The symbol resisted for a moment, glowing an angry red, soaking up the horrific amount of energy pouring from the sorcerer's staff.

Then, inevitably, it broke. A hairline crack ran down the image, shattering the unity of the device and interrupting the runic text beneath. The frigid air rippled with a sudden, searing heat, and then sank back into cold darkness.

Aphael let the power drain back into his staff, panting heavily. All around him, the Rubricae looked on inscrutably.

The ward was broken, and Aphael felt his power instantly magnify. The sense of relief was fleeting. He was humbled, angry and frustrated. There were kilometres of tunnels still to work through, all of them riddled with traps for the unwary.

This was menial work, fit for acolytes, not for commanders. If any of his subordinate Pyrae had been skilled enough to take his place, he'd happily have drafted them into ward-destruction instead of him.

But they weren't, and in any case the greater mass of sorcerers were needed to shepherd the Rubric Marines into combat.

Damn Ahriman. He's made us into a Legion of fools, stumbling around with our puppets in tow.

'Follow,' he muttered, striding out of the chamber and into the next tunnel. The Rubricae smoothly moved to comply. As he went, Aphael could feel the flesh-change accelerating, encouraged by his outburst of anger.

Time was running out, slipping like sand through his fingers, racing towards the horror he knew was waiting. It would not be long now. Not long at all.

* * *

WYRMBLADE LED MOREK far away from the stairway, across the broad floor of the Fangthane and under the feet of the Russ statue. As they went, the air was filled with the trundle of supply transports, the cries of huskaerls ordering their troops back into position, the distant thud of fighting elsewhere in the massive expanse of the Aett. No one gave the Wolf Priest and his mortal hanger-on a second glance.

Morek felt slightly aggrieved about that. If he was going to his death, it would have been nice for someone, just one person, to have cast a sympathetic look in his direction. But, of course, they had no way of knowing what Wyrmblade's business with Morek was. And even if they had, would it have changed anything? Was the power of the Wolf Priests so absolute that there were no sanctions, at all, on what they did with their mortal charges?

That was what I thought, too, and not long ago. Back when my faith was unconditional. The way it ought to be.

The two of them went beyond the statue, out of the Fangthane and into the dark, cold corridors beyond. The noise of fighting at the defensive barricades died away, leaving the chill and isolation of the Jarlheim in its place. Wyrmblade strode powerfully, and Morek had to trot to keep up. As he did so, he felt his exhaustion begin to return – there was only so much fear could do to keep it at bay.

Eventually, Wyrmblade paused before a slide-door in the tunnel wall. He gestured to open it, and ushered Morek inside. Once the door had closed on them, they were alone and entirely sealed off. They stood in a narrow, high-roofed chamber, unfurnished aside from a

single wooden stool and a small fire pit. A collection
of bones was suspended on a length of rope hung over
the flames, twisting gently in the heat. Though mod-
est, the place had the look and feel of a fleshmaker's
abode. Perhaps a rite-chamber of some sort. Or maybe
an executioner's.

'Sit,' ordered Wyrmblade, motioning toward the stool.

Morek did so, instantly feeling even smaller and more
insignificant. The Wolf Priest remained standing, gigantic and threatening, less than two metres away. He kept
his helm on, making his voice, if possible, drier and
more unearthly than usual.

For a moment, Wyrmblade simply looked at him,
saying nothing. Morek did his best not to betray his
trepidation. In normal circumstances, he'd probably
have managed it, but after so many days of constant
fighting the task was difficult.

And he was old. Too old, perhaps. That in itself was a
cause for shame. Not many Fenrisians died from their
age, and it had never been something he'd aspired to.

'Do you know why you're here?' asked Wyrmblade
at last.

The voice wasn't kind, but neither was it unduly
harsh. It was matter-of-fact, stern, authoritative.

'I believe so, lord,' replied Morek.

There was no point in evasion. Wyrmblade nodded,
as if satisfied.

'Then we need not rehearse what brought you to my
chambers. I know why you were there, and what you
saw. Since I discovered your name, I have been watching you. Perhaps you have noticed. I did not feel the
need to hide it.'

Of course not. The Sky Warriors never had the need to worry what a mortal might think of them.

'It has taken me many days to decide what to do with the name Tromm Rossek gave me. As the enemy wears us down to our limits, I can no longer delay. And yet, even now, my mind is still undecided. Your fate has become a burden to me, Morek Karekborn.'

Morek said nothing, but tried to keep his eyes on the skull-mask above him. He'd always told Freija the same thing.

Look them in the eyes. You must always, always look them in the eyes.

That was still the case when the eyes in question were hidden behind the long ivory skull of a slain beast and locked within blood-red, glowing lenses.

'So,' said Wyrmblade, still adopting his chilling, rather prosaic tone of voice. 'What did you think of what you saw?'

'I was shocked, lord.'

Tell the truth. That is your only chance.

'Appalled.'

Wyrmblade nodded again.

'You have been raised in the Aett. Everything you believe in is here. We have made you in our image, lesser versions of ourselves. You were not schooled to question the order of things, nor should you have been.'

Morek listened, still working hard to control his breathing. He could feel his pulse, heavy in his veins. The fire behind him was uncomfortably hot after the privations of the barricades.

'What you saw was forbidden. In different circumstances, your very presence in that room would

410

have been death. The Lord Sturmhjart has been trying to get in there for weeks and without success. If events had not conspired to make the watch laxer than it should have been, the contents of the room would still be secret. So now I have to decide what to do with you.'

Though it was impossible to tell, Morek felt as if the terrible old face behind the mask was smiling – a hooked grin, exposing yellow teeth.

'And as you have been truthful with me, I will be truthful with you, Morek Karekborn,' said Wyrmblade. 'I had resolved to cut your thread. The danger of the work we are doing leaking out has always been so great, and that, you must understand, will never be allowed to happen.'

The prospect of the Wolf Priest ending his life had strangely little effect on Morek. He had already prepared for it. He had been prepared for it every night since the mission to the fleshmakers' chambers. Only the Wolf Priest's strange indecision had postponed the moment longer than it had needed to be.

'If that is my wyrd,' said Morek, even managing to sound half-convinced by it.

'I believe you mean that. You have commendable faith, Karekborn. Though I sense your devotion has been diminished in recent days, which is also not something to be surprised about.'

The Wolf Priest let out a long, whistling sigh.

'Do not think that I have somehow lost my resolve for killing, mortal,' he said. 'I have killed for this work before, and, Allfather providing, will do so again. But I will not kill you. Your wyrd does not end here, locked in this room. That, at least, I can see clearly.'

Morek knew he should feel some kind of relief at that. He didn't. Perhaps it was the fatigue, perhaps it was the loss of faith. Whatever the cause, he found himself wishing for nothing more than sleep, for respite from the endless dark, the endless cold, the endless combat. For as long as he could remember, the Wolf Priests had been an inspiration to him, a tangible link between the mass of humanity and the awesome example of the eternal Allfather. Now, towered over by this near three-metre high behemoth, so close he could see the blade-bites on the ravaged armour and hear the rattle of the breathing through the helm filters, he could summon up none of that lifelong awe. The spell had been broken.

I am not afraid of you. Now, at last, I understand what Freija has been telling me for so long. Daughter, forgive me. You were right.

'But you must be punished, mortal,' Wyrmblade continued. 'If the Heresy taught us anything, it is that transgression must always be met with reprisal. And so I will give you the most terrible gift in my possession.'

The Wolf Priest's helm lowered slightly, bringing the red eyes more on a level with Morek's. They shone dully amid the scorched bone, like rubies set in old stone.

'What you witnessed is called the Tempering. It will change the face of the Chapter forever. Listen, and I will explain how it will destroy and remake all that you have ever been taught to hold sacred.'

CHAPTER NINETEEN

BOREK'S SEAL RANG with the sound of barking gunfire, the thunder of war-engine treads and the spit of oil-furnaces. The Thousand Sons pushed forwards again, ranks of them moving in unison, laying down a close wall of bolter-fire.

Thanks to Bjorn and Greyloc, the enemy had been held at the portals. None of them had yet crossed into the Seal chamber itself, and the many fixed gun positions there were silent and still. The battle raged, as it had done since Bjorn had met up with Greyloc, in the entrance arches, where the Dreadnoughts and Long Fangs had dug in. Just as at the Fangthane, barricades and trenches of adamantium provided cover for the defending infantry. The pattern of battle was simple – endless, repeated attempts by the invaders to storm

413

the perimeter and break into the space beyond, shattering the advantage given to the defending forces by the narrow choke-point.

They had been unsuccessful in that objective so far, but the cost had been high. The kaerls stationed in the barricade zone had suffered under bolter fire, and whole squads had been wiped out in single thrusts. The Sky Warriors weren't immune either, despite their superior armour and weaponry. Aside from the command group, who looked almost invulnerable in their Terminator battle-plate and power weapons, the Hunters and Claws had taken serious casualties going up against the Rubric Marines.

Freija had done her part during the repeated actions, leading her squad of kaerls in support operations, laying down covering fire to allow the Wolves to enter close combat. It had been the hardest, toughest fighting she'd ever been part of. At a given signal from a Sky Warrior, she and her troops would dart from the relative safety of the barricades and lock sights on any Prosperine infantry within range. The *skjoldtar* rifles were more powerful than the enemy's lasguns and inflicted heavy damage, but the kaerls were still vulnerable once out of cover. Dozens had been brought down in previous sorties, caught by las-beams or ripped apart by Rubric Marines before the Wolves could race to assist. Freija had almost had her own thread cut more than once, only saved by her reflexes, her armour, or a good slice of luck.

As the battle had progressed through the days, her fatigue had began to grow, slowing her down and making her aim less sure. Casualties rose as the lack of sleep and constant rotation ground the defenders down. The Prosperine infantry suffered too. After so long locked in a state of semi-constant fighting, the stone floor became ankle-deep in blood, gore and weapon coolant.

Freija had expected the Sky Warriors to look after the sharp end of business and let the kaerls take care of themselves. It would have been in character for them, she thought, to let the mortal support troops suffer the brunt of the firestorm, so long as they were free to close in on the hand-to-hand combat they lived for.

That didn't happen. Once the real fighting began, the Wolves seemed to treat the kaerls almost as equals. It was as if the very act of combat brought them on to the same level. In the normal run of things, a Blood Claw would barely notice a thrall, let alone speak to him. And yet, once the bolter rounds started flying, the distinctions between them suddenly, strangely, ceased to matter.

As Freija had fought on, willing her body to resist the exhaustion that dragged at her muscles, she had found her attitude toward her masters begin to change. She'd seen a Grey Hunter charge headlong into a whole rank of Rubric Marines, his axe whirring, his bolter spitting out a hail of shells. He'd taken down three of them, barrelling one bodily to the ground once his ammo was gone, fighting with his fists once his axe had been knocked out of his hands. He'd kept attacking to the end, expert and brutal, never giving up until a glowing blade was shoved straight into the gap between helm and breastplate, nearly taking his head off.

No fear. No fear at all. He'd been magnificent, the

perfect predator, living up to his breeding as the finest warrior archetype in the galaxy. Freija had found the single-minded arrogance of the Sky Warriors maddening in the past, but in combat she saw why it had to be that way.

They cannot doubt. Not even for a second. They must believe they are the Allfather's keenest blades, his most potent weapons.

Now I see them in their pure state, I am awed by them.

The example had made Freija fight all the harder. She'd been stationed close to Aldr's position, and the Dreadnought had been as immense in defence as his battle-brothers. The strange, almost childlike confusion that had made him seem so vulnerable after awakening had evaporated. Now, no doubt inspired by the peerless example of Bjorn the Fell-Handed close by, Aldr thundered into combat with all the extravagant assurance of his gene-heritage.

He was astonishing, a twin-handed dealer of death, and wherever he came the invaders fell back in disarray. Bolt-rounds clattered harmlessly across his heavy shielding like hailstones, and even the Rubric Marines had no answer to the mammoth claw blades he sent crushing into them. As with the other five Dreadnoughts in the defensive perimeter, Aldr had created islands of stability within the roar and rush of the assaults, islands that lesser warriors could crowd around and use to push out from.

Freija might have imagined it, but the Dreadnought seemed to pay particular attention to her pack. Once, when they'd been caught out of position and lacking in cover, he'd lumbered right between her and the advancing enemy, using his bulk to soak up the incoming fire and launch a vicious, whirling counter-assault single-handedly.

Once safely back under the lee of the barricades, her squad mauled, but still cohesive, Freija had looked back at the rampaging war machine in mute admiration, watching as his fire-swathed shell barged into harm's way with all the swagger of a new aspirant flexing his stone-hard muscles.

Freija kept watching, her gaze held by the thoughtless heroism on display. It thrilled her. For the first time, she felt proud. Proud of her heritage, proud that such gods of war were part of the fabric of her home world. Proud that the Sky Warriors stood alongside her in the trenches, fighting to preserve everything they'd built together on Fenris.

I am not afraid of you.

Freija slammed a replacement magazine into her rifle and prepared to lay down supporting fire. That was her role, her loyal part in the glorious defence of the Aett.

Now, at last, I understand what my father has been telling me for so long.

She looked round to check her squad was with her, then slammed the *skjoldtar* into the firing slot on the barricade crest. She rested her chin against the sights, watching with satisfaction as a line of charging Prosperine infantry came into range.

Father, forgive me.

The recoil of the hammering shoulder-stock bored into her armour plate, slamming against the bruised skin. A rain of covering fire screamed past Aldr, warding him in a mantle of ripping, tearing projectiles, augmenting his already devastating assault potential.

You were right.

WHEN WYRMBLADE SPOKE of the past, his voice took on a different rhythm and timbre. It was akin to the declaiming tone used by the skjalds. The Aett's saga-tellers were all mortals, however, and the Wolf Priest's gigantic frame lent his speech a resonance none of them possessed.

'You know of the Allfather, the Master of Mankind, whom the ignorant venerate as a god, and whom we revere as the mightiest of us all and the guardian of the wyrd. In these darkened days, he dwells in Terra, watching over the vastness of the Imperium from his Golden Throne and contesting the measureless powers that seek to extinguish light and hope from the galaxy. In the past, it was not so. He walked among us, gifting his subjects a fraction of his power, marching to war with the primarchs and ridding the stars of the terror that plagued them.

'It was the Allfather who created Leman Russ, the primogenitor of the *Vlka Fenryka*, and the Allfather who fashioned the Legion that served under his name. For every Legion he created, there was a purpose. Some were blessed with the power to build, or the skill to administer, or the capacity for stealth. Our gift was different. We were made to destroy. Our whole being is destruction. Such was the will of the Allfather. He made us not to construct empires, but to murder them. We were bred to perform the tasks that no other Legion could, to fight with such extravagance that even our brother warriors would shrink from treachery in the knowledge of what we, the Rout, would do to them.

'That power was exercised more than once. Most famously, as you know, against the enemy who now hammers at our doors. But, for all our zeal, we failed in the task of protection. Treachery came, falling like lightning from heaven, and the galaxy was consumed by the fire of betrayal. Though the blackest evil was staunched, much that was great and good was lost. The Imperium is a bleaker place now, and the visions of its founders languish, stillborn and unrealised. We know this, we who preserve the sagas of old. Though many others who rely on the uncertain transmission of the written word and the recorded vox-pattern have forgotten those days, we who live by the recitation of the skjalds remember them all. We know what we were. We know what we were intended to be.

'Now, a new age has dawned. The Age of the Imperium, they call it. The needs of mankind have changed. Instead of twenty Legions, there are many hundreds of Chapters. There are no primarchs to guide them. Instead, the Adeptus Astartes fight in the image of their gene-fathers, rehearsing the capabilities designed for a different future. That is the way of things now, a vision made reality not by the Allfather, but by one of his sons. Chapters no longer march in ranks of tens of thousands or more. They create successors, off-shoots governed by the same gene-seed, so that their primarch's legacy is maintained across the stars. The more successors, the greater the legacy. The sons of Guilliman are the ancestors of hundreds, as are the

sons of Dorn, and so it is that the Imperium is mod-
elled in their image.'

Wyrmblade paused. There was an edge of distaste to
his words.

'This is what has become important. Not prowess.
Not danger. Stability. Reliability. Fidelity. Without
these things, no Chapter lives to exert influence.
Successors – these are what our brothers aspire to
create, to ensure that warriors of their temper flourish
and endure, and to exclude those forged from different
metal.

'And do you suppose, Morek Karekborn, that the
Vlka Fenryka have followed this path? Have we let
ourselves be divided into successor Chapters as the
Ultramarines, the Angels, or the Fists have done?'

'No,' said Morek confidently. 'We are different.'

Wyrmblade shook his head.

'Not that different. We had a successor: the Wolf
Brothers, led by Beor Arjac Grimmaesson. They were
to have been as numerous as we were, and as powerful. They were gifted a home world, Kaeriol, a planet
of ice and fire, just as Fenris is. They had half our fleet,
half our armouries, half our Priests. They were to have
been the first of many, a whole line of descendant Fenrisian Chapters – the Sons of Russ, capable of carving
out a star empire the size of Ultramar. That was the
vision: to be powerful enough to encircle the Eye of
Terror completely, to prevent the Traitors from daring
to leave it ever again. Thus, it was hoped, we would
fulfil our destiny and find a new purpose in the Age of
the Imperium.'

Morek looked up at the skull-mask of the Rune

Priest. The visions he was being asked to absorb were coming too quickly. A glimpse of the galaxy was unfolding in his mind, radically different from the one he knew. Though he'd been off-world many times and seen many wonders, this version of reality was the strangest of them all.

'What happened to them? The Wolf Brothers?'

'They are gone.'

'Destroyed?'

'Not all. Some may yet live, though their wyrd is unknown. They were disbanded, scattered to the six points of the compass. '

'Why?'

Wyrmblade drew in a deep, grating breath.

'For the same reason there can be no further successors to the Rout. The Wolf within. We are too dangerous to be copied. The heritage that makes us powerful also makes us unstable. The Brothers, located far from Fenris, fell quickly into the state of beasts. So it must be with any attempt to splice new growth from the gene-seed of Russ.'

Wyrmblade bowed his head. But then his eyes flashed in the dark, catching a stray flicker of light from the fire.

'Until now.'

REDPELT WAS ON his knees, firing from the waist, watching as the bolt pistol ammo-counter clicked down. His aim was precise, no shot was wasted. Bolts slammed into the oncoming ranks of Rubric Marines, taking down some, exploding against the armour of others.

Then they'd come again, just as they always did, in

remorseless waves, selling their empty souls to break the deadlock at the Fangthane stairway. There were more of them each time, some clad in the shimmering kine-shields of the witches, most relying on the protection of their sapphire battle-plate.

Redpelt exhausted the clip. He calmly knocked the empty container to the ground, grabbed a replacement and slammed it home. By the time he'd resumed firing, the enemy had come no more than two paces closer.

Heavy weapons fire streaked over his head from the Long Fangs, impacting amid the oncoming Traitor Marines. Much of it exploded against the kine-shields in glittering cascades of sparks and plasma-bursts, but some found a weak link and crashed amongst the armoured warriors, causing devastation.

Into those paths of ruin leapt the Wolves, chainswords thrumming, bellowing their litanies of hatred and defiance. Helfist was in the vanguard this time, his power fist rippling, the retrieved blade Dausvjer singing as it arced.

'Contact close, brother!' voxed Redpelt, powering into a sprint and racing after him.

Helfist dropped sharply, evading the stab of an oncoming Rubric Marine, before leaping back up and bringing his own blade to bear. The disruptor-laced edges clashed, sending an explosion of tortured energy out before the swords were withdrawn.

'Fodder,' spat Helfist contemptuously.

There was a strange undertow to his voice, rasping and blood-wet.

By then Redpelt was close at hand, his chainsword

juddering and bolt-pistol pumping. Everything was moving at staggering speed. There were no mortals in this fight. Rossek's Blood Claws did what they always did, fighting with abandon, relishing the unfettered exercise of their kill-urge, keeping Morkai a jaw-snap away and no more. The Traitors met them fearlessly, blocking and thrusting, waiting for the opening, seizing it with cold expertise, moving on to the next task. Both sides were fully committed, locked into a struggle that they knew would preserve or break the deadlock.

The Traitor managed to sweep his fist into Helfist's face, knocking him heavily to the ground. Redpelt let fly with his pistol, throwing the Rubric Marine back several paces in a cloud of detonating rounds.

'Careless, brother,' he jibed over the comm, whirling round to meet the next threat. 'Losing your touch?'

There was no reply from Helfist. Redpelt was soon occupied in hand-to-hand combat with another Traitor, and couldn't look round to check on him.

Helfist hadn't been hit that hard. What was wrong?

The next Rubric Marine slammed into contact, just one of the dozens that crowded into the narrow choke-point.

'Traitor filth!' roared Redpelt, punching out with his chainsword, aiming for the gap under the right shoulder-guard.

The Rubric Marine swung back, letting the whirring blades pass by before jabbing back with his own blade. The movements of both warriors were dazzlingly quick, each one weighted to perfection, each one capable of breaking through adamantium on connection. Redpelt pressed forwards, the kill-urge pulsing in his bloodstream. The blows rained fast, clanging from ceramite and rebounding back.

He had the momentum now. The Traitor fought well, but its weight had been pushed on to the back foot. Redpelt feinted left, then swept his blades up and across, aiming to catch the Rubric Marine under the thick breastplate.

He would have made it. The chainsword would have bit deep, tearing through the plate and into the hollow shell beyond. He would have had another kill, and his helm display would have registered another completion rune alongside the dozens that already lodged there.

He was prevented, not by the enemy, nor by the explosion of a long-range weapon, but by Helfist. The Blood Claw threw himself between the two duelling warriors, slamming into the Rubric Marine and rolling across the ground with it. There was something strange and unsettling about the speed of the manoeuvre. Before Redpelt had even reacted, Helfist had sprung to his feet, slammed Dausvjer into his victim's neck-guard, pulled the blade free, grabbed the stricken Traitor's helm with his power fist and wrenched it off.

His movements were terrifying, like the accelerated gestures of a nightmare. Helfist no longer spoke, no longer joked over the comm. As Redpelt backed away, watched warily for closing targets, he heard a thick, guttural wheezing coming over the comm.

'Brother–' Redpelt started, feeling cold.

Helfist wasn't listening. He was fighting. Fighting like he'd never been able to fight before, not even on the causeways. Rubric Marines charged up to him, and were torn apart. Literally, torn apart. Helfist's limbs passed into a blur of grey, a flailing pattern of devastation, tearing through battle-plate as if it were leather, punching it open and throwing it aside. He plunged into the oncoming ranks of the enemy like a predator let loose amid a herd of slow-moving herbivores, consumed with no thought other than downing as many of them as he could.

'Kyr!' shouted Redpelt, watching his brother move further out of formation.

None of the other Claws could follow him so far out. If they did, they'd be picked off by the Rubric Marines, unable to benefit from the cover of the fixed guns and supporting kaerl squads. Helfist was going to his death.

Redpelt charged toward him. He wouldn't stand by and watch it. He crunched into an oncoming Rubric Marine, putting as much strength as he could into every blow, feeling frustration mount that he couldn't just shoulder it aside like Helfist could. He fought with all the skill of his long conditioning, but it wasn't enough.

They were isolated. Helfist had damned himself.

It was then, and only then, that words came over the comm. They were badly slurred, like a drunkard trying to remember how to speak. Some of Helfist's old voice-pattern was in there, but it was almost gone. The phlegmy tones were more like beast than man, distorted by a mess of growling and slavering.

'Go, brother,' came the snarling, panting voice. 'I cannot protect you.'

Protect me?

Then Redpelt understood. Helfist was killing everything that came close to him. He'd passed too far, and there was no way back. Even Rossek wouldn't have been able to stop him then. The Wolf had taken Helfist, drawn him into its dark embrace and consumed what remained of his old humanity.

Redpelt finally dispatched his foe, but more were coming to take its place. Helfist was now deep within the ranks of the enemy, still fighting like a daemon, still carving them apart like a berserker of legend.

He couldn't follow. No one could follow that path unless the Wolf chose them too. Helfist was doomed, though in his death throes he'd slay more than many of his brothers would do in their whole lives.

Tears of rage started in Redpelt's eyes. They'd fought together since the beginning, since the half-forgotten days on the ice, since the Wolf Priests had first come for them to turn them into immortals. They'd passed through the trials together, learning the way of the Wolves together, gloried in the murder-make together. For a short time, such a short time, it had seemed as if no force in the galaxy could match the raw potency of their combined blades.

I cannot follow. Too slow. Blood of Russ, I was too slow.

Then Redpelt *howled*, a howl of rage and loss, an all-consuming, skirling torrent of pure anger and misery. For a brief moment the bark and echo of the guns were overmastered, and his horrifying cry resounded down the long tunnels of the Aett. Prosperine soldiers looked up from their fighting, thinking some devil of the Fang had come alive to drag them into the dark. Even the kaerls, steeped in the rituals and ways of the mountain, felt their blood run cold.

They knew what the cry meant. The Wolf had come, and claimed one of them for its own.

WYRMBLADE PAUSED BEFORE speaking again.

'The Wolf,' he said at last. 'The curse and the glory of our kind. For a generation of mortals, I have worked on a cure for it. No fleshmaker has ever discovered more than I of the ways of the Canis Helix, perhaps not even those who arrived on Fenris with the Allfather himself. It became clear to me the curse could be eradicated while preserving the glory. This work has been my calling.'

'The Tempering,' breathed Morek.

'Indeed. I have refined the Helix, altered it to deliver the supernatural strength of the Adeptus Astartes without the ravages of the beast within. The products are as powerful as I am, as quick in the hunt and as skilled with a blade, but they do not degenerate, nor do they fall prey to the Wolf. They take the qualities that make us superb, and purge the factors that prevent us from creating successors.'

Morek began to understand. The sickness he'd felt ever since stumbling across the bodies in the laboratorium came rushing back to him.

'The bodies...'

'The ones who came closest to my ideal. They lived for a short time. As of yet, none have survived for more than a matter of hours. Their deaths are... difficult. Yet I have demonstrated that the goal is within grasp. Given more time, just a little more time, I will have set us on a new path, one that promises domination over the stars, the domination of the Sons of Russ.'

Wyrmblade lifted his head proudly.

'Do you see this future, Morek Karekborn?'

Morek struggled to find the words to answer with. Images of Space Marines in gunmetal-grey armour were flitting through his mind, thousands of them, each Great Company drawn from a different Chapter. They fought the same way, killed the same way, swept their enemies before them in a tide of tightly-controlled murder-make. Fenris became just one world at the heart of a sprawling confederation, a temporal power within the greater circuit of the galactic Imperium, a power so mighty that even the Gods of Ruin hesitated as they saw its potential.

And then the vision was gone. The chamber endured, as dark and cold as all the chambers were under the mountain. The Wolf Priest stood before him, waiting.

'It horrifies me, lord.'

Wyrmblade nodded.

'Of course. You are a good Fenrisian. You do not see the alternatives, nor indulge your curiosity about what *might be*. All that matters to you is what *is*, what you can hold in your hands now. The horizon of the future is very close for you. You might die today, or tomorrow, or in a single season, so why spend time worrying about the passage of centuries?'

Morek remained impassive. Wyrmblade wasn't mocking him, just stating the facts of the matter. Until very recently, he'd have taken such a litany as a source of pride.

'But I cannot indulge those comforts,' said the Wolf Priest. 'We are the keepers of the flame, charged with ensuring there are always executioners for the Imperium to call on, always warriors capable of meeting the brutality of our enemies with an equal brutality.

'And, as I look over the runes with the scryers, as I listen to the pronouncements of Sturmhjart and the other Priests, I have no confidence in that future. I see a dark time ahead, an age when the *Vlka Fenryka* are too few to contain the legions of darkness, when we are mistrusted by the masters of the Imperium and feared by its citizens. I see a time when mortals will issue the words "Space Wolf" not as the embodiment of an ideal, but as a byword for backwardness and mystery. I see a time when the institutions of the Imperium will turn against us in their ignorance, believing us to be little more than the beasts we draw our sacred images from.

'Mark these words, rivenmaster: should we survive now, but fail to complete our apotheosis, this is not the last time Fenris will be besieged.'

Wyrmblade looked away from Morek, and gazed at the crozius arcanum at his belt. It hung next to his power sword, the symbol of his office, the mark of his stewardship of the ancient traditions of the Chapter.

'That is why we dare this thing. We can grow. We can change. We can escape the curse of the past. We can move from the margins of the Imperium to become the power at its centre.'

Morek felt the nausea swelling in his stomach, poisoning him and making him dizzy. He'd seen heretics before on other worlds, and always despised them. Now the madness came from the mouth of a Wolf Priest, the very guardian of sanctity.

'And this troubles you, Morek?' asked Wyrmblade.
Tell the truth.

'It makes me sick,' said Morek. 'It is wrong. Russ – honour to his name – would never have allowed it.'

Wyrmblade chuckled, an iron-hard rasping sound that limped out of the helm-grille.

'So you speak for the primarch now, eh? You're a brave man. I'd never presume to guess what he'd have made of this.'

Morek did his best to maintain a steady gaze, but the fatigue and the stress were getting to him. He felt faint, even while seated. For a fleeting moment, he saw the skull on the Wolf Priest's armour leer into a broken, toothy snarl.

He blinked, and the vision faded.

'Why are you telling me this, lord?' Morek asked, knowing he could not stand more revelations. His world had already been destroyed.

'As I said,' replied Wyrmblade calmly. 'To punish you. You have trespassed, thinking yourself equal to the secrets held in the fleshmakers' chambers. Now that arrogance is exposed, and you have tasted just a sip of the terrible knowledge that I bear daily. If I served you the whole cup, you would drown in it.'

'So is that what you wish for me?'

'I do not. I wish you to rest, as you have been ordered. Then I wish you to fight, to hold the line against the Traitor, to sell your position in blood if it comes to that. You will do this in the full knowledge of what has been done in the Valgard.'

The Wolf Priest gestured with a finger, and the fire behind Morek flickered out. Absolute darkness filled

the chamber, and the rivenmaster felt his consciousness begin to slip away almost immediately.

I welcome it. I wish never to wake up.

'We demand that you die for us, mortal,' said Wyrmblade, and his receding voice was as cold as the grave.
'We will always demand that you die for us. It is as
well, then, that you know what you're dying for.'

CHAPTER TWENTY

TEMEKH LOOKED INTO the eye of his primarch. Magnus had a strange expression on his face, part expectant, part resigned.

'The Fang is open to me,' he announced.

Temekh felt a sudden spike of eagerness, quickly suppressed. 'Aphael has been working hard.'

'Yes. He has done well.'

Magnus turned away. In the flickering light of the sanctum, Temekh could sense the raw power bleeding from his image. So much, it was hard to contain. Since casting aside his mortal flesh, the primarch required colossal amounts of energy merely to exist on the physical plane. It was like trying to squeeze a sun into a wineglass.

'I'll protest again,' said Temekh, knowing it was

useless. 'I could be of help down there. The Wolves are still fighting, and you could use another sorcerer.'

Magnus shook his head.

'I'll not tell you a third time, Ahmuz. You have a different fate.'

He looked back at the sorcerer-lord.

'You have your orders for the fleet. Do not deviate from them, whatever happens on Fenris.'

As he spoke, Magnus's outline was curling into nothingness like smoke.

'Of course,' said Temekh. 'But be careful – we have roused a nest of hornets down there.'

Magnus laughed, and the sound rang around the chamber like pealing bells. His body was rapidly extinguishing, sighing out of view and falling into the shadows.

'Careful? I'll take that as a joke. That's good. There was a time when there was more than gallows humour in the galaxy.'

Temekh watched the final shreds of Magnus's visible form slide away. The last element to fade out was the eye, ringed with scarlet and alive with amusement.

As soon as the apparition was gone, Temekh turned away.

+Lord Aphael+, he sent.

+Good to hear from you+, came the reply, sarcastic and weary. +The wards are much weakened. Tell him he may–+

+He knows. He's on his way. Get into position. You don't have long.+

Aphael didn't respond at once. Temekh could tell he was stung by the tone in his sending. Even now, the

Pyrae still thought he was in charge of the operation. That was pitiable, though Temekh didn't feel much like pitying.

+I am close to the bulwark they call the Fangthane+, sent Aphael eventually. +I can be there in moments. It will be good to witness our father in the material universe once again.+

Not for you, I fear, brother.

+He commended you on your labour+, sent Temekh.

He had the faint impression of a bitter laugh, and then the link between them broke.

Sighing, Temekh withdrew from the altar. The air within the chamber felt cold and thin in the primarch's absence. It resembled his own state. He was exhausted by the work of so many days, and his fingers trembled from a long, low level tiredness.

He gestured to the doors, and they slid open smoothly. In the corridor beyond, a silhouette waited for him, a mortal wearing the uniform of a Spireguard captain.

'Have you been waiting long?' asked Temekh, stepping out of the sanctum.

'No, lord,' came the reply.

You wouldn't have told me even if you had.

The man looked strangely nervous, and handed Temekh a data-slate.

'These are reports from the ship-seers,' he said. 'I thought you should see them as soon as possible.'

Temekh glanced at the runes, taking in their import in an instant. The ship-seers had powers beyond those of any loyalist Navigator to see the approaching bow-waves of starships powering through the warp.

The signals recorded on the slate, however, could have been picked up by any Navigator at the start of their training. The fleet coming towards them was approaching fast. Recklessly fast.

'Thank you, captain,' said Temekh calmly. 'Impressive. I didn't believe the interceptor could possibly have made it to Gangava.'

He handed the slate back, and rolled his head stiffly to relieve the ache in his shoulders.

'Very well. Prepare the fleet to break orbit.'

The captain started.

'You cannot mean–'

Temekh's glare silenced him.

'I am tired, captain; you really do not want to test my patience further. Prepare the fleet to break orbit, and wait for my command.'

He flicked a finger, and the doors to the empty sanctum slid shut.

'This game is coming to an end.'

APHAEL STRODE TOWARD the Fangthane, his bitterness fuelling him as powerfully as any chem-stimulant. The tone in Temekh's voice had been unmistakable. While the Corvidae sheltered on the bridge of the *Herumon* in safety, he was once more being thrust into the position of danger.

He didn't mind the danger. He relished combat, as all the Pyrae did. What bothered him was the peremptory manner of his assignment, the assumption that Temekh was in charge now.

Of course, Magnus had always had a soft spot for the Corvidae – the seers and mystics. The more belligerent cult-disciplines had always been the ones that had been reined in and curtailed. Much good it had done. The Corvidae were wayward. If the Thousand Sons had trusted more in the straightforward application of warp-power, perhaps they would have prevailed on Prospero rather than being hamstrung by doubts and visions.

He arrived at the chamber leading to the battle-front. Ahead of him, squads of Rubricae were waiting to enter combat, interspersed with larger formations of mortal infantry. Sorcerers, some of them limping from terrible wounds, walked among them. Far off, hundreds of metres down the tunnels leading to the stairway, came the sound of crashing explosions. The Wolves were being hit hard, but they evidently still held the Fangthane approaches.

'Greetings, lord,' came the reedy voice of Orfeo Cza-mine, the Pavoni commander of operations.

Aphael felt his face distort into an expression of con-tempt. It was entirely involuntary – his facial muscles were now wholly fused with the internal workings of his helm and had a mind of their own. Possibly liter-ally.

'How goes the assault?' asked Aphael, gesturing for his retinue to stand down.

Aphael knew his own voice now resembled a whole choir of speakers, each fractionally out of sync with one another. There was no hiding it, and no hope of the condition improving.

'We are grinding them down, as instructed,' replied Czamine, sounding unsurprised by the bizarre inflec-tions.

'They should have been cleared out of their hole by now,' Aphael said. 'You've had days to wipe them out. I may–'

He broke off. Czamine looked at him quizzically.

'Are you all right, lord?'

Aphael found he couldn't reply. The words formed in his mind, but his mouth no longer obeyed him. He felt the frustration of weeks burn up inside him. Furiously, he clutched his staff with both hands, not yet knowing what to do with it. As his armoured fingers closed over the shaft, witchfire sparked along its length, blazing with a painful, searing light.

Czamine fell back, radiating alarm.

'Lord, you are amongst brothers!'

By then Aphael's movements were no longer his own. The staff began to spin, hand-over-hand, picking up speed with every revolution. The iron whirled, shimmering in the dark from a nimbus of racing witchfire.

He wanted to scream. He wanted to explain.

This isn't me! Help me! Sweet Magnus, help–

But then his thoughts were taken over by another. The presence in his mind that had been growing for days suddenly asserted itself.

+Why should I help you, my son? This is what you were born for. In what time remains to you, relish the moment.+

The staff spun quicker, generating a vortex of rotating energy in its centre. Aphael's hands became a blur, turning over like engine pistons, driving the staff into a whirlwind of dizzying momentum.

Aphael's awareness was now almost gone. What

remained of him spied Czamine hurrying backwards, saw squads of mortals running from him in horror. He watched as the rock walls of the Fang glowed white, before realising that he was lighting them up himself. He was on fire, a caustic, dry fire that drenched the chamber in brightness. Warp-energy was bursting from his eyes, from his mouth, from the chinks in his armour. The flesh-change snarled into overdrive, warping his body into impossible contortions, breaking open the hard shell of his battle-plate and shedding it in rattling slivers.

With all the power that he still had, Aphael somehow dragged three words up from his receding consciousness.

Punish them, lord.

+Oh, I will+, came the response.

Then he was gone. The blaze of light and movement was no longer Herume Aphael. For a few moments, it was nothing at all, just a disparate collection of aetherborn energies, wild and inchoate.

Then there was a massive bang, causing the air to ripple and dust to rain down from the chamber roof. Cracks snaked along the floor, radiating out from the rapidly transforming cocoon of light and noise.

From that point, the whirling gradually wound down. The light faded, burning into a single point of brilliance. As it slowly died, a figure was revealed within it, taller than Aphael had been and far more beautiful. With the final diminishment of the portal, the newcomer stepped clear of the flickering tendrils of illumination.

As soon as he emerged, all those closest fell to their

knees in awe. Czamine bowed low, letting his staff scrape along the ground in submission.

'Father,' he said, and his voice was choked with joy.

'Son,' acknowledged Magnus the Red, flexing his muscles and smiling. 'You have been held up in this stinking place for too long.'

He turned toward the Fangthane stair, and there was a greedy light in his eye.

'Time, I think, to show the Wolves the true meaning of pain.'

ODAIN STURMHJART ROARED his defiance again, his voice cracking under the strain. He'd been summoning the power of the storm for days, using it to divide and demoralise the forces besieging Borek's Seal, and the pressure was beginning to show. His lips were cracked and calloused under his armour, and his throat was raw.

There was no let-up. The sorcerers were powerful, even more so since so many of the wards against maleficarum in the Hould had been taken down. Sturmhjart had little support, and carried almost all the burden of protecting the defending troops from sorcery. A lesser Rune Priest would have given up days ago, overwhelmed by the need to maintain the steady rain of wyrd-sourced power. Only one such as he, steeped in the bottomless reserves of energy gifted by the strange ways of Fenris, could have maintained his position for so long. While he stood, the devices of the enemy were blunted, allowing the warriors of the Aett to charge into battle unhindered. If he fell, their witchery would come into play, turning the tide irrevocably.

And so he stayed on his feet, hurling invective at the silent Rubric Marines as they marched into view, maintaining the flurry of lightning into their ranks, countering the varied powers of the enemy spell-casters and taking the bite out of their aether-born attacks.

It made him proud. After his failure to predict the coming of the enemy, he was able to reflect with satisfaction on what he had done since. The Aett would have fallen already without his untiring efforts. Even if it was still overwhelmed, he had given it precious extra days of life. To fall in battle after inflicting such pain on the enemy was honourable; only an easy, fragile death was a cause for shame.

Sturmhjart stood in the centre of the defensive lines, partially sheltered by the barricades. On either side of him were the gun-lines, still manned by mortal kill-squads. The Wolves' packs roamed ahead of them, preventing the invaders from reaching the trenches. They were supported by the hulking outlines of Dread-noughts and the strange, darting runs of the Underfang beasts. The creatures of the night instilled terror in the mortal Prosperine soldiers, even more so than the Wolves themselves. Many of the creatures had been killed during the repeated actions, but whole packs remained in action, fearless, tireless and horrifying.

Sturmhjart stole a glance to his right, over to where the fighting was fiercest. Greyloc was still on his feet, as he had been for days without pause. His Terminator plate was near-black from plasma-burns, his pelts ripped to tatters and the ceramite beneath cut deep by a hundred blades. But still he fought on, cold and clinical, holding the line together by force of example. He was no longer the White Wolf, more like a coal-black shade of Morkai let loose into the world of the living.

You have surprised me, lord. There is iron beneath that pale skin.

Between them, Greyloc and Bjorn dominated the battle for Borek's Seal. The Thousand Sons were too numerous to be driven back for any length of time, but the invaders had made painfully slow headway since the start of their full-scale assault. The Wolves had forced a deadlock across the barricades, and that in itself, given the numbers of troops in play, was a staggering achievement.

It couldn't last. Eventually, the line would break and the Rubric Marines would sweep into the chamber beyond. Until then, however, no ground would be ceded.

'Fenrys hjolda!' Sturmhjart bellowed, trying, as always, to rouse the Wolves around him to greater heights of heroism. He slammed his rune-staff to the ground, sending up forks of storm-lightning from the cold stone. 'For Russ! For the–'

He broke off. A shadow passed across his hearts, chilling them. The power that sluiced across his runic armour flickered and died. He staggered, putting a hand out to prevent himself falling.

You feel it too, Priest.

Bjorn's voice was dominating, even over the comm. Sturmhjart saw black stars spinning before his eyes, and dizziness wrapped itself around him.

'He is here.'

Greyloc broke from combat.

'What do you sense, Odain?' he voxed, racing back

up towards the Rune Priest's position. Behind him, Grey Hunters struggled to close the gap in the defensive line.

Sturmhjart shook his head vigorously, trying to rid himself of the lingering disorientation.

'He has been here all along. Everywhere and nowhere.'

The sorcerers' attack suddenly stepped up in intensity. Crackling aetheric force whipped out from the attacking ranks, wreathing the oncoming Traitor Marines. For the first time in days, the Wolves began to falter in their defiance.

'He is here?' roared Greyloc, his voice heavy with loathing. 'Show me where he is, Priest.'

He assaults the Fangthane. Even now he lays it to waste.

'Too far away...' gasped Sturmhjart.

'We must reach him,' said Greyloc, his voice urgent. 'There are routes through the mountain, fast ways up. None at the Fangthane can withstand him.'

'Nothing on Fenris can withstand him.'

I can.

Sturmhjart whirled round to face the approaching Dreadnought, still feeling groggy and nauseous.

'You're deluded!' he blurted. 'You cannot sense him as I can. He is a primarch, an equal to Russ himself. This is *death*, Bjorn! This is the cutting of the thread.'

Ominously, the Dreadnought raised his plasma cannon, pointing the heavy, blunt barrels directly at Sturmhjart's helm.

You have a heart of fire. If I had not seen that already, you would be dead where you stand for those words.

Greyloc didn't hesitate.

'The defence of the Seal will be given to Hrothgar of the Revered Fallen – he can hold the line for a little longer. I will go after the Traitor, as will my Wolf Guard. Bjorn will stand with us, and so will you, Rune Priest – your wyrd-mastery will be needed.'

Sturmhjart straightened, looking first at the lowered plasma barrel at the end of Bjorn's gun-arm, then at the blackened and ravaged helm-face of his Jarl. The worst of the sickness brought on by Magnus's translation ebbed. He felt his resolve begin to return, closely followed by shame at his outburst.

'So be it,' he growled, taking up his staff in both hands. 'We will face him together.'

Greyloc nodded, and motioned to his two surviving Terminator-armoured Wolf Guard to follow him.

'Of course, we have to break out of here first,' he said grimly.

Do not worry about that, snarled Bjorn, his voice low and resonant like a starship engine. He swivelled on his axis, training his weapons on the enemy once more. **Tell the Fangs to lay down heavy cover. Now I have prey worthy of a kill, I feel the need to stretch my claws.**

WYRMBLADE LET HIS arms fall slack by his sides. He stood at the summit of the Fangthane stairs, between the massive images of Freki and Geri, the final layer of defence before the hall itself. He was an old warrior, tempered in the fires of a thousand engagements, as inured to surprise or despair as any of the *Vlka Fenryka*.

Yet he couldn't move. The presence before him was

so dominating, so transcendent, that it filled his veins with lead and locked his superhuman muscles into a horrified stasis.

Magnus had come. The daemon-primarch was at the foot of the stairway, attracting tracer fire in glowing, angry lines. The ordnance seemed to explode before it hit him, blooming in starbursts of angry red and orange around his massive frame. The Long Fangs and heavy weapons squads had unloaded all they had at him, pouring streams of flame at the monster's head and chest.

It had no discernible effect. Magnus was a giant, a five-metre-tall behemoth striding through the clouds of promethium like a man pushing through fields of corn. He was radiant, as splendid as bronze, dazzling amid the shadows of the mountain. Nothing hurt him. Nothing came close to hurting him. He had been created for another age, an age when gods walked among men. In the colder, weaker universe of the thirty-second millennium he was unmatched, a walking splinter of the Allfather's will set amid a fragile world of mortal flesh and blood.

As Wyrmblade watched, gripped by a vice of horror, the kill-machine got to work. There were no battle cries, no shouts of rage. The daemon-primarch had retained his phlegmatic humours of old, and cut threads with a chilling equanimity. Wyrmblade saw his Wolves charge up to the shimmering titan, as immune to fear as ever, hurling their bodies into the path of the monster. They were brushed aside, thrown bodily into the stone where their backs were broken.

Still, Magnus strode forwards, reaching the bottom

level of the stairway. The barricades there had held for
days, resisting every attempt to breach them. Box-guns
spat at the primarch, surrounding him in a curtain
of flickering, sparkling impacts. One by one, he tore
them down, ripping them up by their roots and dash-
ing them across the trenches.

Magnus came on. Lauf Cloudbreaker stood in
his path, arms raised in defiance. The Rune Priest
began the summoning, whipping up the storm-wyrd,
contesting the advance of the daemon with all the
art he possessed. The primarch clenched his fist
and Cloudbreaker simply exploded, lost in a ball of
blood, his totems scattered amid the fragments of his
shattered runic armour. Kaerls scrambled to evacuate
the trenches then, all thoughts of resistance quashed
by the immense force striding toward them.

Magnus came on. More Wolves charged to meet
him, still undaunted by the destruction wreaked
around them. Wyrmblade saw Rossek, the grim-faced
Wolf Guard, lumber into contact, his Terminator plate
streaming with golden flames. Grey Hunters went in
alongside, howling with rage. For a moment, the primarch was held, rocked by the sudden assault of so
many blades, each of them wielded with passion and
courage. Rossek even managed to land a blow, causing
Magnus to pause in his rampage.

A single blow. A lone strike with his chainfist, followed up by a hail of storm-bolter rounds. That was
all he managed before Magnus's fists caught him,
hurling him back into the ground, pummeling him
into shrapnel and crushing him into a slick of gore
beneath his ironshod feet. Rossek was gone, taken

down in seconds, his proud life snuffed out with the casual descent of a primarch's boot. The Wolves with him were ripped apart soon after. More fixed guns unloaded their ammunition at the primarch. All were destroyed, torn from their mounts and tossed aside like chaff.

Magnus came on. The Fangthane's six Dreadnoughts waited for him halfway up the stairway, resolute and unmoving. They opened fire as one, launching missiles and plasma bolts in a blistering, crushing flurry of destructive energy. In a few seconds they unleashed enough firepower to level a whole company of Traitor Marines, chewing through heavy bolter ammo-belts and exhausting energy packs. Magnus emerged from the inferno intact, his armour trailing gouts of smoke and flame. As he towered over them, the Dreadnoughts closed up, gunning their massive power fists and lightning claws into life and bracing for impact.

Magnus seized the nearest Dreadnought in one hand and lifted it from the ground. The huge sarcophagus swayed up above the rolling torment of fire, its close-combat weapon flexing impotently, its heavy bolter thudding shell after shell into the impervious hide of the primarch.

Magnus drew his arm back and hurled the Dreadnought against the walls of the stairway. The Revered Fallen hit the surface at speed, shattering the stone and driving a huge rent in the rock. Magnus loomed over the stricken war machine and clenched his fist again. The Dreadnought's armour cracked open, shearing down the middle with a resounding clap of thunder, revealing the seething amniotic chamber within. The ruined scrap of flesh and sinew inside the tank writhed for a moment, still possessed by some primordial urge to survive, before Magnus smashed the plexiglass and dragged it out. With a flex of his mighty fist, the remnants of the Dreadnought's body were squeezed into a slurry of blood and wasted muscle.

Then Magnus turned to take on the rest.

Still Wyrmblade couldn't move. Some power compelled him to stay immobile.

'Lord.'

His limbs were frozen, heavy and sluggish. His sword was rooted to the ground, a dead weight.

'Lord.'

A black curtain of despair sunk behind his eyes.

Nothing can stop this. Even Bjorn could do nothing against this.

'Lord!'

He snapped out of his visions, shaken free by the presence at his elbow. The few surviving Wolves clustered around him at the summit of the stairway. No more than a dozen had escaped the onslaught of the primarch. There were kaerls streaming to join them from the stairway, a couple of hundred perhaps. Below them, the Dreadnoughts fought on, dying one by one under the terrible attentions of Magnus, holding the line for just a few more moments before his relentless march resumed.

The one who spoke was a Blood Claw with blood-drenched armour and teeth studded under the jawline of his helm. Like all the Wolves, he'd seen heavy combat and his plate was dented, burned and blade-scored.

Wyrmblade should have sensed it sooner.

Maleficarum. He is contesting for my mind.

With a huge effort, Wyrmblade fought off the terrible feelings of despair. His troops were looking to him for guidance. The Blood Claw grabbed his arm, yearning for leadership.

'What are your orders?' he asked urgently.

Wyrmblade looked across the faces of those around him. Only hours ago, they had still dared to hope. The barricades had been held for so long. Now, in the space of a few terrible minutes, everything had been destroyed.

He didn't know what to say to them. For the first time since taking the rites of priesthood, he didn't know what to say.

'We will hold him here,' came a clear voice.

All eyes turned to the speaker. It was a mortal rivenmaster with an honest face. Alone among the kaerls, his eyes were not alive with fear. There was a hollowness there, as if the thought of living longer had become somehow abhorrent to him.

'We mortals will hold him for as long as we can,' he went on, speaking calmly despite the roiling explosions moving up the stairway below. 'We are expendable, but you are not. You must go. Seek some way of resisting him in the Valgard. If you hesitate, you will die.'

Wyrmblade looked at the mortal. At last, the final shreds of Magnus's psychic paralysis left him. The rivenmaster looked back, an expression of defiant insolence on his face.

Morek Karekborn. Ah, how I underestimated you.

'The mortal is right,' announced Wyrmblade, recovering his poise and sweeping his blade back into position. 'We will fall back. Our stand will be at the Annulus.'

He gestured toward Morek.

'Take command of what heavy weapon squads we still have. Hold him as long as you can in the Fangthane. The rest of you, come with me. The abomination shall not walk into our holiest chambers unopposed.'

Then he turned, his armoured boots scraping on the stone before breaking into the run that would carry him across the Fangthane and to the transit shafts beyond. The rest of the Wolves came with him, none of them questioning the order, though Wyrmblade could detect the stubborn reluctance to depart from combat. The surviving kaerls struggled to keep up behind them, all now racing freely from the horror in the stairwell. As they went, more crashes surged up from the stairs, punctuated with isolated barks of bolter-fire.

Wyrmblade only looked back once. Morek was already busy, organising the mortals who'd been able to stand alongside him, drawing up the final gun-lines and heavy weapons squads at the summit of the stairs, under the shadow of the snarling wolf images. Beyond them, the bronze leviathan loomed, coming closer.

Brave. Horribly brave. Once the last of the Dreadnoughts was taken down, he'd be lucky if he lasted more than a few seconds.

The Wolf Priest turned back quickly, switching his mind to the present, to survival.

I cannot feel guilt for this. There is more at stake than the lives of mortals.

But as Wyrmblade raced across the empty Fangthane, leaving the powerful primarch behind him, accompanied by the dregs of his command retreating ignominiously upwards in the hope, the faint hope, that things would go differently at the Annulus, a single nagging thought wouldn't leave him alone.

I have no idea how to fight that monster. No idea at all.

THE RUBRIC MARINES were on the rampage. With the departure of Bjorn, Greyloc and the Rune Priest, their powers had been greatly enhanced. Phalanxes of sapphire-clad warriors plunged into battle, surrounded by eldritch whips of energy and spitting cold fire from their gauntlets. Even the remaining Wolves on the barricades were no match for such powers, and fell back in a fighting retreat, pulling back across the rows of trenches to the refuges beyond.

They were covered by the continual fire of the fixed guns and protected by the indomitable presence of the five remaining Dreadnoughts. Hrothgar led them, a huge war machine scarcely less imposing than Bjorn. Under his command, Aldr and others stayed firm in retreat, keeping up constant volleys of fire against the oncoming tide, slowing it down though not halting it. The beasts still fought with undented savagery, launching themselves at the throats of the silent killers, tearing at armour and steel with their strange augmented claws.

Freija could see that it wasn't enough. The departure of the bastion's command squad had robbed the defenders of their most potent weapons. She had watched them fight their way free with growing disbelief, gaping openly as Bjorn had carved a path through the milling hordes and into the tunnels beyond. Russ only knew whether they'd made it to the far side, nor what terrible errand had called them away from their duty on the barricades.

To make things worse, the Thousand Sons seemed to have been filled with a new zeal for combat. They charged into contact faster, their reactions were sharper and their blows landed more heavily. Something had happened to give them new momentum, and the current of the battle had decisively swung their way.

Freija fell back, as ordered, retreating through the massive portals of Borek's Seal and into the cavernous space beyond. Her squad remained in tight formation around her, all of them facing the enemy, all of them firing non-stop. Heavy impacts crashed all around them, many of them bolter-rounds loosed from the approaching Rubric Marines. As the defenders withdrew from their long-held positions at the portals, the guns within Borek's Seal itself opened up, throwing new crashes and explosions into an already deafening storm of sound and light.

There were trenches dug further back, and more lines of barricades. They would fall back and regroup, then fall back again. This was all part of the plan. As long as the Dreadnoughts lasted and the Wolves stood up to fight, they still had a chance. She had faith. After so many years of cynicism, it was a nice feeling to have.

Then she staggered, crying out with pain.

One of her men reached for her, trying to haul her

back to her feet. Stumbling again would be fatal – none of the squad could afford to wait for her to catch up if she fell behind.

Freija's world tilted on its axis. For a moment, she thought a las-beam had hit her, but then realised the pain was internal. Like a spike through her heart, a sharp wave of agony swept through her.

'Rise, huskaerl!' urged her trooper, yanking hard at her armour.

Freija barely heard him. The only thing she saw was a fleeting vision of a bronze-armoured giant striding through curtains of flame, tearing down everything in range of its terrible grasp. Then there was a man in front of him, a mortal, standing defiant as the inferno came for him. On either side of him were wolves, massive and carved from granite. Though their muzzles were locked in snarls, they were static and impotent.

The vision faded, and the rush and fury of the fighting in Borek's Seal returned.

'Father!' she cried, realising what she'd seen.

Her weapon clattered to the ground, dropped from shaking fingers. The trooper made a final attempt to haul her along with him. The rest of the squad was now many metres away, falling back to their assigned muster-point under heavy fire.

'We have to go!' he snapped, urgency in his voice.

'He is gone!' gasped Freija, feeling grief like she'd never known before rise up to choke her. Tears spiked at her eyes, hot and acrid. 'Mercy of the Allfather, he is *gone!*'

The kaerl gave up then, letting her fall to the stone and racing to join his comrades. Freija sank to the ground, careless of the carnage around her. Ahead of her, the Wolves fought a final, losing battle with the remorseless enemy. The line of battle was getting closer. Soon, it would sweep over her like the tide washing away sand.

She didn't care. She didn't even register. Her world had been ripped from under her feet, torn away by the death of the one man who'd given her everything. Days of exhaustion suddenly took their toll, crushing what spirit remained in her.

He is gone.

So it was that, as Borek's Seal was finally breached, and as Traitor Marines stormed the great bastion at the base of Russ's citadel at last, Freija Morekborn, savage warrior-daughter of Fenris, fell to the stone, heedless of everything but her vision of death.

There she remained until the shadow fell across her, the shadow of one of the many warriors who'd come into the Aett with no purpose but to kill. As he lowered his weapon, she didn't even look up.

MAGNUS STOOD IN the Fangthane. His mantle ran with flames, slowly dying out as the glory of his ascent receded. The vast space still echoed from the residual firestorm, but the flashing lights of the guns were long gone. The floor was littered with bodies and broken gun-cases, partly-hidden by the ragged clouds of smoke drifting across it. Freki and Geri had been shattered, their limbs left among the strewn remnants of barricades like burnt offerings.

Across the wide expanse of the stone floor, Rubricae moved in tightly ordered squads, preparing for the push upwards. Spireguard were busy removing the residual defences and repairing the worst of the damage to the stairway. Now that the choke-point had been broken, the upper levels of the Fang lay open.

Magnus knew what he would do. He would crash through the shafts and tunnels, driving his way to the very summit, ripping a trail of flame through the reeling mountain. Then he would break out on to the pinnacle, taking the aspect of a lord of ruin, and watch as his sons tore the remainder of the citadel to pieces. The destruction would be complete and irrecoverable, a fitting riposte to the devastation wreaked on Tizca. By the time he left, the Fang would be an empty, uninhabitable corpse-house.

But he would not do that just yet. There was one task in the Fangthane that remained, one he had been looking forward to for many centuries.

He walked up to the giant statue of Russ.

It was, he had to admit, a good likeness. The ruthless energy of his gene-brother had been perfectly captured. As Magnus approached it, he grew in stature. By the time he drew up to the image, his head was at the same height. They stood facing each other, just as they had done on Prospero. Magnus looked into the unseeing eyes of his old enemy, and smiled.

'Do you remember what you said to me, brother?'

Magnus spoke aloud, his voice pure and powerful. His fingers twitched at his sides, eager for what was to come.

'Do you remember what you said to me as we fought before the Pyramid of Photep? Do you remember the words you used? I do. As I recall, your face was tortured. Imagine that – the Master of Wolves, his ferocity twisted into grief. And yet you still carried out your duty. You always did what was asked of you. So loyal. So tenacious. Truly, you were the attack dog of the Emperor.'

Magnus lost his smile.

'You took no pleasure in what you did. I knew that then, and I know it now. But all things change, my brother. I'm not the same as I was, and you're... well, let us not mention where you are now.'

Magnus put his arms out, grasping the stone shoulders of the statue, pressing bronze fingers into the granite.

'So do not imagine there is a symmetry to my emotions as I do this. I will take pleasure in it, and I will take pleasure in seeing your hearth destroyed and your sons scattered. In the centuries to come, this small act will make me smile, a minor consolation for the hurt you inflicted on my innocent people in the name of ignorance.'

Magnus heaved, and the gigantic statue came free from its base, breaking off at the ankles with a crack of tortured stone. Manipulating the colossal weight easily, Magnus swung the figure into a face-up horizontal position, and brought his knee up under the curved backbone.

'I have waited long for this, Wolf King, and I find that, now the moment is here, it is quite as precious as I hoped it would be.'

With a single, savage, downward thrust, Magnus broke the back of Russ across his knee. The two halves of the statue thundered to the stone below, sending up a slow tidal wave of dust and rubble. The booming sound of the fall resounded from the high vaults of the Fangthane, ebbing like sobs. The head rolled free, still fixed in a grimace of static rage, rocking as it gently settled in the debris.

Magnus paused then, looking down at the ruin of his enemy's image. For a long time, he didn't move. There was a defiant pleasure on his face, the expression of a man who wished to fully enjoy an experience long anticipated.

But behind it, as Ahriman would no doubt have recognised, was a deeper pain, the pain of remembrance. There would always be pain. That was the tragedy of the past, of the things done that could never be undone.

The introspection could not last. As the last of the dust settled in the cracks of the Fangthane walls, Magnus stirred himself once more. He knew his sons would be impatient for more conquest, and he had a duty to them still.

'The final push,' he murmured, speaking to himself. 'The most grievous blow of all.'

He departed then, shrinking in stature back to his old size as he walked, though still towering over the tallest of his servants. Behind him came his Rubricae and their surviving sorcerer-guides. Many had died, but several hundred warriors still remained, all as implacable and dedicated as ever. They marched with their usual eerie, diffident confidence, tramping up the slopes towards the transit shafts. They all followed their father, leaving none behind.

* * *

AFTER THEY WERE gone, mortal Spireguard picked their way through the wreckage of the hall. They were strung-out after weeks of solid campaigning, but they carried themselves with heads held high. They were no longer scared. They had seen the majesty of the Wolves laid low, and it did wonders for their confidence. Many of them believed all of the defending Space Marines had been killed. It was a reasonable belief, given the recent evidence of their senses.

So it was that, a few hours later, none of the sentries noticed the pairs of glowing red eyes at the base of the stairway, moving fast and in pursuit formation. Only when the wolfclaws broke out from the darkness and the booming war cry of the hulking war-engine triggered terror among them once again, did it become apparent they had relaxed too soon.

There were Wolves left alive, and they were hunting.

CHAPTER TWENTY-ONE

REDPELT DIDN'T HAVE time to marvel at the ancient wonders of the Annulus Chamber. In another situation, he'd have lingered over the great stone circle, lost in contemplation of the devices inscribed there. In the current circumstances, that would have been an indulgence too far. He knew the enemy was hard on their heels, sweeping up the transit shafts and tunnels like a rising tide. They would be here soon, ready to finish what they'd started.

So he worked hard, digging in with the few remaining Wolves and the demoralised kaerls. They dragged what protection they could across the doorway to the chamber, piling heavy iron sheeting across the metres-wide portal. All of them knew such flimsy barriers wouldn't last long, but at least it would give the kaerls some cover to fire from.

The mortals looked ready to collapse. They'd been fighting for days already, with only short sleep breaks to keep them from going mad or dying from fatigue. Even their Fenrisian constitutions, about as tough as any in the Imperium, were on the brink of implosion. It was a miracle any of them could still hold their rifles, let alone use them.

Helfist wouldn't have appreciated such things. He'd always been impatient with mortal frailties.

'Why do we still need them?' he'd complained. 'Just breed more Space Marines. Thousands of us. Don't stop until we're all that's left, and forget about the weaklings.'

He'd been joking, but there'd always been an underlying seriousness there. He really didn't see the point of unaugmented humans. Now he was gone, consumed by the very power that had elevated him into superhumanity.

That is the point, brother. We pay a price for our potency.

'Blood Claw,' came Wyrmblade's dry old voice.

Helfist snapped round. The Wolf Priest stood there in his half-ruined armour, dark against the angry light of the hearth-fires.

'You will have to hold the Annulus for a little while without me.'

For a moment, Redpelt couldn't believe what he was hearing.

'Forgive me, lord. I don't under–'

'There is something of the utmost importance I must attend to. Russ willing, I shall be back before the enemy reaches you. But if I am not, then hold the line until I return.'

Redpelt felt a roar of anger building up within him. He knew he was on the edge of his strength, and knew the penalty for defying a Wolf Priest, but what Wyrmblade intended was madness. There was nothing, *nothing*, more important than defending the last and holiest chamber of the Aett against assault.

'You cannot,' he said, keeping a lid on his temper with difficulty. 'We need you here, lord.'

Wyrmblade shook his head.

'Do not attempt to argue with me, Blood Claw,' he said. 'I know how you feel, and I will go as swiftly as I may.'

For a moment longer, Redpelt considered protesting. Hel, he even considered hammering the Wolf Priest to the floor and forcing him to stay.

As that thought crossed his mind, it forced a weary smile, the grim acceptance brought on by utter desperation.

Have we been reduced to this?

'If you miss the action, I will claim the primarch as prey,' said Redpelt. 'You'll have to live with that shame.'

Wyrmblade laughed in his strange, cynical way.

'You deserve it, Blood Claw. But you will not fight Magnus alone. Take my oath on it.'

Then he turned and strode through the makeshift barricades, pushing his way past the working kaerls. Redpelt watched him go for a while, then cast his eyes back over the remaining defences.

Twelve Wolves, a mix of Claws, Hunters and Long

Fangs. A few hundred kaerls, rammed into the narrow approaches to the Annulus Chamber or taking up positions within it. A couple of heavy weapons, but mostly sidearms, and those low on ammo.

Then he looked over to the Annulus stones, only a few metres away. The image of the Wolf that Stalks the Stars sat in the centre of the circle, the emblem of the Chapter. Russ himself had stood before that device once, surrounded by his mighty retinue, all warriors without equal.

So few left. So few, to defend the very heart of our realm.

Redpelt let out a shuddering sigh. He was in danger of letting the events of the past few hours get the better of him. He could imagine Helfist laughing at that, taunting him as he always had done.

Not now. There was work to be done.

'You! Mortal!' he roared, striding over to where a gang of kaerls was struggling to carry a fresh barricade into place. 'Not there. I'll show you where.'

And then he was busy again, consumed by the need to make the Annulus as secure as possible. They did not have long. As the defenders worked, the sounds of the coming storm could be heard, far below them, lost in the endless maze of tunnels. It was still a long way off, but coming closer with every heartbeat.

MAGNUS STALKED THROUGH the corridors of the Aett, pausing only to destroy the meagre wards against sorcery that still lingered in the upper reaches of the Jarlheim. Behind him came the slow-moving squadrons of Rubric Marines.

There was almost no resistance. The tunnels and

shafts were empty, or surrendered quickly by scattered bands of mortal defenders, bereft of hope and leadership. Magnus knew that Wolves still fought on down in the lower levels, pinned back by his troops and suffering a slow strangulation. The few defenders in the upper levels capable of mounting any kind of fight must have retreated to the summit, hoping against reason to hold the last redoubt for a few more hours.

That defiance did not surprise him, though he couldn't summon much admiration for it. He'd never expected them to roll over and give up. The Wolves had kept attacking him as he'd swept up the Fangthane stairway, even though they must have known they would die in the attempt. That big warrior, the one with the chainfist and the sound of bitterness in his battle cry, his strikes had even hurt.

Magnus looked around him with disdain. These were, he knew, the levels where the Sky Warriors dwelt. The surroundings were as squalid and bare as the rest of the benighted mountain. Though the Fangthane had a kind of bleak grandeur, there was really very little in the Fang to be impressed by. It wasn't much more than a big rock, half-carved open, cold and shivering with mountain draughts.

Czamine, the Pavoni sorcerer-lord, came alongside him then, striding hard to match his primarch's pace.

'Lord, do you have more orders?' he asked. 'I have sent squads into the side tunnels to destroy the remaining wards. We can cause much damage there before we engage the last defenders.'

Magnus nodded.

'Do that. Burn, crack and maim everything you find.

Pay special attention to the totems and charms. The Wolves have an inexplicable weakness for them, and it will hurt their souls to have them broken.'

'It will be done. And then, the summit.'

'Indeed, though you will be alone there, at least for a time.'

Czamine inclined his helm questioningly, though he didn't dare voice a query.

'I have an appointment of my own to keep,' explained Magnus. 'When you've finished smashing what remains of the artefacts, look for me again at the pinnacle.'

Magnus didn't bother to hide the look of anticipation on his face then.

'Russ's chamber is close, my son, the one he called the Annulus. You will have the honour of taking it. We will meet again there, once the last hope of this wretched Chapter has been extinguished.'

WYRMBLADE ENTERED THE chamber of the fleshmakers. He went hurriedly, passing through the many interlinked rooms swiftly. The vacated spaces were still brightly lit, but looked mournful in their emptiness. He hadn't encountered enemies in the tunnels leading from the Annulus to his own domain, but he knew it was only a matter of time before they arrived. He had precious moments; moments he could use to salvage the essential elements of his research before all was destroyed. He had little idea what to do with it after that, but something would occur to him. It always did.

Wyrmblade strode through the empty fleshmaker labs, hardly seeing the bare metal slabs where the bodies had lain. After so long detained in the Fangthane, it felt odd to be back in those antiseptic spaces, bathed once more in the harsh light of medicae glowglobes reflected from the walls of white tiles.

Wyrmblade approached the inner sanctum, the place where the Tempering programme had been conducted in secrecy for so many years. The blast doors were shut, just as he'd left them. He prepared to issue the voice-activation release, forcing his pulse to lessen as he did so. Agitation would only interfere with the mechanism.

It was then that he stopped. He looked around, down the long rows of silent machinery, the pristine operating slabs.

There were no bodies. Frar, the Grey Hunter who'd been brought here by Morek, was gone. All the others were gone. It was as if no trace of them had ever existed. It was then that he realised the truth.

He'd not arrived at the laboratorium first.

Turning slowly, knowing the consequences of what he did, he opened the doors.

The Tempering chambers lay beyond. They were in disarray. The birthing tubes were shattered, their contents dribbling across the tiled floor. The corpses of the experimental Sons of Russ lay on the floor, trampled and torn apart. The vials were all destroyed, broken into glistening shards of glass. In the rooms beyond, the cogitators crackled, consumed by flames. Irreplacable equipment, some of it dating back to the days of Unification on Terra, had been entirely devastated, and priceless inner mechanics were now strewn open like entrails.

It was gone. All gone.

Wyrmblade took in the ruin of his life's work in an instant. Then his amber eyes flickered up. Most of his attention was drawn to the man standing in the centre of the destruction.

No, not a man. He was smaller in stature than he had been on the stairs of the Fangthane, but still greater than any Space Marine. His golden mantle hung from three-metre-high shoulders, encasing a breastplate of bronze. Amniotic fluid dripped from his fingers. His single eye glistened with triumph.

Wyrmblade drew his sword, and the dragon-edge slid from the scabbard with an empty hiss.

'Do you really intend to fight me, Thar Hraldir?' asked Magnus calmly.

'With all my hearts,' said Wyrmblade, igniting the blade's disruptor field.

The primarch nodded.

'Of course you do. But know this first, old man. The future you envisaged was worth striving to prevent, and so what remains of my Legion has been sacrificed for it. There would have been no invasion of Fenris without your meddling, Wolf Priest. In the last moments you have alive, reflect on that.'

Then Wyrmblade roared with all his old, bitter fury, charging toward the giant primarch and sweeping the blade towards his neck. The dragon-sword, carved with the flowing image of the wyrm, screamed in its turn, hurtling over the bronze breastplate and toward its target.

Magnus drew his own weapon in an instant. His movements seemed casual, unhurried, but they somehow had effect instantly. One moment, he was unarmed and relaxed; the next, he was restored to the fiery angel he'd been in the Fangthane.

The swords clashed, and the clang of the metal edges resounded from the walls.

Wyrmblade moved as if he were a Blood Claw in the prime of conditioning, twisting his blade in tight, sharp arcs, crying aloud with every strike. The weariness of the long battle fell away from him, freeing his limbs to move with their old crushing, dazzling speed.

In all his hundreds of years of service, he had never fought more finely, had never perfected the channelling of kill-urge more completely. Wyrmblade whirled, ducked and thrust with sublime energy, driven by an anger and loss that consumed him utterly; a burning, terrible grief that, for a few moments, lifted his artistry beyond even that of the Wolves of Fenris and into the category of legends.

Magnus parried him with an unconscious ease, moving just as smoothly, deploying his blade with all the remorseless skill of his heritage. It was almost as if he were allowing the Wolf Priest his last moment of perfection, gifting him a final flourish of martial sublimity before the end had to come.

But it couldn't last. Wyrmblade, for all his furious energy and control, was to a primarch what a mortal was to a Space Marine. As even his age-hardened muscles tired of their furious assault, the dragon-blade dipped for an instant, leaving an opening. It only took one stroke from Magnus's sword, just a single thrust aimed directly at Wyrmblade's chest. The primarch's eldritch blade passed through the armour smoothly.

Impaled on the metal, Wyrmblade spasmed. He struggled for a little longer, desperately trying to pull himself from the bite of the sword. His own blade fell from his fingers, its energy field still fizzing angrily.

The Wolf Priest coughed up blood, hot and black, and it sprayed across the inside of his helm.

For a final time, his vision came to him. Space Wolves, as numerous as the stars, bringing war to the darkest reaches of the galaxy, shaping the Imperium in the image of the Wolf King and making it as vital and powerful as Russ had been.

'It was... done... for Russ,' he gasped, feeling the cold clutch of death steal upon him.

Then he went limp, slumping heavily on his enemy's sword.

Grimly, Magnus withdrew the blade, letting Wyrmblade's body crumple to the floor.

'If that is so, then you failed him,' remarked the primarch, looking down at the ravaged corpse impassively. 'This struggle is over.'

'Not while you live, betrayer!'

Magnus snapped his gaze up. Amazingly, there were warriors charging towards him. A Terminator-clad giant, his wolfclaws blazing with angry lightning. A Rune Priest, flanked by two bodyguards, his staff crackling with forks of aether-born power. And behind them, moving more slowly, something massive and lumbering. Something he recognised from long, long ago.

THE RUSSVANGUM HURTLED into the orbital engagement zone, its lances blazing. The escorts flew hard in its wake, opening fire with every weapon they possessed. The arrival of the Wolves' battle fleet was devastating, wrapped in fire and fury.

The Thousand Sons fleet did not engage them, but began to pull away from Fenris in a move that had clearly been planned for. The *Herumon*, the only vessel in the armada capable of taking on Ironhelm's flagship, powered out of harm's way smoothly, turning on its axis and heading directly for the jump-points.

Space Wolves frigates and destroyers headed straight into the heart of the enemy, throwing broadsides against the flanks of the ponderous troop ships as they screamed past them. The golden vessels began to burn, their shields buckling under the fury of the assault.

But an orbital war was not what Ironhelm had come for. He could see the dark circle of destruction about the Fang even from the realspace viewers. Kilometres-wide, it stained the pristine reflective expanse of Asaheim like a wound in pale flesh.

As he looked at it, his mind was taken back to the ranks of Wolf Brothers, howling in mockery and anguish even as they were cut down. The air of the Gangava pyramid had been noxious, infused with madness and horror. Breaking free of that battle had been the hardest decision he'd ever made. Lost in a world of rage, he'd barely recognised Kjarlskar when the Wolf Lord had fought his way to his side. Even then, even after he'd heard what had happened on Fenris, a part of him had resisted the call to come back.

The depth of his folly had been revealed in an instant. It would have been less painful to have kept on fighting, to have lost himself in the kill-urge, to have gloried in the righteous drive to purge the tainted from existence.

He still saw the faces of those he'd killed. Tortured faces. Faces that masked a dreadful awareness. Somewhere deep down, the Wolf Brothers knew what they'd been twisted into.

We keep the danger close.

'To the pods,' he growled, stomping from the bridge and down to the launch bays. On every ship of the fleet, Jarls of the Great Companies did the same. Dozens of drop-pods were already primed for planetfall, each one carrying a full payload. Thunderhawk engines thrummed into life in the hangars, waiting for the all-clear to burst out into the troposphere and into cannon-range.

The entire Chapter had achieved orbit, sweeping away resistance with the same contemptuous ease as the Thousand Sons had so many days ago. The massed landings were only moments away.

Ironhelm boarded his pod impatiently, leaned back against the adamantium walls and felt the restraint cage slam into place. The shell-doors hissed closed, and launch klaxons began to blare.

'Land me on the summit,' he snarled over the comm.

That would be dangerous, with no margin for error – the bulk of the pods were being sent down to the causeways. The operators of the bays knew better than to argue, though, and the coordinates were duly set.

'Clear to launch, lord,' came a voice over the comm.

'Do it,' ordered Ironhelm, bracing for the release of

the clamps, and then the dizzying, whistling descent towards the surface. It could not come soon enough.

I am coming for you.

The launch-tube doors flew open, and the pods began to fall. In every direction, Wolves vessels powered into battle, tearing apart any enemy ships too slow to evade their guns.

He knew what the enemy would be thinking now. He knew that, all along the causeways, entrenched Spireguard battalions would be looking up, realising that their fleet was deserting them and that they were being left to fend for themselves. It was then, as they watched the skies darken, that the same terrible thought would enter every one of their terrified minds. He took a cold pleasure in that.

This is the planet of the Wolves. And they have come to take it back.

STURMHJART SPREAD HIS arms wide, kindling a rage of storm-energy. Fists of lightning raced out, engulfing Magnus in a nimbus of coruscating brilliance. The sigils on the Rune Priest's armour exploded into life, burning heartblood-red.

Greyloc and his two Wolf Guard leapt into action, snarling with pent-up rage. They went for Magnus like a pack taking down a *konungur* – one at the throat, one at the breast, one at the legs. Their armour shimmered from Sturmhjart's protective aegis as they charged into combat.

Greyloc was fastest. He got his talons up into the primarch's face, raking and tearing. Magnus fell back, rocked by the speed of the assault. Though he stood over a metre taller than the Terminator Marines, the pace and ferocity of the attacks pushed him on to his heels, and he stumbled.

Magnus the Red, son of the immortal Emperor, primarch of the Thousand Sons, *stumbled*.

'For the Allfather!' roared Greyloc in triumph, his whole being consumed by the awesome, feral power of the hunt. Like Wyrmblade before him, the absolute hatred engendered by Magnus lent him, for a time, truly astonishing power. 'For Russ!'

Greyloc bludgeoned the primarch back another pace, howling his hatred in scarcely intelligible frenzy. Magnus got his sword in place, but it was cracked aside by a savage swipe of wolfclaws.

A Wolf Guard made contact, plunging his talons into Magnus's leg. Sturmhjart bellowed with kill-pleasure at that, and his wyrdfire roared with even greater intensity. The other Wolf Guard crunched his claw into the primarch's chest. The Wolves had the scent of blood in their nostrils, and it made them awesome.

Magnus staggered again, crashing into the wall behind him, breaking it open, demolishing it as he passed through. Greyloc leapt after him, closely followed by the others. Sturmhjart kept on their heels, consumed with an inferno of raging wyrd-flame. The four Wolves harried, stabbed and hammered at the retreating daemon-primarch, their fists flying and blades biting. There was no let-up, no respite, just a flurry of horrifying blows, each one sent hurtling into contact with a visceral, remorseless passion.

They drove the daemon-primarch back further, tearing through another wall, laying waste to everything around them. The noise of roaring and slavering was deafening, a hideous cacophony of hate-filled defiance that rose, booming, into the narrow space of the fleshmaker halls.

'Death to the witch!' bellowed Greyloc, utterly possessed by kill-urge, his whole body pumping with furious energy.

He was fighting at such a pitch of perfection that it made him want to scream aloud. Greyloc could feel himself burning up as he fought on, damaging himself irretrievably through the very action of such unrestrained violence. There was no retreat from this, no possibility of recovery. He was fighting himself to death, using up every gram of potential in his mortal body.

I am the weapon.

Nothing less would do. He was contesting a living god, and only his indomitable faith, his unshakeable certainty, his complete commitment, would possibly match up to that awesome task.

My pure state.

So he pushed Magnus back again, giving him no time, no space. Another wall crashed into ruins, destroyed by the lightning-crowned rampage of their furious progress.

They burst through the rubble into a wide, open space. They'd broken out of the laboratorium and into a hangar of some kind, one of the many hundreds that studded the mountain near the summit. There was a single gunship left on the apron, ruined and black from heavy battle-damage. At the far end of the launch bay, a gale roared past. The thundering of the vengeful wind boomed around their ears, fresh from the frigid airs of Asaheim, harsh and howling.

The soul of Fenris. It shares our fury.

The Wolves tore onwards, wreathed in Sturmhjart's wyrdlight, bellowing defiance, landing blow after blow, each one of which would have ended another fight but in this case merely prolonged it.

But their strength, for all its extravagant majesty, was fixed by clear limits. Magnus was a child of the Emperor, one of the peerless twenty who had lit the fires of the Great Crusade, and his poise could only be disrupted for a short time. The onslaught had been horrendous, the worst he had endured in a thousand years, but his strength was near-infinite and his guile scarcely less so. He straightened, towering over his assailants, and remembered what power lay within his gauntlet-grasp.

One of the Wolf Guard let his defences slip for a fraction of a second, and that was enough. Magnus's fist crashed into his face, hurling him out of contact and sending him flying metres through the air. The Wolf Guard crunched heavily to the ground, his helm smashed in, and didn't get up.

Sturmhjart was next, caught by a devastating blast of witchfire from Magnus's outstretched hands. The Rune Priest bent double, clutched by sudden, agonising pain.

'*Hjolda!*' he cried, writhing in apoplexy, blood spraying from his armour-joints.

Magnus clenched his fist, and the ceramite shell exploded, throwing a storm of flesh and bone across the hangar floor. Then the primarch whirled back to face Greyloc and the surviving Wolf Guard. The equanimity had been wiped from his face, and his wine-red hair hung in straggling clumps around him. He was bleeding, and limped from a deep wound to his leg. Only once before had his physical form sustained such wounds, and the remembrance of that pain enraged him.

'You have angered me, Dog,' Magnus snarled, backhanding the Wolf Guard viciously out of contention, breaking his back with a messy snap. Then he lowered a crackling fist at Greyloc.

He never loosed the witchfire. A spinning ball of plasma hit Magnus directly in the torso, throwing him across the hangar. Another impacted, and another, knocking him further back. Limbs flailing, doused in supernova-hot bolt-residue, Magnus slammed into the carcass of the downed Thunderhawk. He smashed it apart as he crashed into it, his golden fists plunging through the crushed adamantium superstructure like a raging child trapped in a doll's house.

You know nothing of anger, Traitor, boomed Bjorn, lumbering from the wreckage of the hangar wall and punching another flurry of plasma bolts from his arm-cannon. *This* **is anger.** *This* **is hate.**

The bolts impacted, one after the other, each aimed with exact precision. Magnus was enveloped in a furious, screaming inferno, a stream of starbursts that bludgeoned him back further, smashing him deep into the wreckage of the gunship.

He still stood. He fought back. For a moment, it looked as though the primarch would rip the Thunderhawk's structure apart completely.

Then the promethium tanks ignited.

The explosion was titanic, rocking the entire hangar and sending a blast-wave sweeping across the apron. Magnus was engulfed by a bulging sphere of white-hot destruction, an orb of flame that raced out, surging up to the hangar roof and running along the stone like quicksilver. Greyloc was hurled to the ground. Cracks raced across the apron, deep and gaping. The wind howled, dragging tongues of flame through the tortured air.

Only Bjorn endured. He kept firing, over and over, pouring more plasma into the raging torrent of destruction.

When Magnus finally emerged from the heart of it, his face was contorted with murder. Skin hung from the bone, smouldering and blistering. His golden mantle was black, his bronze armour scorched. His mane of hair was gone, replaced by a flesh-tattered skull. His lone eye was star-red, burning like metal on the blacksmith's forge. Huge gashes had opened in his flesh, revealing a lattice of shifting, luminous colour beneath. The physical cloak he'd draped over his dae-monic essence had been ripped open, snatched away by the furnace.

Magnus leapt from the inferno, straight at Greyloc, streams of fire trailing him like an angel's wings. Bjorn swept his plasma cannon round, but too slowly. The wounded primarch crashed into the Wolf Lord as he struggled to regain his feet. Magnus felled him with a hammer-blow from his clenched fist, still flaring with raging promethium. Greyloc's head cracked against the stone, and for a moment his guard was down.

Magnus plunged with both hands, tearing up the Jarl's breastplate with grasping fingers. Silver-gold warp-energy blazed out, dissolving the ceramite in hissing clouds. Magnus delved deep, seizing both Greyloc's hearts in his crackling fists.

The Wolf Lord *screamed*, his limbs going rigid with agony. With a sickening wrench, Magnus ripped the beating organs free, hauling them from Greyloc's still-living chest, snapping the clutching trails of gore, and hurled them aside.

For a moment, the Wolf Lord retained consciousness, somehow managing to hold the gaze of his killer.

Beneath his helm, his white face was harrowed but defiant. His eyes reflected, for the final time, a fleeting vision of a snow-smooth plain, of prey moving under the harsh sun, of the icy wind against his naked arms.

My pure state.

Then the arms went limp, and the blood-glare from his lenses died.

JARL! ROARED BJORN, his voice distorted by loathing.

Still firing a stream of plasma bolts, the Dreadnought strode right into the primarch, his lightning claw blazing with angry disruption. The two giants came together in a crash of warp-energy, promethium, and steel on steel.

As Magnus and the Fell-Handed fell into terrible, devastating combat, the storm around them whined to a new pitch of vitriol. The ground beneath their feet cracked open further, tearing chasms in the plascrete floor. The ancient Dreadnought, fuelled by the greater rage, forced the distracted primarch on to the defensive again, gouging at Magnus with his talons and blasting him from close range. At such proximity, the terrible plasma backdraft affected Bjorn nearly as badly as his enemy, but he maintained the barrage nonetheless.

Step by step, shrouded in smoke and trails of fluid energy, the two fighters staggered towards the open hangar bay in a grotesque, swaying embrace, each trading hammer-blows of crushing, heart-stopping force. There was no shielding left over the portal. Beyond the plascrete edge of the apron, the bare rock carried on for a few metres before plunging down sheer. They reached the precipice, blazing away at each other with strikes of such brutality that the rock edges crumbled under them.

Magnus had been hurt. He'd been hurt more profoundly than any mortal had hurt him before. His shock at that translated into his movements, which had become strangely halting and erratic. All his easy grace had left him, and he fought like a bar-room brawler, clubbing at the heavy armour of the Dreadnought even as Bjorn thundered back.

They got closer to the edge. More rocks broke away, streaming down the steel-hard flanks of the mountain in tumbling trails. The drop was nearly vertical. They were thousands of metres above the causeways, duelling in the high heavens like the gods of Fenrisian myth, surrounded by the lancing tongues of lightning and the death-cry of the gales.

Far below them, there was fire and slaughter. The Wolves had landed in their hundreds, and now ran amok across the stone, cutting threads at will. Columns of them were streaming towards the broken shells of the gates, entering their own citadel again with the deadly light of pursuit in their eyes. The skies were studded with the outlines of drop-ships and the dark trails of Thunderhawks. Far above that, surrounded by leaping bursts of chain lightning, heavier ships were slowly descending through the upper atmosphere.

They both saw it. Even as he fought, Bjorn let slip a triumphant snarl.

Ironhelm is here, witch, he taunted, plunging his claw hard into the bronze armour and twisting the blades. **This is death for you.**

Magnus seemed beyond speech. The flesh around his mouth was ragged, burnt ebony by the clinging promethium and torn into a gash by the Dreadnought's slashing strikes. He grabbed the barrel of Bjorn's plasma cannon, clamping claw-like fingers over the red-hot muzzle.

Bjorn fired it again, engulfing Magnus's wrist in a searing holocaust of energy. The primarch clung on, absorbing the terrible heat, twisting and crushing the blunt barrel-end into a blocked mess. His gun rendered useless, Bjorn switched to his claws, driving them again at the primarch's ravaged face. The talons connected, tearing more of the flesh from the daemonic essence beneath.

Stone pillars broke and crumbled from the cliff edge, and a filigree of cracks ran under Bjorn's mighty feet. Both titans teetered on the very lip of the chasm, exchanging blows even as the icy abyss beckoned them down. The harsh wind of Asaheim clutched at them, dragging them closer to oblivion.

It was then that Magnus, weary, wounded and burned as he was, seemed to remember his dread authority at last. He let fly with a broken hand, and fluorescent warp-energy spat from his outstretched fingers. Bjorn's claw crumpled, withering amid a storm of varicoloured madness. The talons flexed wildly, then cracked apart.

Weaponless, the venerable Dreadnought powered in close, attempting to grapple with the primarch and bear him over the edge. Magnus evaded the manoeuvre, punching out with his other hand. Though bereft of a blade, the daemonic flesh was still potent enough to crack Bjorn's sarcophagus open, rending a jagged tear in the long face-plate. Bone icons shattered, and runes were cloven asunder.

Bjorn reeled then, finally exposed to the full power of the primarch's wrath. Magnus cocked a flaming fist, aiming for the eye-slit. Bjorn could do nothing. The blow came in hard, tearing up the reinforced plate, rocking him back on his central axis, forcing him closer to the edge. Magnus swung round, positioning himself on surer ground, pushing the Dreadnought half over the drop and holding him in place one-handed. The ground supporting Bjorn's clawed feet gave way, dissolving in a mini-avalanche of rubble and ice-blades.

'You were on Prospero,' hissed the primarch, his voice a horrific echo of what it had once been. 'I recognise your soul-pattern.'

Bjorn tried to reply, but his vox-generators had been destroyed. He could feel systems failing all over his artificial body. At last, the hellish existence he'd been forced to endure for so long looked like coming to an end. He couldn't be too sorry about that.

'Did you really think you could kill me?' Magnus rasped, sounding both incredulous and furious. His free hand kindled with fresh witchfire. 'If my brother could not, what hope have you?'

It was then that Bjorn saw the shape careering down the slope above. A huge, armour-clad warrior, loping down the sheer ice-face toward them. Far above that was the profile of a drop-pod embedded near the very summit of the Valgard.

Within his cracked shell, what remained of Bjorn's ancient mouth smiled.

IRONHELM POUNCED, LEAPING through the air, hurtling fast, arms outstretched. He crashed into the locked figures with the force of a Land Raider at full acceleration. There was a hard clang as armour smashed into armour. The ledge shattered, and all three of them wheeled over the broken edge of the precipice, rolling down the steep slopes in a cloud of broken stone and flying ice.

Ironhelm's head snapped back as he hit something at speed, then his arm crashed through a rock outcrop, smashing it open. He slid and tumbled, falling over and over, destroying the flanks of the mountain in his fall. He had the vague impression of Bjorn crashing straight through an ice-field before the Dreadnought's huge body passed out of view. Showers of snow were everywhere, blinding him. He heard Magnus crying aloud and caught snatches of daemonic flesh flashing close to him before being torn away by the descent.

He fell, and fell, and fell. There was nothing to break the whistling plummet except loose snow and fire-blacked stone. Ironhelm slammed into a fresh outcrop and felt it shatter before he corkscrewed away. Everything was in motion, disorientating and whirling in a white-out of sensory deprivation.

Then, with a sickening crash, he hit something bigger. Even cocooned in his Terminator plate, the impact was staggering. Ironhelm blacked out, his body bouncing like a whip-crack before grinding painfully to a halt.

It was a ledge, one of the thousands of steps in the jagged upper reaches of the Fang, a hundred metres wide and high up the dizzying cliffs of the ultimate peak.

Ironhelm felt awareness return almost immediately, and knew then how much he'd been damaged. Pain surged through his body like a roaring fire, blazing across his tortured joints and spliced bones. He could feel the steel plate in his skull rattle loose. That meant his cranium was fractured, a prognosis consistent with the sun-hot agony that buzzed behind his eyes.

He snarled with anger, and thrust himself to a half-sitting position. Magnus was there too. The two of them had come down together, kicking and flailing. There was no sign of Bjorn, though there was a long gouge running down the rock behind the primarch, torn out of the stone like a plough's furrow. Snow and pack-ice still fell in clouds, laced with biting slivers of rock.

The primarch was on his feet. All semblance of his old form was gone. There was no golden mantle, no bronze plate, no beautifully inscribed greaves with images of the zodiac glinting in the sunlight.

What remained was a being of energy, a vaguely man-shaped network of pulsating warp-matter, vivid and unsettling. The only fixed point within the skin of shifting aether-essence was a single eye, garnet-red and blazing like a circle of fire.

The wind skirled around the ravaged primarch, frigid and tearing, trying to snatch him from the mountain-edge and dash him to the ground below. The planet's soul knew what kind of abomination had been unveiled, and screamed to hurl it back into the warp.

Magnus took a single, pain-filled step towards Ironhelm's broken body, and the eye shot a look of distilled venom. He swayed in the wind.

Ironhelm clambered to his feet, ignoring the blazing agony throughout his mighty frame. He felt blood slosh in his boots, pooling in his armour-joints. The pain kept him conscious, kept him focused. He had travelled across the warp for this encounter with all the speed and fury he could muster. *Twice.*

'Witch,' he spat, feeling the blood-rich saliva slap against his face-plate.

His frostblade had been lost during the crashing descent, but his Terminator armour had other weapons. His right wrist held twin storm bolter muzzles embedded in the curve of the plate, while his left hand was enclosed in a hulking power fist. Trusting in his prowess with both, Ironhelm lumbered into a heavy, rock-fracturing charge towards the wavering form of the primarch. As he powered into the barrelling run, he loosed both bolter barrels. The rounds punched into Magnus's flesh but didn't detonate. They seemed to disappear entirely, though the impact clearly hurt the daemon-primarch. Magnus roared with pain and anger, bracing to meet the charge of the Great Wolf with his bare hands.

Ironhelm felt his legs burn as he thundered into contact. His armour boosted him, propelling tons of dense flesh, bone, ceramite and adamantium into the body of the primarch. As he connected, he swung his power fist in a massive, hammering arc straight at Magnus's shimmering face.

Magnus veered from the path of the fist expertly, keeping his body supple, and rammed his own fists into the Great Wolf's breastplate, slamming him back across the ice. Ironhelm staggered against the slick surface. Magnus swept in for another strike, but Iron-helm managed to get his power fist round in time. It connected on the full, and the blow felt like punching a bag of bones.

Magnus was hurled away, crashing into the cliff edge. As his body hit the mountainside it shimmered, like a hololith flickering on low power. The primarch's expression was a mix of incredulity and anguish.

He had been diminished. Terribly diminished.

Ironhelm laughed ferociously, charging again, using his massive bulk to generate momentum. Magnus rose to meet him, his fists blazing with witchlight. The two came together with a sickening crunch. Ironhelm felt his bolter-arm shatter, blasted apart by a discharge of white-hot fire. He also felt his power fist strike home, rocking the daemon-primarch on his flickering heels.

Ironhelm snarled with the raw pleasure of the fight. After so long hunting ghosts and being taunted by apparitions, he was in his element at last. With every fresh strike of his tormented arms he felt a little more alive. The pain was immaterial. The only thing that existed for him was the contest, the test of arms, the exercise of his peerless capacity for controlled violence.

That capacity was stoked by rage, the rage he had cultivated ever since leaving Gangava. The faces of the Wolf Brothers clustered into his mind, still howling their horror and pain. The faces of the slain on Fenris were among them too, growling in accusation. Greyloc had been right. The dead had all been sacrificed on the altar of his hubris, and now they demanded retribution.

He intended to deliver it. The power fist crunched again into Magnus's aether-woven flank, slamming the primarch back against the cliff face. The one-eyed visage blazed with pain as Magnus was crushed against the sword-sharp rock. His whole frame juddered, rippling like a flame caught in the wind. The wounds bit deep, sending shockwaves across his patterned flesh. Far above, the storm crashed in furious triumph, hurling void-cold gales around the mountainside. Ironhelm hit him again, and again, pummelling him against the rock-blades of the Fang's flanks.

Magnus cried out then, a cry of pain that had not been heard since the Wolf King had destroyed his first body. It echoed from the rock, outmatching the wind; outmatching the thunder of artillery from below as the Wolves tore through into the mortal troops on the causeways. In that cry was the weariness of ages, the despair of a demigod bred to fathom the deep mysteries of the universe and instead locked in grubby conflicts amid the dirty snow of a world of barbarians. It was a cry of loss, of waste, and of the infinite futility of an endless war that he had never wanted.

Ironhelm heard that cry, and grinned savagely. He kept going, hammering away at the abomination before him, his limbs working like a mighty engine, lost in a storm of blood-frenzy.

'Fight me, witch!' he roared. 'Raise those hands and fight me!'

For a moment, it looked like Magnus had lost the will to. He absorbed the punishment, his back arching against the cliffs. Trails of fire still clung to his ravaged outline, the residue of his tortuous ascent through the Jarlheim. His eye was open, staring with pain. He looked lost, cast adrift on the summit of the death world he had sworn to ruin.

But then, just as before, he began to remember himself. From somewhere deep within, a new flame kindled. The primarchs had been bred, above all, to survive, to endure all that an immeasurably hostile galaxy could throw at them. Their residue of power was near-inexhaustible, a well on to the deep ocean of the Emperor's matchless potency. Even now, even after enduring so much, having absorbed so much pain, his essential strength, the core of fire that fuelled him, remained inviolate.

His back straightened up. Magnus caught one of Ironhelm's incoming punches with his palm, clutching at the power fist and holding it in fingers of fire. With his free fist, he lashed out, catching the Great

Wolf full in the face. Ironhelm reeled, and staggered backwards.

Magnus raised himself up higher. The wounds on his body flared crimson as they healed themselves. Aether-born lightning crackled where his feet trod. The single eye burned again, an ingot of molten iron amid the ice. He opened his fist, and a neon deluge burst from his palm, dousing Ironhelm in consuming, wracking electric fire. The Great Wolf was driven back toward the edge and beaten down to his knees, wrapped in the raw quintessence of the immaterium.

The torrent broke off. Ironhelm rocked to the ground, his armour charred and smoking. He didn't get up.

Order had been restored. The demigod looked down at the broken challenger, the last of the many Wolves who had stood up to face him.

'You should have stayed on Gangava,' Magnus rasped, his fractured voice playing across insubstantial vocal cords like the fingers of Hel's harpist. To the extent he still resembled a human at all, he looked exhausted.

'Gangava no longer exists,' coughed Ironhelm, tasting blood in his mouth as he tried to rise. 'Orbital bombardment. Atoms now.'

His bolter-arm had been twisted out of shape, and hung limp. His power fist smoked from the ruinous touch of the primarch, and the ceramite cover was blistered and cracked. All he had left was his native strength. They both knew that would not be enough. He clambered to his feet with slow, agonising effort.

Magnus drew closer. The patterns on his warp-wound flesh were gyrating faster, spinning into new and strange formations. Something was changing within him again. His brief sojourn into physical space was coming to an end.

'Gangava served its purpose,' he said.

Then the primarch launched himself at Ironhelm, sweeping at him like a vengeful bird of prey. His arms stretched wide, bursting with more neon blades of aether-matter.

Ironhelm had nothing left to counter the assault with, and no time to evade the embrace. He stood up to the onslaught, and when it hit him his fangs were bared under his helm, his fists clenched, raging in defiance.

The world disappeared in pain. Ironhelm felt his armour torn open, cut into ribbons by the rending power of the warp. Dimly, he was aware of his organs breaking open, bursting with hot, wet pops. He could hear the sound of cracking across his chest, and only half-knew it was his own ribcage. His vision swam out of focus, replaced by a white wall of searing, writhing witchlight. The hurricane of power, the full and final expression of the primarch's mastery, tore through him like a tempest of the Helwinter, terrible, frigid and inexorable.

He didn't fall. Somehow, he maintained his position on the edge of the drop, dug into the shattered stone and beaten down across it. When the agony ended, he was on his back, broken open, prone before the wrath of the Emperor's son.

One eye still worked to see his death come for him. In that sense, if in no other, the two of them were equal.

Ironhelm coughed a gobbet of something slimy and

hot from his mouth. From far below he could hear the distant thunder of his Chapter's war machines. Already he knew they must have penetrated the Aett. His Wolves would hunt down every invader in those halls, one by one, driven by the remorseless focus that had always been their badge of honour. The fact that they would come too late to save him was unimportant.

'The Aett endures,' he rasped, his voice a wet scraping whisper. 'You ran out of time. I'll take that victory.'

Magnus's body loomed over him. The patterns on his flesh were still moving, still whirling. He was less than opaque now, and the wind snatched at him. For the moment, he held back from the killing blow. He looked death-cold.

'What victory?' he said. 'You wished to kill me. Such as you could never kill such as me, Harek Ironhelm – I am beyond your vengeance now.'

Then Ironhelm laughed, despite the fact it made his punctured lungs flare with fresh agony.

'Kill you? No. I failed in that.' The choking laughs died out. 'But I hurt you, Traitor. We hurt you here. We cut the threads of your sons and broke your witches' sticks. We tore that smile off your face and ripped the skin from your back. And I have lived to see it. That's worth losing some bottles in a fleshmaker's tray for. Blood of Russ, you bastard, I lived to see you *howl*.'

Then Magnus spoke no more, but pulled his fist back. By the time he released the blow that would kill Harek Ironhelm where he lay, the Great Wolf was laughing again, hacking up blood against his voxplate, strung out on the spikes of pain all over his body, crushed against the side of the mountain with no hope of recovery, but laughing like old Russ himself in the morning of the galaxy.

CHAPTER TWENTY-TWO

Forty days.

From the first arrival of the Thousand Sons in orbit over Fenris to the slaying of the last Spireguard mortal within the Aett, forty days had passed. That number was given to the skjalds, who implanted it into the sagas. Those sagas were declaimed, and the Dreadnoughts took them down into the cold vaults of the Underfang with them so they were never forgotten.

Alongside that number were the names. Vaer Greyloc, the White Wolf. Odain Sturmhjart and Lauf Cloudbreaker. Thar Ariak Hraldir, the one they called Wyrmblade. Tromm Rossek, Sigrd Brakk, Hamnr Skrieya and the other Wolf Guard. Garjek Arfang of the Iron Priests, and eight Dreadnoughts of the Revered Fallen.

Of the Grey Hunters, Long Fangs and Blood Claws of the Twelfth Great Company, twenty-two lived. Twenty-one of those had been in Borek's Seal, still fighting when the relief forces arrived at the portals. The only survivor in the Valgard was a Blood Claw, Ogrim Raegr Vrafsson, the one they called Redpelt. When Egial Vraksson of the Fifth broke into the Annulus Chamber with his Wolf Guard, Redpelt was standing over the central stone, surrounded by Rubric Marines, guarding the sacred image with his own body. He had been long in the Red Dream after that, but lived.

Countless kaerls had given their lives in the defence of the Aett. Their names were not recorded.

It was not known by what means the Traitor Marines escaped vengeance. Many did not, it is true, and were killed in the tunnels. But others, including most of the sorcerers, disappeared from Fenris at the same time their fleet achieved the in-system jump-points. The Wolf Priests speculate that Magnus himself departed in the same manner, though there were no witnesses to his leaving. When Harek Eireik Eireiksson's body was discovered, there were some who believed the Great Wolf had indeed killed the primarch. Though the rumours persisted for many years, the wisest among the Rout knew that it was not in Ironhelm's wyrd to do such a thing, and prepared for the day when evidence of the Crimson King would emerge once again.

None of the mortal soldiers brought to Fenris by the Thousand Sons were saved by their fleet. When the returning Wolves made planetfall, the troops were slaughtered in their thousands. The fires of their destruction darkened the air of the planet for a month, so that the tribes out on the ice cowered in their shelters and cried out against the coming of Morkai.

But the darkness passed. In time, the Sky Warriors came among them again, taking the best and bravest to fight for the Allfather.

So it had ever been. So it would ever be.

THE FIRES OF the Hammerhold had never gone out. Now they roared more angrily than ever, working hard to replace the weaponry that had been destroyed.

Aldr stomped across the long bridge in convoy with his brothers. He had no wish to return to the dark. None of them did. But the long task of driving the enemy from the last recesses had been completed, and the sagas had been memorised. There was nothing left for them to contribute, and so the Revered Fallen went back to the Long Sleep.

They went alone, unaccompanied by the living. In time, an Iron Priest would come to read the rites and prepare the tomb-cradles. For now, the fellowship of Dreadnoughts was left alone, given a little time to reflect on their sojourn in the world of vital flesh before leaving it again. The living respected that, knowing how important the niceties of ritual were.

All except one. Freija Morekborn walked with Aldr, seemingly unwilling to leave him even as the Underfang portal beckoned.

Aldr couldn't say he was sorry about that. It had been irresponsible of him to pick her from the floor of Borek's Seal and carry her from danger. She had failed in combat, and such weakness was habitually met with execution on the field. But he owed her for other things, and debts were important on Fenris.

What will you do now?

Freija gave a weary smile.

'I've been given penance. For the moment, I still serve in the kaerls. I prefer it in the ranks. I didn't cover myself in glory at the Seal.'

It was weak.

'I know. I recognise my weakness, and will strive to correct it. I believe I can overcome my flaws.'

Your mind wanders where it should not. You are made to serve.

In the past, Freija would have balked at such words. Now, she merely bowed her head.

'That is a lesson I will learn,' she said. 'I have the example of my father.'

She looked back up at Aldr then.

'Morek never doubted. In the face of that horror, he never doubted. His faith in the Sky Warriors was complete even at the end, and I will work to match it.'

Aldr said nothing, and they walked together for a while in silence.

The Dreadnought knew that, next time he awoke, he would recognise no faces. It was a sober thought. Perhaps the second awakening would be easier. Perhaps it was something that became less excruciating the more one did it.

He doubted it.

The portal to the Underfang drew closer. He kept walking, though each step was harder to make.

'I know I'm too curious,' interjected Freija, just as they reached the point where she couldn't follow. 'I know it's a weakness. But tell me one thing.'

Aldr halted.

'The beasts, the ones who fought with us at Borek's Seal. What were they? You said they were weapons, but who made them?'

Aldr hesitated. For a horrible moment, he realised how fully he would miss their conversations. He would miss this mortal's endless questioning, her bluntness, her lack of poise. It was beneath him, to feel that way about a thrall, but he would miss her all the same.

You said you would strive to improve yourself, he replied. **Start now. Cease your questions. That knowledge is not for you.**

Freija broke into another weary smile.

'You are right,' she said. 'I have offended you again. I will leave.'

At that, Aldr made to move off, to follow his brothers into the tunnels. His powerful leg-motors whined as he stepped across the portal. Freija fell back, at last respecting the sanctity of the occasion.

You never offended me, he said, his voice thick, before stalking off back into the dark.

BY THE FLICKERING light of the hearth fires, two voices echoed in the chamber. Both were impossibly deep, resonating from ancient armour. One belonged to Jarl Arvek Kjarlskar, who would soon be elevated to Great Wolf in place of Ironhelm. The other belonged to Bjorn the Fell-Handed, who had been Great Wolf before and had since passed beyond such titles.

The venerable Dreadnought had been recovered from the mountainside a day after the last fighting had been completed. His life-sign had been so faint that no auspex had picked it up. Only a visual scan of the Valgard slopes had marked his final resting place. He'd torn half the pinnacle down in his fall, grinding a huge wound in the bare rock before lodging in a deep crack between two mighty spurs. Retrieving him had taken two days, and his physical recovery had taken many more. Even now, his sarcophagus bore the signs of battle, and the Iron Priests still had much work to do before he could rejoin his brothers in stasis.

There were Wolf Brothers on Gangava?

'Yes, lord. A Great Company, or something close to it. They'd been corrupted, and were wholly given over to the enemy.'

So you destroyed them.

'Lord Ironhelm wished to finish them himself, but we had tidings of the siege here, and I persuaded him to break from combat. The city was destroyed from orbit, and a squadron left behind to ensure the devastation was complete.'

Bjorn grunted with grim satisfaction.

It sickens me. What purpose did the Traitor have in this?

'He meant to detain us on Gangava. He knew Ironhelm would not refuse combat with corrupted brothers. He was right. Had news not come of the battle here, we would have hunted the last of them for many days, and the Aett would have fallen in our absence.' The Jarl's voice was speculative. 'But that could not have been all. We were shown the weakness of our successors in that place. With all that has transpired here, I do not believe that could have been an accident.'

You speak of the Tempering.

'I do not know the details. Only Ironhelm and Wyrmblade did. Possibly Jarl Greyloc too, since he was close to the Wolf Priest. But we all knew the goals of the programme. It cannot be chance that the flesh-maker chambers were destroyed before the Chamber of the Annulus was assaulted.'

It should never have been done. It was a betrayal of the primarch.

Kjarlskar shrugged, his massive shoulder-guards moving only fractionally.

'Perhaps. In any case, it cannot be restarted. None now live who understand Wyrmblade's work, and the equipment is destroyed. We will remain alone, the sole inheritors of Russ's mantle.'

As it should be. If I'd known of the work, I'd have destroyed it myself.

Kjarlskar had to suppress a smile. He could well imagine the Dreadnought doing just that.

'Then you should be content, lord. You have fought a primarch and lived, and the Aett was defended. Soon the sagas will be full of your deeds and no one else's.'

Bjorn gave no indication of a smile.

Not my deeds. Greyloc held out the longest, and this is his victory.

'So it will be recorded,' said Kjarlskar. 'But I do not think it will be remembered that way.'

A FIRE BURNED on the pinnacle of Krakgard, the dark peak overlooking the Fang where the dead had been honoured since the age of the primarchs. The summit of the mountain was flat and smooth, having been carved out in the days of the Allfather and hallowed in the long years since. The entire Chapter was assembled across its expanse, standing in rows of grey, their heads bare and exposed to the biting elements.

The sun was low in the sky, and the shadows were long. The flames leapt, red and angry, sending sparks floating high into the dusk.

Kjarlskar stood before the blaze, the heat of it pressing against his back. The Rune Priest Frei was with him, as were others of the Lords of the Wolves.

'Sons of Russ!' he cried, and his voice carried far across the wind-whipped heights. 'As is the way of our kind, the bodies of those who died in the defence of Fenris are now committed to fire. Here lies Jarl Vaer Greyloc, and the Rune Priest Odain Sturmhjart, and the Wolf Priest Thar Ariak Hraldir. So do we reverence them for their sacrifice. As their mortal bodies burn, it kindles our everlasting hate for the ones who did this. Remember your hatred. Keep it vital, and forge it with malice into one more weapon in the Long War.'

The rows of Space Wolves listened intently, each one of them as silent as stones. In the front rank stood twenty-three warriors, removed slightly from their brothers. They were the survivors of the Battle of the Fang, the last of Greyloc's company. Redpelt was there, his face still badly scarred. There were few Blood Claws left to stand alongside him. It hadn't been decided how best to reconstitute the packs yet, but many believed Redpelt would not serve in one again, instead choosing the path of the Lone Wolf. The death of his comrades had hit him hard, and such a path was an honourable response.

As Kjarlskar spoke, he stared into the flames, watching as the bodies of the fallen turned to ash. He carried Brakk's force-blade Dausvjer at his belt, the last weapon his battle-brother Helfist had taken into combat. Though none assembled there knew it yet, the sword had a powerful wyrd set upon it, and would find a place in the sagas millennia hence. For then, though, it was merely a weregild, and a reminder, and a warning.

'The Great Wolf, Harek Eireik Eireiksson, does not lie here,' said Kjarlskar. 'His body has been taken to the place where he fell fighting the great enemy. I have ordered that a shrine be built there, a place of pilgrimage to test the endurance of the faithful. Let it serve as a memorial to his unwavering devotion. Let it also serve as a memorial to his blindness. Never again will we allow ourselves to be drawn into a war not of our own making. This is the lesson we will draw, and we will use it to improve ourselves further.'

Set aside from the twenty-two veterans of the siege, shunning as ever the company of his brothers, was Blackwing. The Scout had recovered much of his poise on the journey back from Gangava. He'd since been assigned the task of rebuilding the Twelfth's void-war capability, though few expected him to last long in the position. He'd already fallen out with the Chapter's armoury over requisition plans for new fast-attack frigates, insisting on an engine-heavy design that most thought of as wildly impractical.

As Kjarlskar spoke, he looked up at the stars, mild tedium playing across his dark features. Ceremonies bored him, though he'd been satisfied by his manoeuvre

over Fenris being placed in the sagas. It was some
compensation for losing the *Nauro*, the only element
of his life on Fenris he'd ever felt much affection for,
and the only element he ever would.

'We will rebuild,' said Kjarlskar. 'The Aett will be
restored and made even greater. The last taint of the
enemy will be scrubbed from the ice, and the remnants of his forces on other worlds hunted down and
destroyed. The Twelfth Great Company will be rebuilt,
its honour intact and its packs restored.'

The Great Wolf swept his golden eyes across the
assembled companies.

'No recovery will take place for our enemy. We have
broken them. Never again will they mount such an
operation, for they have been reduced to petty war-
bands of knowledge-thieves, roaming the galaxy for
scraps of hidden trinkets. Their shame knows no limit,
and their poverty knows no equal. They have come
here, led by their primarch, and failed.'

Kjarlskar's eyes blazed then.

'Remember that, brothers!' he cried. 'They failed.
This will be the greatest lesson of all, the truth we will
carry with us as we march once more to war in the sea
of stars. Our faith defines us. Our loyalty defines us.
Our hatred defines us. So it is that we endure while
the Traitor falters.'

His voice shook with fervour.

'In a thousand years men will still speak of this battle. For as long as the Imperium of Man stands, skjalds
will tell of the Battle of the Fang, and hope will flare
in the hearts of the loyal. Whenever the flames of war
return, they will remember what we have done here,

and find the strength to rise up and accept the test.'

Kjarlskar thudded a fist against his breastplate.

'*This* is our legacy. *This* is our purpose. *This* is why we fight.'

Then he lifted the clenched gauntlet in a gesture of defiance, pride and acclamation.

'For the Allfather!'

And across the summit of the Krakgard, two thousand warriors of the *Vlka Fenryka*, the Space Wolves of fearsome repute, slammed their fists on their battleplate and raised them up to the heavens. The roar of their massed response rose high into the darkening sky, a war cry that was already ancient, already feared, and as bold and exuberant as the dawn across unbroken snow.

For the Allfather. For Russ. For Fenris.

ABOUT THE AUTHOR

Chris Wraight is a writer of fantasy and science fiction, whose first novel was published in 2008. Since then, he's published books set in the Warhammer Fantasy, Warhammer 40,000 and Stargate: Atlantis universes. He doesn't own a cat, dog, or augmented hamster (which technically disqualifies him from writing for Black Library), but would quite like to own a tortoise one day. He's based in a leafy bit of south-west England, and when not struggling to meet deadlines enjoys running through scenic parts of it.

Read more about his upcoming projects at *www.chriswraight.wordpress.com*

SWORD OF VENGEANCE ~ CHRIS WRAIGHT

WARHAMMER HEROES

An extract from
Sword of Vengeance
by Chris Wraight

HELBORG FELT THE ash-hot air stream past him as he spurred his horse into a gallop. Schwarzhelm had committed his troops, drawing attention away from the Reiksguard and leaving the field clear for the charge. The squadron comprised fewer than fifty horsemen, including himself and Leitdorf – a laughable force with which to threaten a host of thousands.

The wedge of riders around him tightened. Their massed hooves drummed on the packed earth as the knights swept towards their target. Half a mile to their left the walls of Averheim rose up into the storm-raked air, vast and dark. Ahead of them were file upon file of marching infantry, each clad in close-fitting plate armour and bearing a crystal halberd. Somewhere beyond them was Volkmar. The Theogonist's position had been obvious enough from the vantage of the rise, but was now lost in the smoke and confusion of the battlefield.

The success of the charge all depended on speed and power. The first blow would settle things.

'Karl Franz!' roared Helborg as the first lines of the enemy came into view. The dog-soldiers before him turned to face the onslaught. Too slowly. They'd be ripped aside.

'The Emperor!' replied the Reiksguard, crying aloud as one. Skarr was at the forefront of the charge, his ravaged face enclosed in steel and his blade flashing.

Rufus Leitdorf rode on his left shoulder, leaning forwards in the saddle and with the Wolfsklinge unsheathed at his side.

'For my father,' he murmured, too low for the others to hear.

The gap shrank, closed and disappeared. The wedge of cavalry, a steel-tipped spear of white and red, slammed into the defenders. Grosslich's infantry were ridden into the mire or cut down by the precision of the Reiksguard sword-work. Helborg kicked his horse onwards and it leapt into the press of Grosslich's rearguard, lashing out and kicking its hooves as it laboured through the mass of bodies.

Startled by the sudden onslaught, the resistance was weak. A group of heavily-armoured dog-soldiers attempted to form a line against the charge.

'Take them!' cried Helborg, pulling his horse's head round to meet the threat.

The Reiksguard wheeled, every horseman controlling his steed superbly. Without any drop in speed, the knights galloped at the wall of iron and steel. They crashed into the defence again at full tilt, breaking open the nascent line of shields and scattering the mutants. Some knights were knocked from the saddle or raked with a desperate halberd-stab from below, but the wedge remained intact, tearing forwards, heading ever further into the files of the corrupted troops.

'D'you see him?' shouted Skarr, crouching low in the saddle, his helmet drenched in blood and his sword still swinging.

'Not yet,' replied Helborg, impaling a dog-soldier with a downward plunge before bringing the Klingerach smartly back up for another victim.

Helborg felt stronger than he'd done since leaving Nuln. His shoulder spiked with pain, but he ignored it. Like Schwarzhelm, he lived for combat. Creeping around in the hinterland of Averland had been a drain on his soul. Now, surrounded by the filth he'd dedicated his life to eradicating, the tang of blood on his lips and the thunder of hooves in his ears, he was back where he belonged.

'Keep on this course!' he bellowed, directing his galloping steed towards a fresh attempt to halt them. 'Rally to the Theogonist when we see him. Until then, kill all who get in your way.'

With that, Helborg swerved to avoid a looming dog-soldier, carving a deep gash in the mutant's shoulder as he passed, before powering onwards to the line of mustering defenders.

His eyes narrowed under the visor and a warm smile creased his battle-scarred face. The hooves of his horse thudded as he hurtled towards his next target.

'Sigmar preserves those who fight,' he murmured to himself, licking his cracked lips with anticipation. 'Blessed be the name of Sigmar.'

* * *

SCHWARZHELM STRODE FORWARDS and the Rechtstahl trailed a line of ripped-free gore behind it. He'd dismounted once the press around him had got too close and now went on foot amongst his troops, carving his way towards the sundered Imperial lines. Kraus was at his side, hammering away with his blade.

There seemed to be no end to the mutants, horrors and dead-eyed mortals looming up out of the dark, faces blank and blades swinging. The assault on Grosslich's flank had almost stalled. Bloch's men were capable of holding their own but the Averlanders were less accomplished. Schwarzhelm had seen dozens of them running from the field, crying with fear and leaving their weapons in the mud behind them. Those that remained were now surrounded, enveloped in the endless ranks of Grosslich's legions. The mutants exacted a heavy toll for any forward progress. Only Schwarzhelm kept the drive going, hauling his men forwards by the force of example.

'No mercy!' he roared, stabbing the Rechtstahl through the wheezing throat of a mutant and ripping it out. 'Keep your formation! Fear no traitor!'

He knew time was running out. They were too deep in to disengage.

'Where now?' panted Kraus, fresh from felling his man. His armour looked big on him, as if the weeks in the wild had physically shrunk the honour guard captain.

'This is the right course,' said Schwarzhelm, dragging a halberdier back out of harm's way before crushing the skull of his looming assailant. 'Unless the Empire army has fallen back to–'

With a scream, something dark and clawed flung itself from the enemy lines. It was cloaked in rags and had talons for fingers. The halberdiers shrank back, bewildered and terrified.

Schwarzhelm brought the Rechtstahl round quickly. Steel clashed against bone, and a flash of witch-light burst out from the impact. Kraus leapt forwards, blade at the ready.

'Get back!' roared Schwarzhelm, his sword dancing in the firelight, parrying and thrusting at the scuttling creature. 'Your blade will not bite this.'

Kraus fell away, blocking instead the advance of a slavering dog-soldier. Schwarzhelm worked his sword with speed, matching the spider-sharp movements of the horror. Every time the Rechtstahl hit, a blaze of sparks rained to the ground. The creature leapt at him, screaming with frustration, talons lashing.

Schwarzhelm ducked under the scything claws, shouldering his mighty pauldrons to the assault and swinging the blade fast and low across the earth. The horror reacted, spinning back on itself to evade the strike, but too late. The Sword of Justice sliced through sinew and iron, taking off the creature's legs and leaving it writhing in the blood-soaked mud.

Schwarzhelm rose to his full height, spun the sword round and plunged it down, pinning the horror's torso as he'd done with Tochfel in Averheim. It let out a final screech of pain and fury before the light in its eyes went out.

With the destruction of Natassja's pet, the dog-soldiers began to withdraw. None of them could stand against Schwarzhelm. In the shuffling confusion the halberdiers were finally able to push them back.

'Morr's blood,' spat Kraus, looking at the twisted carcass still twitching in the slime of the field. 'What is that?'

'Another one I failed to save,' replied Schwarzhelm grimly, stalking back to the front line. At his approach, the dog-soldiers fell back further. Soon his massive shoulders were busy again, hacking and parrying, driving the mutants inwards.

'Reikland!' came a voice then from further down the line of halberdiers. Schwarzhelm recognised it at once. Bloch. The halberdier commander was still unstoppable, as tough and enduring as old leather.

Schwarzhelm whirled round, hope rising in his breast. Drifts of smoke still obscured the battlefield beyond a few paces and the ash-choked darkness did the rest, but he could see the shadows of men running towards them.

'Hold your positions!' he bellowed, his gruff voice cracking under the strain. He couldn't afford for his troops to get strung out.

Then, suddenly, there were halberdiers around him. They weren't Bloch's men, but wore the grey and white of the Reikland. They looked exhausted, their faces streaked with blood and their breastplates dented.

'Against all hope...' one of them stammered, limping towards Schwarzhelm like he was some shade of Morr.

Bloch burst from the right flank after him, grinning like an idiot.

'We've broken through, my lord!' he cried, exposing the bloody hole in his smile where something had knocked half his teeth from his jaw. 'These are our men!'

Even as he announced the news, more Imperial troops emerged from the gloom. There were dozens, possibly hundreds.

'Maintain the assault!' growled Schwarzhelm, glowering at Bloch and pushing his way past the limping Reikland troops. 'You pox-ridden dogs, form up like you're in the army of the Emperor.'

Bloch's men immediately responded, swinging back to face the dog-soldiers and charging the disarrayed lines. Their commander disappeared with them, in the forefront as ever, hefting his halberd with brutal enjoyment.

Schwarzhelm turned on the nearest Empire halberdier. Everything was in flux. They were still heavily outnumbered, and their only hope lay in restoring discipline.

'Who's the senior officer here?' he demanded.

'I don't know, my lord. Kleister is dead, and Bogenhof is–'

'You'll do then. Get these men into detachments. Four deep, ten wide. Do it now. Follow my lead, and we'll clear some space around us. This isn't over yet.'

The halberdier looked back at him, first with surprise, then with a sudden, desperate hope.

'Yes, my lord!' he cried, before rushing to form his men up as ordered.

Schwarzhelm turned back to the fighting. If there were any more of those creatures, he knew he'd be the only one who could take them on.

'What now?' asked Kraus, hurrying back to his side.

'Get in amongst these men,' said Schwarzhelm, striding without break to catch up with Bloch's men. 'Get them organised and follow me. There'll be more of them as we go, and they all need leading.'

'So where are we taking them?'

Schwarzhelm turned back to shoot Kraus a murderous look.

'Grosslich must have seen us by now,' he said, his eyes narrowing under his helmet. 'He's here somewhere, and when I find him, he's my kill.'

Then Schwarzhelm stalked off, massive and threatening, his sword thirsting for the blood that followed it whenever it was drawn.